Embracing the Darkness

The Darkness Trilogy - 2

Cassie Sanchez

Embracing the Darkness

© 2022 Cassie Sanchez

All rights reserved. No portion of this book may be reproduced, stored in a retrieval system, or transmitted in any form or by any means—electronic, mechanical, photocopy, recording, scanning, or other—except for brief quotations in critical reviews or articles, without the prior written permission of the publisher.

Publisher's Note: This novel is a work of fiction. Names, characters, places, and incidents are either products of the author's imagination or used factiously. All characters are fictional, and any similarity to people living or dead is purely coincidental.

Cover and Interior Design by:

Karen Dimmick

ArcaneCovers.com

Maps created by:

Sarah Waites, Illustrated Page Design

theIllustratedPage.net

Published in the United States of America, by Silver Labs Press.

ISBN 979-8-9868224-1-9

*This book is for you, Mom and Dad.
You're either walking by my side or residing in my heart.
You've always been a light in my darkness.*

Cast Of Characters

MAIN CAST - MAGICAL ABILITY
Commander Jasce Farone (FA-rone) - Vaulter/Amp
Kenz Haring - Shield
Kord Haring - Healer
Amycus Reins (AM-i-cus) - Air
Caston Narr, Second in Command - Amp

SUPPORTING CAST
Flynt Culbrim - Fire
Delmira (Del-MEERA) Temay - Shield
Maera (MAY-ra) Sandor - Natural
Emile (EM-i-lee) Karch - Earth, Amp, Vaulter
Lander Karch - Natural
Maleous (MAL-i-us) Haring - Healer
Alyssa Nadja, General - Natural
Aura (OR-a) Danel - Air
Jaida Farone - Psyche

PANDAREN COUNCIL
Queen Lorella Valeri

Alaine Darbry - Lady of Torrine (TOR-een)
Serena Wuhl - Lady of Wilholm
Larkin Haldron - Lord of Bradwick
Dirk Rollant - Lord of Carhurst

FOUR KINGDOMS - MAGICAL ABILITY

ALTURIA - Shade Walkers
    Prince Nicolaus Jazari
    Commander Eris Faez

TERRENUS - Gemaris
    Archduke Kraig Carnelian
    General Tobias de Sille

BALTEN - Strength and Speed, Defenders
    King Leonid Morzov
    Consort Natasha Lekov

VASTANE - Unknown
    Queen Evelina Siryn
    Garan, Bodyguard

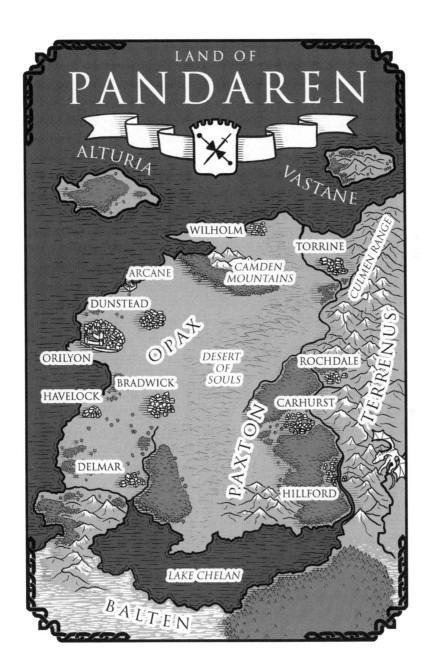

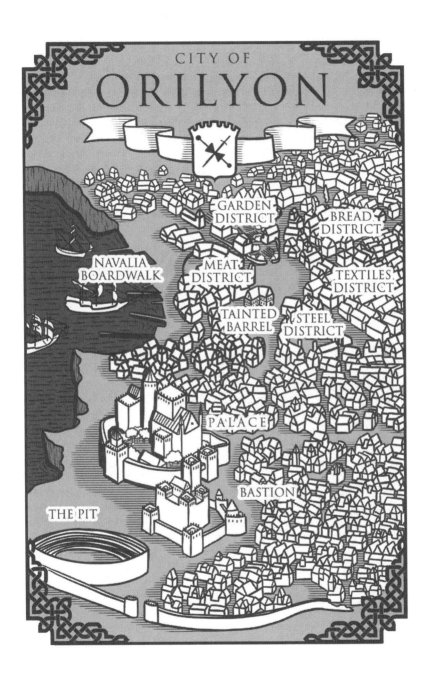

Prologue

Delmar, Opax
Four Years After the Vastane War

Jasce Farone and his younger sister, Jaida, walked through the village of Delmar after spending the afternoon in the Nisene Forest. Sweat dampened their heads and dirt covered their clothes. It had been another day pretending to be warriors battling the evil Fae in the north. Jaida always insisted on imitating a princess, which Jasce thought was silly. She could be anything—why a princess? He liked to pretend to be a magical warrior who wielded two swords made of fire and ice.

"Hey, you two. Your mother is looking for you," the blacksmith, Braxium, said as he sat on a stump whittling a piece of wood. His brown, scraggly hair lay across broad shoulders that hunched as he concentrated on the fine details.

"Thanks," Jasce said, and tightened his grip on Jaida's hand. He pulled a few leaves from her blonde hair and wiped a smudge of dirt off her pale face. Jasce longed to help Braxium finish the dagger he'd been working on, but if their mom was searching for them, then that meant trouble. He'd visit the forge tomorrow when he wouldn't have to babysit his sister.

Cassie Sanchez

"Can we not go home?" Jaida asked, her bottom lip quivering.

"It'll be fine, Jai. I'll protect you."

At eight years old, she only came to his chest and had to look up at him. She had gray eyes like their mother's—the prettiest color he'd ever seen. She nodded and they continued walking toward their cottage at the end of the lane. Even from a distance, he could see their mom, Lisia, pacing out front and chewing on her thumbnail. She wore traveling clothes, black pants and a dark green tunic, and had tied her blonde hair into a messy knot on the top of her head.

It must be bad, he thought.

After the war with the Vastanes, their father, Barnet, had started drinking and grew more paranoid, always questioning their mother, asking where she went. Things continued to get worse as Hunters raided villages, searching for Spectrals and hurting anyone who got in their way. He had never heard his father yell at their mother like he had the day she'd inscribed a tattoo on Jasce's arm. She said it would protect him and to keep it hidden, so that's what he did. But his father had found out, and ever since then the drinking and yelling had become daily occurrences.

"There you are," their mother said. A crash sounded behind her, causing Jaida to jump. Their mother handed satchels to them and led them into the forest. "Quickly now. We're going on another adventure."

Jasce knew she only said this to lessen the fear of their enraged father and his tirades. How many nights had they spent in the forest? Jasce didn't mind, but he knew that with each time, Jaida became more scared.

The sound of breaking dishes and yelling pursued them as they navigated the familiar path leading away from their cottage.

"Mommy, tell us a story," Jaida said, hiking up her dress to hop over a fallen tree.

Jasce rolled his eyes. "You've heard them a hundred times." He pressed his hand against his rumbling stomach and hoped his mother had packed enough food. He had just turned twelve, and hunger was his constant companion.

"I have a new one tonight, but after dinner," their mother said. She

Embracing the Darkness

smiled over her shoulder and grabbed Jaida's hand, leading her deeper into the woods.

Dusk settled, and lightning bugs flickered in the distance. The soft hoot of an owl sounded from a tall pine, and a breeze infused the air with cedar and wet moss. The gurgle of the Galinas River, low this time of year, lay to the east, zigzagging through the forest and emptying into Lake Chelan.

Jasce lit a fire, pleased with himself at how quickly he got it started, while his mother and sister set up camp. He inhaled the smell of stew cooking in a small pot resting on the coals. Once their bellies were full and stars pierced through the blackness of night, their mother laid their bedrolls in a circle around the fire, like she did before every story time.

She leaned back on her hands and stretched her long legs, crossing her ankles. "A long time ago, two powerful beings, named Theran and Cerulea, visited Pandaren. They were light and dark, standing over ten feet tall, and full of magic."

"What was Cerulea wearing?" Jaida asked.

Jasce shoved her. "Who cares?"

Their mother chuckled and tapped her lip. "She wore a beautiful silver gown and had long black hair that seemed to hold the starlight captive."

Jaida gasped and her eyes widened.

"What kind of magic did they have?" Jasce asked, not caring about dresses and hair.

"Theran had Physical magic. He could control the elements—water, earth, fire, and air—and was also magnificently strong and fast. Cerulea, on the other hand, had Mental magic. She could move objects with her mind, sense magic, heal with just a touch, create a glowing shield, and travel through space as if disappearing."

"Ooh. I want to be her," Jaida said, rubbing her legs.

"Yes, she does sound fabulous." Their mother gathered Jaida in her arms, sitting her on her lap, and waved Jasce over. He leaned into her, and even though he was too old, he savored the security she offered. "Anyway, because there must be a balance in all things, Theran and Cerulea had to drain their magic every one thousand years and give it to people they found worthy. And thus, the Spectrals were made, as was the Heart of Pandaren."

Jasce snorted. "That's a dumb name."

Jaida smacked him on the shoulder. "No, it isn't, and quit interrupting."

He opened his mouth to argue, but his mother continued telling the story.

"The Heart is a magical crystal; some say it's the creator and sustainer of all the magic in the land. Soon after giving their magic and creating the crystal, Theran and Cerulea returned to their world with the small amount of power they had left. For a time, Pandaren was at peace. But, as with all things, the lust for power and control tainted the minds of certain people. Wars broke out, Mentals fought Physicals, families divided. It was a dark time." She paused, staring through the forest toward home. "Theran and Cerulea returned and were heartbroken over what had become of the people, so they separated them into five tribes, sending four to different lands. The Spectrals remained in Pandaren as did the Heart, but Theran and Cerulea further divided it into four separate Stones."

"Why would they do that?" Jaida asked.

"Quit interrupting, Jai," Jasce said, smirking.

"You two knock it off," their mother said, but there was no bite to her words. The fire reflected in her gray eyes, which were crinkled around the edges. "They separated the Heart and hid it so no one person would have too much power, for if someone could control the Heart, they could manipulate magic and those with it. But before they split it, a young girl named Namaha snuck into the chamber. She was a curious thing, like someone else I know." She squeezed Jaida, who giggled. "A noise scared Namaha, and she accidentally dropped the Heart. She quickly returned it to the pillar, but a sliver of crystal had broken off. Not wanting anyone to notice, she stole it and escaped to the coast where no one would know. Namaha was a Psyche and didn't know the sliver she carried belonged to the Empower Stone of the Heart."

"The what?" Jasce asked.

His mother swept the hair out of his face. "The four Stones of the

Embracing the Darkness

Heart affect magic differently. The sliver that came from the Empower Stone strengthened magic. Over time, Namaha grew more and more powerful, able to influence large groups of people with her mind. She set herself up as queen, married, and had a son. When her son turned eighteen, she gave him a ring that contained the small piece of the crystal, and that ring was handed down through the royal family. Years turned into centuries, magic lessened as more and more Naturals were born, and the story of the Heart and Theran and Cerulea became one of legend. To this day, no one knows where the four Stones are or where the magical ring went."

The fire sputtered and sparks drifted into the night sky. Jasce wondered what it would be like to have power like Theran or Cerulea. He'd easily be able to protect his mother and sister from his father, or even the Hunters.

Their mother switched stories, describing flying beasts that dwelled on the other side of Pandaren, and magical beings slipped to the back of his mind. Her comforting voice accompanied the crackle of the fire and the musical chirp of frogs. His sister soon drifted off to sleep, but he forced himself to stay awake until his eyelids refused to cooperate.

His mother settled Jaida onto her sleeping mat and covered her with a blanket. She knelt next to him and mussed his hair. "You need to rest. I'll wake you up with the sunrise."

Jasce smiled. His favorite time of day—sharing the sunrise with his mother as the light chased away the darkness.

Chapter One

The Palace in Orilyon
Fourteen Years Later

Commander Jasce Farone shoved open the towering front doors of the palace and marched down a corridor lined with portraits of Pandaren's royal family. The muddy footprints in his wake didn't concern him, nor that two weeks' worth of dirt covered him. The last thing he needed was to be called back to another meeting, especially when he'd obtained a good lead on his sister's location.

Five months, he thought as he massaged the tension from his jaw. It had been five months since discovering Jaida was alive, and his need to find her had consumed his thoughts. He would find her. Persuading her not to hate him was another matter. He could still picture her arms raised as discarded weapons hurtled his direction, her anger and pain like a hurricane attacking the shore.

Jasce ran his fingers through his wet hair. The rain, splattering on the stained-glass windows, had accompanied him from northern Opax to the kingdom city of Orilyon. Early summer along the coast brought the monsoon season with a vengeance, and fierce thunderstorms frequented the afternoons, matching the tempest raging through him.

Cassie Sanchez

A brilliant spark of lightning illuminated the hallway, followed by a crash of thunder that made the portrait of the late king rattle next to the one of Queen Valeri. Her eyes seemed to glare at him from the canvas as he trudged down the hall, unable to escape her harsh stare from a painting or in real life.

The queen was losing her patience with his lack of answers, and her frustration was tangible. After the Battle of the Bastion, as it was now called, Queen Valeri promoted him to commander of the new Paladin Guard. Not only was he in charge of recruiting and training the troops, but she also wanted proof of Drexus's death since Jaida and Vale had taken his body. Jasce didn't know how the Fire Spectral could've survived since his blade had gone straight through the man's chest. His sister had begged him not to kill Drexus, but his need for revenge had overpowered any other emotion.

Jasce pinched the bridge of his nose and swallowed his anger at his mounting failures. On top of not being able to find his sister or the proof the queen required, Spectrals had been reported missing all over Pandaren. He despised going into another council meeting without substantial information, and he would not be able to solve anything sitting around a table with a bunch of nobles.

He nodded to the saluting guards along the hallway leading to the War Room. He'd walked down this corridor many times, but as the Angel of Death—the most lethal assassin in Pandaren. Back then, the Watch Guard soldiers had saluted out of fear. Now, besides a few of the Naturals who still didn't trust the ex-Hunter, most of the men and women under his charge respected him as their commander. He was one of them, training and fighting alongside his army instead of brutally disciplining them, as Drexus had done.

He opened the ornate doors and strode inside. Rain pelted the windows overlooking the queen's gardens, and a raging fire in the hearth brought a soothing warmth to the room, which hadn't changed since the days of Drexus's influence. An enormous map of Pandaren occupied half the wall, with the Desert of Souls separating the countries of Opax and Paxton, along with displaying the surrounding kingdoms: Balten to the south, Terrenus in the west, and the two northern islands of Alturia and Vastane.

Embracing the Darkness

Gazing at a colorful tapestry of two magical beings holding a glowing crystal was Amycus. A smile curved Jasce's lips as he observed his mentor, not surprised that the Air Spectral was the first to arrive. With his scarred hands linked behind his back, the blacksmith studied the gold and yellow threads that wove throughout the fabric like streams of morning light.

Amycus turned from the tapestry and smiled. "You're back, I see." He had removed his blacksmith apron, but a leftover smudge of soot lined his cheek. His long brown hair, streaked with gray, hung loosely on his shoulders.

Jasce's smile slipped. The Spectral seemed to have aged since the last time he saw him, the lines around his eyes and mouth deeper.

Jasce rubbed his face and sat at the oval table dividing the room. He winced at the squelch his soaked clothes made against the leather chair. "Just got here," he said, not hiding the irritation in his voice.

"Where were you this time?" Amycus asked.

"I was in Wilholm when I received the summons." Being in Wilholm had dragged up memories Jasce had suppressed for years, and the familiar anger that had been his incessant companion crawled its way to the surface. Barnet Farone had moved north after the shame of what he'd done to his family became too much to bear. Jasce had tried not to notice his father's broken-down home when he scoured the town for information about his sister. He didn't want to remember the feel of his father's blood splattering his face as his screams were forever silenced.

As Azrael, he'd relished blood and death, but Jasce was desperately trying to bury that part of his past. He thought he'd been successful until he saw the dilapidated cottage. How it was still standing, Jasce didn't know. It seemed the cottage was as resilient as his past.

Amycus sat opposite Jasce and rested his elbows on the table. "Any news on your sister?"

Jasce leaned back and crossed his arms. "I was tracking a lead about a missing Earth Spectral, thinking maybe it was Vale. Jaida's too smart to use her Psyche magic—that would be a beacon pinpointing her location." There weren't very many Psyches alive, and none as powerful as Jaida that he was aware of. He was making progress, following rumors and whispers, but whenever he seemed to get close, the trail dissipated like smoke in the wind.

Jasce rubbed his temples. The headache brewing behind his eyes was developing into a migraine. With every false lead, unease grew, and it was taking its toll. The anger he felt in Wilholm pulsed through him and made his fingers tremble.

"Jasce, we'll get to the bottom of this," Amycus said, concern lining his eyes. "But you don't have to do it alone."

The doors to the War Room opened and a rush of soothing magic settled Jasce's fury. Ink-black hair and mesmerizing green eyes made his pulse jump as his fiancée entered. Kenz had bewitched him the first time he saw her, when she and her brother, Kord, had rescued him from Bradwick Prison. His attraction had been immediate, but hers took longer. She had hated him because his Hunters attacked a village and killed her former fiancé. Over time, though, Kenz started seeing him as a man and not just a killer. She'd even saved his life. He still couldn't believe she'd said yes when he'd asked her to marry him. Even though she seemed happy in Orilyon, part of him felt guilty that Kenz and her family had left their home in Carhurst.

Caston, an ex-Hunter and now Jasce's Second in Command, followed Kenz into the room. Kenz laughed at something Caston said, and a flutter of jealousy flashed through Jasce's gut, but quickly vanished when she smiled at him.

Kenz quickened her pace, causing the small metal cuffs on her wrists to jingle. She'd previously worn gauntlets to help control her shield, but Amycus had created smaller bands, and to anyone who didn't know better, they looked like nothing more than fancy bracelets.

Jasce stood, wrapped his arms around her, and inhaled her citrusy scent. Their magic swirled and joined, igniting a fire inside him. His magic responded to hers differently than any other Spectral's, which had almost gotten him killed until he learned to control the distraction. But now he let her magic fill him as he savored its calming presence. She was his anchor to the light, to all that was good in his world. He hugged her tighter and cursed the queen for calling this meeting.

"I missed you," he whispered in her ear, smiling when he felt her tremble.

Embracing the Darkness

She pulled away and grinned up at him. Kenz stood at five-eight, but still had to tilt her head back to meet his eyes. "I missed you, too," she said, giving him a quick kiss on the lips.

"Welcome back," Caston said, sitting on the other side of Amycus. He wore the Paladin Guard uniform: a black tunic and pants lined with deep purple, his rank embroidered in gold over his heart. He scratched at his goatee and wrinkled his nose. "You could've cleaned up first."

Jasce threw his Second an inappropriate gesture.

"Any luck?" Jasce asked. He had sent Caston and a few guards to the Desert of Souls to search for Jaida and Vale, but based on the man's face, he'd come up empty as well.

Caston shook his head. "I really hate going to the desert. Next time, send someone else."

Kenz huffed. "You're such a baby."

"I just don't like how that place smothers my magic. It's unnatural."

"Actually, what's unnatural is the fact that you have magic, but we won't go there," Amycus said, his blue eyes sparkling. Caston had been a Natural, but had endured the same experimental procedure as Jasce, giving him Amplifier magic.

"Anyway," Caston continued, ignoring Kenz and Amycus, "have the other teams reported in?"

Jasce inspected the gilded ceiling. "All but Flynt and General Nadja."

"Shouldn't they be back by now?" Kenz asked.

He was about to answer when a deep voice interrupted him.

"What is that awful smell?"

Kord's large six-four frame practically filled the entryway. As Kenz's older brother, he shared the same hair and eye color, although Kord's hair always looked like he spent his free time battling windstorms. As far as anyone knew, Kord was the most powerful Healer in Pandaren, which was why he oversaw the Sanctuary, the medical facility located inside the Bastion.

"Do I smell that bad?" Jasce whispered to Kenz.

She patted his cheek. "Yes"

Kord rested his large hand on Jasce's shoulder, sending his healing magic through Jasce's weary body. "Glad you've returned, safe and sound. Maleous drove me crazy asking about you. He wants to show you a new move he's mastered but be warned. His mother isn't thrilled with the fighting techniques you've taught him."

Jasce chuckled. "I'll make it up to Tillie. I brought back those spices she wanted, so I'll be in her good graces."

"Smart move," Kord said, sitting next to him and stretching his long legs under the table.

The remaining members of the queen's council, all Naturals, trickled in. It had been Queen Valeri's hope to unite the Naturals and Spectrals after years of unrest. And it needed to start in this room with the leaders of the largest towns.

"I'll see you later. Don't dawdle," Kenz said, giving him a wink. Jasce admired her lithe form and a fierce longing rushed through him. He could only hope the meeting would go quickly. Kenz waved at Lady Alaine Darbry from Torrine, who smiled back. Lady Serena Wuhl whispered to Lord Larkin Haldron, both having territories in Opax while Dirk Rollant, Lord of Carhurst in Paxton, spoke outside with Captain Reed, whom Jasce had fought alongside. Reed inclined his head and took up a chair in the hallway across from Kenz.

The council members greeted one another, but there always seemed to be an underlying tension when Jasce was in the room. Even though the Naturals knew he was on their side, some of them, namely Lord Haldron, still harbored resentment toward the former Angel of Death. He didn't blame them. He had brought death and destruction to nearly all the villages in Opax. But he also didn't care what any of them thought, especially Haldron. For the peace of this council, and ultimately Pandaren, he tamped down his disdain for the portly man dressed in his fancy robes—his smirk accentuated by the pencil-thin mustache clinging to his upper lip.

They all stood as Queen Lorella Valeri entered, her purple gown trailing behind her. She sat at the head of the table with the Valeri coat of arms on the wall above her. "The Gathering is less than two weeks away and there are still reports of missing Spectrals."

Lady Darbry snuck a glance at Jasce and then focused on the queen. "What do missing Spectrals have to do with us and the Gathering?"

Embracing the Darkness

"I want your personal guards to help find answers," Queen Valeri said.

Lord Haldron squared his broad shoulders. "If I may, I thought the Paladin Guard was tasked with this assignment."

Jasce bristled. "If *I* may, the Guard is stretched thin recruiting and training soldiers, preparing for the Gathering, and searching for Jaida and Vale."

Lord Haldron's face reddened and he puffed out his chest. "That's not a good enough reason. There are disappearances happening near my territory, and I'd expect—"

"You don't care about Spectrals, Larkin, so don't act like you're concerned with their welfare."

Lord Haldron stood and leaned on the table. "How dare you!"

Jasce mirrored him, his teeth grinding together. He wanted to punch the smug look from the councilman's fat face.

"That's enough, gentlemen." The queen's voice cut the tension like a sharpened blade through butter.

Lord Haldron scowled at him and sat.

"Jasce," Kord whispered at his side. "Let it go."

He tore his gaze from the noble and was met with wide-eyed stares from the other council members. Kord scanned Jasce's body as if something uncertain lurked under his skin, while worry etched along the creases of Amycus's eyes.

Jasce took a deep breath, released the hilt of his dagger, and sat. He traced the fire-shaped tattoo on the top of his hand. As the Angel of Death, he had a symbol inscribed on his arm for every Spectral he'd killed. The final tattoo he'd received was the one for Drexus, the Fire Spectral who had murdered his mother and taken his sister. Azrael had worn the marks as a badge of honor and power. Jasce wore them as a reminder of who he never wanted to be. However, he had never anticipated the challenge of reining in his temper or changing former habits.

Queen Valeri leaned forward. "The search for the fugitives is no longer the priority." Jasce opened his mouth, but the queen raised her hand, silencing his protest. "I need all of you to help with the effort of solving the mystery of the missing Spectrals. I cannot have my people disappearing when the other kingdoms arrive."

Cassie Sanchez

Jasce shook his head. For the last three months, all anyone talked about was the Gathering—a time when the five kingdoms assembled to broker trade agreements and establish general welfare for each country. The event hadn't happened in over twenty years because of the war with the Vastanes and the following unrest in Pandaren, but now Queen Valeri was back in power, and to make her land prosperous again she needed the other kingdoms.

"I still can't believe you invited the Vastanes," Lady Wuhl said, her mouth pursed as if she'd sucked on a lemon.

Lord Rollant sighed. "Serena, we've been over this a hundred times."

"Yes, and we'll go over it a hundred and one more times. They didn't ravage your land, did they? How many people did you lose in the war?" Lady Wuhl's brown eyes darted to the queen and then back to Lord Rollant, who raised his hands in surrender.

Amycus rested his arms on the table. "If we prohibit the Vastanes from joining the Gathering, we are showing weakness and fear."

"We can't trust the Vastanes, and I'm not too sure about the other kingdoms," the queen said. "Which is why I called this meeting. We need to prepare for our"—she looked at the ceiling—"guests, and I need everyone united." She studied each member of the council, ending with Jasce. "The Paladin Guard must be ready."

After another hour of discussing security, namely how to deal with the different types of magic from the Baltens, Terrenians, and Alturians, Queen Valeri stood and exited the room, followed by the nobles. Jasce shoved his chair back and stalked after the queen.

"Jasce, don't—" Amycus started to say. The closing door silenced his words.

"Your Majesty," Jasce said, pushing through the other council members as Kenz and Captain Reed rose from their chairs in the hallway. Kenz's brow furrowed while Reed acknowledged Jasce and then followed Lord Rollant down the corridor.

Queen Valeri turned, her sculpted brow raised.

"I need to continue the search for my sister. I'm getting close, I—"

The queen lifted her hand, and he pressed his lips together. She'd done that twice now, and his anger bubbled to the surface. She waited

Embracing the Darkness

for the hallway to clear while her guards stood at the end of the corridor with their hands resting on the hilts of their swords. Rain pummeled the windows and lightning slashed through the turbulent sky.

"Commander, I need you to focus on the Gathering and the missing Spectrals. Currently, Jaida isn't a threat." Her brown eyes held an edge of steel. "That's my final word."

The train of the queen's gown slid around the corner, and Jasce's hands shook with the need to hit something. The air shifted as slender fingers laced with his. He closed his eyes, letting Kenz's magic flow over him, a soothing balm that settled his nerves and quieted his anger.

"Come on," she said, a seductive glint in her eye. "Let's get you cleaned up, and you can tell me what that was all about."

Jasce scanned her face, from the freckles that bridged her nose to her soft, full lips, and desire pulsed through him. This is what he needed—to lose himself in the woman he loved, the one who understood him, scars and all.

Chapter Two

Dawn peeked through the curtains, sending a shaft of light across the floor. The last thing Jasce remembered was collapsing into bed, exhausted. He blinked away the fatigue and thought about the ten days that had passed since the meeting with the queen, when he had obeyed orders and abandoned the search for his sister.

Ever since the announcement of the Gathering, Jasce and Caston had worked nonstop getting their soldiers ready, and they still had a lot to do. Both men used their expertise as Hunters, thinking of ways someone could infiltrate the palace. Along with thwarting any sort of assassination attempt, they also had to plan for the different forms of magic from the visiting kingdoms. But the biggest concern was the Vastanes. Even though it was widely believed they didn't have magic, no one on the council trusted the Vastane queen. Queen Evelina Siryn claimed she wanted peace, but her father had been killed in the war. Jasce knew all too well how addicting vengeance could be.

The staff at the castle had labored tirelessly to make sure everything was ready for the upcoming festivities. Hallways were shined so reflections could be seen in the black marble floors, and the guest rooms had been cleaned where not a trace of dust was found. The gardeners had trimmed the hedges to perfection and the grounds resembled a tropical paradise, with flowers and shrubs exploding with color. Even the people of Orilyon were excited with the news of the Gathering; the streets clear of trash, storefronts glimmering, fountains sparkling. On the outside, everything looked perfect.

Last night, Jasce had another late night of meetings, and when he'd arrived at his and Kenz's suite, she was asleep on the couch, an array of leather straps and paint forgotten on the table. Her skills in carving and decorating belts and scabbards had spread through the Bastion, where many of the soldiers donned her work. What had started as a hobby had grown into a full-time job.

Coming home late and finding her asleep had become their new routine. She'd seemed more tired than usual. Granted, she'd been training harder than normal to prepare for the tournaments held during the Gathering, but what she desired most was to be promoted to captain, with her sights set on general. She had applied again last week.

He swallowed the guilt. If Kenz had been any other soldier, he would have already promoted her. But she wasn't. His captains and generals were the first to step into the fray, and that was the last thing he wanted for her. His need to protect her had caused more than a few arguments, and he'd learned to keep his feelings to himself. She had something to prove, and he wasn't sure how long he could put off this decision, knowing he was being unfair and was running out of time and excuses. Even Caston had brought it up during their last meeting.

Jasce listened to her gentle breathing as the room grew lighter with the rising sun. The blanket had slipped to her waist and her bare shoulder lifted with each breath. Definition in her arms and back proved how hard she'd been practicing. When he'd first met Kenz, she was already a competent fighter. Now, she was one of his best soldiers.

He traced his fingers down her back, circling each bone along her spine.

To hell with it, he thought. They could both be late for their morning responsibilities.

He kissed her neck and shoulder blade, smiling when a soft moan escaped her lips. She rolled over and opened sleepy green eyes. The

Embracing the Darkness

blanket shifted, exposing her breasts that were pebbled in the cool air. He leaned down and gently swirled his tongue along her delicate skin.

"Hi," she mumbled, playing with the hair that fell across his face.

"Hi." Jasce lifted his head and trailed kisses over her eyelids and down the tip of her nose. She wrapped her arms around his neck and pulled him closer. She smiled against his mouth, and he knew she felt how much he wanted her. "I've missed you. And as your commander, I order you to be late for training."

She laughed and slid her fingers down his scarred back. "Are you suggesting we neglect our duty to the Guard and the queen?" Her hands began a tortuous journey along his body.

"What queen?" He captured her mouth and desire erupted deep inside him as their magic merged. He explored her curves, pulling the blanket lower to allow the morning glow to illuminate her pale skin. Where his fingers went, his tongue followed, savoring every part of her. Kenz moaned and gripped his shoulders, her hips jerking underneath him as she cried out.

Jasce licked his lips and pulled himself to eye level. "I need you. Desperately," he whispered.

She breathed deeply. "Then take me."

He didn't need to be told twice, relishing the feel of her surrounding him. She gasped and he waited a breath before slowly moving with her. It was agony and bliss at the same time. Their magic swirled in a seductive dance that made him crave more, calming him yet igniting a fire that threatened to burn out of control.

"Kenz," Jasce sighed as he moved faster, going deeper. With her, he was whole. With her, his past became a blurry image, loosening its suffocating grip.

Their lovemaking was vigorous and passionate, and as she wrapped her legs around his waist, he couldn't restrain himself any longer. She threw her head back and cried out, which broke him as he lost himself in the release.

He collapsed half on her, his breathing rapid. She ran her hand up and down his back in a soothing motion. He'd almost drifted to sleep when she asked, "Want to talk about it?" She lovingly traced the scars from the times Drexus had whipped him.

Cassie Sanchez

"Not really," he muttered against her breast. She had this uncanny way of knowing when something troubled him. It was annoying and endearing at the same time.

"Amycus says keeping things in the dark gives them power. I'm here if you want to talk."

Jasce grunted and pulled her closer, needing the comfort of her warm body. He lifted himself onto his elbow to gaze at her beautiful face. "Am I abandoning Jaida?"

She toyed with her bracelets. "You and your teams have searched most of Opax for her and Vale. I've barely seen you. If she only knew how hard you've tried…"

"I was getting close. I know it. And then the queen ordered me to stop the search and focus on this bloody Gathering." He scoffed and rolled onto his back. "Obedience to the queen or loyalty to my family."

"She isn't your only family, you know."

He sighed and wrapped an arm around her, tucking her into his side. "I know." He couldn't believe his luck, but how long would fate be kind to him? He didn't deserve the woman in his arms, her acceptance, or her love. But he would do everything in his power to protect her and try to one day be worthy.

Seagulls cried as dawn shifted and the sky grew brighter. He did have a family with Kenz and Kord. Soon he'd have a wife, a brother and sister, and even a nephew. The thought filled him with hope, and yet the feeling of failure tugged at the corners of his mind. Jaida was out there, somewhere.

Kenz brushed the hair out of his face and swallowed. "There is something—"

A knock on the door interrupted her. She rolled her eyes and glanced out of the bedroom toward the living area.

The knock came again. Louder.

"Just ignore it." He rolled over and smiled. "What were you going to say?"

"Quit ignoring me." Caston's voice rumbled from the other side of the door. He rapped his knuckles again loudly.

Jasce swore and forced himself off the bed, securing a blanket around his waist. "What?" he asked, practically ripping the door off its hinges.

Caston raised his brows and then looked away, a sheepish grin on his face. "Sorry, but I received word the Alturian ships were spotted on the outskirts of the Marinus Shoals."

Jasce raked his fingers through his hair. "Have you told the queen?"

"I was on my way."

Jasce sighed. He thought he'd been busy before, but as each kingdom arrived, he'd have fewer moments to rest. "Let Queen Valeri know and gather one squadron. I'll meet you on the docks."

"You still have a little time." Caston winked and marched down the hall.

Jasce shut the door and leaned against it. He rubbed his temple and thought of everything that still needed to be done.

Kenz emerged from their room wearing an emerald silk robe he'd brought from one of his last scouting missions as a peace offering. "Headache?" she asked.

"The Alturians are close." He closed his eyes as she brushed the hair from his face. "Now, what did you want to tell me?"

"It can wait. You're busy."

"I'm never that busy."

She ran her hand down his naked chest and thoughts of Alturian ships vanished. He untied the robe, letting it puddle around her bare feet, and trailed a finger between her breasts and along her stomach, enjoying the way her muscles quivered under his caress. She arched her back and sighed his name.

Caston was right—he definitely had time.

Royal-blue and emerald-green sails emerged on the horizon like peacocks fanning out their feathers. Three Alturian ships sliced through the water, kicking up foam as seagulls flew overhead. The smell of brine and fish wafted on the breeze, and the docks bustled with fishermen preparing their nets and boats. Merchant vessels floated in the harbor as a steady stream of skiffs, loaded with supplies, sailed across the bay. Vendor stalls along the Navalia Boardwalk opened for business, and the city buzzed with excitement for the first kingdom to arrive after twenty years of war and isolation.

Jasce tugged at the collar of his doublet as sweat trickled down his spine. Even in the morning, the heat glimmered off the wooden planks of the dock, and the humid air wrapped around him like a wet blanket.

The Alturian ships lowered their anchors, and a tall man with ebony skin climbed down a ladder into a smaller boat, followed by his guards.

Must be Prince Jazari, Jasce thought, squinting into the distance. Men and women dressed in jewel-tone clothing filled the other boats and sailed toward the dock.

The Alturians were known for their exotic spices and fine cloth. The Gathering, along with establishing peace between the nations, would also increase trade and commerce. When the Spectral conflict broke out after the Vastane War, the steward had closed Pandaren's borders and ceased all business with the surrounding kingdoms, forcing the country to become self-reliant, but the restrictions had taken its toll. If the negotiations ran smoothly, all the kingdoms would benefit.

Jasce approached Caston, who had a squadron of soldiers standing behind him. "Are we ready?"

Caston crossed his arms. "The Trackers are in position. Do you think this will work?"

Amycus had told them about the Alturians' Shade Walking magic. Shade Walkers manipulated shadows for camouflage, and powerful Walkers used the shadows to travel short distances, which made them excellent spies. During one of their many strategic meetings, Jasce had suggested using Trackers since they could sense the different forms of Spectral magic. There was a chance they might also perceive the Alturians' powers.

Drexus had used a Tracker when the Hunters raided villages in search of unregistered Spectrals. In his dreams, Jasce was still haunted by the white eyes of one of those Trackers. She had warned him of a powerful Psyche right after she'd plunged Jasce's dagger into her chest, freeing herself from Drexus's chains. Her blood stained his hands, just

Embracing the Darkness

like the rest of the Spectrals he had killed, even if hers hadn't been intentional. Guilt rose inside him. He hadn't even known her name.

"Let's hope so," Jasce said as he spotted the four Trackers stationed in different areas around the dock. He'd been fortunate enough to find them during the transition of power between Drexus and Queen Valeri. The closest Tracker, Indago, glanced his way, or at least it looked like he was staring at him. It was hard to tell with their white eyes. Who knew what they saw? They were a mysterious group that kept to themselves. Indago tilted his head as his vacant gaze studied him, sending a shiver down his spine.

"They've always given me the creeps." Caston grimaced. "Anyway, I don't expect trouble from the Alturians. Lord Haldron is causing more of a headache than anyone else. Why are nobles so annoying?"

Jasce snorted. "Because they're nobles."

Lord Haldron had insisted on being present when each kingdom arrived. It seemed the noble didn't trust Jasce's ability to be diplomatic. Lord Rollant and Captain Reed also stood nearby, speaking with Amycus and Kenz. Supposedly, Lord Rollant had an acquaintance in Alturia traveling with the prince. How the lord from Paxton knew someone in Alturia, he couldn't guess.

Jasce glanced at all the dark corners and alleys. Security against people who disappeared among the shadows would be a challenge. "I don't trust any of our visitors, including the Shade Walkers. Keep your eyes open."

Caston saluted and returned to his post. Jasce drifted to the end of the dock and rested his arms on the wooden railing. Dark clouds lined the horizon, threatening another afternoon of rain. Fishermen laughed while they cleaned their early morning catch, and a breeze blew the coppery stench of blood and brine across the harbor.

The Alturian prince stepped onto the docks and smiled brightly. The man was tall and thin, his dark skin rippled across taut muscles in his arms, shoulders, and legs, and Jasce could tell by his movements that the prince was a competent fighter. The Shade Walker seemed to glide along the pier, his silver hair glimmering in the sun.

Jasce approached and bowed slightly. "Welcome to Pandaren, Your

Highness." He snuck a glance out of the corner of his eye to see Kenz and Amycus smirking.

"You must be Commander Farone," Prince Jazari said, smiling. "I've heard quite a lot about you. Please, call me Nicolaus."

Jasce dipped his chin. "Very well. Nicolaus, this is my Second, Caston Narr, and may I present Lord Haldron of Bradwick and Lord Rollant of Carhurst." As the two men bowed before the prince, Reed caught Jasce's stare and rolled his eyes. Jasce bit back a laugh.

He noticed an Alturian woman watching him, her sculpted brow arched. She didn't wear the custom Alturian robe as the other delegates, instead donning a crimson tunic and gray trousers. A scimitar sat on her hip, the curved sword scratched and dented, and a bow and a quiver of arrows was strapped to her back. Her sable skin, violet eyes, and silver hair braided down her back made her an imposing and intriguing woman.

While the prince addressed the others, Jasce glanced at Indago, who nodded. The Trackers sensed the Alturians' magic.

Prince Jazari inched closer, and his silver eyes sparkled as he studied the woman Jasce was observing. "This is Commander Eris Faez. She is most interested in touring your facilities. We have heard much about the Bastion, even on our island across the sea."

"I'd be happy to arrange a tour once you are settled," Jasce said. Her eyes never left his as she gave him a curt nod.

The prince rubbed his hands together. "Let's get this show on the road, shall we?"

"Allow me," Lord Rollant said, and led the Alturians to the carriages waiting to take them to the palace with Lord Haldron tottering behind. Indago and his fellow Trackers scanned the dock one last time and followed the entourage up the hill.

Caston crossed his arms as he stared at the procession. "They'll be hard to watch with that shade-walking thing they do."

"I want a Tracker present in all meetings with the queen." He released his top button and gazed at the sky. The sun drifted behind the clouds but did little to soothe the oppressive heat. "Remember when all we did was train and hunt? I don't recall Drexus having to do all this delegation nonsense." He shoved his hands into his pockets.

Embracing the Darkness

Caston chuckled. "Yeah, well, things were a bit different then." He patted Jasce's shoulder. "One down, three to go."

"I already need a drink," Jasce mumbled, and followed his Second down the boardwalk toward Amycus and Kenz, who waited with the horses.

Chapter Three

Dark shadows, barely visible against the gray sky, took shape on the horizon, and dust swirled below as carriages made their way toward the outskirts of the city. Even though the people had been warned of the Terrenians' means of travel, screams still echoed through the streets.

Jasce raised his brows as Amycus bobbed on his toes with a grin plastered on his face. He nudged Kenz and pointed toward the blacksmith. She smiled. Even he had to admit it was exciting to see the Terrenians' wyverns after hearing stories of the legendary beasts.

Jaida would've loved this, he thought, and the knot in his stomach tightened. As a little girl, she'd always wanted to fly, especially after listening to the tales their mother told. They'd jump off fallen logs in the forest as they pretended to save Pandaren from the evil invaders. What would their lives have been like if not for Drexus? What if his mother hadn't been killed, his sister taken, and him made into a monster? Jasce sighed. Focusing on what-ifs left him hollow inside. Unable to change the past, he pushed the memory aside and observed the wyverns gliding effortlessly toward Orilyon.

"Have you ever seen one?" Jasce asked Amycus, who reluctantly pulled his gaze from the dozen flying beasts.

"A long time ago, after the war, I traveled to Terrenus and ran into the archduke and his wyverns."

The Terrenians dwelled on the other side of the Culmen Range, east of Paxton. They had kept to themselves, rarely venturing into the small villages that nestled along the western edge of the mountains.

"What were you doing in Terrenus?" Kenz asked, her brow furrowed.

Amycus returned his gaze toward the wyverns. "I was searching for information and interested in the Gemari magic. Their ability to use their gems to create weapons and shields is quite impressive."

Jasce had researched Terrenus during his preparation for the Gathering. Certain Terrenians, called Gemari's, were born with magic and had gems implanted in their chests. And only a Gemari could be in a position of power or in the military. Their magic reminded him of Spectral Shields, like Kenz. She couldn't form a weapon, but she had learned to use her shield for offense as well as protecting those around her.

Kenz tapped the hilt of her blade. "Producing a sword with a thought would certainly be convenient."

"Indeed," Amycus answered, giving her a wink.

"I've heard those mountains aren't easy to get across," Jasce said. The wyverns and their riders wouldn't have any problem, but all those carriages traversing through the dangerous trails must have been grueling.

Amycus chuckled. "I was a lot younger and headstrong when I made the trek."

Kenz and Amycus talked while Jasce surveyed the security lining the perimeter. He had transformed one of the Guard's outposts into a large paddock to house the wyverns. His soldiers, Naturals and Spectrals alike, stood side by side waiting for their guests. He'd stationed Aura, a powerful Air Spectral, and a group of Airs as an additional safety measure just in case a wyvern flew off course. As if she could feel his stare, she turned and gave him a subtle nod. Her long white hair billowed in a breeze that always surrounded her.

The ground trembled as the largest wyvern landed, stamping an enormous clawed foot and shaking its head like a horse shakes its mane. People had filled the streets and rooftops to get a better view of the

Embracing the Darkness

legendary creatures, creating another security issue for Jasce and the Guard.

Another wyvern landed, opened its massive jaws, and roared. Emile squeaked while Maleous and Lander shared a laugh.

Jasce had been so entranced by the mysterious beasts, he hadn't seen the kids approach. "What are you three doing here?"

Maleous, Kord's son, kept his gaze fixed on a wyvern with red scales and black horns. "Dad said we could as long as we stayed out of the way."

Jasce pointed to the wyvern paddock. "You think this is out of the way?"

Maleous shrugged and then gave his aunt and Amycus a quick hug while the other kids said hello. Amycus knelt next to Emile and whispered in her ear. She shook her head and stared at her feet.

"Where's Kord?" Kenz asked. "I thought he'd want to see this."

Maleous rubbed his neck and glanced at Jasce. "There was a . . ." Using air quotes, he finished, "misunderstanding."

Jasce arched a brow. "What kind of 'misunderstanding'?" He copied the young Healer with air quotes of his own.

"I guess a Natural got into it with a Fire. Dad wants you to come by after this."

He sighed. If it wasn't one thing, it was another. He inclined his head toward Emile's older brother, Lander. "Shouldn't you be training?"

Lander crossed his arms. "Someone has to watch out for these two."

Jasce pinched the bridge of his nose and then nodded toward the Air Spectrals. "Stay behind Aura and keep your distance. Tillie will have my head if something happens to any of you."

The three kids rolled their eyes and jogged over to the Air Spectrals. Kenz squeezed Jasce's arm. "I better go with them. I don't want Tillie having my head, either." She followed them and hugged Aura. The two laughed at something Emile said.

Jasce caught Amycus frowning at Emile. "What is it?"

"I'm just concerned about what the three types of magic are doing to her."

"Are the side effects getting worse?" Drexus, in his quest for building a Spectral army, had experimented with combining magic. Emile had survived the procedure, and now had both of Jasce's powers alongside her Earth magic. She'd recently complained of headaches and shaking limbs, so Jasce and Amycus had been keeping a close eye on her.

"Maera is working with her."

Jasce was about to ask more when the remaining wyverns landed, and the spectators cheered.

The winged creatures varied in color and size, all as unique as the Gemaris on their backs with gems glowing from each of their chests. The wyverns had blue, red, green, or black scales that shimmered like metal. The talon-tipped wings, easily twenty feet wide, folded as their riders dismounted. Powerful hind legs with lethal claws quivered as their large gold eyes scanned the crowds, their nostrils twitching. Jasce had read that the wyverns, a smaller version of the dragons that lived across the sea, were apex predators known for their intelligence and hunting in packs. Based on the beasts now striding through the enclosure, he believed every word.

Caston, who'd been stationed on the other side of the paddock, jogged over. "Those are amazing," he said, breathless, as he gazed at the winged creatures.

Jasce crossed his arms. "Do you think the archduke will let us ride one?"

"I certainly hope so."

Archduke Kraig Carnelian slid off the black wyvern and stretched his back. The man stood at about five and a half feet, but his muscular frame made up for his lack of height. His long brown hair and beard was the custom for the men of Terrenus as were the leather and metal breeches they wore.

The archduke exited the paddock and opened his arms wide. "Amycus, my old friend. It's been a long time."

The creases around Amycus's eyes deepened. "It's good to see you, Kraig." The men exchanged a brief hug. "This is Commander Farone and his Second, Caston Narr."

Jasce and Caston stepped forward. "Those are incredible," Jasce said, eyeing the largest wyvern flexing its powerful wings.

Embracing the Darkness

The archduke puffed out his chest. "They are indeed. I'm sure we can arrange for you to ride one."

Jasce glanced at Caston and winked. "That would be fantastic. Thank you." He motioned to a soldier standing behind them. "In the meantime, General Seb Brin, an Earth Spectral, will be your liaison. Whatever you need, please don't hesitate to ask."

The archduke raised his bushy brows at Seb. "An Earth Spectral?" He shook the general's hand, then looked at Jasce. "I know my friend Amycus here is an Air, but what type of magic do you have?"

"I'm an Amp and a Vaulter."

"Two types? I didn't think that was possible. At least, not without consequences." He studied Jasce's chest as if he could see the two powers flowing through him.

Amycus stepped forward and steered the archduke toward the waiting carriages. "Yes, well, let's get you settled. The Alturians are already here, and the other kingdoms should arrive in the next few days." Amycus nodded to Seb, who followed.

Jasce grabbed Seb's arm. "Get me any information you can. I need to know exactly how their magic works. Is that clear?"

The Earth Spectral saluted. "You got it."

Mounting their horses, Jasce and Caston maneuvered through the villagers attempting to inch closer to the paddock to observe the legendary creatures.

Caston scratched his goatee. "What did he mean by that? What consequences?"

Jasce rubbed the scar where his magic-suppressing tattoo used to be. "Two types of magic can kill you or make you insane."

"Well, that explains it."

Jasce jerked his head and scowled at Caston. "What's that supposed to mean?"

Caston raised his hands. "Whoa. I was just kidding around." He lowered his voice. "Are you all right?"

Jasce massaged the back of his neck. "Sorry. Just tired."

Caston's brows furrowed. "You've been under a lot of stress with the Gathering and wedding plans."

Groaning, Jasce peered over his shoulder to where Kenz and the kids had moved closer to the wyvern paddock. "I can't deal with a wedding right now."

Caston's lip quirked as he followed Jasce's gaze. "Have you mentioned that to her? Because she and Maera were talking cake and flowers the other day. It was enough to make my eye twitch."

"No, I haven't said anything. I've barely seen her these past few weeks. There never seems to be a good time to talk."

"Pretty sure you had time the other morning." Caston laughed as Jasce glared at him.

If he was being honest, he didn't want to discuss the wedding. He had so many other things to tend with, and that was without the disciplinary issue with his recruits Maleous had mentioned.

The sound of a whip cracking through the air had Jasce spinning in his saddle, causing his horse, Bruiser, to grunt. Bruiser had been his horse during his time as a Hunter and had always been a loyal, stable presence. He patted the horse's neck and grimaced as memories of Drexus's whip slashed through skin and muscle.

"Jasce, what is it?"

He swallowed and surveyed the area. Lightning arced through the dark sky, followed by thunder and roars from the wyverns. "Nothing."

Caston's brow wrinkled, but he kept his horse moving.

The Balten king, Leonid Morzov, and his consort reached the gates of Orilyon the next morning. Jasce had received word after the Alturians arrived that the caravan had already passed Delmar. Balten, a land in the south, spent most of its days covered in snow and was known for its harsh environment and even tougher soldiers. They were a warrior race famous for their furs, weapons, and whiskey.

A squadron of guards waited near the southern entrance into the city to escort the Baltens to the palace. Caston leaned against the archway, flipping his dagger from hilt to blade. Jasce gritted his teeth and tried to ignore the repetitive movement.

"Will you knock it off?" Jasce finally said as the light from the blade flashed in his eyes.

Embracing the Darkness

Caston grinned and flipped the dagger faster. "Does this bother you?"

He scowled at his Second, who snickered and replaced the knife in its sheath.

"You look like hell, by the way," Caston said, a flicker of worry crossing his face.

"Thanks." He'd only managed a few hours of sleep, and exhaustion was catching up to him.

"Would you look at that?" Caston said, his eyes wide.

A tall woman with tattoos peeking out from her sleeves and across her chest opened the lead carriage's door, and two white catlike creatures, easily the size of ponies, hopped down. Their red eyes scanned the terrain as if looking for their next prey. The closest soldiers wisely stepped back, allowing room for the cats and the imposing woman.

One cat hissed and jumped out of the way as the other vomited. Jasce's laugh morphed into a cough when the woman glowered at him.

"Busted," Caston said out of the corner of his mouth.

"Shut it," Jasce replied.

The woman scratched the first cat's ears and whispered to it, then motioned to a Balten soldier standing guard at the entrance to the carriage. The king emerged, his eyes surveying the area. Jasce had seen that expression before from his Hunters. Warriors and assassins always knew their surroundings, able to locate any hidden threat or potential weapon.

King Morzov was a powerfully built man, rivaling Kord's size and strength. His copper-red hair hung to his shoulders, and a gold circlet lay on his head. Tattoos crept up his neck and decorated his hands. An armored chest piece covered a cream tunic that hid even more tattoos, if the stories were true.

The king took the cats' leashes from the woman, who strode to his other side, giving orders to the Balten soldiers. The rest of the court followed while Jasce's guards directed the wagons and carriages toward the palace.

The Baltens' magic was the most mysterious compared to the other attending kingdoms. Based on what he'd researched, the warriors could tap into a power that gave them speed and strength, similar to the

Cassie Sanchez

Amplifier Spectrals. One legend stated that a warrior could summon their Defender to fight alongside them, if only for a short while.

"Your Majesty," Jasce said, bowing. "Welcome to Pandaren. I'm Commander Farone." He introduced Caston and the other council members, who had again wanted to be part of the welcoming committee.

King Morzov inclined his head. "Commander. It's been a long time since I've visited Opax and the wonderful markets of Orilyon. We are eager to begin trade negotiations."

Lord Haldron stepped forward and jutted out his chest. "As are we."

Jasce refrained from rolling his eyes. Lord Rollant, Lady Wuhl, and Lady Darbry introduced themselves as the king fiddled with his goatee, flecked with gray, and peered out from the archway toward the city center as if imagining all he could buy or sell.

The woman who had soothed the cats stared at Jasce, her short blonde hair looking almost white with the morning sun. She was armed to the teeth with small blades across her chest, two swords hanging at her hips, and daggers sticking out of her boots.

King Morzov noticed Jasce's stare, and his mustache quivered. "This is my consort, Natasha Lekov, and also my general."

Jasce inclined his head. "Consort Lekov, welcome. I've heard many stories about your training regimen."

The consort's lips curled. "The Hunters are infamous in our region as well. The competitions should be very telling regarding who has the better system."

Jasce's shoulders tightened at the insinuation. "We don't train our recruits like that anymore."

"But," Caston said, cutting in, "I think you'll find our Paladin Guard up to the task." He shot Jasce a look.

The king's eyes sparkled as he stared between his consort and Jasce. He chuckled and crossed his arms over his broad chest. "This will be entertaining."

Jasce forced a smile. "And who are your . . . pets?"

King Morzov ran his tattooed hands across both cats' heads. Their eyes drifted closed, and purrs rumbled from their chests. "Ah, yes. These are Khioshkas, common in our region. This is Arseni, and the larger one

Embracing the Darkness

is Dasha. I promise you, they are very well-behaved. Now, where is Lorella? She owes me a case of wine for a bet we made years ago."

"The queen told me to tell you she's waiting in her receiving room and hasn't forgotten the wager." Jasce stumbled forward as the king slapped him on the back and laughed a deep, rumbling laugh. The consort signaled her guards, and they mounted their horses to ride up the hill toward the palace.

People moved out of the way as the Balten carriages wove through the streets. "You better go with them," Jasce said.

Caston saluted, hopped onto his horse, and galloped after the visitors with a squadron of soldiers flanking him.

Jasce strolled past the city archway and down a limestone path. He gazed out to sea, the cool breeze drying the sweat at his temples. Whitecaps crested along the waves, churning the usually tranquil water of the harbor into a chaotic dance of froth and foam. Only one more kingdom left. Figures the Vastanes were the last to arrive.

Chapter Four

Later that day, Jasce stood guard near the door to Queen Valeri's receiving room. The afternoon rain had cooled the temperature, but a mugginess filled the air. Prince Jazari, King Morzov, Archduke Carnelian, and Amycus sat on the covered veranda drinking tea with the queen.

Jasce stifled a yawn as he listened to the royals talk. The queen had insisted he stand guard, but the lack of sleep was making it difficult to focus. He would've chosen General Nadja for this drudgery, but she hadn't yet returned from their scouting mission.

He busied himself by examining the queen's chamber, having only been invited to this room a few times. The place was spacious, with white couches and blue rugs decorating the marble floor. Paintings of Pandaren's landscapes lined the wall, from the Merrigan Sea to the imposing mountain ranges separating Paxton from Terrenus. On the wall behind a gurgling fountain rested a crooked picture of a bowl of fruit. Jasce frowned at it, wanting to straighten the gilded frame.

The cascading water sent a shiver down his back, and the hairs on his neck rose. A memory flashed, and he could vividly see the fountain in Dunstead when Spectral emotions had overcome him. He'd lost himself to the rage and had removed an innocent man's head. It seemed no matter how hard he tried to change, his past lurked in the shadows where the Angel of Death's presence refused to lessen its grip.

Jasce caught Amycus staring at him with wary eyes, the dark circles underneath stark against his pale skin. The older man raised his brows in silent question, but Jasce shook his head and rested his hand on the hilt of his dagger, feeling its comfortable weight. He focused on his breath and willed the headache away. He needed to get some sleep, otherwise he'd be no good to anyone.

"So, Leonid, how was your journey from Balten?" Queen Valeri asked, stirring her tea.

"Uneventful. Your people have been very hospitable."

"I'm glad," she said. "Now, what do we know about Queen Evelina Siryn?"

Prince Jazari placed his porcelain teacup on the table. "Queen Siryn seeks knowledge and information like other men crave gold, and her libraries are quite extensive."

Archduke Carnelian leaned back and crossed his muscular arms. "Unlike her father, who simply wanted power. Thankfully, you and your Spectrals stopped the war."

Grief flashed through Queen Valeri's eyes. She'd lost her husband right after they defeated the Vastanes. Rarely did she show any sorrow, seeming to force it down with pure determination. Nothing and no one would stand in her way to better Pandaren. "Yes," she said, "you all were quite fortunate."

The Balten king stroked his goatee. "I wonder why King Siryn had his sights set on Pandaren. No offense, but what made your land so special?"

Jasce raised his brows. The Baltens were known for their honor and speaking the truth. Sometimes, their method was harsh, just like the region they lived in.

Queen Valeri narrowed her eyes. "No offense taken. Besides our shipping industry, the farms in Opax and natural resources in Paxton are very valuable, as you know."

Prince Jazari cleared his throat. "I've heard Queen Siryn's medical team might rival your Healers, Lorella."

The queen scoffed. "I doubt that. Kord Haring and Maera Sandor

Embracing the Darkness

have transformed our Sanctuary into something remarkable instead of what it used to be. Drexus Zoldac's ways were archaic, as were his experiments with magic."

Archduke Carnelian glanced over his shoulder and spied Jasce. "Commander, you were part of those experiments, weren't you?"

Amycus coughed and the archduke patted him on the back. Prince Jazari snickered as he glanced between Jasce and the Gemari.

Jasce held his stare and nodded. There were only a few times in his life he'd welcomed death, and one of those was when he'd received the Amplifier serum. He hadn't been sure he'd survive the process. No one had known he already possessed magic, either, including him. The two magics had fused together, and the consequence was the ability to feel other Spectrals' emotions. This weakness had made the Angel of Death a liability and led to his team of Hunters betraying him.

King Morzov swiveled in his chair. "We've heard about your power, Commander. It is quite impressive." Jasce tore his gaze from the archduke and focused on the king. "What was it like? You can't deny that the Watch Guard, especially your Hunters, were thoroughly trained and lethal."

The sheer curtains fluttered from the ocean breeze, and rain splattered on the balcony. A distant rumble of thunder filled the silence.

Jasce approached the table. "Commander Zoldac's methods were efficient, his discipline harsh. But yes, the Hunters were very skilled." He could still hear the crack of the whip, feel the pain from the grueling workout sessions, and sparring until his hands bled.

The Alturian prince regarded Jasce, his gaze drifting over his body as if he could see the magic within him. "The stories of the Hunters with their skull masks made it across the sea to our country. How many are there?"

The queen poured more tea. "We no longer have Hunters, Nicolaus. Commander Farone and his Second are the only two left from that barbaric system."

"Of course." The prince inspected his fingernails. "Commander Faez would like to see your soldiers train. What do you call them again?" he asked Jasce.

"The Paladin Guard." Jasce laced his hands behind his back.

Archduke Carnelian lifted his chin. "Our soldiers aren't as adept in the art of killing as yours, or the Baltens, but with the Gemari and our wyverns, we do okay."

The prince's silver eyes sparkled. "I'd also like to get a closer look at those magnificent creatures."

The archduke's smile grew. "By all means. I'm happy to give you and anyone else a demonstration of what they can do. They are remarkable."

Amycus leaned forward and addressed the Balten king. "Leonid, I think you'll be impressed with what Jasce has accomplished. Having Naturals practice alongside Spectrals is no easy feat."

Jasce stood a little taller. At least someone had noticed. He had worked hard with the Guard, and even though there were still some issues he needed to deal with, they were making progress. Of all his duties as commander, instructing the recruits is what he loved most. He'd take that responsibility over sitting in meetings or guarding the queen any day.

When Queen Valeri had informed him he'd be working for her, he hadn't known what to expect. Based on previous experience before the shift in power, he'd thought she was docile. Now he knew better. She would do whatever, and use whoever, to protect her lands. And currently, he was her tool to do just that.

His nails dug into his palms. He was no one's pawn. He was the most powerful Spectral in Pandaren.

"Commander?" Queen Valeri examined him with her brow furrowed and nodded toward King Morzov.

Jasce blinked. "I'm sorry. What were you saying?"

"Consort Lekov is eager for the tour of your facilities as well," the Balten king said. He pursed his lips at his teacup. It looked like a child's mug in his large warrior hands. "Honestly, Lorella, don't you have something stronger?"

They laughed, and Queen Valeri signaled to a servant, who disappeared through a side door.

"That'll be all, Commander," Queen Valeri said.

Jasce curled his lip, and his pulse quickened. He wasn't some sideshow for their entertainment. Did they not understand who he was? He shook his head. Or had been.

Amycus cleared his throat. The archduke raised his brows, his eyes darting from Jasce to the queen.

"Don't send him away, Lorella," Prince Jazari said, leaning back in his chair. "We have lots to discuss. I want to know his thoughts on the tournaments."

Jasce opened his mouth, but voices in the corridor had him turning. The queen's personal guard entered with Caston on her heels, his lips pressed in a hard line.

"I'm sorry to interrupt, but the Vastane ships have arrived."

As one, they peered toward the harbor. In the distance, white sails glided across the water like giant seabirds, graceful and serene. The peaceful image was at war with the nerves in the room.

Jasce inhaled and inclined his head to the queen. "Let the games begin."

Chapter Five

J asce leaned against a column, away from the overcrowded docks, and rubbed his forehead. The Guard and council members were on high alert, as no one knew what to expect from Queen Evelina Siryn. After the Vastane king was killed in the war, she'd been thrust into power as a teenager. Her father had sought dominion but, according to the Alturians, she valued knowledge. The queen's focus was in medicine, and she had insisted on meeting with Kord and Maera when she arrived.

A large hand rested on his shoulder, and a tingle ran up his neck into his head. Kord's magic flowed over him like a gentle breeze. He closed his eyes and inhaled the salty air. "You know, if you bottled that you'd make a fortune."

Kord chuckled. "Pretty sure that wouldn't end well for me."

Small transfer boats made their way from the Vastane ships toward the docks.

Kord crossed his arms and examined him. "Another headache, huh? You've been getting those a lot."

"Who wouldn't with all of this going on?" He looked past his friend at the waiting council members. Everyone had wanted to be present for the Vastanes' arrival. Lord Haldron and Lady Wuhl each had a small squadron of their personal guards stationed around the dock, even though Jasce had told them it was unnecessary as he had soldiers posted throughout, some undercover as fisherman and dockhands. But, just as a few nobles didn't trust the Vastanes, they didn't trust him, either.

He fisted his hands as he thought about how he'd almost died fighting Drexus, the blood spilled as he protected Naturals and Spectrals alike. And still, they looked at him as a traitor, as the Angel of Death.

"Hey, you okay?" Kord's brow wrinkled as he scanned his face.

"Yeah, just tired." How many times had he given this excuse? He huffed out a breath. He was getting tired of saying he was tired.

Kord studied him, concern tightening the skin around his eyes. "You sure that's it?"

Jasce stepped out of his reach as Caston approached in full armor with a sword on each hip. "Commander, it's time."

Jasce nodded and marched down the dock, past the waiting council members, with Kord at his heels. A few nobles widened their eyes as they looked him up and down. He wore his armored chest piece, his two swords rested against his back, and his dagger was in its sheath on his thigh. It wasn't welcoming, but he didn't care. He'd rather be prepared than proper.

He signaled to Amycus and Kenz, also wearing their armor, to join him. Amycus had his scimitar sheathed along his back and Kenz's bracelets glowed. Jasce wasn't expecting a fight on the docks, but he wanted to present a powerful front, just in case the Vastane queen had any ideas.

Jasce faced Amycus and Kenz. "I want you two on the other end of the boardwalk. Stay alert." They both nodded and wove through the crowds of vendors and townspeople.

Wood creaked as the skiffs docked. Four bodyguards disembarked, three of them matching Kord's size, but Jasce could tell the most dangerous was the smaller guard by the predatory way he moved and how he scanned the area with lethal precision. His dark eyes finally settled on Jasce, and the corner of his lip lifted, making the scar along his cheek pucker. He inclined his head and then held out his hand to help the Queen of Vastane out of the boat.

"Damn," Caston said, keeping his voice low.

Embracing the Darkness

Jasce had heard rumors of the queen's beauty, but the stories didn't compare to the woman who emerged. She wore a silver gown that complemented her golden skin, and her blonde hair was intricately woven around a diamond-encrusted crown. A ruby pendant nestled between her breasts and eyes the color of a tropical sea found his. Jasce's gut tightened.

He took a deep breath and stepped forward. The guards surrounded their queen, and he couldn't help but smirk as he eyed them. His magic pulsed, readying itself. They were no match for his power or skill as an assassin.

"Ah, the Angel of Death. I've so longed to meet you," Queen Siryn said, her red lips tilting up at the corners.

"It's Commander Farone, Your Majesty." He bowed, never taking his gaze off her guards.

"But the Angel of Death has a nicer ring to it. Don't you think?" The queen's eyes hardened as she peered at the soldiers behind him. "All of this for me?"

Kord moved by Jasce's side. "Queen Siryn, I'm Kord Haring, lead Healer of the Sanctuary. On behalf of my staff, we are pleased you are here." Jasce gave his friend an incredulous look.

The queen raised a brow. "Mr. Haring. I've heard about you as well. Your abilities are renowned. My personnel"—she looked over her shoulder as her people disembarked—"are very interested in sharing notes."

"It's an honor. We'll schedule a tour for tomorrow, before the Welcome Ball."

The queen's eyes slid to Jasce. "And will you be offering a tour as well, Commander?"

He searched for Caston, since he was their designated tour guide, but his Second was talking animatedly with Lord Haldron, whose face had turned different shades of red.

"Commander?"

He forced a smile. "I'd be happy to show you our facilities."

Lord Rollant approached and cleared his throat. "We are glad you arrived safely, Your Majesty," he said, bowing. "I'm Lord Rollant of

Carhurst. Our guards will see you to your quarters and get you anything you need."

Jasce's shoulders stiffened under the queen's stare. The gleam in her eyes shifted into something predatory. "Anything I need?" She smiled coyly, and then addressed Lord Rollant. "Very well."

Jasce pivoted out of the way as the guards and council members escorted the Vastanes to the castle.

Kord crossed his arms, watching the group climb into carriages. "That was interesting."

"Not sure that's the word I'd use."

"If Kenz sees the queen act like that with you, we're going to have a diplomatic incident."

Jasce pinched the bridge of his nose. "I really need a drink. Do we have time?"

Kord grinned and smacked him on the back. "Always, my friend. Always."

Jasce inhaled the smell of ale and sweat, and although it wasn't the most palatable combination, it was inviting nonetheless. He had spent many nights at the Tainted Barrel as a Hunter when he was a member of the Watch Guard, and he found it continued to give him comfort even as those days were behind him. He greeted Jerome, the bartender, and strode toward his usual table in the corner, facing the room and door. Kord settled beside him with a large tankard and leaned against the wall.

"It seems our guests have truly invaded," Jasce said, nodding across the tavern. A group of Gemari and Balten soldiers surrounded a scarred table that wobbled as a Balten slammed the Gemari's hand onto the surface. The Alturians observed the competition and managed the bets.

Delmira and Kenz ambled in and passed the group, earning a few salacious glances from the visitors. Jasce glared at one Balten soldier who whistled. Kenz rolled her eyes and pulled Delmira past the crowded tables. Laughter and clinking glasses sounded throughout the tavern.

"Why do boys feel the need to arm wrestle?" Delmira asked, eyeing the Balten flexing his massive biceps.

Embracing the Darkness

"To impress the ladies," Jasce said as Kenz sat. He draped his arm over her shoulder and kissed her cheek. The Balten who'd whistled glanced at her and then at Jasce, who winked. The warrior raised his brows and turned back to his companions.

"If you want to impress me, use your brain instead of what's hanging between your legs," Kenz said.

Kord coughed and spit foam across the table at Delmira, who jumped.

Jasce laughed and patted him on the back, then squeezed Kenz's shoulder and pulled her close. "That's not what you said the other night."

Kord pointed at him. "First, no. Second"—he wiped his chin and glowered at his sister—"where did you learn to talk like that?"

"I work out with a bunch of men. What do you expect?"

"She has a point," Delmira said, getting to her feet. "Want anything?"

Kenz shook her head. Another slam followed by cheers caught Jasce's and Kord's attention.

"I'd put money on you," Jasce said with a mischievous smile.

Kord chortled but resumed his drinking. Aura joined them, and it almost felt like old times in Carhurst. A warmth grew in Jasce's belly as he laughed with his friends.

After a few tankards and some nudging from Jasce, Kord finally wandered over to the arm-wrestling table. Jasce knocked back another shot of whiskey and slid out of the booth, rubbing his palms together. "This ought to be good." Aura, Delmira, and Kenz all rolled their eyes.

"Boys," Aura muttered.

He stood behind Kord and placed a coin on the table. Wagers came in as more patrons surrounded the group, most going in the Balten's favor.

The large warrior eyed Kord. "You're big," he said with a heavy accent.

"So I've been told." Kord rested his elbow on the table and waited for the Balten to grab his hand.

"You can't use your magic, Matvey," a Gemari said, his muscular arms crossed and a grin on his face. Jasce hadn't missed that a few Terrenians had bet on Kord.

Matvey laughed. "Yeah, yeah, I know. I won't need to."

Kord arched a brow. "Shall we?"

Matvey nodded and clasped Kord's hand.

"On three," an Alturian said, standing beside Jasce.

The Alturian counted, and cheers rang out as Kord's and Matvey's hands shook and biceps bulged. The Balten gaped at Kord, whose face remained relaxed, his lips turned up into a smile. Matvey grunted and pushed. Kord's arm dipped an inch, and Matvey sneered.

Kord's shoulders bunched as he settled into his chair. His jaw muscle ticked, and his eyes narrowed. Matvey swore, a word Jasce wasn't familiar with, and his companions laughed. The warrior's hand drifted closer to the surface.

Jasce crossed his arms and smiled. He knew Kord would win.

Matvey's knuckles were an inch from the surface when the man's eyes glowed. Suddenly, Kord's hand crashed onto the table. Boos and yells echoed through the tavern.

"He used magic!" said one of Jasce's soldiers.

Jasce shoved Kord out of the chair and gripped the Balten's hand. "You want to use magic, then let's use magic."

Matvey swallowed and tried to pull away. Jasce's knuckles whitened and the veins bulged on his arm.

"Jasce, don't," Kord said.

Jasce focused on his Amplifier power and pushed against the Balten soldier. His anger burned and he let it empower him. Matvey grunted as Jasce forced his arm closer to the surface. The man's eyes glowed again, but he was no match for Jasce's added strength.

He slammed the Balten's hand down while Jasce's other hand wrapped around the hilt of his dagger. Matvey yelled, his eyes wide as he stared at the blade pinning his palm to the wood.

The tavern fell silent.

Jasce leaned forward and whispered. "Not so strong, are you?"

Kord swore, pushed him out of the way, and removed the dagger from Matvey's hand. Chaos erupted as the Baltens and Paladin guards exchanged blows. Fists flew and chairs splintered. Shade Walkers disap-

Embracing the Darkness

peared among the shadows, reappearing and catching the Gemaris off guard as the crystals in their chests ignited and luminous swords and daggers appeared out of thin air.

"Stop!" Kenz's voice broke through the din. Her lips drew into a straight line as indigo light forced the soldiers back. Delmira used her own shield to subdue a group of Gemaris and Alturians.

Blood dripped down Jasce's chin and his arm trembled as he squeezed Matvey's neck. The Balten's toes scraped the floor, and his face had reddened around bulging eyes. A familiar glow fluttered over him as his name was called. He released Matvey, who stumbled, seconds from passing out, and Kenz's shield shrank around Jasce. The room fell silent. He blinked and noticed his bloody dagger on the table, not remembering grabbing it, or using it. Only anger. The consuming rage reminded him of . . . No, he thought, and lowered his head. He didn't want to travel down that path again.

Kord stepped between them and reached for Matvey, who jerked away. Kord raised a hand. "I'm a Healer."

Matvey didn't take his eyes off Jasce.

Jerome emerged from the other side of the bar. "Okay, everyone. This round's on me. Let's all just settle down." He flashed Jasce a glare.

Jasce realized Kenz's shield was still enclosing him, and only him. He looked at her.

"You good?" she asked.

He licked his lips and nodded.

The shield disappeared.

He inhaled and returned his dagger to its sheath. "Matvey, please accept my apology. I don't . . ." He was at a loss for words. As commander of the queen's army, this could lead to strained relationships with the Baltens at the least. At the most, it could turn into a war. The Baltens were a proud race, and King Morzov wouldn't be pleased.

Jasce counted the seconds while Matvey continued to glower at him.

Finally, the warrior glanced at his healed hand. "I probably deserved that." Nervous chuckles rumbled from the onlookers as he approached Jasce and leaned in close. "But if you stab me again, it will be the last thing you ever do."

Jasce bristled, but Kord cleared his throat. Feeling the hairs on his neck rise, he peered over his shoulder to see a short, pudgy man leave the tavern. Lord Haldron looked back, a smirk lining his face.

"That doesn't bode well," Kord said, following Jasce's stare.

"No, it does not." He ran his fingers through his hair. "I need to inform the queen what happened before that weasel does." He moved toward the exit just as Caston sprinted through the door. He approached Jasce and saluted, then whispered in his ear.

Jasce stiffened.

"What is it?" Kord asked.

"Flynt and General Nadja have returned."

Chapter Six

The sound of Jasce's boots reverberated off the stone walls as he strode down the corridor with Caston and Kord on his heels. "Where are they?" Jasce asked.

"Sanctuary," Caston replied, his voice tight.

Jasce's shoulders tensed. Someone on the team must have been injured, otherwise they would've met in the Bastion's command room. He picked up his pace, tempted to vault straight to the medical facility.

He pushed through the doors of the Sanctuary as one of the junior Healers, Pilar, led Flynt and General Alyssa Nadja, covered in dirt and dried blood, to an exam room. Jasce scanned the area for the other members of the scout team.

Kord jogged over and swore when he saw the gashes across Flynt's arms and chest. He did a quick survey of Alyssa, but she waved him off.

"He needs your attention," she said. Pilar handed her a glass of bubbling liquid wafting with a mint and lavender aroma. She sniffed it and then guzzled the contents.

Flynt winced as he rested on the pillow, his arm folded over his chest. Kord sat next to him and examined his wounds. Jasce stood on the other side, his arms crossed, while Caston leaned against a counter, fiddling with his dagger.

"What happened?" Jasce asked as Amycus and Kenz entered. Amycus pulled up a chair while Kenz hugged Alyssa. Both Jasce and Caston had trained with Alyssa during their early days at the Watch Guard, and her talent, discipline, and leadership skills had made her an easy choice when Jasce promoted her to general. Now, Jasce was more grateful than ever for his decision.

Flynt swallowed. Dark smudges under his amber eyes lay stark against his ashen face. He raked a hand through his short, red hair and grimaced. "We were attacked. The others didn't make it."

Amycus leaned forward. "Attacked by who? Jaida?"

Alyssa set her glass on the table, weariness marring her face. "Not who. What." Bruised skin showed through her torn uniform, and her brown hair, normally tied in a tight knot, lay tangled down her back.

Jasce glanced at Amycus, whose eyes narrowed. Months ago, after the Battle of the Bastion, Queen Valeri had revealed a black claw with lethal talons that had been found in the desert. Neither he nor Amycus had ever seen anything like it. The queen had tasked them with obtaining information on it, but the search for Jaida and the missing Spectrals, plus preparations for the Gathering, had forced the mysterious creature to the back of their minds. Jasce hadn't thought about it in weeks.

"We were returning from our mission when rumors of strange noises were reported on the outskirts of Bradwick," Alyssa continued. "Markel was on watch and disappeared without a trace—all we heard was his scream. We were following some tracks through the forest when it attacked Flynt."

"My fire barely affected the Snatcher."

Jasce raised his brows. "The what?"

"Snatcher. That's what the locals are calling it." He flinched as Kord placed his hands on the wounds.

"How did it take down Markel?" Kenz asked. "He's one of our most powerful Amps." Jasce wondered the same thing.

The general scrubbed a hand down her face. "I don't know. It was strong, seemed intelligent, too. It didn't attack the Naturals—acted like we weren't even there, unless we provoked it."

Embracing the Darkness

Jasce went completely still. "You mean it only targeted the Spectrals?"

"That's what it looked like. Both my men were killed trying to rescue Ada. The Snatcher took her, too. We never found their bodies."

Caston addressed Alyssa. "Did you get a good look at it? Do we know what we're dealing with?"

"It's about the size of a small horse, and wicked fast. The eyes were creepy white orbs."

Amycus rested his arms on his legs, staring at nothing. "How many were there?"

"Only one."

Jasce jerked his head around. "One of these took out the entire team?" It wasn't a question, but he didn't understand how a single creature could be so lethal against highly trained soldiers, three being Spectrals.

He pulled his gaze from his general and frowned at Kord. "What's wrong?"

Kord's brow furrowed. "He isn't healing. I don't know why."

Flynt looked from his chest to Kord. His wound wasn't closing, the flesh jagged and raw. Kord's power normally worked in seconds, maybe minutes, depending on the severity of the injury. The gash across Flynt's chest should already be a scar.

Amycus knelt in front of Flynt. "How is that possible?"

"I don't know." Kord leaned closer to the wound, pressing the edges with a finger. "It looks like teeth caused this, very large teeth." Kord looked at Kenz. "Go get Maera and have her bring the trauma kit, please."

Kenz nodded and maneuvered through the cots to the storage rooms.

"The thing knocked me on my back after it went through my fire and sank its fangs into me," Flynt said, a tremor in his voice. "If Ada hadn't blown it off course, I'd be dead. It was going for my throat."

Jasce looked from the jagged marks on Flynt's chest to his face, and his eyes widened. Sweat beaded on the warrior's upper lip and his body trembled. Jasce lowered the protective wall that sensed Spectral emotions and terror crashed into him. He quickly raised it again. He'd never seen fear in the Fire Spectral. Anger and jealousy, but never fear.

Amycus tapped his lip. "Flynt, can you spark your fire?"

He flicked the ignitor on his wrist and a green flame appeared, then immediately sputtered out. He swore and tried again with the same results.

"So whatever this thing is, it's blocking Kord's magic as well as yours," Amycus said.

Kenz arrived with Maera and Maleous. Kord sighed when his son approached and shot a glare at Maera.

She waved her hand as she knelt next to Flynt. "Don't blame me. He insisted on coming."

"He's barely twelve. Surely you have some authority over him."

Maleous jutted out his chin. "It's not a big deal, Dad. I've seen worse."

Jasce snorted and earned a scowl from Kord. The Healer shook his head. "He needs stitches."

Maera opened her bag and started cleaning the jagged laceration. Jasce grimaced at the chamomile and medicinal scent drifting through the air. He hated that smell. He'd spent countless hours in this room with physicians dressing the wounds on his back. He balled his hands into fists and peered around the Sanctuary.

Caston stood over Maera's shoulder as she threaded the needle with immense dexterity and calm, something Jasce had admired even when they'd first met. Drexus had used Maera's son, Rowan, as leverage to force her to perform the experiments at the Arcane Garrison. Experiments Jasce had endured. Her son currently trained at the Ironbark compound now, completely safe, though Jasce hadn't checked on him in some time. He made a mental note to visit the garrison once the Gathering was finished.

"Flynt, any information on Jaida or Vale?" Jasce asked, trying to keep his voice level.

Flynt eyed the needle and gulped. "We questioned a few of the locals but came up empty."

Jasce swallowed the disappointment. It seemed they hadn't gone north or east. Hell, they might not even be in Pandaren. A part of him hoped so—at least his sister would be safe from this Snatcher, whatever it was.

Maera handed Maleous a bandage. "Might as well make yourself useful." The kid grinned and wrapped the cloth around Flynt's chest.

"Kord, I want you and Maera to analyze whatever is suppressing his magic," Jasce said, then placed a hand on Flynt's and Alyssa's shoulders. "I'm glad you both made it back."

His general gave a weak smile and sat on the cot opposite Flynt's.

Jasce addressed Caston, Amycus, and Kenz. "We need to talk." He had seen the panic in some of the Healers' eyes and didn't want news of this creature's power spreading through the palace, especially with the kingdoms now taking up residence.

Unlike the War Room, the Bastion's command room was anything but elegant with its gray stone walls, a scarred table with mismatched chairs, and a hearth to take out the chill during the winter. Ash and bits of charred wood filled the grate.

Amycus tapped his finger on the table while Jasce regarded a map identical to the one in the palace. The Desert of Souls carved through Pandaren, a harsh landscape that was home to the Brymagus plant known for suppressing magic. He rubbed his neck, remembering the collar Drexus had forced him to wear. Even though he hadn't had his magic for very long, wearing the collar had felt like he was drowning.

"So, what's going through your minds?" Kenz asked, sitting next to Amycus. Jasce had told Kenz about the claw months ago, but lately they'd been preoccupied with other pressing matters.

Caston leaned back in his chair with his arms crossed, his dark eyes focused on the ceiling. "It seems like this Snatcher, whatever it is, can combat our magic."

"And yet is also targeting it," Amycus added, rubbing his hand along his jaw.

"It's obviously lethal. Do we know how many there are?" Kenz asked.

Caston shook his head. Jasce faced the map but stared at nothing, deep in thought. "I'd bet my two swords that the missing Spectrals are related to these Snatchers."

"It makes sense, if this thing is attracted to them," Kenz said.

"We need to find out. Caston, send guards with tracking skills—Naturals only—to those villages that reported missing Spectrals. And do it quietly."

Caston stood. "You want me to go, too?"

"No, I need you to help with security and training. And to attend meetings."

Caston laughed. "The first two, yes. That last one? You're on your own." He opened the door and strode toward the barracks.

Jasce swore. He really hated meetings. And he was about to have another to update the queen on the Snatcher.

"Lorella isn't going to like this." Amycus grimaced as he rose from the table. Kenz furrowed her brow as she reached out to help him.

Jasce approached his mentor, his eyes darting over his face, noticing the gray in the whiskers along his jaw. "Are you okay?"

Amycus looked at them with a wariness lining his face. "Just a sparring injury. Nothing serious." Jasce tilted his head. He couldn't remember the last time the blacksmith had sparred. He was about to press when Amycus continued, "You, however, look awful."

Jasce leaned against the table and shook his head. "I had forgotten about that claw, and with everything else, I don't have the time to deal with this, too."

Amycus patted his shoulder. "Let's see what Caston's scouts learn. In the meantime, get some rest. I have a feeling you're going to need it." He shut the door behind him.

Jasce huffed. He didn't have time to rest, either.

He turned to Kenz as she rose from the table. "Does he seem all right to you?"

She stared at the closed door. "Everyone's on edge these days, especially with the Vastanes."

Jasce groaned. "I need to inform Queen Valeri about the bar fight, too."

She smiled but it didn't reach her eyes. "Want to tell me what that was about?"

He massaged the back of his neck. "I lost my temper. Probably just stress."

She nodded and bit her lip.

Embracing the Darkness

"What is it?" Jasce asked.

She reached for his hands. "I know the timing isn't great, but . . ."

"If this is about your promotion to captain, I've already put the request on the agenda for the next military meeting with the queen."

Kenz's mouth dropped. "Well, no, that wasn't what I . . . really?"

"Not quite the reaction I was expecting after months of your pestering."

Her eyes lit up. "I'm going to be a captain?" Her grin grew, and he couldn't remember the last time she'd been so happy. He should've promoted her sooner just to see that smile.

"I'm going to recommend it, but the rest of the generals have to approve, which they will." She wrapped her arms around him and mumbled a thank you against his chest. He rubbed his hands down her arms. "I don't like it. I need you to know that. You'll be on the front lines, and I won't be able to protect you."

She pulled back and gazed up at him. "I'll be on the front lines with you."

He kissed the tip of her nose. "We'll talk more and hopefully have a proper ceremony when this Gathering is finished. But you get to tell your brother."

She laughed. "Coward."

"Damn straight. He's got a mean right hook."

She gave him another hug and jogged out of the room.

He traced the toe of his boot along the floor and hoped he hadn't made a huge mistake. If anything happened to her . . . he swallowed. He wouldn't play the what-if game.

Things would be fine, he told himself as he walked toward the queen's chambers. He exited the compound and glanced at the night sky—menacing clouds eclipsed the stars and moon, and an angry surf crashed against the shore. He was not looking forward to informing Queen Valeri about the creature, especially at this late hour. The events of the Gathering would soon begin, and any answers he had now only led to more questions. It was imperative his team keep the news of the Snatcher quiet. He didn't want fear snaking its way through the Bastion or the palace.

When fear was involved, mistakes happened.

Chapter Seven

The next morning, Jasce and Kenz visited Kord and Tillie's home. It had become a tradition to have breakfast once a week, and he usually looked forward to this time, especially Tillie's cooking, but he couldn't relax with everything he still needed to do. Every minute of every day, something required his attention, and he felt pulled in too many directions. He rubbed his temples as Kord updated him on Flynt's condition.

"He's finally able to use his magic. The venom burned through his system pretty fast, so that's some good news," Kord said, raking his hands through his hair, making it even messier. "Maera and I discussed ways to flush the venom, in case this happens again."

Jasce grimaced at his dirt-covered boots and tried to wrap his mind around the creature that wiped out most of his team. "Whatever this Snatcher is, it really caused some damage. I wonder if it has the same effect on all Spectrals." Almost half of the Guard comprised Spectrals, and to not have their magic would put them at a disadvantage if a fight came. And he had a feeling a fight was coming. The timing of these creatures with the missing Spectrals and the Gathering was just too perfect, and he didn't believe in coincidences.

The question was why. He wondered if the Snatchers were only drawn to Spectrals, or could they also be attracted to the other kingdoms' magic? If that were the case, the dignitaries would have to be told and their people warned.

Kord rested his feet on the coffee table and leaned back in his chair. "Where did it come from? In all my time in Paxton and the other places I've traveled, I've never heard or seen anything like what Flynt and Alyssa described."

Jasce glanced into the kitchen where Tillie and Kenz discussed wedding plans. Maleous, Lander, and Emile seemed occupied with a game, but those three excelled at getting into trouble. With what Maleous saw the day before, he'd bet Lander and his sister knew all about the Snatcher. He'd have to have a word with Lander to keep quiet. He didn't want the other recruits finding out, especially the Spectrals. The last thing he needed was trepidation among his Guard.

He faced Kord, keeping his voice low. "I've never seen Flynt scared like that. Whatever attacked him left him spooked."

"Hopefully Caston's trackers will bring back some information. The queen and council members are all tense."

"Tense is an understatement." He massaged his forehead again.

"You have another headache?" Kord removed his feet from the table and leaned forward, his green eyes scanning Jasce's body, which always made him squirm.

"Just a lot going on."

"You sure that's it? You look terrible."

Jasce huffed out a breath. "I've heard that a few times." Kord touched Jasce's head, and the pain disappeared. "Thanks."

"Anytime." Kord returned his feet to the table.

A cry made them turn toward the kitchen. Maleous's face drained of color as he gaped at Emile, whose hand gripped his arm, her knuckles white with the strain.

"Emile, let go," Lander said as Jasce and Kord rushed over. Tillie knelt next to her son and tried to pry Emile's fingers loose.

"Don't, please!" Emile cried out.

Jasce froze as he looked at her face. "Her eyes." They had changed

Embracing the Darkness

from hazel to black, and the veins in her neck stuck out as she bared her teeth.

Lander grabbed her shoulders. "Emile."

Kord knelt next to Tillie and placed a hand on Emile's arm. He closed his eyes, his brow furrowed.

Emile gasped and released Maleous, who fell back and clutched his elbow.

She shook her head, and her eyes returned to their normal color. She regarded Lander as tears streaked down her cheeks. "I was on that table again, and he . . . he," she covered her face and a sob escaped.

Kenz wrapped her arms around Emile and glanced at Jasce.

"Kord," Tillie said, nodding to Maleous.

Kord tore his gaze from Emile. A muscle in his jaw pulsed as he noticed his son's arm bent at an unnatural angle. He placed his hands on Maleous's. "Work with me—you need to learn to heal yourself as well as others."

Maleous had inherited his father's magic, and Jasce often wondered if he'd be as powerful. The kid didn't have experience in healing himself, though, which he supposed was a good thing. Maleous closed his eyes and breathed deeply.

Emile lowered her hands. "Oh, Mal. I'm so sorry."

Lander scooted closer to his sister. "What did you see this time?"

"This time?" Jasce asked. "How often has this happened?"

"She's been hallucinating for a couple of weeks," Lander said. "It's happening more and more. Sometimes it's the experiment Drexus performed on her and other times it's . . ." He snuck a glance at Jasce.

"It's what?"

"She sees you with your Hunter mask. She sees the Angel of Death."

Jasce's protective wall slipped, and he stumbled back. He could sense Emile's fear, along with Kenz's and Kord's worry, and something else he didn't have time to name as tremors racked his body. He squeezed his eyes shut and rested his hands on his knees. Voices sounded muddled, as if spoken through water.

Breathe, he thought as he focused on his magic, imagining himself stacking brick upon brick while he fortified the barrier. A gentle hand rubbed down his back and Kenz's magic flowed around him. Hers felt different than normal, but he pushed that notion aside and relaxed into the comfort she offered.

With a final breath, he solidified the wall. Standing, he squeezed Kenz's hand and gave her a half smile. She kissed his cheek and knelt next to Maleous.

"That's very good, son," Kord said as the boy's arm healed. He grimaced but his color slowly returned.

Emile's eyes darted around the room. "I'm sorry."

"You have nothing to be sorry for," Jasce said through his teeth. Drexus did this—put two more types of magic inside the Spectral—a *child*—in his lust for domination. And now it was affecting not just her, but her friends and family.

"Does Maera know this is happening?" Kord asked, getting to his feet.

Emile nodded.

"Both Amycus and Maera are helping her," Jasce said, remembering Amycus's concern over Emile the other day. Whatever they were doing didn't seem to be working.

"All right. How about some cookies?" Tillie asked, forcing a smile and leading Emile and Maleous into the kitchen. Kenz followed, while Kord mumbled about getting more coffee.

Jasce wandered into the living room with Lander on his heels. Lander swallowed and then glanced toward the kitchen.

"Yes?" Jasce asked.

"Do you think she'll be okay?"

Jasce sighed. He was responsible for Emile's plight. If Bronn hadn't seen him help Emile and Lander, Drexus would never have used the girl against him. Jasce was forced to reveal the secret to combining magic, which was using a Healer's blood, otherwise Emile wouldn't have survived the procedure. And now she was suffering the consequences.

"If anyone can help her, it's Maera and Amycus," Jasce finally answered.

Lander bit his lip.

"What else is on your mind?" He thought he had a pretty good idea. Emile and Maleous returned to the living room, handing Lander and him each a cookie. They sat next to Lander on the couch.

Embracing the Darkness

Lander looked at his sister and then at Maleous. "I wanted to ask you about the creature."

Jasce crossed his ankle over his knee and contemplated the three kids. Emile and Maleous were about the same age as when he'd been taken to the Watch Guard, and Lander was only sixteen. Sorrow washed over him at the childhood he'd never known. He envied these kids who were loved and protected.

"Uncle Jasce?" Maleous asked, rubbing his arm. Emile wiped crumbs off her dress and Lander rested his elbows on his knees, staring at him.

"Normally, I would tell you three to mind your own business," he said. "But considering Mal helped treat Flynt . . ." He arched a brow at Maleous, who lowered his head trying to hide his grin. "This creature—locals are calling it a Snatcher—is hunting Spectrals and seems impervious to magic. And it's lethal."

"I heard Healers were missing, too," Maleous said, sneaking a glance at his dad through the kitchen doorway.

"That's true, but you're safe here and at the Bastion. Just don't go looking for trouble."

"I bet those Snatchers wouldn't stand a chance against a wyvern," Maleous said. Lander and Emile both agreed.

"Have you been going to the wyvern paddock? I'm pretty sure I told you to stay away from there. They aren't pets, you know."

Maleous rolled his eyes. Jasce was about to threaten them when Kord ambled in and handed him another cup of coffee. The kids huddled together on the couch, whispering. Kord raised his brows and then shrugged.

Jasce sank into the cushions and inhaled the smells drifting through the open window from the Bread District. He often wondered if Kord regretted moving his family from Carhurst to Orilyon. Things seemed to be working out for them, as Tillie would one day take over the bakery where she currently worked since the owner was older and had no children of her own. And Kord was thriving at the Sanctuary. But would they have been happier if they hadn't moved? They'd be safer, that's for sure.

Tillie's and Kenz's discussion of wedding cakes drifted to the back of his mind as he mulled over the four visiting kingdoms. He needed to oversee the final details of the Welcome Ball and the tournament—four competitions, one every week, that would test the strength, skill, and wit of those competing. The first was the Gauntlet Run, followed by sword fighting, grappling, and archery. He still had a lot of work to do and didn't have time for much else, least of all planning a wedding.

And if he was being honest with himself, he couldn't think about celebrating, not with Jaida out there somewhere with the Snatchers roaming around and Spectrals missing. A wedding was not a priority. He loved Kenz—did a big ceremony really need to prove that? When he'd asked her to marry him after returning to Carhurst, he had just wanted to start a new life with her, not have a grand celebration.

Jasce tapped his finger on the arm of the chair, the rhythmic sound the only noise in the room as he realized everyone's eyes were fixed on him. Kord sighed, and he knew he'd missed something important. Both Kenz and Tillie stood in the living room. He hadn't even seen them move from the kitchen.

"What?"

Kenz took a deep breath. "I asked what you thought of Amycus walking me down the aisle?"

"I don't care who you have walk you down the aisle."

Kenz's eyes widened. Kord rubbed his forehead, and Tillie bit her lip. In all his years at the Watch Guard, he'd never attended a wedding and wasn't sure of the importance of Kenz's question, but based on everyone's reactions, he had made a colossal mistake.

Jasce massaged the back of his neck. "That didn't come out right. I just meant—"

"You really don't care about any of this, do you?" Kenz interrupted.

Tillie left the room, jerking her head at Kord and the three children. Kord glanced over his shoulder and winced.

Jasce was in serious trouble.

"Look, Kenz, I love you, and I don't need a wedding to validate that. There's a lot going on right now. I don't understand why you want to rush this."

She rested her hands on her hips. "There will always be a lot going on with us, but it would be nice if you could engage."

Embracing the Darkness

He pushed up from his chair, and a flutter of anger entwined with his magic. "Do you understand what's happening? The responsibilities I have? And you want me to 'engage'?" he asked, using air quotes.

She stepped closer and scowled. "Yes, I understand what's happening. Don't talk to me like I'm some simple-minded idiot."

"You know I don't think you're simple-minded or an idiot. Even though, right now, you're acting like one."

A groan sounded from the hallway.

Jasce clenched his fists as he tried to snuff out the rage bubbling to the surface. "If you're going to eavesdrop, Kord, you might as well come out and be comfortable."

"I'm acting like an idiot?" Kenz's voice softened—the telltale sign she was about to explode.

He needed to rein in his temper. Why was he getting so angry? It was the same sensation from the council room with Lord Haldron. He stared at the ceiling and counted to ten. "Until the Gathering is finished, the mystery of the Snatcher is solved, and I find Jaida, my mind will not be on a wedding."

"You've been obsessed with finding Jaida and pushing me to the side in the process."

"If Kord was missing, I'm damn sure you'd be obsessed with finding him."

"Do I need to remind you she tried to kill you, and me for that matter?" Kenz stood toe to toe with him, her green eyes flashing. "She doesn't want you."

Jasce stiffened and stepped back. The truth in that statement eclipsed the fury seething inside him. Jaida hadn't wanted him. She'd chosen Drexus over her own flesh and blood.

Kenz closed her eyes and sighed. "I'm sorry. I didn't mean that."

"Save it." He strode for the door.

"Jasce, wait."

The door shut, and it took all of his self-control not to ram his fist through it. Why couldn't she understand his need to find his sister? To make things right? Kenz, as a Shield, knew what it meant to protect those she loved. He hadn't saved Jaida when she was young, and he hadn't been able to save her during the Battle of the Bastion, either.

Cassie Sanchez

Jasce tipped his head back. The clear, blue sky mocked the storm raging inside him. His failure with Jaida hung like a millstone around his neck, and he wouldn't be free from the crushing weight until he found her and tried to restore their relationship. If he had to do it alone, then he would. It was, after all, what he was used to.

Chapter Eight

Jasce rode Bruiser through the crowded streets of Orilyon toward the Bastion looming in the distance—its tall, gray turrets a dominating presence visible from anywhere in the city. The sun burned down on him, the air as oppressive as the words echoing in his mind.

She doesn't want you.

Kenz's comment cut like a knife to the heart. But even though Jaida had tried to kill them, she had also stopped Drexus, which meant his sister still cared for him. He would do whatever it took to make things right.

Jasce rode past the Garden District. Its floral fragrance tickled his nose, and the colors rivaled the gardens at the palace. The busiest areas were the Meat and Textiles quarters, especially with the upcoming parties in honor of the Gathering.

Sadness and longing swept through him as he rode through the Steel District. To beat a piece of metal into submission sounded like a good idea. If only that would help relieve some of his frustrations.

He also replayed Queen Valeri's lecture from the night before when he reported on the Snatchers. Unfortunately, it seemed Lord Haldron hadn't wasted any time informing the queen.

"A bar fight? Really?" she had asked as she stared down her nose at him.

He had no excuse and still didn't exactly understand why he'd lost control like he had. "It won't happen again, Your Majesty."

"It better not. Thankfully, I'm on good terms with the Baltens. If it had been a Vastane, we'd be having a much different conversation." She leaned forward and narrowed her eyes. "I will not allow you to ruin my plans. I gave you that rank, and I can easily take it away."

He'd been tempted to resign right there as being commander wasn't what he had expected. It didn't seem like Drexus ever had to deal with these issues.

He fisted his hands as the smell of steel and smoke reminded him of when he assisted Nigel, the old blacksmith at the Bastion, when Jasce had been a Hunter. He'd helped him fix swords and daggers, and together, they'd created the first model of his specialized armor that was worn by most of the Guard. Images flashed through his mind of Drexus's sword piercing through Nigel's back, soldiers dragging away his body, leaving only a smear of blood. Drexus had killed the blacksmith simply because Nigel hadn't wanted him experimenting on Spectrals. He didn't deserve to die that way. Jasce had held the dying man as he uttered his last words: *"Don't give in to the darkness."*

Easier said than done.

The guards patrolling along the walls saluted him as he rode through the massive gates of the compound. He hopped off Bruiser and handed him to the stableboy. His body thrummed with energy, and the anger he tried to bury clawed its way to the surface. He focused on his magic and the tug that occurred before he vaulted. In mid-stride, he disappeared.

The comforting sounds of clashing steel filled his ears as he materialized in the training yard. A few recruits jumped at Jasce's sudden appearance. Ignoring them, he scanned the area for his Second, finding him near the archery range. Caston was the only person Jasce could spar using his amplified strength and speed since he had received the same serum. Caston lifted a brow and said something to Aura as Jasce strode toward a sparring ring. He grabbed a blade from the weapons rack and waited for the ex-Hunter.

Embracing the Darkness

"I see you're in a mood," Caston said, selecting a practice sword and giving it a twirl.

Jasce grunted and cracked his neck. He needed to hit something before he exploded.

The side of Caston's lip quirked. "All right, then. Let's do this."

The two assassins crossed blades, and the collision sent a shock wave across the yard. In no time, an audience surrounded the fighters. Jasce lunged and swung his weapon at Caston's head, who raised his blade, blocking the strike. Caston performed a counter move that had Jasce twisting and parrying. Both men tapped into their magic and their sparring became a blur of metal and muscle.

Jasce flipped over his Second and brought his sword down. Caston pivoted and deflected the attack, following with one of his own. Jasce ducked, and the air from the passing blade blew his hair off his face.

"What are you doing?" Maera stood on the outside of the ring with her arms crossed. "We have visitors." She pointed to the upper balcony, occupied by the Balten consort and the Alturian commander.

Caston winked at Maera, and Jasce used the distraction to his advantage. He thrust his sword, connecting with the hilt of Caston's, and twisted, flinging his weapon out of the ring. A loud cheer echoed off the walls.

Caston glanced from his fallen blade to Jasce and sneered.

He didn't have time to dodge before Caston's fist connected with his jaw. His head jerked to the side and blood pooled in his mouth. Caston spun and kicked him in the chest, sending him flying.

Jasce spit out the coppery warmth and got to his feet.

Caston crossed his arms. "You've had enough?"

"Not even close," he growled and charged. He spun at the last moment, and his elbow cracked against Caston's eye. He lunged, attempting to throw Caston over his shoulder, but the ex-Hunter swept his leg and knocked Jasce off balance. Caston seized him around the middle and slammed him onto the ground.

"Okay, that's enough!" Maera called out to the jeers of the recruits.

They grappled, fists and feet flying. Blood and sweat dripped down their faces. Dirt stung Jasce's eyes. Finally, he maneuvered his leg around Caston's neck and anchored his arm to keep Caston from moving.

"Yield," Jasce said.

Caston tapped his arm, and Jasce released him. They both fell back, panting, while a couple of wyverns flew overhead, casting a momentary shadow.

"Feel better?" Caston asked.

"Much. Thank you."

"You know, as your Second, I had to let you win."

Jasce snorted.

Footsteps sounded. Blonde hair and angry hazel eyes peered at them. "You two are idiots," Maera said.

Caston raised to his elbows and squinted against the sun. "I hear you're a sucker for a proper idiot."

She pressed her lips together and tried not to smile. Jasce sat up, glancing between Caston and Maera. Was his Second flirting? He stood, wiped the dust off his pants, and helped Caston to his feet. Applause broke out, and Caston bowed while Jasce used his shirt to wipe the grime off his face.

Maera shook her head. "Come on. Let's get that taken care of," she said to Caston, pointing to the gash on his forehead. He wiggled his eyebrows at Jasce and followed her to the Sanctuary.

Jasce glanced at the balcony, but the two visitors were no longer there. Shaking his head and wondering what was going on between Maera and Caston, he left the sparring ring. His mind had finally settled, and his body was relaxed, if a little sore. Caston was an excellent fighter, almost as good as him, and during the last few months he had become a trustworthy friend, a completely different relationship than what Jasce had experienced when he was Drexus's Second. He'd simply been Drexus's pawn in his plan to conquer Pandaren.

He stared at where the whipping post had once stood. The first task he'd accomplished as commander was to burn that pole to the ground. Never would the crack of a whip sound through the compound again, not as long as he was in charge.

Someone cleared their throat and Jasce wheeled around. Kord leaned against a pillar with his arms crossed.

"Took you longer than I expected," Jasce said, nodding to a few sixth-year recruits who passed by.

Embracing the Darkness

"Couldn't rush out. I don't want Kenz mad at me, too."

Jasce sighed. "Yeah, only one of us should be in harm's way."

"My thoughts exactly." Kord's green eyes, like his sister's, penetrated as if he could peer into the depths of Jasce's soul. "What was that about?" He inclined his head toward the ring.

Jasce ran a hand through his damp hair. His soldiers resumed their activities at the various stations around the yard, the Water Spectrals taking a break to create a mist to cool off the recruits running through the obstacle course. A young Psyche practiced launching various items at a few Shields while Airs worked with Aura and Amycus.

"Have you ever felt torn in so many directions that you feel ripped apart?" Jasce asked.

Kord chuckled. "Pretty sure that's the definition of being a husband and father." He reached out, and Jasce flinched. Kord tilted his head and then pressed his fingers against his eye. Immediately, warmth rushed to the wound and lessened the swelling. "In all seriousness, yes, I know the feeling."

Jasce used a piece of leather to tie back his hair. He hadn't realized how long it'd grown. "How do you handle it so well? You never seem to annoy Tillie. You're always kind and have that blasted grin on your face."

"I'm sure Tillie would say otherwise."

He remembered first meeting Kord, envying his lighthearted manner, wondering what it was like to have so much peace that your resting expression was a smile.

Kord trudged beside him through the courtyard as the sounds of clanging swords drowned out the noises sifting through his head. The Healer rested his large hand on Jasce's shoulder and said, "It takes practice."

Jasce huffed out a breath.

Kord continued, "You have a lot of responsibilities and things pulling for your attention, but you need to remember what's most important."

"And that is?"

He pointed at Jasce's heart. "What's in here—love, friendship, family. And you're not in this alone." Kord patted him on the back and sauntered off toward the Sanctuary, calling over his shoulder, "Don't forget the tour you're supposed to be giving."

Jasce swore, having forgotten completely. Now he'd be late and filthy.

He rubbed his chest. Love, friendship, family. What he really wanted to do was talk to Kenz. She was his light and his anchor to all that was good.

"Duty first," he sighed, and headed for the barracks. Being commander definitely wasn't what he'd thought it'd be.

Chapter Nine

Jasce led Balten Consort Natasha Lekov, Commander Eris Faez of Alturia, and Queen Siryn with her guard, Garan along the breezeway of the Bastion, where they could observe the recruits training below. He'd already shown them the arena where the tournament would be held, and spirits were high for the anticipated Gauntlet Run occurring in two days.

Resting his hands on the wall, Jasce peered into the practice yard and located Kenz sparring with Flynt. He almost felt bad for the Fire Spectral as she used his momentum, flipped around his neck, and brought him to the ground. He couldn't help but smile.

Commander Faez stood next to him as she observed a group of soldiers on the climbing wall.

"How does Shade Walking work, exactly?" Jasce asked, aware of Queen Siryn watching him, as she had for the past hour. The Balten consort joined them, crossing her arms and leaning a hip against the wall. Shade Walkers were known for guarding the finer details of their magic.

The corner of the commander's lip quirked. "Are you asking as a commander or as a fellow magic wielder?"

"Both."

"Ours is similar to your Vaulter magic."

Jasce raised a brow.

"We've done our own reconnaissance, Commander. Some Shade Walkers can use the shadows to travel through spaces as well as camouflage themselves."

"Yes, but how effective are you if there are no shadows?" Queen Siryn asked.

Commander Faez narrowed her eyes. "We have our ways." She meandered along the breezeway, focusing on the recruits running through their afternoon exercises.

The Vastane queen shrugged, and her blue gown shimmered like a stream rippling over polished stones. A gold pendant with a ruby the size of Jasce's thumb sparkled in the sun. Queen Siryn raised her brows as he forced his gaze from her chest. Shaking his head and shoving his hands in his pockets, he backed away from the balustrade.

Consort Lekov peered into the courtyard. "Commander Farone, this is very good. I'm impressed."

"Thank you." He marveled at the colorful tattoos decorating the Balten's arms and neck.

The consort pointed to his arm. "It seems you are like us. What do your marks mean?"

"When I was a Hunter, I'd tattoo a symbol for every Spectral I killed. Mine aren't honoring my people or my past like yours but are a reminder of who I never want to be again."

She ran a finger along the images inked into his forearm. "If we cling to our pasts, it's difficult to move forward." Jasce forced himself to hold her stare as her amber-colored eyes searched his.

And if our pasts cling to us? he wanted to ask. Instead, he said, "Your soldiers are welcome to train with my recruits." He tugged on the sleeve of his tunic.

She lowered her hand. "I'd like that very much. We will join after the tour."

"We?" Queen Siryn said, leaning closer to Jasce.

"Yes, Your Majesty. I practice with my soldiers. One needs to keep their skills in top form." Consort Lekov frowned at the gown the Vastane queen wore.

Embracing the Darkness

The queen drummed her fingers on the balcony, a coy smile on her lips. "There are other skills one needs to hone besides batting around a sword." She drifted along the walkway, whispering to Garan as her attendants followed closely behind.

Jasce's gaze darted between the women, all warriors, yet only two used steel. He knew how to handle the consort and the commander as fellow soldiers, but Queen Siryn battled in ways he wasn't comfortable with. She was playing a game, one he recognized but didn't know how to navigate. As Azrael, he'd have no problem taking whatever she was offering. As Jasce, and engaged to Kenz, he'd tell her to shove off. But as Commander of the Paladin Guard and a member of the queen's council, he swam in uncharted waters, a feeling he didn't enjoy.

"I really don't like her," Consort Lekov said as she glared after the Vastane queen.

Jasce snorted. He had many responses to that, but the warning from Queen Valeri kept battering against his skull. *I need you to behave. You are my liaison between the Guard and the other kingdoms. Not an assassin. Are we clear?*

"Is it wise to have your non-magical soldiers work alongside the magical ones?" the Alturian commander asked, her attention on a group of third-year recruits throwing daggers.

"They practice basic fighting skills together, and then we separate the Spectrals to work on their specific magic. It's safer this way, as many are still learning to wield their magic as a weapon," Jasce said.

Flynt, resuming his duties and leaving Kenz to spar with another soldier, worked with the other Fires and Waters. At first, Jasce had separated the two elementals, but when the Fires kept destroying anything made of wood, the instructors decided to have the Waters train alongside. Flynt currently instructed a group of teenagers, showing them the method for forming fireballs and hurling them at specific targets. A recruit launched a fireball, and it exploded into a straw training dummy. A few Naturals dove out of the way, some laughing, others cursing the young girl. Flynt patted her on the shoulder while the Water instructor, Noelani, extinguished the flames.

Amycus and Aura worked with the Airs. By the looks of things, they were teaching them how to create a shield made of solid air. Amycus leaned against the water barrel, letting Aura do most of the teaching. He glanced up, and his eyes narrowed as the Vastane queen strolled along the walkway.

A crash from across the yard drew Jasce's attention. He swore when a section of the climbing wall cracked and shattered. The ground quaked and someone yelled as the entire structure teetered. Amycus's arms shook while he used his magic to slow down a recruit who'd fallen from the top, but the girl fell too quickly. Jasce was about to vault when Aura sprinted over and raised her hands to stop the recruit and bring her safely to the ground. Amycus stared wide-eyed at his hands, dismay etched along his face.

Recruits took refuge on the outside edges of the courtyard. As the dust cleared, Jasce could make out Emile standing at the base of the climbing wall holding her head. She screamed, and the ground trembled and undulated across the training area. Cobblestones and dirt rose, trapping her legs, while a large fissure snaked through the yard. With a loud crack, a section of the wall sheared off.

"Emile!" Jasce felt the tug as darkness surrounded him. He reappeared next to her, and his entire body shuddered when the wall pressed down on his shoulders and back.

Emile sat on the roiling ground, her feet encased in sand and rock.

Nearby shadows shimmered, and Commander Faez appeared, her form solidifying as she dragged a soldier clear of the debris.

Jasce gritted his teeth. "Emile, honey, come back to me."

Her eyes, black as night, widened. She jerked away from him, her mouth open in a silent scream.

Sweat dripped down his chest as he dropped to a knee. "You're safe. No one will hurt you."

Caston raced across the yard and shuffled under the fallen structure. He barked orders to nearby Amps to help, and then crouched next to Jasce and pushed up with his back and arms. Two Spectrals, a man named Eli and a teenage girl named Mila, slid under the wall and helped brace against the crushing load. Jasce inhaled, getting his feet underneath him.

A fierce wind blew his hair off his face. Amycus and Aura had their

Embracing the Darkness

hands raised and used their magic to help absorb some of the weight while Flynt pulled the recruits out of harm's way.

Kenz tried to use her shield, but the angle of the wall blocked its path. She lowered to her knees.

"Don't even think about it!" Jasce shouted.

Her eyes darted along the collapsed surface and to the Amps holding it up. "Then what's your plan?"

"Working on it."

Caston grunted and shifted his shoulder to balance out the pressure. "Work faster."

Jasce scanned the courtyard and spotted the Alturian commander tending to some recruits. "We need Faez."

"Who?" Caston asked, following Jasce's line of sight.

A commotion sounded from the other side of the yard, and Lander pushed through a group of soldiers. He crawled to his sister, his face leached of color, and grabbed her shoulders. "Emile, look at me." His eyes were wide, but his voice remained calm. "You need to find yourself."

Emile jerked her head toward her brother. "Please don't do this." Tears streamed down her face and her entire body shook. "Keep him away from me."

"Who?" her brother asked.

"The Angel," she panted, pulling at her hair. Her black eyes located Jasce. "You're evil, and a monster."

He tried to ignore her words and focus on his magic, drawing from his Amplifier power to hold up the fallen structure.

The ground quaked and the fissure snaked toward them.

"Jasce!" Kenz yelled. Amycus grabbed her and said something he couldn't hear. The shifting wall reverberated through his skull.

Lander glanced over his shoulder and then brushed the hair off his sister's face. "Focus, Emile. The Angel of Death is dead. Come back to me, please."

Jasce glanced at Caston, who winced.

Emile gripped Lander's hands and took a tremulous breath. Her eyes cleared and the ground around her legs receded.

A cry had them all turning as Mila lost her footing and fell to her knees. Both Jasce and Caston groaned as the wall pressed down. Cracks splintered along the edges, and someone screamed.

Kenz threw up her shield, protecting recruits from the falling debris.

They were running out of time.

Jasce yelled at the Alturian commander. "Get them out of here!"

Commander Faez disappeared in the shadow of a pillar, materialized seconds later, and wrapped her arms around Lander and Emile. They merged with the shadows and vanished.

Jasce called out to the other Amps. "Eli, Mila, on the count of three, get free." Eli's biceps bulged under the strain, and Mila bit her lip. The wall dipped lower.

"What?" Caston's eyes widened as he shifted his feet.

Jasce yelled to Aura and Amycus to use their air shields to protect Eli and Mila. He looked at Caston, whose arms shook. Jasce's spine felt like it was compressing into solid bone. "The second they're clear, I'm going to vault us out of here."

"No! I hate it when you do that."

Jasce spoke to the Amps. "One, two—"

Caston edged closer to Jasce. "Seriously, another way?"

"Three!"

The Amps leaped out, and both Jasce and Caston grunted as the full weight of the structure fell on them. Jasce dug deep into his magic, further than he'd had to go in a long time. He wedged his shoulder under the wall, held on to Caston, and focused on the other side of the courtyard. Something inside him fractured, and he yelled as darkness and pain erupted.

A pillar cracked as their bodies collided with the marble. Recruits cried out and soldiers rushed to where they had materialized. A cloud of dust covered the training yard.

Caston rolled to his knees and retched while Jasce lay flat on his back, his chest heaving.

"I really hate it when you do that," Caston said, gagging.

Amycus and Kenz pushed past the recruits and sprinted to where they had fallen.

Jasce sat up and stared at his trembling fingers.

Amycus leaned closer to him. "Jasce?"

Embracing the Darkness

"What?" he asked, lowering his hands.

Amycus opened his mouth and then shook his head. "Nothing. You just . . . it was nothing."

Kenz wiped the dust off Jasce's face. "Are you all right?"

He nodded and focused on her green eyes as her magic embraced him and settled his nerves.

Kord and two other Healers ran into the yard. He relayed orders while he knelt in front of Jasce, resting a hand on his arm. "You okay?"

Warmth rushed through his body. "I'm fine. Check on Emile." Kord narrowed his eyes and glanced at Caston.

Caston raised his hand, his face still tinged green. "I'm good."

Kord tended to Emile while Flynt, Aura, and Commander Faez helped the younger recruits. Jasce would have to thank her later for her assistance. Her Shade Walking was impressive.

He stood, pulling Caston to his feet. "Thanks for your help back there."

Caston ran his hands through his brown hair, tiny streaks of gray clinging to his temples. "That's what Seconds do, save their commander's skin." He patted Jasce's shoulder and walked across the yard to help with the cleanup.

Jasce watched Kord carry an unconscious Emile toward the Sanctuary. Adrenaline rushed through his system, and his heart pounded in his ears. He inhaled a cleansing breath and thought about Emile losing control over her magic. The side effects were getting worse, fast.

A shiver ran down his spine. The power he'd tapped into holding up the wall and then vaulting was something he hadn't experienced before. When was the last time he'd used his magic like that? He couldn't remember—most of his day was spent teaching recruits, which he loved, or doing the queen's business, which he currently loathed. The adrenaline coursing through his veins made him feel alive, and deep down, he wanted more.

After changing into a clean shirt, he met with the staff and his generals to prepare for the Welcome Ball the following evening. One hour in and his eye twitched. Two hours later and a headache brewed like the storms that formed over the Merrigan Sea. And he still had one more person he needed to meet with before settling things with Kenz.

News of the incident on the training grounds had already made it to Queen Valeri, so by the time Jasce arrived at her quarters, she was focused on other issues and didn't give him her standard lecture.

The fallout of the accident with Emile concerned him, though. A few Naturals were already wary of Spectrals, and now they had another reason not to trust those with magic. What if Emile had directed her magic at someone instead of herself? Who knew what she could really do? All he knew was that her symptoms were rapidly getting worse. He hoped Amycus and Maera could come up with a solution to help the poor kid.

He strode along the vacant corridor of the garrison toward the sleeping quarters. What he really needed was a drink, or three. His anger at Kenz had dissipated like smoke. He'd been so focused on his sister, the Gathering, and missing Spectrals that he'd neglected the one person he loved most. He was a fool. And if history had taught him anything, he had learned that he and Kenz made a formidable team.

Her magic flowed over him before he opened the door. Entering the room and breathing in her scent, he took comfort from her magic as it swirled with his. She laid on the couch reading a book, one leg dangling, her bare foot scraping the ground. The fire sparked behind her, creating a soft glow in the room.

Kenz raised her head as he entered and leaned against the closed door.

"I'm an ass. I know that," he said, holding her stare.

She arched a brow, and the corner of her lip lifted. She sat up and put the book on the side table. The cuffs on her wrists jingled as she got to her feet. The metal glowed blue, and indigo light shot out, pinning him to the door. Her magic enveloped him, soothing him, which quickly evolved into hunger as she approached, her cream tunic and dark green pants accentuating her lithe form.

"Is that your idea of an apology?"

He chewed the inside of his cheek. "Pretty much." He trailed a finger down the shimmering wall and raised his brow as goosebumps formed on her arms. "But if you lower your shield, I'd be more than happy to show you how sorry I am."

A flush crept up her neck, but she kept her voice even. "I don't know. I was in the middle of a good book."

"How about you let me prove it? If I'm wrong, you can go back to your book. What are you reading?"

"*The History of Pandaren.*"

"Seriously?"

Kenz tapped her lip. "There's a legend of a magical crystal—it's very engaging. You might have your work cut out." She twisted her wrists and lowered the shield.

He pushed off the door and wrapped an arm around her waist, pulling her close. "I'm always up for a challenge."

Her body fit against his perfectly, and a fire ignited deep in his core. He gripped the hem of her tunic and pulled it over her head, his breath catching at the sight of lace. He ran his hands down her sides, and she arched her back as his thumbs caressed the tips of her breasts. He kissed the sensitive skin behind her ear, trailing his tongue down to her collarbone. A small moan escaped her lips. She reached for his shirt and yanked it off.

He picked her up and groaned as she wrapped her legs around his waist. His mouth captured hers, tongues twirling in a seductive dance while he gently laid her on the rug in front of the fire, admiring the way her skin glowed from the flames. He kissed down the center of her body while peeling off the barriers blocking him. She gasped as his lips explored every part of her, savoring her until she cried out his name as he took her over the edge.

Jasce hovered over her, getting lost in the deep emerald of her irises. She ran her hands down his body, sliding her fingers under the band of his trousers.

"I should let you get back to your book, since it's so engaging," he said, his voice husky.

Kenz laughed and flipped him onto his back—a move he had taught her. She kissed his neck and her touch sent flames of desire to every part of him. He moaned as she ran her hands along his body and removed the rest of his clothing.

"Maybe you should." Her smile was pure evil.

He pushed up on his elbows. "I am sorry."

"I am, too," she whispered, trailing a finger down his chest.

His heart pounded as she straddled him, and desire for her threatened to consume him. With a growl, he flipped her over and nipped at her bottom lip.

She let out a sexy laugh, replaced by a sigh as he deepened the kiss. He settled over her and drowned in her beauty. He could never get enough of her body, and the need to cherish her overwhelmed him as he claimed her, shuddering at the softness surrounding him. She moved with him, and they surrendered to the pleasure.

Later, as he stroked her back, the fire warm against their cooling skin, he asked a question that had bothered him for a while. "Do you regret coming here?"

Confusion flashed through Kenz's eyes. "What are you talking about?"

He ran a hand through his hair and leaned on his elbow. "You left everything for me. I just don't want you to resent me."

She smoothed the wrinkles on his forehead and kissed his nose. "I love you, Jasce Farone, and regret nothing."

He gave a small smile. "I love you, Kenz Haring, and I will do better. I promise."

She smiled and ran her tongue across his lips. "How about you start now?" He laughed, picked her up, and carried her into the bedroom, shutting the door behind them.

Chapter Ten

A buzz of excitement filled the Bastion and the palace as the Gathering officially commenced with a Welcome Ball honoring all the kingdoms. After hours of trying to teach the recruits, Jasce surrendered and gave everyone the rest of the day off. He and Caston ran through security one last time before getting dressed for the festivities.

He was tugging at his doublet, the top button already tight around his throat, when he entered the Sanctuary. Lander sat next to Emile's bed, talking quietly. Jasce pulled up a chair, and the young soldier stood and saluted.

"At ease," he said, waving his hand at Lander and then focusing on Emile. "Hey, kid, how are you feeling?" A silver collar peeked out over her nightgown. It took all his restraint not to yank it off.

"I'm okay, just tired," Emile said.

Lander huffed. "She's not okay, Commander. Your magic is causing this." The teenager's face paled. "I mean . . ."

"I understand what you mean. It's fine."

But was it? Was his magic causing her to lose control?

Heels clattered along the floor as Maera approached, flipping through a chart. "Commander," she said. She was dressed in a midnight-blue gown with her blonde hair piled on the top of her head in an elaborate twist.

"Maera, how many times have I asked you to call me Jasce?"

The corner of her lips lifted. "Not when I have patients. Speaking of which, Lander, you need to rest. I promise, she's in capable hands."

The young man patted Emile's shoulder. "I'll bring you dessert from the party."

She grinned as he rose from his chair, giving a final salute to Jasce and exiting the Sanctuary.

Jasce caught Maera's stare and frowned. "What is it?"

She smiled at Emile. "I need the commander to move something heavy for me. You should get some sleep."

Jasce ruffled Emile's hair and followed Maera into a separate room. Equipment whirred, and vials of different colors sparkled along the walls. His shoulders tensed at the memories of when Drexus had forced Maera to siphon his magic. The layout was eerily similar to the facility at the Arcane Garrison.

He crossed his arms. "What's going on?"

She leaned against the counter. "A while back, Queen Valeri asked me how much I knew about Drexus's experiments and if I could reverse the procedure."

He narrowed his eyes. "What did you tell her?"

"The truth. I'm very familiar with what Drexus was doing, and I believe there is a safe way to remove magic."

"Why would the queen want to remove magic? Did she have someone in mind?" He thought he knew the answer to this question, but prayed he was wrong.

"Look, Jasce," Maera said, holding up her hands. "Drexus wasn't the only evil Spectral. There are some powerful people out there, and we have to be able to stop them."

"Powerful people. Like my sister? Like me?" Anger churned inside him. "So when I find Jaida, the queen will take her magic? Or if I went rogue, you'd steal mine. Is that it?"

She held his hand. "That wouldn't happen."

He pulled away and paced the room. He could still hear the screams of the Spectrals who had died during Drexus's procedures while their bodies either burst into flames or dissolved into a puddle of water."

"I didn't risk my life to defeat Drexus and the despicable things he was doing to have it start all over again."

"It wouldn't be like that, and you know it. I value life and will do everything I can—"

He held up his hand. "How long have you been working on this?"

"Since the queen hired me." She sighed. "After the incident with Emile, Queen Valeri has moved up the timeline for starting the experiments."

He swore. "You're going to remove Emile's magic?"

"Not until I know it's safe. And Kord will be there."

"I thought you and Amycus were working with Emile to fix this."

"We are, but nothing is helping. She can't wear the collar for the rest of her life. Suppressing magic like that has negative effects, too. We're out of options." She took a step forward, her palms raised. "It will be different, I promise."

"You can't promise that! You have no idea what will happen." He raked his fingers through his hair. "Did Kord agree to this?"

She bit her lip and nodded.

Caston strolled in, fiddling with the cuffs of his jacket. "Hey, Maera, you ready . . ." He looked up and lifted a brow. "What's going on?"

Jasce stepped away from Maera and unclenched his fists. He glanced out the door to where Emile's small body lay. How could they put her through another experiment? He wheeled around and pointed at her. "You touch her and so help me—"

"Jasce," Maera said.

"That's Commander to you." He stomped past a wide-eyed Caston and scared a junior Healer, who squeaked as he stormed out of the Sanctuary. The anger consuming him was all too familiar. He stopped at his rooms and uncorked a bottle of whiskey. The heat from the alcohol rushed down his throat and warmed his belly. He breathed in between gulps and tried to settle the fury swarming through him.

He was late and needed to get to the ball. How he was going to act like everything was okay was beyond him. The desire to strangle the queen had him draining the bottle.

Cassie Sanchez

Tables ladened with food lined the far wall of the ballroom—the colors and aromas as succulent as any tropical garden. Ice sculptures reflected the light from the chandeliers, and an orchestra played background music while the guests, dressed in their finery, arrived. The Orilyon court circled like vultures, searching for an opportunity to meet the visiting rulers, while the lords and ladies from the smaller villages vied for position near the council members. Women craned their necks to view the head table where Prince Jazari sat along with the rest of the dignitaries.

Jasce had stationed soldiers around the room, some wearing evening attire pretending to be guests. He scanned the upper balcony, unable to see his sharpshooters or their crossbows, but he knew they were there.

The four Trackers stood guard near the entrances, nostrils widening as they sniffed the air, searching for magic. As Jasce walked by, Indago's white eyes followed him. He tried not to cringe from the man's intense gaze, as if the Tracker peered into his soul. For the second time, he wondered what the Spectral saw and was tempted to ask, but he thought better of it with the mood he was in.

After his rounds, he approached the high table where Kenz and Delmira, his two strongest Shields, guarded the queen. He stood next to Kenz and observed the guests mingling on the dance floor.

"Where have you been?" she asked out of the side of her mouth.

"Checking on Emile."

She sniffed. "Have you been drinking?"

He wiped a speck of lint from his shoulder. "Only a little."

"Doesn't smell like a little."

Queen Valeri cleared her throat. "Commander, we've been waiting for you." Her tone sounded pleasant, but her eyes spoke a different story.

The queen glared at him as he sat next to her. She was as safe as he could make her, with Amycus on one side and him on the other. Thankfully, his anger had reduced to a simmer, and he no longer wanted to strangle her.

He avoided Kord, who kept looking at him with his brows raised

Embracing the Darkness

but was unable to say anything with the dignitaries separating them at the table. King Morzov discussed establishing new trade routes through the Arakan Mountains with Amycus while Prince Jazari talked to Archduke Carnelian, comparing Shade Walking and Gemari magic. Across the table and down a few chairs sat Queen Siryn, who'd been observing Jasce since he arrived. He tried focusing on the Balten king's words but felt the heaviness of her stare.

"Leonid, please. Let's just enjoy this meal. We'll have plenty of time to discuss business during our meetings," Queen Valeri said, taking a sip of her wine. "Besides, I know Mr. Reins and Commander Farone have wanted to talk weapons with you."

Amycus's eyes twinkled as he explained how he and Jasce had both worked in the forge and perfected the interlocking armor the soldiers wore.

"So, Commander, you're also talented with your hands?" Queen Siryn asked.

Jasce choked on his drink and coughed. Prince Jazari patted him on the back and chuckled.

"Evelina, give the man a break," Archduke Carnelian said, wiping ale from his beard.

"I only meant that yesterday was such an impressive display of the commander's power. And now I learn he's a skilled blacksmith." She played with the pendant on her neck. "Honestly, Lorella, you are fortunate to have Commander Farone by your side." She raised her glass to him, her blue eyes sparkling.

"Hear, hear!" Prince Jazari said, lifting his drink and sneaking a glance at Kenz. His smile widened.

Jasce cleared his throat, thankful the next course had arrived. He was about to take a bite from the quail legs when he caught Amycus staring at Queen Siryn, his brows furrowed as he tapped his finger on the arm of his chair. Dark circles under his eyes made the blue of his irises deeper. He looked thinner than he had a month ago. It seemed the strain of the Gathering was affecting everyone.

"Well, I for one am excited to see the challengers compete tomorrow in the Gauntlet Run. That's an impressive obstacle course," Prince Jazari said as he summoned a waiter for a refill of his wine.

Kord rested his arms on the table. "My Healers might say otherwise. I have a feeling we'll be very busy. Who came up with the swinging blades? Honestly."

Jasce suppressed a cough and looked away.

Kord leaned back in his chair and crossed his arms. "I'm not surprised."

"Mr. Haring, please allow my staff to assist you. They are all proficient in the healing arts and will be invaluable to you," Queen Siryn said.

"Thank you, Your Majesty."

"Yes, that's very generous of you, Evelina," Amycus said with a bite to his voice.

Jasce looked between Queen Siryn and Amycus. A thunk under the table had the blacksmith wincing while Queen Valeri gave him a stern look.

The Vastane queen barely spared Amycus a glance and resumed her conversation with the archduke. They discussed the wyverns while Kord and King Morzov talked about a new type of sword the Baltens had developed.

"Your Majesty," Archduke Carnelian said between bites of his braised lamb. "What's Pandaren's policy if something were to happen to you?"

King Morzov raised his brows while Prince Jazari shook his head. Queen Siryn held her fork in midair as her eyes darted between Queen Valeri and the archduke.

Queen Valeri slowly lowered her glass, her knuckles white as she gripped the stem. "Excuse me?"

Both Jasce and Amycus shifted closer to her, and Jasce signaled Kenz and Delmira. Kenz's bracelets glowed blue, while Delmira's gauntlets sparked a bright yellow.

The archduke wiped his mouth with his napkin and placed it on the table. Tension cut like a sharpened blade through smoke. "Well, it's common knowledge that you don't have an heir, so the question remains: What happens if, magic forbid, you were incapacitated? Your country is in a precarious position. I believe I speak for the rest of us

Embracing the Darkness

when I say we can't afford for Pandaren to go through another civil war."

"Kraig, you're out of line," Amycus said.

King Morzov drummed his fingers on the table. "Well, the archduke broaches an interesting subject, even if the timing is poor."

Queen Siryn bit her lip while Kord rubbed the back of his neck, wincing slightly.

Queen Valeri lifted her chin and focused on each dignitary. "I appreciate your concern, but we have measures in place. The ruler of Pandaren can assign someone to lead in the event there is no heir."

"A non-royal could rule Pandaren?" the archduke asked, his brows disappearing into his shaggy hair.

"Are you volunteering to give Lorella an heir, Kraig?" Queen Siryn asked, wicked amusement flashing in her eyes.

The archduke cleared his throat. "A unified Terrenus and Pandaren is an option, of course. We are more alike than the other kingdoms."

"You are mistaken," Queen Siryn said. "All of our people resided in Pandaren eons ago, before the tribes journeyed to their own little parts of the world." She patted the archduke's hand. "You really aren't that special."

The archduke sputtered.

Jasce sat up straighter. He hadn't known that the Vastanes had once lived in Pandaren. But who was he to question it? Their libraries were renowned, and the queen was very knowledgeable. He glanced at Amycus, who gave a slight nod.

"In our country, the leader of our military would take that role, at least temporarily, until my son was of age. But Andrei is a little too young for you, I think," the Balten king said, giving Queen Valeri a wink.

The queen laughed. "Commander Farone lead Pandaren? Magic help us." A few others tittered but stopped when they looked at Jasce.

His stomach clenched. Was she actually insulting him in front of everyone? Kord held Jasce's stare, attempting a smile that didn't meet his eyes.

The thought of ruling hadn't entered his mind. Not since the days he worked for Drexus, who'd developed plans to take over the country and had wanted the Angel of Death by his side. Something oily slithered inside him—the thought of more power and not being under someone else's authority had a certain appeal.

Queen Siryn trailed her finger along the rim of her glass. "Oh, I don't know, Lorella. The commander seems more than capable."

The queen's nostrils flared. "Yes, well, this discussion can wait until we have our meetings."

The Vastane queen inclined her head. "Of course."

Amycus cleared his throat and conversed with the Balten king while the archduke finished his meal. Queen Siryn smiled at Jasce as if they shared a secret joke.

He snuck a glance at Kenz, who glared at the Vastane queen.

"Tell me, Commander, who is that delectable creature? The one that looks like a sea goddess, albeit an angry one. She is truly mesmerizing," Prince Jazari said as he examined Kenz.

He had noticed the prince staring at Kenz all evening. Even he was having a difficult time keeping his eyes off her. The green dress she wore highlighted every curve, the low-cut neckline showing more of her than he wanted others to see.

"That's Kenz Haring," Jasce said, glowering at the prince. "My fiancée."

Queen Siryn's gaze darted between Jasce and Kenz. A shadow flickered across her face but disappeared as quickly as it had come.

"Fiancée, huh? You're a lucky man. What magic does she have, as I don't see any weapons tucked away in that dress?" The prince chuckled at his own joke.

Jasce reached for his dagger and winced as another thunk sounded under the table. The queen and Amycus gave him a look. He took a breath and suppressed the rage. "She's a Shield."

"Ah," said the prince.

"She's also being promoted to captain and competing in all the contests."

"Is she? That will be exciting to watch. Especially if she wears that dress."

Jasce swallowed as a jagged edge of anger sliced through any calm he had. He could see himself grabbing the man's head and slamming it into

Embracing the Darkness

the table, then elbowing him in his perfectly straight nose, possibly even cutting out his tongue.

The prince held up his hands, his silver eyes wide. "Commander, I was only admiring the scenery. I didn't mean any offense."

"Commander Farone," Queen Valeri said, "please see to the security at the north end of the ballroom. It seems a little lax."

He held the queen's stare. Silence weighed heavily as all eyes focused on him. Kord slowly lowered his drink, and the tapping of Amycus's finger sounded like a countdown. He knew he needed to leave before he did something rash, remembering how he had behaved at the tavern.

He pushed back his chair, straightened his doublet, and dropped his napkin onto his plate. Concern lined Kenz's face. He gave a slight shake of his head and strode away from the queen and her guests.

King Morzov's deep voice carried, even though he kept it low. "You're lucky he didn't stab you, Nicolaus. You shouldn't tempt the Angel of Death."

Prince Jazari mumbled something, but Jasce couldn't hear it over the blood pounding through his ears. How dare the queen dismiss him. The security was fine, and they both knew it. The prince had lusted over Kenz the entire dinner, and the Balten king was correct: No one should tempt the Angel of Death.

Jasce flexed his hands and choked down the rage. He needed to pull it together. Leaving the ballroom, he slid out a side door onto the terrace and welcomed the breeze floating off the ocean. He inhaled the saltiness and squeezed the top of the wall, still warm from the afternoon heat. The gardens below shimmered with the soft glow of flickering torches.

His heart rate finally settled, and his breathing returned to normal by the time he counted to one hundred. He knew he needed to get back inside, but being alone with the cool of night soothed him. He drummed his fingers on the wall. Ruling Pandaren, although a monumental headache, would be better than taking orders from the queen.

A hand touched his shoulder. He spun, seized their arm, and twisted while pressing his dagger to a pale throat.

Queen Siryn gasped and held on to Jasce's wrist.

He immediately released her and pressed against the balcony. "Your Majesty, forgive me. I didn't—"

She rested a hand on his arm. "No, Commander, it's my fault. I'm sorry, I should've announced myself. You are quite nimble and strong—impressive."

He narrowed his eyes. Had Queen Valeri ever complimented him before? He couldn't remember a time when she'd been impressed with him as a warrior or the leader of her army. And then she'd laughed at the thought of him ruling Pandaren. An image of him sitting on the throne flitted through his mind.

The queen smiled, and her eyes reminded him of a summer storm over the ocean. "You'll have to ignore Nicolaus. He's always appreciated beauty, but his heart is already taken."

"By who?"

"I'll let you figure that out on your own." She leaned her hip on the railing and closed the distance between them. "Your skills really are magnificent. I look forward to watching you compete."

The side of her hand brushed up against his. The music and voices from inside drifted away. The breeze rustled Queen Siryn's hair and the scent of her perfume clouded his thoughts.

"Jasce, are you—" Kenz emerged onto the balcony and froze, her eyes narrowing.

He quickly stepped away from the queen. He hadn't realized how close they stood.

"Kenz, I . . ."

The queen's lip curled. "Ahh, the fiancée. That's my cue, then. See you tomorrow, Commander." Queen Siryn glided past Kenz, who scowled, her hands fisted on her hips. She slowly turned toward him.

He raised his hand. "That wasn't what it looked like."

Glasses clinked and music floated from the ballroom. A flash of lightning lit up the sea, the smell of rain lingered on the breeze.

Kenz wandered to the railing and leaned over, peering into the garden. "Be careful with her. She couldn't stop looking at you throughout dinner. I wanted to throw a fork into her eye."

He smiled and pulled her toward him. "Just like I wanted to cut Prince Jazari's tongue out."

"That's disgusting," she said, pressing her hands on his chest. "Now, do you want to tell me what's wrong?"

Embracing the Darkness

His smile dissolved. "What do you mean?"

"Why were you drinking on duty? You'd beat one of your soldiers if they showed up drunk."

"I wasn't drunk."

She crossed her arms and waited. The breeze blew his hair into his face, and he absently thought about getting a haircut. "There's just a lot going on. I needed to take the edge off." He didn't want to talk about Emile or Kord. Not tonight. Tracing his thumb along her jaw, he said, "You look beautiful. Have I told you?"

"Nice deflection," she said, and the corner of her mouth lifted. "Only a few times. But I won't object to you telling me again."

Jasce kissed her, running his tongue on her lower lip. "You're beautiful and I can't wait to get you out of that dress."

"Shouldn't you be thinking about security?"

"You're making it difficult."

She teasingly bit his lip and then stepped out of his embrace. "Actually, you really do need to check on security. One of the Alturians was using their Shade Walking magic against a Gemari. Anyway, Caston asked me to find you."

Jasce sighed and led her inside. He rested his hand on her lower back and felt her warmth flow through him.

She gave him a quick kiss. "But if I ever see you in that position again with that Vastane hag, I will throw you over the balcony." She playfully slapped his cheek and sauntered to a table where Flynt, Tillie, and Aura sat.

He rubbed the back of his neck. Knowing Kenz, she probably would knock him off the balcony.

Queen Valeri proceeded to her throne while the other dignitaries dispersed to different areas of the room. Jasce took up position on one side while Amycus walked up the dais and whispered to Delmira, who sighed and headed straight for the food table.

Amycus gave him a wry smile. "I decided to give her a break. Is that all right?"

"I don't know." Jasce smiled and patted him on the shoulder. "How's your air shield?"

A shadow flickered over his face. "It'll do."

Queen Valeri stood, and the room fell silent, all eyes turned toward the throne.

"I want to officially welcome our esteemed guests who have traveled great distances to take part in a long-standing tradition. Here's to the start of the Gathering—forging new friendships and strengthening the bonds between nations." She raised her goblet. "Welcome to Pandaren." The queen sipped from her glass and returned to her seat as the ballroom erupted with cheers. The orchestra played a lively tune, inviting couples to the dance floor.

King Morzov approached the throne with Consort Lekov and gave a bow. "Thank you for a wonderful evening. We are going to retire now." The king stood eye to eye with Jasce and inclined his head. "I look forward to the tournaments and seeing the strength of your competitors."

"Likewise." Jasce glanced at the consort. "I didn't see your name on the list."

She crossed her arms. "I have to evaluate my soldiers. Plus, someone needs to supervise the king."

"Ha!" King Morzov said. "It's a miracle I survived forty years before I found her."

Consort Lekov rolled her eyes, and the king led her out of the ballroom, followed by a squadron of soldiers, some the size of Kord. Jasce's men and women who planned to compete would have their work cut out for them.

"I think he's my favorite," Queen Valeri said. Jasce raised a brow and was about to respond when she held up her hand. "I need to reiterate how important the negotiations are for Pandaren and our economy, especially with the Alturians. I can't have what occurred at dinner happen again. Is that clear?"

His jaw throbbed from grinding his teeth. Amycus gave a slight shake of his head.

Jasce kept his face blank, but inside, his anger burned. "Yes, Your Majesty."

Embracing the Darkness

The queen fixed her attention on Amycus. "That goes for you, too. We can't afford an incident."

The blacksmith nodded, and the queen focused on the couples dancing. After a while, she rose and bid the guests good night. She exited through a side door, followed by her ladies-in-waiting and two guards.

"About bloody time," Jasce murmured, walking down the dais. He caught Maera's gaze and looked away. He'd deal with her later, after he spoke to the queen regarding Emile's magic.

Amycus crossed his arms. His eyes found Queen Siryn, who talked with Prince Jazari and the archduke. Lord Rollant and Lady Darbry joined them, while Lord Haldron and Lady Wuhl loitered on the other side of the room, both frowning.

"What's the story between you two?" Jasce asked.

Amycus threaded his fingers behind his back. "I just don't trust her."

"Who does?"

Tillie and Kord approached. Jasce scanned the area for Kenz, finding her with Delmira and Aura and a few Gemaris who were putting on a display of their magic. Now that the queen had retired, it seemed the visitors were keen to show off.

"Why do I have a bad feeling about all of this?" Kord asked, his arm wrapped around Tillie and holding a delicate flute in his massive hand.

"Because there's some intelligence behind the brawn." Jasce ignored Kord's scowl. "We have Shade Walkers, Gemaris, lethal warriors, and the Vastanes all in one room. And now a play for the throne since the queen doesn't have an heir. I mean, what could possibly go wrong?" he asked, rubbing a hand down his face.

"No wonder you have dark circles under your eyes," Tillie said, taking a sip of the bubbling pink beverage.

Kord took a drink and grimaced. "This is awful." He placed it on a nearby table and studied Jasce. "Remember, you don't need to take this all on by yourself. We're here for you, okay?"

His nails dug into his palms as he thought about Emile and what Kord and Maera were planning.

Kord tilted his head and lowered his voice. "What's wrong?"

Jasce inhaled. He'd had enough confrontations for one night. "Nothing." There was still time to change the queen's mind regarding removing Emile's magic.

Amycus rested a hand on Jasce's shoulder. "We'll get this figured out. Just one thing at a time."

He nodded. "I'm going to do another sweep and then double-check the security for tomorrow's tournament. I'll see you in the morning." He surveyed the room and gave instructions to both General Nadja and Caston, then headed to the Bastion. Security was as tight as he could make it, and he needed a reprieve from the noise, the politics, and the people. He removed his doublet and drew in a deep breath. Grabbing a practice sword, he went through an exercise sequence, letting the motion and familiarity settle his mind. His thoughts drifted to Jaida, and he hoped she was okay and that Vale was taking care of her. He'd abandoned the search for his sister. But what could he do? He was stretched thin, pulled in too many directions, while being at the beck and call of Queen Valeri.

Life was easier as the Angel of Death.

Jasce tilted his head back and focused on the stars. As Azrael, he'd had one purpose and was good at it. Now, he found himself in uncharted waters, swimming upstream, and if he wasn't careful, he could be swept away.

Chapter Eleven

The arena, nicknamed the Pit, was a hive of excitement as spectators marveled at the Gauntlet—a lethal obstacle course comprising moving bridges, rolling logs, swinging weighted spheres, and blades that could cleave a man in two. The course was designed to test the physical and mental strength of the competitor, along with coordination and flexibility.

The Pit wasn't usually open to outsiders. In the days of Drexus, the Hunters had trained and bled in this arena, and the commander had kept their activities hidden from the Watch Guard—the less anyone knew about the assassins, the better. The mystery surrounding them and their infamous skull masks had incited fear in the soldiers, nobles, and citizens of Pandaren.

But today, the gates had been thrown open to allow entrance to those fortunate enough to win a ticket. Special areas along the lower level of the arena had been erected for the visiting kingdoms, with plush chairs and coverings to protect the royals from the sun. Vendors peddled their wares, and the smell of roasting meat and sweet pastries filled the air. Some stalls even sold trinkets to ward off magic, not that they did any good.

Archduke Carnelian's scowl was visible from across the Pit as he slouched in his chair. He was flanked by his guards, their different colored gems sparkling in the afternoon light. He had brought up the lack of an heir again in their meetings, but his plans for uniting the kingdoms were met with resistance from the other rulers. If Pandaren and Terrenus joined, they'd be a dominating force with the Spectral magic alongside the Gemari. Jasce sensed there was something else behind the archduke's motive for wanting to marry the queen. He just couldn't figure out what.

Dark clouds formed in the west and threatened the afternoon rains, which Jasce welcomed as he sought the shade and waited for Queen Valeri to enter Pandaren's viewing box.

The other council members filed in, with Lord Haldron leading the way and talking with Lady Wuhl.

"Those beasts are getting closer," Lord Haldron said to Lady Wuhl, his voice lowered.

"I've heard the same thing. Something needs to be done." They strayed to the back of the box, whispering and sneaking glances. Jasce shook his head. He'd sent out more scouts to search for the Snatchers and they'd either returned with only stories or rumors, or they didn't return at all.

Lady Darbry found an attendant, snatched a drink off the tray, and took her seat, while Lord Rollant strolled past with one of his personal guards. Jasce glanced around, wondering where Captain Reed was.

Amycus approached and leaned over the railing to observe the competitors warming up. "What are your thoughts about an heir for Pandaren? Interesting that the archduke brought it up again."

Jasce looked over his shoulder to make sure the nobles couldn't hear but kept his voice low just the same. "I'm glad we have a plan. A vote from the council to elect the next ruler is strategically wise. And one I won't have to worry about winning."

"You might be surprised at how many support you."

Jasce snorted. "I wouldn't even vote for myself, even though I'd rather give orders than receive them. As long as it's anyone but Haldron."

Amycus tapped the railing, his eyes drifting toward the Terrenus box. "Why now, though?"

Embracing the Darkness

Jasce followed his gaze. "I was thinking the same thing. He could've come to Pandaren's aid years ago. The timing doesn't make sense."

Murmurs rumbled through the stands as the Vastane queen entered, accompanied by her guards and a few of her nobles. She spoke to two attendants dressed in white, who bowed and made their way into the Pit. They stopped near Kord, who shook their hands and introduced them to Maera. Queen Siryn smoothed her royal-blue dress and sat. She caught Jasce staring and wiggled her fingers in a playful wave.

Jasce still hadn't spoken to Kord about removing Emile's magic, and it grated on his nerves that anyone would try to steal a Spectral's power. A knot in his stomach tightened as he observed Kord interacting with the Vastane attendants. Emile had been through enough. He was about to ask Amycus about it when squeals from a group of ladies snagged his attention.

Prince Jazari, donning a forest-green tunic lined with silver, strolled to his booth. He waved to his enthusiastic fans.

Amycus chuckled as the women flaunted the Alturian scarves they had purchased. "He's quite a character."

"Do you trust him?"

Amycus nodded. "I do."

King Morzov entered next with Consort Lekov at his side. As they strode past the prince, the king whispered to his consort, who tucked her chin, hiding a laugh. As they settled in their box, a Balten attendant approached the consort and pointed to a group of competitors warming up near the Gauntlet. Consort Lekov scowled and then said something to the king. She hopped over the wall and stalked toward her soldiers.

The crowd cheered as Queen Valeri entered the stadium, followed by Caston and Delmira, whose gauntlets glowed yellow. The council bowed as she glided into the box and took her seat. She wore the colors of Pandaren, the purple and gold shimmering under the waning light of the sun. The clouds marched across the sky, their conquest nearly complete as thunder rumbled in the distance.

The queen acknowledged the other royals and then surveyed the competitors. "Commander Farone, are we ready?"

"Yes, Your Majesty. The Gauntlet is set and teams assigned." Each competitor would earn points for their team depending on how well they performed. For Pandaren, Jasce had chosen eight of his soldiers, all who had strengths suited for the different trials. Flynt and Kenz leaned against a column, silver collars peeking out over their chest pieces. Two other Spectrals were chosen along with three Naturals, picked by General Nadja.

"Good. Then why aren't you down there?"

Jasce crossed his arms. "Your safety is more important than these games."

The queen's lips curved upward. "I appreciate that. However, I have Amycus, Caston, and Delmira up here, and the rest of the council. I'm well protected. And I don't want to lose. Is that clear?"

"You want me to compete?"

The queen rolled her eyes, an action Jasce considered very unqueenly. "Of course I do. Why wouldn't I?"

"I just thought—"

"That's a dangerous pastime," Caston said, smacking him on the shoulder.

Jasce muffled a curse and glared at his Second. Spotting Kord across the arena, speaking with his Healers, he focused on his magic, felt the tug, and disappeared.

Kord jumped as Jasce materialized by his side. "I hate it when you do that!"

Jasce smirked and surveyed the other competitors. The soldiers of Balten and Terrenus were strapping on armor provided by the Guard to protect them from the swinging blades. Consort Lekov grimaced as she held a chest piece between her fingers.

"Consort Lekov, I didn't think you were competing," Jasce said.

"I am now, as one of my men didn't show. He's probably slumped over a bar, which he'll pay dearly for." She dropped the armor, rubbing her hands together as if they were covered in filth. "However, I will not be wearing that."

Jasce opened his mouth to comment when he felt Kord's large hand on his shoulder, giving it a firm squeeze.

"Consort Lekov, I must insist you wear armor for your protection," Kord said, a warm smile on his face.

She pointed to Jasce. "Is he?"

Embracing the Darkness

"Jasce isn't competing."

"Actually, I am. The queen ordered it. But I'm not wearing armor."

The consort placed her hands on her hips. "Then I won't, either."

Kord sighed. "Yes, but you're more important than Commander Farone."

Jasce rolled his eyes. Any other time or place, he would knock Kord to the ground, but diplomacy sucked the joy out of everything. "Would you rather use your own—as long as it doesn't have any magical capabilities?"

Consort Lekov narrowed her gaze and nodded, snapping her fingers at her guard, who hurried toward the west wing of the Bastion where the Balten soldiers resided. "I assume you will also wear a collar."

Jasce clenched his teeth. The last time he'd worn one was when Drexus had captured him and almost whipped him to death. If it hadn't been for Kord, he'd be dead.

Kord squeezed his shoulder again and handed him the silver ring. "Yes, all Spectrals who compete are required to."

The consort inclined her head and returned to her soldiers.

"I can't tell if I like her or not," Jasce said, scratching the scruff along his jaw. "And if you squeeze my shoulder one more time, I'm going to knock you on your ass."

Kord laughed, tightening his grip on his arm. "No, you won't. The queen is watching."

"Which one?" He glanced at the stands where both queens observed him. Amycus looked from Jasce to Queen Siryn, his brows furrowed.

A swish of blonde hair caught Jasce's eye. Emile and Maleous ran toward them from the Healer's tent.

"Uncle Jasce, are you competing?" Maleous asked, a grin plastered on his face.

"Yep," he said, ruffling the boy's hair. "How are you feeling?" he asked Emile.

"Better." Her hand rose toward the collar around her neck and then lowered. "Safety precaution," she mumbled.

Jasce bristled. There had to be another way to help this kid.

"We have to give these out," Maleous said, lifting a box filled with the collars.

"Good luck," Emile yelled over her shoulder as they ran across the arena.

"Don't those two ever just walk?" Jasce snapped the collar around his neck and winced as his magic disappeared. Breathing deeply, he focused on relaxing his muscles and envisioned the task ahead.

Kord handed him a chest piece. "And you are wearing armor—at least this."

Jasce slid the covering over his head. "Kord, I need to talk to you." Across the Pit, Emile laughed at something Maleous said. This probably wasn't the best time to bring up Maera's experiments, but he hated having this wedge between them. "It's not like you to keep things from me."

The Healer dropped his arms by his side. "Jasce, I—"

"I can't believe you agreed to remove Emile's magic after all she's been through."

Kord's mouth gaped. He snapped it shut and cleared his throat. "Oh, I thought . . ." He waved his hand as if swatting a bug. "I'm sorry. I haven't had the chance to tell you with everything going on, but I won't let anything happen to her."

Jasce scanned the crowd. His eyes stopped on Lord Haldron. "I know that. But what if this gets into the wrong hands? Would you want your magic taken against your will?"

Kord followed Jasce's gaze and crossed his muscular arms. "Maera will have safety precautions. Trust us, okay?"

He stared up at his friend and nodded. He trusted Kord with his life. Maera, too.

"Good. Now be careful out there. And see if you can talk my sister out of participating."

Jasce huffed. "Yeah, right."

He strode over to his team, and their eyes widened as they noticed his collar.

"Sir, I didn't know you were competing," Alyssa said, glancing at Kenz and Flynt, who both shrugged.

"Neither did I." He adjusted his chest piece. "The fastest time with fewest injuries wins. Oh, and the queen informed me she doesn't like to lose."

Embracing the Darkness

Flynt chuckled. "No pressure or anything."

Jasce eyed the Fire Spectral. "You good? You don't need to do this if you aren't at full strength."

"I'm fine. It just took Kord longer than usual."

Kenz sidled up to him while the team dispersed to the waiting area around the Gauntlet. "What's going on? You have that look."

"What look?"

"The look that says something is about to happen and Mean Jasce might come out."

Laughing, he tied back his hair. "Mean Jasce?"

Kenz tilted her head, resting her hands on her hips. She was too perceptive for her own good.

Jasce glanced up at the viewing boxes again. "I find I don't enjoy politics."

She snorted. "What's there to enjoy?"

"The dignitaries are playing some sort of game with their own agendas, and I don't trust a single one of them. Plus, missing Spectrals have been reported on the outskirts of Bradwick."

Kenz frowned. "The Snatchers are getting closer."

"Seems like it. At least that's what the council members are saying. And now I have to compete in this bloody course."

"No pun intended?"

Jasce pulled her close and double-checked the straps of her armor, making sure she was secure. "Your brother wanted me to ask you to bow out of this one."

Kenz's lifted her chin and glared at Kord. "Will he ever stop trying to protect me?"

He tucked a stray hair behind her ear. "Nope, and neither will I. Please be careful. Time the blades, don't rush. Quick feet."

Kenz gave him a mock salute. "Yes sir."

Shaking his head, he followed her to where his team waited. He couldn't worry about Emile, politics, or the Snatchers—he needed all his wits and skills to not only get through the Gauntlet, but to win.

Chapter Twelve

A celebratory dinner for the completion of the Gauntlet Run occurred in one of the larger dining rooms in the palace. Laughter and clinking glasses sounded throughout the room, especially around the Pandaren tables. After the judges tallied the points, Jasce's team had the fastest and cleanest runs, making them the winners of the first trial.

Individually, Garan, the Vastane guard, came in second while Kenz and Consort Lekov tied for third.

Both Kord and Jasce had held their breaths as Kenz ran the obstacle course. Kord swore when a swinging blade nipped her shoulder and when she stumbled on the rolling logs. When she finished, she'd had a huge grin on her face. Jasce had often wondered what she did when he was searching for Jaida. Now he knew.

The Terrenians scored the worst, but that didn't surprise Jasce. There were other challenges that suited their skill set, especially the grappling and sword fighting trials. The Alturians had scored fourth, and the Vastanes third, despite Garan's impressive run.

Jasce glanced at the Baltens' table. They were in second place and only a few points separated them from his team. He'd known they were tough competitors, and now he figured the competition would come down between the warriors from the south and Pandaren. A chair sat vacant next to Consort Lekov, and he wondered what had happened to the missing soldier.

Queen Valeri nodded to Jasce as she entered the dining hall, her pleasure at him winning the first trial evident on her face. He'd had the cleanest race with no injuries and received the fastest time.

"Look who's the queen's favorite," Caston said, elbowing him in the side.

Jasce grunted. Rarely was he ever in the good graces of the queen. "You would've won if I hadn't been down there."

Queen Valeri joined the other royals at the high table. Jasce sighed in relief that she hadn't forced him to sit with them. He scanned the room for Kenz and Kord, who wove their way through the tables decorated with the banners of the five kingdoms.

His smile slipped, and he rose from his seat. Dark smudges under Kord's eyes stood out against his pale face. "What's wrong?"

Kord waved him off and plopped into the chair. "I'm fine."

"His magic is drained," Kenz said, frowning.

Caston scratched his goatee. "I thought you healed quickly."

Kord rested his chin on his hand. "I do. But there were a lot of injuries from that blasted trial. Swinging blades—honestly, I would beat the tar out of both of you if I wasn't so exhausted."

Jasce and Caston glanced at each other, trying to hide their grins, and then directed their gaze across the dining hall, feigning interest in a group of musicians.

"I just need food and sleep." Kord rubbed his face and focused on Jasce. "Because of that performance, you've got a target on your back."

Jasce sighed. "When haven't I? Anyway, that's why I have Caston." Kenz cleared her throat. He smiled and added, "And your sister."

Kord glanced at Kenz and shook his head. Flynt, Aura, and Delmira joined them, already halfway through their pints of ale. Delmira laughed at something Aura said while Flynt winked at one of the Alturians. Her cheeks blushed as she whispered to her friend.

Servants arrived with platters of food, and a collective sigh flowed through the cavernous room.

Queen Valeri rose from her throne and lifted her glass. "To all those who competed in the first trial, congratulations on a job well done. The next challenge will occur in one week. In the meantime, rest and enjoy all that Orilyon offers."

A cheer resounded, and forks scraping plates drowned out any conversation.

Kenz wrinkled her nose at her plate loaded with food.

"Are you going to eat that?" Flynt asked, reaching across to stab at a piece of meat.

She shook her head. "I'm not hungry."

Prince Jazari strode toward them, and Jasce scowled when he sat in the empty chair next to Kenz.

Jasce raised a brow. "Your Highness, do you need something?"

"Nicolaus, please," he said, winking at Kenz, whose eyes widened.

Jasce squeezed his fist under the table, his nails digging into his palms.

The prince relaxed into the chair, holding a glass of wine up to the light and swirling it. "What I need is to get away from the archduke. He really is a bore and won't stop talking about the Heart of Pandaren."

Caston leaned forward. "The what?"

The prince's silver eyes gleamed with mischief. "You've heard the story of the Heart of Pandaren, haven't you?"

Caston looked between Jasce and Kord and shrugged.

A memory clawed its way to the surface. The forest, the crash of dishes thrown in a rage, Jasce's mother's voice permeating the night. He remembered bickering with Jaida while their mother told them a story about the origin of magic in Pandaren. Jasce narrowed his eyes as he focused on the prince.

"Ah, well, it's an old tale. Your friend Amycus might be aware of it. He seems rather knowledgeable. And I would bet my crown the Vastanes know of it."

Kenz lowered her glass and pivoted in her chair. "What's the story?"

Prince Jazari grinned, his white teeth sparkling. Caston cleared his throat and nodded at the bent fork in Jasce's hand. Jasce sighed and loosened his grip.

"Thousands of years ago, or so the legend states, two magical beings, Theran and Cerulea, came to Pandaren and lived among the five tribes, searching for those worthy to receive magic. However, as with any magic, there needs to be balance, so Theran and Cerulea created a crystal called the Heart of Pandaren."

"What does it do?" Kord asked.

"Wait a minute," Kenz said, sitting up straighter and pushing her plate away. "I read about this." She looked at Jasce. "Remember the other night?"

"I do, but I was a little preoccupied." He smiled at the blush creeping into Kenz's cheeks.

"With what?" Kord asked.

Jasce raised his brows. "Do you really want to know?"

Caston laughed as Kord glanced at his sister, his eyes widening. "Nope."

"Anyway," Kenz said, flicking her hand at them. "This Heart, or whatever it's called, is in four pieces, right?" She looked at the prince, who nodded, his eyelids heavy.

Jasce was seconds from ripping the man's head off. "I thought it was just a myth, a bedtime story."

"Not according to our information," the prince said, "which is always accurate."

Caston leaned forward. "Always?"

"Always."

Jasce kept himself from rolling his eyes. "So, what does this Heart do? How does it affect magic?"

"Well, the people misused the crystal's power. Seems things don't change." The prince took a sip of wine and licked his lips. Aura and Delmira grinned at each other. He raised his glass and nodded at the two Spectrals. "Theran and Cerulea split the Heart into four Stones and hid them throughout the land, but not before separating the five tribes. Surely you've noticed how Shade Walking is comparable to Vaulting and the Baltens' magic is like your Amps?"

Now that Jasce thought about it, there were some similarities. "That doesn't explain the Gemaris and Vastanes."

"The Gemaris create weapons using magic, similar to your Shields." The prince glanced at Delmira and Kenz.

Embracing the Darkness

Delmira rested her arms on the table. "Yeah, but the Vastanes don't have any magic."

Flynt snorted. "The gods must not have liked them either."

"There is some debate about whether the Vastanes possess magic," Prince Jazari said.

Jasce sat up in his chair. "Debate? Among whom?"

"Among the Alturians."

Caston slid Jasce a guarded look. "But I thought your information was always correct. We need to know if the Vastanes have magic."

"Agreed," the prince said, glancing around the dining hall. "Have your white-eyed people . . . what do you call them again?"

"Trackers," Jasce said.

"Yes, have your Trackers noticed anything?"

"Not that I'm aware of, but I'll find out." Jasce glanced at the empty Vastane table. Even Garan wasn't at the festivities.

"It can't be that powerful if no one has noticed," the prince said.

"You mentioned four Stones. What do they do?" Kenz asked.

Prince Jazari scooted closer to her, his silver eyes shining. Jasce cleared his throat and raised a brow.

"They each affect magic differently. One creates and another destroys, while one strengthens and the other suppresses."

"Like the Brymagus plant?" Flynt asked.

The prince leaned forward. "Have you ever wondered how the plant gets its magic?"

Jasce looked at Amycus, who sat with the archduke and his aide. If anyone would know about the magic of the Brymagus plant, it would be Amycus or Drexus. Jasce's shoulders tensed. Had Drexus known about the Heart of Pandaren?

"And no one knows where these Stones are?" Aura asked.

"No, but there is another story, and we haven't verified if it's true or not, that a sliver of the Empower Stone—the part that strengthens magic—has been passed down through the centuries through Pandaren's royal family, usually as a piece of jewelry." The prince glanced over his shoulder at Amycus and then back at Jasce. "I wonder, have you come across a Spectral with an impressive amount of magic?"

Everyone's heads swiveled toward Jasce. Even with his two forms of magic, one of them rare, he wasn't abnormally strong in either. And Amycus was powerful, but he'd never noticed him wearing jewelry.

Jasce kept his face blank and shook his head, ignoring the ice flowing through his veins. He remembered Drexus owning a ring, and an image of a wall of black fire surrounding him and Kenz flashed through his mind. Drexus had been extraordinarily powerful, and so had Jaida. Was it possible his former commander had the piece of the Empower Stone? Is this why Queen Valeri wanted proof of his death?

Prince Jazari held his stare. A glint shone in his eye, as if he suspected Jasce wasn't telling the truth. "Anyway," he finally said, "if you decide to search for the Stones, I'd love to join you. For informational purposes, of course."

"Of course," Jasce said.

The prince turned to Kenz. "You were quite remarkable today. I heard Consort Lekov wasn't happy. She's not accustomed to losing. Or tying."

The corner of Kenz's mouth slid upward. "She might as well get used to some female competition."

The prince laughed, his gaze drifting over Kenz's face. "Beautiful and full of fire. You're a lucky man, Commander Farone."

Jasce's voice was steel wrapped in silk. "Yes, I am."

Prince Jazari stood and straightened his tunic. "I'll ask a server to bring you another fork." The man winked and sauntered off toward where his soldiers sat.

Jasce squeezed the mangled utensil, and a jolt of rage ran through him, the hairs on his neck standing to attention.

Kenz reached across the table, resting her hand on his. "Jasce, he's just playing around. Don't let him get under your skin."

He swallowed and squeezed Kenz's hand. She was right, of course. He couldn't allow the prince to annoy him. Again, he warred with diplomacy and wanting to punch the man in the face.

A soft snore had Jasce turning. Kord's chin rested on his chest.

Kenz shook her head. "I'll see you later. I'm going to take this big lug home." Kord startled awake when she nudged him. "Come on. Let's get you back to Tillie." He mumbled something and trudged off with Kenz.

Embracing the Darkness

Delmira and Aura wandered across the dining hall toward a group of Baltens, while Flynt ate the rest of Kenz's dinner.

"You seem a bit on edge." Caston stared at him, the skin around his eyes tight.

"No, I don't," Jasce said.

"That fork would say otherwise."

Jasce peered at the high table and wondered who else knew about the Heart of Pandaren. A stirring slithered through his gut. To have that much power . . . He thought again about Drexus and his black fire. If Jasce had the Empower Stone, he'd be unstoppable.

The corner of his lips curved into a smile.

Chapter Thirteen

Queen Valeri held an emergency council meeting the next morning, secretly so as not to alarm their guests. She had received reports from nearby towns of more missing Spectrals and sightings of the mysterious creatures people were calling Snatchers. The last group of soldiers Caston had sent out hadn't returned from their scouting mission, and members of the Paladin Guard were getting nervous.

Indago walked the perimeter of the War Room, his white eyes scanning the shadows for Shade Walkers. After Jasce's talk with the Alturian prince and witnessing Commander Faez's Shade Walking abilities when the climbing wall fell, having a Tracker present in all council meetings became a necessity.

Jasce's jaw ached from clenching his teeth. He tried to relax, but every time Indago drifted by, he sensed the Tracker's eyes probing him, as if searching through the murkiness of his soul.

"What are we going to do? Bradwick is brimming with fear, people won't leave their homes, and commerce is down," Lord Haldron said.

Jasce refrained from rolling his eyes. "What about Delmar and Havelock?"

Lord Rollant leaned forward. "The Snatchers seem to be concentrated around the central part of the country. My scouts are telling me that only Spectrals are being targeted and left for dead, their bodies almost unrecognizable."

"Why Spectrals?" Lady Darbry asked.

"It has to do with magic," Jasce answered. "When my team returned, they reported the Snatchers were barely affected by it."

Kord rubbed his jaw. "Maera and I think the creature's teeth must have some sort of venom that blocks magic."

Lord Haldron's face reddened as he glowered at Jasce. "And when, Commander, were you planning on telling us?"

Jasce bared his teeth. "You're on a need-to-know basis, Larkin."

Kord sighed and rubbed his forehead. "Not helping," he murmured.

Lord Haldron pushed back from the table and opened his mouth, but the queen interjected. "Commander Farone is on my orders. The point is, it seems they are getting closer to Orilyon, which obviously poses a problem."

Lady Wuhl rested her forearms on the polished wood. "Yesterday, after the competition, one of my guards reported some unusual activity at night coming from the Desert of Souls."

Lord Rollant drummed his fingers. "I sent my captain to investigate the desert, as we too have heard the rumors."

So that's where Reed had been, Jasce thought, wondering how much Lord Rollant and the captain knew about the Snatchers. He snuck a glance at Amycus, who had remained quiet. Jasce had meant to talk to him about what he'd learned from Prince Jazari but hadn't been able to find him after the celebration dinner.

"It doesn't sound like they're rumors anymore. What are they doing in the desert?" the queen asked.

"According to Captain Reed, there were areas of disturbed ground," Lord Rollant said.

She arched her brow, her back straightening. "Disturbed?"

"Yes. And there were no traces of the Brymagus plant."

Amycus steepled his fingers under his chin. "It makes sense, since

Embracing the Darkness

the plant suppresses magic and these Snatchers, whatever they are, seem able to resist our powers."

Lady Darbry lifted her hands off the table. "What? Are these creatures eating it?"

Jasce remembered what the prince had said last night about the Brymagus plant. Could a piece of the Heart be in the Desert of Souls?

"If Spectrals are ineffective against these Snatchers, can Naturals fight them?" Lady Wuhl asked.

"The Paladin Guard should be able to handle them," Jasce said. "One of these took out four members of my team, but now we know what we are dealing with. We'll be better prepared."

"Are the other kingdoms aware of these creatures?" Lady Wuhl asked, glancing around the room.

"As of now, no," the queen said. "But how long we can keep it from them, I don't know, especially with the Shade Walkers. Who knows what they've overheard? Prince Jazari has spies everywhere."

"We may have another problem." Jasce tapped his finger on the arm of his chair. "What do you know of the Heart of Pandaren?" He examined the queen closely. A shadow passed over her face, and if he hadn't been watching, he would've missed it.

Lord Haldron laughed. "That old myth? You can't be serious. I thought you were smarter, Commander."

"According to Prince Jazari, it's not a myth," Jasce said, keeping his eyes fixed on Queen Valeri. "And it would explain the archduke's interest in Pandaren. Your Majesty?"

She glowered at him, and her knuckles whitened as she gripped her chair. Rumbles resounded as the other council members processed what he had reported.

Queen Valeri sighed, but her eyes hardened. "Guards, leave us." Everyone turned as the soldiers vacated the premises. "What I say must remain confidential. If I get any inclination that one of you revealed this secret, you will be guilty of treason and hanged. Is that clear?" She glanced at Indago, who scanned the room, sniffed the air, and then nodded.

Lord Haldron's mouth dropped open. "You mean it's true?"

"Do I have your word and your allegiance?"

All the council members mumbled their consent.

"Your Majesty," Amycus warned, shaking his head.

So, the prince was correct, Jasce thought. Amycus was aware of the Heart. He wondered if the old man knew about the broken-off sliver from the Empower Stone.

Queen Valeri lifted her hand. "Only the ruling family knows the story of the Heart of Pandaren." She repeated the same tale the Alturian prince told. "The locations of the four Stones aren't known, and the previous rulers had decided not to search for them. The Heart was broken apart and hidden for a reason. Spectrals cannot get their hands on any part of it."

"Spectrals won't be the problem," Jasce said, getting to his feet. The energy coursing through him made sitting impossible.

"And do tell. Why do you think that, Commander?" Lord Haldron's thin mustache quivered as his lip curled.

Jasce fisted his hands. Lord Haldron had never trusted Spectrals and would probably be thrilled to have them all wearing collars again. He paced the room and forced himself to relax, aware of the eyes following him.

"I don't think most Spectrals are aware of the Heart. But as it was Prince Jazari who told me, I'd wager the other kingdoms also know, and if they're using the Gathering to search for the Stones, then we have another security issue."

Jasce peered out the window and ignored the chattering of the nobles. Streaks of rain snaking along the glass blurred the gardens below. He'd gone to sleep last night wondering what it would be like to have the Heart of Pandaren in his possession, even just one piece. He'd dreamed of himself on a throne, power like he'd never experienced coursing through his veins. Kenz was by his side, a crown framing her head, her green dress hugging her curves, red lips parted in a seductive smile. In the middle of the night, awakened by intense longing, Jasce had made love to Kenz, satisfied with the sound of her moans as he moved them both to oblivion.

Lord Haldron calling his name ripped him from his thoughts. "You should have told the council immediately. How long have you had this information?" His face reddened.

Embracing the Darkness

Lord Rollant fiddled with a loose thread on his vest while Amycus lowered his head and sighed. Kord and the other nobles stared at Jasce.

Jasce bristled but kept his face neutral. "Settle down, Larkin. I only found out last night." He fought the desire to smack the twitching mustache off his pudgy face. "This could be why the archduke is so interested in aligning with Pandaren," he added, addressing the queen. "Your Highness, it might be wise to suspend the tournament. I can't monitor the games, search for the Snatchers, and deal with the other kingdoms looking for this crystal."

Lord Haldron's lips pursed as if tasting something foul. "If we stop the Gathering, we will look weak and ruin all trade negotiations."

The control Jasce had on his temper snapped. He stalked toward the table and rested his hands on the glossy wood. "Is it possible for you to shut up for just a moment?"

"Jasce," Amycus said, his eyes wide.

Kord rubbed his forehead and mumbled, "*So* not helping."

Lord Haldron's face turned crimson. "I tire of your insubordination, Commander. I fear you're not up to the task the queen has set before you." A glint of victory sparked in his eyes. "Especially after your bar-room brawl. You are not equipped to lead Pandaren's army or even be in this meeting."

Tension coursed through the room like the storm raging outside. Jasce tried to quench his fury. Tried and failed. "There are other things you should fear right now."

Lord Haldron's eyes narrowed, but the color that had seeped into his face faded. Lady Darbry and Lady Wuhl gaped at Jasce while Lord Rollant focused on the queen, his brow furrowed.

"That is enough," Queen Valeri said, rising to her feet. "I will not suspend the Gathering." She scrutinized each of the council members, her brown eyes like granite. "We have a week until the next challenge. Commander Farone, take a team to Bradwick and find out what the hell is going on."

Jasce focused on his splayed hands while everyone silently left the room. Everyone except Kord and Amycus.

The chair creaked as Kord leaned back and crossed his arms. "Okay, out with it."

Jasce looked out of the corner of his eye at his friend. Amycus toyed with his bottom lip as he watched Jasce lower himself into his chair.

"Out with what?" Jasce asked.

"That's the second time you've lost your temper with Larkin," Amycus said. "What's bothering you?"

"You mean besides the fact he's a pompous ass?" Jasce asked, earning a snort from Kord.

Amycus chuckled and laced his fingers together, his kind eyes patiently waiting.

Jasce traced an amber vein running through the table. "Why did the queen select me for commander? Why not Caston or someone more qualified?"

"You are qualified," Amycus said. "Lorella's not the woman she was before her husband died. She's bitter, harder, but she's always pushed those who hold a high rank, to force them to become better."

"She's definitely pushing." Jasce sighed and leaned back. "I feel like I'm not sure where to step, fearing I'll make the wrong decision. Playing this game, acting the part, is exhausting, not to mention the Snatchers and missing Spectrals. I'm trying to regain control but end up grasping thin air."

Kord rested his arms on the table and peered at Jasce. "The only thing you can control is yourself—how you react and the choices you make. Trying to control the queen or the nobles, or even these tournaments, will leave you impotent."

Jasce smirked. "Impotent?"

Kord rolled his eyes. "You know what I mean."

Amycus shook his head. "I think Lorella made an excellent choice having you lead her army. You inspire people, and not every leader can do that. You need to trust yourself and know that you'll make mistakes. Everyone does."

Jasce rested his chin on his hand. He'd never had friends who encouraged him like these two did. And if Kenz or Caston were sitting here, they'd be by his side as well. He needed to adjust the way he approached things. Like in a sparring match, sometimes one needed to pivot and reassess.

Embracing the Darkness

"So, what do you know about the Heart of Pandaren?" Jasce asked Amycus.

"Nicolaus and his big mouth." The blacksmith shook his head. "I found out about the Heart after the war, when Drexus was coming into power. I needed something to help Spectrals and had read about this magical crystal."

"I think Kenz was reading the same book," Jasce said.

Amycus smiled. "I'm not surprised. Always curious, that one. Anyway, that's when I traveled to Terrenus and met Kraig and his wyverns. Who better to talk about a magical crystal than a Gemari?"

Kord leaned forward. "You crossed the Culmen Range?"

Amycus nodded.

"Did Drexus have the sliver of the Empower Stone?" Jasce's pulse throbbed in his neck as he waited for Amycus to answer.

The blacksmith lowered his eyes and gave a slight nod. "He did. Which is why the queen wanted you to find his body. To retrieve the ring."

Jasce raised his brows. "So that's why she wanted proof."

"Yes. Plus, she really despised him," Amycus said.

Makes two of us, Jasce thought.

Kord looked between Amycus and Jasce. "Do you think Jaida and Vale have it?"

Jasce drummed his fingers on the table. "It's a likely possibility." Another reason to find his sister. If anyone discovered she could have the sliver of the Empower Stone, her life would be in danger, more than it was now. The rhythmic strum of his fingers quickened as guilt coiled in his gut. He should've never stopped searching for her.

"Stop." Kord rested his hand on his. "You're making me antsy. And don't stab me."

Jasce shot him a look. The Healer chuckled and pushed back from the table, mumbling about being late for dinner. Jasce's stomach rumbled. When had he last eaten?

"I think I should go with you to search for the Snatchers," Amycus said.

Jasce stood. He needed to plan for that trip and gather the team he was taking. "No. I'm limiting the number of Spectrals I take. Besides, how are you feeling after your sparring injury?"

Amycus's brows furrowed followed by a slight widening of his eyes. "Oh, yes. I'm all healed up. Anyway, please be careful."

Jasce frowned. "See you later, then." As he left the room, he glanced over his shoulder to see Amycus staring out the window at the darkening sky.

Chapter Fourteen

"I'm going and you can't stop me. That's my baby sister," Kord said, already dressed in black leather pants and a brown tunic with his baldric of knives crossing his huge chest.

Jasce raked his fingers through his hair and bit back a curse. His friend had seemed more protective of Kenz since the Gathering had started, objecting to her guarding the queen and competing in the games. Jasce understood; he would have acted the same with Jaida. He rubbed Bruiser's neck. His black coat shimmered in the sun as his large body quivered.

"You are aware she's twenty-six, right? An adult?" Jasce asked.

He'd been honest with Amycus about wanting to limit the number of Spectrals since the Snatchers seemed attracted to magic. He hadn't wanted to bring Kenz, either, but not having a Shield was foolish, and if he'd taken Delmira, Kenz would've had his head.

Kord shot him a look. "We still don't know what we're dealing with, and having a Healer is sound strategy."

He secretly agreed and didn't have time to argue since his team was waiting outside the gates. And of all the staff at the Sanctuary, Kord was the only Healer who was skilled with a sword. "Fine. But I'm telling Kenz you called her 'baby sister.'"

Kord mumbled under his breath as they mounted their horses. Jasce smiled and imagined the look on his fiancée's face when he told her what big brother had said.

He rode next to Kenz for the three-hour journey inland, the stifling heat worsening the farther they rode from the coast. She looked pale, but every time he asked if she was okay, she nodded and smiled. General Nadja and Captain Reed brought up the rear, with Kord in the middle.

They rode into Bradwick at dusk and stopped outside the Raven Inn and Tavern, where Lord Haldron's captain waited. After leaving their horses in the stable, the group entered the inn and were greeted by the sounds of clinking glasses, laughter, and the smell of ale. Jasce strode to the bar, his need for a drink intensifying along with the headache behind his eyes.

"You okay?" Kenz gave him a wary look as he slid next to her, keeping his back against the wall.

He took a long swallow of whiskey, relishing the slow burn down his throat and into his stomach. "I'm fine."

She raised her brow and held his stare. "For an assassin, you're an awful liar."

He forced a smile and gripped her hand. "Really, everything's fine. Just a lot on my mind." The night before, he'd told her about his conversation with Kord and Amycus regarding the Empower Stone, and she'd spent most of the night with her nose in a book. Now, she looked seconds away from falling asleep. "Can I get you something?"

She shook her head. "No, thanks."

"Are you sure you're all right? You're pale."

She opened her mouth but snapped it shut as Kord and Reed sat, both gripping tankards of ale. Kord rested his hand on her arm and her color returned. Jasce was about to ask what was going on when Alyssa wove through the tables, followed by a short, balding man with Lord Haldron's emblem etched onto the chest of his cape. Jasce shared a glance with Reed, who raised his mug to hide his laugh.

Kord kicked him under the table and Jasce bit back a curse. "What was that for?"

"You know what."

"He's wearing a stupid cape."

Embracing the Darkness

Kenz snorted as Alyssa approached. She pressed her lips together. "Commander Farone, this is—"

The caped man stepped forward and jutted out his hand. "I'm Captain Marin Dacier. My men are at your disposal, and if you need anything at all, please let me know."

Jasce stood and shook the captain's hand. "Thank you. I'd appreciate a private room to talk to any witnesses."

"Yes, of course. I'll have that set up right away." The captain spun, forcing Alyssa to duck as his cape almost smacked her in the face.

They all watched him trounce through the tavern to speak with the owner.

Alyssa shoved Reed over and took a long swig from his tankard. "Hey, get your own," he said, grabbing the half-empty mug.

She rested her arms on the table. "The locals are nervous. As far as we know, there are only a few registered Spectrals in Bradwick."

Jasce leaned forward. "Registered? The queen ended that."

"It seems Lord Haldron still wants to keep track of them." She cringed. "Of you."

When Steward Brenet and Drexus were in charge, all Spectrals had to be accounted for—their name and type of magic. If any were caught without being on the list, they were captured and taken to Edgefield Prison. That had been Jasce's job, as a Hunter and as the Angel of Death. But since Queen Valeri took over, she'd ended that practice.

"That bastard," Jasce said through clenched teeth as a surge of rage rushed through him. He squeezed his glass so hard a crack etched down the side.

"Jasce," Kenz said, grabbing his hand and prying his fingers loose. Her eyes widened when she looked at him. "You need to settle down."

"It doesn't bother you they're still forcing Spectral registration?"

"Yes, it bothers me, but now is not the time to lose your temper. We'll sort it out when we get back."

He inhaled and peered around the table before swallowing the anger. She was right. He'd deal with Lord Haldron later.

Jasce motioned to his general. "Go on."

"Currently, an Amp is missing. Disappeared two days ago in the Silver Glade Forest."

"We'll start there. Meet at the stables at dawn."

~

A soupy mist clung to the ground as Jasce and his team rode toward the forest. He tensed when they passed Bradwick Prison, where he'd been tortured for three days. A part of him wanted to find the warden and return the favor. Of course, if he hadn't been captured, Kord and Kenz wouldn't have rescued him. He'd either be dead or—he shivered at the thought—have become a monster in his quest for revenge.

Dismounting from his horse, he pulled his cloak tighter against the morning chill and tied back his wet hair, then double-checked his chest plate, making sure it was secure.

Kenz shook her head as she approached and tightened his straps. She looked up at him and gave a seductive smile. He knew what she was thinking. Months ago, she'd helped him remove his armor after he'd discovered Drexus was the Fire Spectral he'd been searching for. The desire that had coursed through him as her knuckles scraped his bare skin had literally brought him to his knees.

He tucked a piece of hair behind her ear. "Be ready. The Snatchers seem resistant to our magic, but hopefully your shield will slow it down."

She traced the veins on his hand. "And you won't do anything stupid?"

"Who, me?" Jasce gave her a quick kiss and turned toward the rest of his team. "General, you've seen this thing in action. What can we expect?"

Alyssa straightened and clasped her hands behind her back. "It's fast and strong. It rears onto its hind legs before it attacks, so that might give us an edge. The creature is attracted to magic, so you three"—she peered at Jasce, Kenz, and Kord—"watch your backs. Fight in pairs. We didn't do that last time." Sadness etched along her eyes.

Jasce rested his hand on her shoulder and gave it a squeeze. "You heard the general. Stay alert and stick together."

He was securing the horses when he noticed Kord pulling Kenz aside and whispering in her ear. She shook her head and forced a smile.

Embracing the Darkness

A knot formed in his belly. He couldn't be sure what they were discussing, but he didn't like sending either of them into the forest. He shoved the unease aside and paired off his team, assigning each Spectral with a Natural.

The Silver Glade Forest came alive with the rising sun as birds chirped and animals skittered on the ground through the rustling bushes. The teams set off, Kord and the general going east and Kenz and Reed heading west.

Jasce trudged deeper into the forest with Captain Dacier on his heels.

"Is it true? Are you the Angel of Death?" the captain asked.

"Not anymore."

"Ah. Well, we're glad you're here, no matter what name you go by. However, I wouldn't let the warden know you're back. He was quite annoyed with your escape last year."

"I bet."

The creaking of ancient trees bending in the breeze and the crunch of shimmering pine needles filled the silence.

Jasce stopped and held up his hand. Kneeling in the soft dirt, he peered at a mark in the soil.

Captain Dacier looked over Jasce's shoulder. "What did you find?"

"A footprint." He scanned the clearing. A fissure ran through a large tree trunk and droplets of blood peppered the ground. "I think our Amp might have run into the Snatcher here."

He stood, wiping dirt off his knee, and surveyed the area. He whistled, signaling his team to join him as he examined another print, at least eight inches long, with claw marks leaving deep grooves in the soil. This was bigger than the one the queen's soldier had found a few months ago.

A snapping twig had him reaching for his dagger. Captain Dacier pointed his crossbow into the trees.

Indigo light shone as Reed and Kenz emerged through the brush. "Just in case someone has a happy trigger finger," she said, twisting her wrists and lowering her shield.

Jasce chuckled while Captain Dacier mumbled under his breath and wiped the sweat off his brow.

Kord and Alyssa joined them a few minutes later.

Jasce pointed to the print and the split tree. "Pretty sure our Amp was here. Not much of a fight, though."

"How can you tell?" Captain Dacier asked.

Alyssa knelt next to some tracks on the far side of the clearing. "Because when an Amp fights, there is usually a lot of destruction due to their strength and speed."

Reed approached the general and swore at the blood saturating the ground.

"Looks like it dragged the body through here," Kord said, indicating a path of broken branches and a trail of crimson.

"Weapons ready," Jasce said. "Kenz, we'll follow you. General, you have our back." He gripped his dagger and shifted out of the way for Kenz to pass.

"You think it wise for her to go first?" Captain Dacier whispered, glancing between him and Kenz.

Her back stiffened but she kept walking.

"She's my strongest Shield and an excellent fighter. There's no one else I'd rather have leading us."

Kenz looked over her shoulder and blew him a kiss. Her bracelets glowed as they pushed through the underbrush following a trail of blood. Kord walked next to his sister with his sword drawn.

Jasce removed his cloak and shoved it into his bag as the trees thinned and the sun melted away the chilly mist. The bloody tracks had disappeared, but now and then, a broken branch or a faint claw mark in the dirt led them closer to the rocky crags on the edge of the forest.

Signaling for Kenz to stop, Jasce examined another print with his finger. He squinted at the rocks and bushes. The hairs on his neck bristled. The birds had stopped chirping, and an eerie silence settled over the forest.

"What is it?" Kord asked.

Jasce replaced his dagger and drew both swords. "We're no longer the hunters." His eyes scanned the forest. "Everyone fan out. Kenz, ready your shield."

Kord raised his sword and stepped closer to Kenz, while Captain

Embracing the Darkness

Dacier and Alyssa lifted their crossbows. Reed positioned himself next to Jasce and unsheathed his weapon.

"Commander?" Captain Dacier said near a copse of bushes. His face had drained of color and his mouth pursed.

Jasce jogged over and swore.

"What?" Kenz asked, her shield shining brightly among the shadows.

"The Amp. Or what's left of him." The man's throat was torn, and his chest and stomach were in ribbons.

"What would do such a thing?" the captain asked.

A low growl sounded from behind a boulder.

Jasce pivoted and tightened his grip on his swords. "We're about to find out."

A Snatcher emerged, followed by answering growls as two more crept from the bushes. White eyes were sunk into narrow skulls and muscles quivered under leathery black hides. Their forearms were longer than their back legs and ended in three-inch claws. One snapped its jaw, revealing jagged, yellow teeth.

The first creature's head tilted as it stepped closer to Jasce.

"What the hell is that?" Kenz said, drawing her sword and enclosing the group with her shield.

The other two creatures stalked forward, one aiming for Kord and the other circling along the far side.

"Kenz, put your shield around you and Kord," Jasce said, twirling both blades as he observed the closest Snatcher. It was the size of a small pony, and he bet it was as fast as it was strong.

Kenz opened her mouth to argue.

"That's an order. Do it now."

Her jaw pulsed. "On the count of three."

"One."

Jasce stepped farther from Kenz, keeping the creature focused on him.

"Two."

The third Snatcher reared back on its hind legs.

"Three!"

As soon as the indigo light shrank to surround Kord and Kenz, the

Snatchers attacked. One went right for the shield, causing her to cry out. Her wall sputtered but held. Kord pushed her behind him and raised his sword. Alyssa and Captain Dacier fired their arrows, targeting the Snatcher charging from the opposite side of the clearing, while Reed and Jasce fought the third one.

Jasce spun and slashed with his swords as the Snatcher leaped for his throat, completely ignoring Reed. He dodged and the creature shot past him, crashing into a rock. The beast shook its head and snarled.

A yell had Jasce looking over his shoulder. His general held her stomach and blood oozed through her fingers. Her crossbow lay on the ground. Captain Dacier gripped his sword and stood between the Snatcher and the general.

"Reed, go! I've got this." Jasce kept his eyes on his Snatcher, which circled him and lifted its snout, its large nostrils widening. Matching it step for step, he peeked out of the corner of his eye and felt a tinge of relief. Kenz's shield shimmered brightly.

The muscles in the Snatcher's back legs tensed as it extended its claws.

Jasce flipped through the air, using his speed and strength, and landed behind the creature. With a twist, he brought his sword around. His strength and the steel in his blade cut through the Snatcher's neck cleanly.

Reed and Captain Dacier fought the other creature while Alyssa lay on the ground, blood soaking her armor.

"Lower your shield, I need to help her!" Kord shouted at Kenz. She shook her head, her green eyes wide.

The first Snatcher dug its claws into the dirt, let out a shriek, and rammed into Kenz's shield. Indigo light traversed across its leathery skin, and the creature squirmed. Kenz fell to her knees, and blood dripped from her nose as the beast attacked again.

Captain Dacier cried out as the other Snatcher pounced on him, its yellow jaws snapping. Reed yelled and kicked the creature off.

Kenz's shield sputtered.

Jasce felt the tug and darkness swallowed him. Before he disappeared, the creature attacking Reed swiveled its head and scanned him with probing white eyes.

Embracing the Darkness

Jasce appeared in front of Kenz's shield as it disintegrated. The Snatcher roared and darted around him, its claws extended and maw opened.

Kord shoved his sister aside.

Kenz grunted and tried to get to her feet. "Kord, no!" she screamed as the gleam of the creature's claw swiped through the air.

Chapter Fifteen

Jasce slammed into the Snatcher's side and knocked it off Kord. Growling, it twisted and collided with him, smashing him into the ground. He used all his strength to keep the beast from tearing out his throat and punched it in the side, which gave him time to grab his dagger. Blood spurted in his face as he sliced the blade across its neck.

He pushed the Snatcher off, got to his feet, and glowered at the corpse. "Reed, you good?"

"It's down, but General Nadja needs help."

He spun in their direction and froze. Kord lay motionless on his side, his back to him.

"Kord!" Kenz cried as she crawled over to her brother. Blood stained her lips and chin.

"Please, no." Jasce sprinted to his friend and rolled him over. Half of his face was the color of parchment. Kord's hand covered the other half, blood flowing through his fingers, staining his tunic.

Kenz removed Kord's hand and gasped. Three deep gouges carved from his forehead, across his eye, and down to his jaw.

"Why did you push me out of the way?" Kenz asked, shaking. "I had it under control." Tears spilled down her cheeks, cutting through the dirt and grime.

"I couldn't risk you and the baby," Kord whispered, his voice laced with pain.

Kenz gasped and her hand flew to her mouth.

Jasce's blood ran cold. "What did you say?"

Kord swore under his breath. Kenz looked up at Jasce, guilt and horror lining her face.

"You're pregnant?" he asked.

She bit her lip. "I'm sorry. I was . . . I was waiting for the right time."

"The right time?" His knuckles whitened as he fisted his hands. How could she not tell him? Or Kord. How could they both keep this secret from him?

"This isn't a good time, either." Despite the blood dripping down his face, Kord lumbered to his feet. "I need to check on Alyssa."

Jasce gaped at Kenz, disbelief making it hard to breathe. He snapped his mouth shut and looked away. Kord was right. This wasn't the right time. The right time would've been before they left when he would've insisted Kenz stay behind.

He shook his head and ripped off a piece of his tunic, holding it against Kord's face to staunch the bleeding. Captain Dacier sat next to Alyssa and pressed against the wound in her stomach. She writhed on the ground, biting her lip, and focusing on the sky.

Jasce led Kord to her, watching the blood drip down Kord's neck. "Why aren't you healing?"

Kord grimaced. "I need to help her first." He knelt, placed his hands on the general, and closed his eyes. Blood flowed faster from the gashes in his face. He swore as Alyssa cried out. "Grab my kit. My magic isn't working."

Jasce picked up Kord's bag without looking at Kenz and placed it on the ground next to him. "Those aren't bite wounds."

"It looks like the claws must also carry venom that suppresses magic." Kord swiped at the blood running down his face.

Kenz grabbed the torn material from Jasce and held it to her brother's face while Kord worked. Jasce dropped to his knees and helped wrap the general's midsection. He gauged the distance between the clearing and the tavern. He'd been testing his vaulting strength and knew he

Embracing the Darkness

could vault that far alone. He studied his general, whose expression twisted in pain, her chest rising rapidly. Kord also needed immediate attention, but he couldn't leave Kenz out here. Who knew how many Snatchers lurked in the forest?

Pregnant? Jasce clenched his jaw.

Focus on the mission, he thought.

"Reed, you and Captain Dacier bring that thing back to the tavern." Jasce pointed to the dead Snatcher closest to them.

"What are you going to do?" Reed asked.

"Vault them to the inn."

Kenz's head shot up. "What? How?"

"One at a time," he said without looking at her. He focused on Reed. "Stake out a perimeter until I get them out of here." Reed nodded, picked up his fallen sword, and jogged to the other side of the clearing.

Kenz stood while holding the fabric to Kord's face. "Is this a good idea? I'm concerned—"

His body vibrated with restrained fury. "You're concerned? How about being concerned with telling me the truth?"

She opened her mouth, but he stopped her with a look. He wrapped his arm around her and vaulted. The Raven Inn's door was closed, but a light flickered through the window. Thankfully, the tavern was empty.

"Get the owner and supplies," he said, leaving her on the doorstep.

Reed and Captain Dacier jumped when he reappeared seconds later. He stalked across the clearing toward Kord and Alyssa.

Kord sat on his haunches, holding the blood-soaked fabric. "Take her," he said without looking up.

Of the two, the general's wounds were more life-threatening, so he didn't argue. He dug into his well of magic—deeper than he had when saving Emile. Power coursed through him, fueled by a burning fury. He focused on that anger, allowing it to feed him and his magic.

He appeared again on the doorstep of the inn. A fire was lit, and Kenz and the owner's wife, Gaeline, sorted bandages and herbs. Gaeline yelped when he entered, holding Alyssa in his arms. He placed her gently on the table and strode for the door. He stumbled at the entrance but gritted his teeth. Pressing his hand against the frame, he closed his eyes and imagined an abyss of power, a never-ending supply of magic. Something deep inside beckoned him closer and a dry, brittle sound resembling a laugh cut through the pulsing in his ears. He shoved the sensation away and vaulted to the clearing.

His last time vaulting back completely drained his magic. He and Kord collapsed in front of the inn. Kenz ran outside and helped lift her brother off the ground.

Jasce struggled to his feet. "Get the general upstairs. You'll need to stitch her wounds."

Kenz helped Kord to a chair and studied Jasce. "Are you all right?" she asked.

"No, Kenz, I'm not."

She bit her lip and tears welled in her eyes. A part of him wanted to gather her in his arms and comfort her, but he kept his feet rooted to the ground.

His body and mind were exhausted, and his magic depleted. His protective wall crumbled, and he couldn't stop the barrage of emotions surging from her and Kord. He groaned and almost dropped to his knees. Pain, guilt, worry, and sadness slammed into him like waves crashing against the shore. He rested his hands on a nearby table. Drops of sweat splashed onto the wooden floor, and his entire body shook.

He closed his eyes and focused on his breath. Finally, the sensation subsided as a kernel of magic flickered to life.

He straightened to his full height. Kenz stood in the middle of the room, her arms wrapped around herself and her eyes wide. "Just go. I'll take care of Kord."

Sadness lined her face, but she nodded, and with the help of Gaeline, she guided Alyssa up the stairs.

Kord leaned back in the chair. He held his hand over his damaged eye and breathed deeply as blood dripped through his fingers. Jasce lurched toward the bar and grabbed a bottle of whiskey. He closed his eyes, swallowing the bile that burned the back of his throat.

Gaeline shuffled down the stairs. "She seems to have it handled. Do you need help?" The woman twisted her hands in front of her gray dress.

Embracing the Darkness

He lifted his head and tried to fill his lungs with air. "I need rags, a needle, and thread."

She brought the items and placed them on the table. "Do you know what you're doing?"

"Yes."

The woman swallowed and took a hesitant step back. He handed the bottle to Kord, who drank deeply. He hissed in pain as Jasce cleaned the wound.

"So, this is what that feels like," the Healer said through gritted teeth.

Jasce pointed to the whiskey. "It helps numb the pain."

Kord took another drink. "Pain is inescapable. Suffering is a choice."

Jasce grunted as Kord quoted the mantra he had used during his time at the Watch Guard. Pain was inescapable, that part was true. But at this moment, it didn't feel like he had a choice in the suffering. Being deceived about his future wife's pregnancy hurt him more than he'd willingly admit. He'd been trained to block despair, sorrow, and loss. Drexus had whipped those emotions out of him. But as a Hunter, his hardened heart hadn't experienced the debilitating feelings currently carving through his soul. He wanted to escape this sensation, shove the sentiments down, and bury them under hatred and rage.

Gaeline handed him the needle and thread once he finished cleaning the wound. He took a drink from the bottle and sighed as the warmth soothed his anger and lessened the tremble in his hands.

Kord winced as Jasce pushed the needle through his skin. "Can you feel any of your magic returning?"

The Healer exhaled through his clenched jaw. "Not yet. I guess we were wrong about the teeth."

"We'll have Maera dissect it," he said as he worked methodically. Visions of the battle flashed through his mind as the needle pierced skin: Kenz's shield disintegrating, Kord pushing her out of the way, claws slicing through the air. The words that followed.

I couldn't risk you and the baby.

Jasce swallowed and glanced at his friend. "Why didn't you tell me?"

Kord moaned when the needle pierced his ravaged skin. "It wasn't my secret to tell. But I didn't mean for you to find out that way. Neither of us did."

Jasce focused on the task at hand. Their betrayal brought back too many memories of his past. Three silhouettes on a hill, arrows sticking out of his body, Bronn's fist pummeling him. The Hunters who had betrayed him were dead now, but that didn't ease the nausea swirling in his gut.

Kord flinched as Jasce worked. "Almost done," Jasce said.

Gaeline mopped up the blood. "Those are very good stitches. You don't look like a physician."

"I'm used to sewing myself up." He tied off the last stitch. "This is easier."

Kord inhaled and sank into the chair. "Easy for you to say."

Jasce forced a smile. "Try to focus all your magic to your eye. I don't know if—I mean, can you see?"

The minutes ticked by and Kord opened both eyes. The uninjured eye was its normal green, but the other resembled sea glass, as if the creature had literally ripped the color out.

Kord's jaw tightened, and he shook his head.

Jasce rubbed a hand over his mouth. His best friend was blind in one eye because he hadn't been fast enough. Grabbing the whiskey, he strode toward the fireplace, his hand leaving bloody prints on the bottle. He finished it in a couple of swallows. Failure and alcohol churned like a maelstrom in his stomach.

"Jasce, don't," Kord said.

"Don't what?" His voice resembled a blade grinding against a whetstone.

"I know you. This wasn't your fault."

Jasce peered into the hearth. The flames devoured the logs and reminded him of Drexus's black fire destroying his family's cottage, of how he hadn't been able to protect his mother or sister. Once again, the crushing weight of defeat pressed against his chest, making it difficult to breathe.

Rage hammered against any self-control he had left. He yelled and threw the bottle into the fire. Gaeline yelped as it exploded into flames. His chest rose and fell rapidly as the alcohol ignited, devouring the logs.

Embracing the Darkness

He lifted trembling palms stained with blood.

A hand rested on his arm, and he spun, reaching for his dagger.

Kord's two-colored eyes widened. "It'll work out. I promise."

"You can't promise that, Kord." Jasce turned from the fireplace. "You should probably check on Kenz and the general."

Kord chewed the inside of his cheek as the wood crackled. He sighed and trudged up the stairs, leaving Jasce alone by the dwindling fire.

Chapter Sixteen

Captain Dacier arrived at the Raven later that afternoon with the horses, while Reed rode to Orilyon with the Snatcher's corpse.

After cleaning up and changing clothes, Jasce returned to the tavern, observing the locals from the table where he and his team had sat the previous evening. Gaeline had given him regular updates on Alyssa and Kord, along with providing him something to eat. She had that motherly worried look about her, and he tried to smile whenever she passed by.

The night crept along as the patrons came and went. The tavern slowly emptied, and he still hadn't gone upstairs to the inn. He wasn't ready to talk with Kenz, and if he was being honest, he didn't have the courage to cope with the hurt of her betrayal. He was a bloody coward.

Mumbling a curse, he grabbed another bottle from the bar and sat in front of the hearth. The warm glow of the embers did nothing to thaw his insides.

Pregnant, he thought, staring into the flames. How could she keep this from him? And why?

Jasce put the pieces together. It made sense now why Kenz had been determined to have their wedding so soon, why she'd been so tired and not eating. For over a month, she'd kept this secret.

Rage built again inside him, but he didn't let it explode. Instead, it simmered. He'd used anger in the past to help him focus, and he would need every bit of concentration to deal with the Gathering, the Snatchers, and the Heart of Pandaren.

And Kenz's pregnancy.

Jasce contemplated his magic—how he'd vaulted six different times, three carrying people. He'd traveled deeper into the well of his power than ever before, but after the adrenaline had worn off, his mind and body had been weak and vulnerable. He longed to return to that state of deadly purpose where his blood pumped, his muscles burned, and his focus was unbreakable. That sense of importance, of being alive, had flowed through him again, and he craved more.

Footsteps sounded on the stairs, and he could tell by the gait who it was. He took a long pull from the bottle. After a day of hiding, he still wasn't ready for this conversation.

Kenz padded across the empty room and sat in the chair opposite him. She had changed out of her bloody fighting leathers and wore leggings and a tank top that showed off the definition in her arms.

"I'm sorry. It was wrong for me not to tell you."

"Why?" His gruff voice grated through the silence.

She wove her fingers together and stared at her feet. "At first, I wanted to be sure. And then with all the strain you're under searching for Jaida and handling the Gathering, I—"

He slammed the bottle on the side table. "You're going to blame this on me? Seriously?"

She looked up and unshed tears made her eyes sparkle like emeralds. "No. It's just that I've barely seen you and . . ." She sighed. "I tried a few times to tell you. And then after you promoted me, I didn't want you to change your mind. I wasn't sure how you'd react."

He rubbed his temple and struggled to extinguish the anger longing to break free. She was right. If he would've known she was pregnant, there was no way he'd allow her anywhere near a battle, let alone leading the troops as their captain.

He lifted his head. "And how did you think I'd react?"

"A baby is a lot. I didn't know if you'd be happy or not."

"But instead of giving me the chance, I had to find out when you

Embracing the Darkness

and Kord were covered in blood and my general was dying. Brilliant plan, Kenz." He pushed out of the chair and stopped in front of the dwindling fire. Goosebumps pebbled on his bare arms as the last ember winked out.

The chair creaked as Kenz stood, and she wrapped her arms around his waist. Her heart thumped against his back, and the tears she'd tried to keep from falling soaked his shirt. Her magic, usually a fluid dance with his, stumbled, struggling to connect. He wondered if she could sense the change.

"Please forgive me," she whispered.

A part of Jasce yearned to storm off into the night. That's what Azrael would've done. But that's not who he wanted to be. He had changed, or was at least trying to, and hated this wedge between them. He rotated in her arms, his eyes flitting over her face. He loved her so much it made his chest ache.

He wiped away a stray tear with his thumb. "I already have."

But forgiving her didn't erase the hurt. This was the problem with loving someone. Love opened him up to a pain he couldn't ignore. His mantra echoed in his mind. Physical pain he could suppress—something the Watch Guard had taught him to do since he was a child—but loving Kenz created a vulnerability he didn't know how to combat. He couldn't have one without the other, it seemed, and he wouldn't have it any other way. Loving Kenz had changed him from a monster into a man capable of caring.

She swallowed and nodded. Her eyes drifted to his mouth, and a hunger quivered through him. He leaned down and pressed his lips to hers. She sighed, and he savored the way her chest fit against his. Their magic swirled faster, its normal rhythm returning, and he groaned as her tongue swept into his mouth. He slid her top over her head and cupped her breast with one hand as he held onto the base of her neck and deepened the kiss. She removed his shirt, and he shuddered when her soft skin pressed against his.

He needed her closer—to drown in her heat and the silkiness of her skin.

Jasce picked her up, placed her on the table, and gently laid her back. He ran his tongue over her sensitive flesh, smiling against her breast as she moaned. He trailed kisses across her stomach and hesitated.

He looked up through strands of his hair. "Is this okay?"

She raised herself to her elbows. "Most definitely."

He realized he was about to make love to his fiancée in the middle of an empty tavern—and he didn't care. He pulled down her leggings as she undid the ties of his pants. They both hurried, their heavy breaths filling the silence.

"Now, Jasce. Please."

He didn't need any encouragement. All he wanted was to be so deep inside her he lost who he was; to forget his past, not worry about the future, and just be one with the woman he loved.

The table rocked as he took total possession of her.

She ran her hands along his chest and wrapped her legs around his waist. "I love you," she whispered, bringing his face closer to hers and kissing him softly, intimately. He immersed himself in her tenderness and loved her thoroughly until their magic exploded and they both tumbled over the edge.

Watery light peeked through the window, and voices from downstairs floated up the hallway. Kenz threw her arm over her face and groaned.

Jasce chuckled while he laced up his boots. They may have only gotten an hour of sleep. He was used to it. Kenz was not. "We need to get moving. I want to see what Maera thinks of our little pet."

She rose to her elbow and lifted her brows. "Little pet? Interesting choice of words."

Jasce placed a kiss on her forehead. "I'll meet you downstairs." He took one last look at her, the covers twisted around her naked body, before heading to the tavern.

Kord hunched over a table while drinking a cup of coffee. His color had returned and the jagged edge across his face had started to heal.

"Quit analyzing me. I'm fine." His deep voice was rugged with sleep.

"Now you know how that feels, too." Jasce signaled to Gaeline for a cup of coffee and sat on a chair, spinning it so his arms rested on the back. "It looks like your magic is returning. I need to remove the stitches."

Kord looked up slowly. Jasce tried not to wince when he saw the clear eye staring out from the damaged skin. "Can I finish my coffee first?"

"Sure," Jasce said, taking a deep drink from his and relishing the jolt of caffeine. He'd need a lot more to get through this day.

"Listen, I'm sorry about how you found out about the baby. I hope you aren't too angry with Kenz." Kord raked his fingers through his already mussed hair. "I did try to convince her to tell you, just so you aren't furious with me, too."

"Well, it makes sense why you were so protective of your 'baby sister.'" He pulled his dagger from its sheath.

Kord leaned back warily. "What do you plan to do with that?"

"Take out your stitches."

"Oh, hell no. Go find something else."

Jasce laughed and had Gaeline bring him a small pair of scissors. He quickly cut the threads and watched as Kord's magic returned and slowly healed the wounds. He'd now have three scars carving through his face from his forehead to his jaw. Jasce wondered what Tillie would think. Knowing her, she'd think her husband was even more handsome.

Kenz came down along with Alyssa, who limped toward the table with her hand pressed against her stomach. Jasce started to rise from his chair, but she waved him off.

Kenz kept her face blank while she scanned Kord, but Jasce could see the grief in her eyes as she hugged herself.

"You look more dashing, at least," she said, unable to hide the wobble in her voice.

Kord tied a piece of fabric across his forehead to cover his injured eye. He studied his sister, his one green eye penetrating her feigned toughness. He wrapped his muscular arm around her waist and pulled her close. "I'm all right, you insufferable nag. It's just an eye."

Kenz released a shaking laugh against his chest and wiped away a stray tear. "Can another Healer help you get your sight back?"

Kord sighed. "We can try when we return to Orilyon, but I think, because of the venom, the damage might be permanent."

Jasce pulled his focus from Kord and Kenz and finished his coffee. He didn't want to think about his friend losing his sight in one eye. He stood and addressed Alyssa. "You good to ride? You can stay here a few days to recover."

"No, Commander, I'll be fine."

Jasce held her forearm and peered at her face. She hid the pain well, but he could still see it. "Next time, be more careful. That's an order."

She gave a weak smile and saluted.

Kord released Kenz and approached the general. "Let me look at you. My magic has partially returned."

He led the general to the table as Captain Dacier entered the tavern to wish them a safe trip and to give Jasce a letter for Lord Haldron. "We will keep you updated on any changes. For now, I've established a curfew and encouraged Spectrals not to go out alone. So far, we've had no incidents in town, and I'd like it to remain that way."

They said their goodbyes to the captain and Gaeline and readied their horses for the trip to Orilyon. Kord rode next to Alyssa, touching her now and then to give her his healing magic.

"Thank you for helping my brother," Kenz said, bringing her horse alongside Jasce's.

"You never need to thank me for that."

"I will always thank you for protecting my family, soon to be yours."

Jasce glanced at her from the corner of his eye. They hadn't discussed the wedding since his colossal blunder over a week ago. "Are you wanting to get married before the baby is born?" He still couldn't believe she was pregnant and hadn't wrapped his brain around the fact that he was going to be a father. He clenched his teeth at the roiling in his stomach.

Kenz reached for his hand and gave it a quick squeeze. "We'll find the right time."

"What were your parents like?"

Kenz lifted her brows.

"What?" Jasce asked.

"Nothing. I just wasn't expecting that question." She ran her fingers through the horse's mane. "They were wonderful. We had our disagreements, but I always knew they loved me. They died when I was nine."

Embracing the Darkness

"I'm sorry." He despised the platitude but wasn't sure what else to say. He had known her parents died in the war and were powerful Spectrals, but he hadn't realized she'd still only been a child.

She shrugged, but he could see the tightness around her eyes. "Why do you ask?"

"I'm just concerned about what kind of father I'll be. I didn't have the best example, and after everything I've done, who I was . . ." It was his turn to shrug.

Her fingers interlocked with his as they rode through the field, the sun making the grass shimmer like gold. "I can understand that, but you do have two excellent examples." He frowned at her, and she smiled. "Amycus helped raise me, especially through the teenage years. He knows a little something. And you have Kord, who is an amazing dad."

He nodded. They couldn't erase his past, but they would hold him accountable and help him along the way. For the first time in days, his shoulders lowered as some of the tension melted away.

Chapter Seventeen

When Jasce arrived at the Bastion, most of the soldiers were in the dining hall. He'd left Kenz and Kord at Kord's home, telling them he'd check on them later. His stomach rumbled, but lunch would have to wait, as well as the queen's debriefing, which he could guarantee would irritate her. He needed to get to the Sanctuary and find Maera to see what she had discovered regarding the Snatcher.

Caston leaned against a column, cleaning his nails with the tip of his dagger as Jasce shoved open the main doors to the compound. He scanned Jasce's face. "I should've gone with you. You look like hell."

"Why does everyone keep saying that?"

Caston pushed off the wall, falling in step with him. "Reed caused quite a commotion, bringing that thing in here. There was no way to keep it a secret from our esteemed guests."

"Perfect." That was all he needed, to have worried dignitaries hassling him over security issues. As he strode down the corridor toward the Sanctuary, he didn't miss the wariness in some of his soldiers' eyes.

They wove through the beds and exam tables to a back room, where they found Maera hunched over the dead Snatcher.

"Hello, Maera," Caston said, running a hand through his hair.

She jumped and dropped her scalpel. "Oh, hi. I didn't hear you come in." Her gaze flicked between Caston and Jasce and a flush ran up her neck.

Jasce raised his brows, and the side of his lip lifted.

Caston bent down, retrieved the scalpel, and handed it to her. She was about to say something when her eyes widened.

"What?" Caston asked. Jasce followed her gaze and swore. Prince Jazari stood at the doorway, rubbing his hands together.

Jasce stepped in front of the exam table and held up a hand. "Your Highness, you're not allow—"

The prince maneuvered around him and patted him on the back. "I heard you were examining the creature that's wreaked havoc in your villages." He peeled away the white sheet and whistled.

"Heard, huh?" Jasce said, knowing the Alturians were using their Shade Walking to gather intel, even with his Trackers in place.

Amycus entered, followed by King Morzov and Archduke Carnelian. Jasce rested his hands on his hips and stared at the ceiling, blowing out a sigh. "Does everyone know?"

Amycus squeezed his shoulder. "It seems so. I'm glad you're back safely." He glanced around the Sanctuary. "Where's Kord and Kenz?"

"Kord was injured. Same with General Nadja." Jasce hadn't been fast enough—the thought had circled inside his mind on the long ride home and still haunted him.

Amycus rubbed the scruff along his jaw. "The magic in those Snatchers must be powerful to affect Kord that way. I'm glad he and Kenz are all right." He avoided looking at him.

Jasce wondered if Amycus knew about the pregnancy and anger knotted in his stomach, but now was not the time to discuss it.

King Morzov approached the exam table. "What is this creature?"

The archduke leaned closer to the carcass. He picked up a scalpel and lifted the top lip to examine the yellow teeth. "I've never seen anything like this." He addressed the other two dignitaries. "Have you?"

The Balten king shook his head.

Prince Jazari tapped his chin. "No, but I can do some investigating. If that's all right with you," he said, leveling his gaze at Jasce.

Jasce pinched the bridge of his nose. "Fine, but update me immediately if you find anything."

Embracing the Darkness

"Done," the prince said, returning his gaze to the corpse.

"I wonder where it came from," Amycus said, his voice quiet as if talking to himself.

Queen Siryn entered, followed by Garan. Her brows raised as she neared the table. "What do we have here?"

Jasce sighed and kept his back to the dignitaries to speak to Caston. "You might as well inform Queen Val—never mind."

Caston looked over his shoulder and winced. The queen stood in the doorway with her hands on her hips and anger churned in her brown eyes.

"Commander Farone, it seems I was the last one invited to the party."

Jasce bowed. "Your Majesty. I was hoping to obtain more information before I briefed you. They"—he looked around the room—"were not invited."

"We'll discuss this later." She examined the carcass, her lips pursed. "What have you learned about this creature?"

Jasce stood next to her. "It's powerful, fast, and lethal. It is definitely attracted to magic and yet, has a strong resistance to it. One of them eventually broke through Kenz's shield."

Amycus lowered the claw he was observing. "One of them?"

Jasce nodded. "Yes, there were three."

Prince Jazari leaned against the table. "I would assume there are a lot more out there. That would explain the rumors from different locations occurring at the same time."

Maera lifted its claw and snipped the long nail. Liquid seeped out. "Looks like the claws have venom, too."

Jasce rubbed the tension from his neck. "It seems so."

"So, there are many of these creatures skulking around," King Morzov said, crossing his powerful arms.

"Yes, and based on reports, they're headed this way," Jasce said.

Amycus nodded. "That would make sense. If the Snatchers are attracted to magic, the Bastion has the highest number of Spectrals in one place."

"Well, maybe you should send your Spectrals away, for our safety," Archduke Carnelian said.

Jasce shook his head. "That's a stupid idea."

Caston ran a hand down his face while Maera bit her lip and busied herself on the other side of the room.

The archduke puffed out his chest. "Excuse me?"

Queen Valeri glared at Jasce. "I'm sorry, Kraig. My commander speaks before thinking." Jasce opened his mouth but snapped it shut as she raised her hand.

"I actually agree with Commander Farone," Queen Siryn said, looking between the dignitaries. "It seems the Spectrals are also competent soldiers. Am I right, Leonid?"

Jasce narrowed his eyes at the Vastane queen, who gave him a quick wink.

The Balten king nodded. "Consort Lekov and I have observed them training, and they are efficient with their magic and fighting skills. Sending them away would lessen the Paladin Guard by almost half. Plus, are these creatures attracted to all kinds of magic or just Spectrals?"

"We don't know, but there is a way to find out," Jasce said to the archduke, who bristled.

Queen Valeri's nostrils flared. "I, of course, will send none of my soldiers away, but your safety is of our utmost concern. Meet me in the council room to discuss our next steps."

The archduke inclined his head and exited the Sanctuary, followed by Prince Jazari and King Morzov.

Queen Siryn examined the creature and then approached Jasce. "I'm glad you've returned safely. Your soldiers are fortunate to have you leading them."

Jasce didn't miss the look she gave Queen Valeri as she glided from the room with Garan behind her.

Queen Valeri fisted her hands on her hips. "She's up to something."

Jasce crossed his arms. "Why, because she compliments me?"

"Jasce," Amycus said, but he stopped as the queen wheeled around.

Her eyes narrowed to slits. "I didn't realize flattering speech and a few winks were what you needed to do your job, Commander." She stalked toward the door. "Be in the council room in five minutes and keep your damn mouth shut."

Embracing the Darkness

Amycus sighed. "She's just on edge. But please try not to provoke her." He patted his shoulder as he walked out the door.

Caston leaned against the counter next to Maera. "That wasn't your best moment."

"I know." He raked his fingers through his hair. "I'll meet you at the compound after the meeting. We may need to outfit our Spectrals with collars." The idea made him sick, but it might be the only way to protect them from the Snatchers. "Maera, when you're finished analyzing that thing, I want it destroyed."

Jasce left the Sanctuary and stormed through the corridors of the Bastion.

Keep your damn mouth shut? How dare she speak to him that way. If it weren't for him, her army would be weak and useless. She should be thanking him instead of insulting him.

He ran his hands down his face. He needed a drink, food, and sleep. He stopped at the kitchens for a slice of bread and a piece of meat, choking them down as he crossed the training yard past a group of first-year recruits practicing with wooden swords. He longed to skip the meeting and work with the kids, but his comment to the archduke had dug him further from his queen's good graces, and he couldn't afford to make another mistake.

He swallowed the last piece of bread and walked to the palace to sit in on another useless meeting when he should be hunting the Snatchers.

Chapter Eighteen

Jasce analyzed the map of Pandaren and the red markers indicating where the Spectrals had gone missing. Lady Darbry's soldiers had spotted Snatchers in northern Paxton, near Torrine and the Culmen Range. Lord Haldron had received information that a Spectral had been found dead around Delmar and Lake Chelan with similar injuries to the body he and his team had discovered in the Silver Glen Forest. But based on intelligence from his Guard, it seemed the creatures were getting closer to Orilyon. The council members devised a plan to evacuate any non-military Spectrals and recruits under the age of sixteen. He'd wanted Kord to make Tillie, Maleous, and Emile return to Carhurst until things settled, but he wasn't surprised that Tillie had refused, claiming they were a family and they stuck together. Kord had taken collars for Maleous and Emile, just in case.

Jasce had sent two squadrons of non-magical soldiers to the outskirts of Orilyon to set up camp and wait.

He rubbed his forehead. He hated waiting.

During the meeting, the royals had discussed safety measures. Jasce had suggested canceling the Gathering but was immediately voted down. King Morzov was eager for the games to continue and wanted to discuss the sword fighting trial that was to be held in a few days. Jasce caught Prince Jazari rolling his eyes while Queen Siryn seemed lost in thought with her brows furrowed.

The archduke again brought up concern for Queen Valeri's safety, insisting she divulge her plan if something were to happen to her, especially with the Snatchers getting closer. Jasce wondered who the queen would choose. The idea of ruling Pandaren was growing on him, but he suspected he'd be Queen Valeri's last choice. Her displeasure with him was tangible.

A swish of fabric had him turning. Queen Siryn shut the doors behind her, holding a decanter and two glasses. "Hello, Commander. I figured you could use a drink. I know I do. I absolutely abhor meetings." The golden liquid swirled as she placed it on the table and handed him a glass. "You received my message, then. Thank you for staying."

He took the drink. It had surprised him when Garan had given him a note in the hallway after the meeting, and curiosity had gotten the better of him. Maybe the Vastane queen had information about the Snatchers that she didn't want to share with the other kingdoms.

She sat and crossed her legs, eyeing him like prey.

He chose a chair across the table and tasted the liquor. He raised his brows at the smooth, smoky flavor.

"You must have a lot on your mind with the tournament, the Snatchers, and the Heart of Pandaren."

"You know about the Heart?"

The queen grinned. "Oh, Jasce. Everyone knows about that." She took a slow perusal of his body, her eyes settling on his lips. "Why do you think Kraig is so eager to unite with your queen? Honestly, if the woman would simply tell him who would take over, it would end the discussion. My money is on Amycus, although he doesn't look too healthy. She should pick you."

The Vastane queen was indeed up to something. He just wasn't sure what. "She won't. Now, do you have a point or just want to share a drink?"

Queen Siryn's smile sent shivers down his spine. "I believe there's a certain Psyche you're looking for."

The glass was halfway to his mouth, which had turned as dry as the desert. He forced himself to lean back, feigning boredom. "I don't know what you're talking about."

"The stories of the Angel of Death are renowned: lethal, efficient, brilliant. But never foolish."

A muscle in his jaw throbbed. "What does that have to do with anything?"

"It means you don't play games. It's not your style. You know exactly who I'm talking about."

Jasce finished the contents of his glass, willing his heartbeat to return to its normal rhythm. "Where's Jaida?"

The queen wiped imaginary lint from her dress. "She's safe. She and her Spectral friend are all healed up. My scouts found them near the Camden Mountains. They needed help, so we helped them."

He leaned forward. "Was she injured? Is she okay?"

Queen Siryn refilled his glass. "Jaida's fine, physically."

"What do you mean?"

"She seems a little unhinged. Of course, being a Psyche can do that. Or so I hear."

He gritted his teeth. Drexus had made her that way, filling her head with his lies and a hunger for power.

The queen reached across the table and pried his fingers off the glass. "Careful now. Don't want any of your precious blood to spill." She stood and sashayed toward the window, her hips swishing seductively. The waning sunlight shone through her drink, making it shimmer like gold.

He looked away and inhaled a calming breath. What had happened that Jaida and Vale needed help? And after he'd searched for months, it was the Vastanes who'd found them. Jasce's head shot up. "Why did you have scouts in Pandaren?"

"That's of no consequence." She took a sip from her glass but kept her back to him. "Your magic, as well as your sister's, are quite rare, making you both valuable. I'd be a fool to release her without something in return."

He pushed from the table, blood rushing through his ears, and unsheathed his dagger. "I could make you."

She twirled around and smiled when she saw his knife. "Garan is right outside. Any harm comes to me, any scratch or hair out of place, and he will kill your precious sister."

He smirked, replacing the blade. "So she's close by."

The queen raised a brow. "Smart, powerful, and insanely attractive. Lorella really doesn't appreciate what a treasure you are. She could have you ruling at her side instead of being her lackey. At least, that's what I'd do."

"I'm not interested in ruling anything."

"Are you certain about that, Commander?"

"I just want my sister."

She rolled her eyes. "Yes, you've made that perfectly clear. But I have wants, too."

"And what do you want?"

"Isn't it obvious?" She chuckled when Jasce glared at her. "I want the Empower Stone. Bring it to me and I will release her."

Jasce walked around the table. "Why are you interested in the Stone? You don't have magic." At least, he didn't think the Vastanes did.

"The Gemaris can't get their hands on it." Her blue eyes hardened to ice. "Any magical being who finds even one piece would cause chaos. I'd rather be in charge of it than be at someone else's whim, especially Kraig's. I'm sure you can understand that."

Jasce crossed his arms and tapped his finger against his bicep. "Tell me about the Heart."

She sighed and stared at the ceiling. "It's a magical crystal that's been split into four Stones. The Empower Stone strengthens magic. The Creator and Abolish Stones—those should be self-explanatory. And the Inhibitor Stone suppresses magic. All the pieces are somewhere in Pandaren."

"And if you're lying?"

"I have no reason to keep secrets from you." She winked, and a chill spread through his veins. "Anyway"—she pulled a ring from her bodice—"this should convince you."

A gold band with a clear crystal lay in the center of her palm. Jasce's shoulders tensed as his magic thrummed. "Where did you get that?" he whispered.

"Ah, you recognize it."

Embracing the Darkness

His pulse quickened. He'd seen Drexus fidgeting with that ring during his training. And when he'd cut off Drexus's hand, he remembered twitching fingers and the golden band surrounded by black fire.

He reached for it but quickly dropped his arm. "How did you get this?"

"They had it with them. So you see, it's quite simple. The Empower Stone for your sister."

He tore his gaze from the crystal as adrenaline rushed through his system.

She passed by him and placed it near the decanter. "This will guide you to the Stone."

"Then why don't you search for it. Why do you need me?"

The queen huffed out a laugh. "I'm sure Lorella would approve of Vastane soldiers traipsing through her lands." She smoothed the folds of her dress and then peered at him. "Be careful. That's a powerful gem. And I'd keep it hidden, especially from the Gemaris."

He forced himself not to move toward the ring. "How do you expect me to search for the Empower Stone with the Gathering taking place?"

"You're resourceful. I'm sure you'll come up with a plan."

"I wouldn't know where to start. It could be anywhere in Pandaren."

"According to certain sources, the last known resting place was somewhere between the Camden Mountains and the sea."

Jasce narrowed his eyes. "I want to see my sister before I agree to anything."

"I figured as much. And you will. But not until after the second competition. Oh, and this remains between you and me. I'd hate for something to happen to her, or anyone else you care for."

"Any harm comes to her, and I'll rip you to shreds." He prowled forward, fingers brushing the hilt of his dagger.

The creak of the door had Jasce jerking.

Amycus wavered at the entryway and frowned. "Evelina."

She placed her drink on the table. "Go ahead and finish that. And remember what I said."

Jasce palmed the ring as he grabbed the glass. If anyone would recognize it, Amycus would.

As Queen Siryn glided past the blacksmith, Jasce's heart thumped in his chest. While Amycus focused on the queen and Garan retreating down the hallway, he slid the ring into his pocket.

Amycus shut the door and approached the table, worry crinkling the skin around his eyes. "What's going on?"

"She wanted to discuss the Snatcher. Thought I might know more than I had revealed in the meeting." Jasce finished his drink in one swallow. The lie had come too easily. He lowered himself into the chair and rubbed his face.

Amycus's breath hitched as he sat next to him. His gaze darted along the table and then at the closed door.

"What is it?" Jasce asked, keeping his hands away from the ring. It felt like a lead ball in his pocket.

Amycus licked his lips and stared at him. "Nothing." The blacksmith didn't look well. His face was pale, and his forehead glistened. "Whatever she's up to, you can't trust her."

"I don't."

The blacksmith glanced back at the closed door and then peered at Jasce. "I'm here if you want to talk."

A part of Jasce desperately wanted to open his soul and reveal everything to the old man. Not only was Amycus his mentor, he was a reliable friend. What would he think about Drexus's ring hidden in his pocket, or that the Vastane queen had his sister? For now, he needed to keep this information to himself, for he had no doubt Queen Siryn would make good on her threat. Too many lives were at stake if he revealed what he knew.

It seemed everyone was keeping secrets these days. But at least he was getting close to finding Jaida. She was alive and safe, if he could believe the queen.

Jasce clenched his fists. He was now at the mercy of not one, but two queens, and neither of them cared for his or his family's best interests.

He finished his drink, mumbled about having to train recruits, and

Embracing the Darkness

trudged from the room. Amycus's stare pierced his back until he rounded the corner.

∼

The whip snapped through the air and Jasce bit back a curse with each strike.

"Your compassion makes you weak." Drexus's voice mocked him as skin and muscle were stripped away. Blood poured down his legs. A tooth cracked as he clenched his jaw. He would not cry out.

He glared over his shoulder at his commander, and his breath caught in his throat. It wasn't Drexus wielding the whip, but a man who wore a Hunter's mask. Two swords peeked over his shoulders, and piercing blue eyes filled with hatred stared back.

Azrael, the Angel of Death, lifted his arm and cracked the whip again and again.

Jasce shot up out of bed and winced at the imaginary pain in his back. Sweat covered his body, and his chest pounded. He turned and placed his feet on the cold stone floor and put his head between his knees. Bile burned his throat.

It was just a dream, he thought, repeating the words over and over until his heart rate settled. He glanced at Kenz and allowed her gentle breathing to soothe his nerves. Moonlight drifted through the window, illuminating her black hair and pale skin.

"Just a dream," he whispered, desperately wanting to hold her yet repulsed by the malevolence churning inside him. He'd dreamed before of the time Drexus had almost killed him, but never had it been Azrael doling out the punishment.

Drexus's ring sparkled on the nightstand. The pull from the crystal beckoned him like a lodestone, calling to his magic—a moth to the flame.

With shaking hands, he grabbed the ring and let the crystal's power flow through him. His spine stiffened, and he stifled a groan as his magic opened its arms in a welcoming embrace.

He quietly dressed and snuck out of his room, glancing at Kenz before shutting the door. The Bastion's corridors were empty besides a few soldiers keeping watch as he made his way to the forge. Jasce breathed in the smell of ash and metal and ran his fingers along a steel rod waiting to be transformed into a beautiful sword.

Plopping down on the stool, he focused on the empty hearth. He was so tired of fighting. He never imagined he'd feel that way since combat had once defined him. But he had tasted freedom when he lived in Carhurst, as he worked in Amycus's forge and had family dinners in Kord's kitchen. Simple—no more bloodshed or death at his hands. The life he had envisioned would be as easy as breathing.

"Finish this mission and you can have it," he mumbled. Once the Gathering was over and he'd rescued Jaida, he'd take the life he wanted with Kenz at his side. Fear tightened in his gut at the notion of being a father. Would he be like his own father: angry, standoffish, cold? His temperament already leaned that way, but he was making progress on changing those habits.

He placed the ring on the table and crossed his arms. The light from the candles flickered on the crystal, making it sparkle. He remembered the prince's words, that this gem had to have come from the part of the Heart that strengthened magic. The other three parts—create, destroy, and suppress—would be just as valuable. He wondered what it would be like to possess that kind of power.

He trailed his thumb over the crystal. If he possessed the Empower Stone, he'd be fast enough to save those in harm's way—unstoppable and no one's pawn. His magic pulsed as his lips curved into a smile.

He wandered toward the hearth, the bricks covered in soot, and lit a fire. The kindling sparked to life, and heat caressed his face. Dancing flames mesmerized him as they engulfed the wood. He grabbed the tongs hanging on the wall and placed the ring inside. The metal glowed, and the crystal pulsed with power. A tremor slid down his spine as his magic responded to the gem.

He pulled the tongs from the fire and placed the glowing band on the table. With a quick strike from a hammer, the gold cracked, and the crystal skittered toward the edge. He slapped his hand on it before it tumbled off. A rush of magic coursed through him, and something deep

Embracing the Darkness

inside stretched its arms wide, as if waking from an eternal slumber. He moaned and tipped his head back, allowing himself to level out.

His magic purred, and power coursed through him. With this small sliver alone, he felt invincible. And if he found the Empower Stone? He wouldn't have to answer to any queen.

He wouldn't have to answer to anyone.

Chapter Nineteen

Jasce watched the wyverns with a longing to take one and fly away somewhere, anywhere. The archduke's beast roamed the length of the paddock, its black scales reflecting the rising sun as it stretched its leathery wings toward the warmth and shuddered. All the wyverns had spiked tails—a trait bred into them, according to the archduke. Combined with their powerful hind legs and massive jaws, they were lethal hunters.

Jasce had returned late in the evening from an outing to an island off the coast of Orilyon. Pleasure boats had sailed across the turquoise waters in the morning and returned after the sun had set, the royal guests happily exhausted and a little drunk. He didn't want to admit to the envy that snaked through him as the dignitaries and the nobles enjoyed the food and drink. Many lounged on chairs basking in the warm sun, while others reveled in the refreshing water of the Merrigan Sea. As he had guarded Queen Valeri, he had to stop himself from fidgeting. The sensation of spiders crawling along his skin made him cringe. He'd resented the queen for ordering him to attend. With everyone away, it would have been the perfect time to search for Jaida, but he suspected Queen Valeri wanted to keep a close eye on him.

And he understood why. He'd spent any free time vaulting through the streets of Orilyon but hadn't had any luck locating his sister. It seemed the queen wasn't the only one aware of his recent excursions, either. He'd caught Kenz giving him wary looks, as well as Amycus. The dark circles under Jasce's eyes and his lack of patience were telltale signs that he wasn't getting enough sleep. They knew he was up to something, but for Jaida's sake, and theirs, he couldn't tell them what. Not with all the spies lurking around the Bastion and the palace. Even with the Trackers monitoring the meetings and other events, it was a known fact that Prince Jazari's Shade Walkers searched for information.

He yawned as the sky shifted from deep purple to a light pink. The little sleep he did get was plagued by nightmares, and a dull pain had taken up residence behind his eyes.

At least reports of the Snatchers had lessened. The nobles had distributed messages, giving their towns instructions regarding the creatures, and Spectrals were doing whatever was necessary to keep themselves safe. A few nobles wanted members of the Paladin Guard to help monitor their lands, but both Jasce and Queen Valeri had said no, at least until the Gathering was concluded. There were still three trials remaining, which meant weeks of pandering to the dignitaries.

Jasce didn't mind Prince Jazari's company if Kenz wasn't around, but he preferred spending time with the Baltens and learning about their ancestors and magic. King Morzov and Consort Lekov were the most accepting of him as a warrior.

The archduke, however, couldn't keep his eyes off a leather band Kenz had made for Jasce. He'd woven the crystal from Drexus's ring inside and no one was the wiser, or so he thought. He'd first noticed the Gemari staring at it during their meeting and again on the island. Every time the man approached him, Jasce made sure he was mysteriously needed elsewhere. Standing in front of the wyvern paddock probably wasn't such a smart idea. But he longed for a reprieve. Just a moment to not think about Jaida or the Heart of Pandaren.

The sound of a bottle breaking startled him. Cursing, he spat a glob of blood onto the ground. His tongue still bled from when he'd bitten it during the night. The latest nightmare had him stumbling for the bathroom to retch up his dinner.

His father's dilapidated cottage. Candlelight flickering off the

Embracing the Darkness

sharpened edge of a dagger. But instead of Barnet Farone lying drunk in his bed, it had been Jasce. Blood covered everything, including Kenz, her vacant eyes staring at him accusingly. The Hunter's mask grinned over him as Azrael whispered, "Compassion makes you weak."

He leaned against the fence and tried to relax into the warmth of the rising sun while a Terrenian handler worked with a smaller wyvern, attempting to get it used to a saddle.

He repeated his mother's words—*here it comes; the light chasing away the darkness*—unable to remember when he'd taken the time to enjoy a sunrise. His finger rubbed along the crystal in the leather band around his wrist. He'd felt more powerful than he ever had, his body stronger, his mind more focused. He had a mission—find the Empower Stone and rescue Jaida. Once he had that section of the Heart, he'd no longer be a pawn. And Queen Siryn was delusional if she thought he'd just hand that power over. He'd take his sister and whatever else he wanted.

"Hi, Uncle Jasce."

He jumped, and his hand immediately moved toward his dagger. Preoccupied with his thoughts, he hadn't heard the kids approach. Maleous was dressed in his training leathers, while Emile wore a simple brown dress. The silver collar sparkled as if mocking its true purpose.

"You two aren't supposed to be here," Jasce said, smirking. He'd suspected they had been coming to the paddock to watch the wyverns ever since the Terrenians arrived.

"Emile wanted to see them before . . ." Maleous started, and then he looked away, his jaw set.

"Before what?" he asked, glancing between the two kids.

Tears welled in Emile's eyes. "Maera is removing my magic tomorrow."

Jasce swore. "Tomorrow? I thought she was still in the testing phase."

"There were successful experiments with some Guard members who'd received the Amplifier serum." She moved closer to the fence. Her knuckles whitened as she gripped the metal, and her eyes darted between a smaller wyvern and the sky.

Jasce figured she wanted to fly away, too. "You don't have to do this."

Maleous straightened his shoulders. "That's what I said."

She looked out over the paddock. One female, a brilliant green beast with small horns, strolled over. Emile took a piece of raw meat from her pocket and tossed it to the animal, which it caught in midair. "Whenever I take the collar off, I lose control of my magic. I can't live like this, and I won't have Mal or Kord healing me all the time."

Maleous reached out and then lowered his arm. His cheeks flushed.

"Isn't there another way?" Jasce swiped at the blood on his lip. Anger and hopelessness battled inside him.

Maleous stepped closer and signaled for him to kneel. He bent over and the boy touched his face, his eyes narrowed in concentration. A tingling warmth ran through his mouth and the pain lessened.

Jasce stood and swirled his healed tongue against the inside of his cheek. "Thanks, kid."

Maleous's lips curved into a smile. The boy's healing magic wasn't as strong as his father's, but for his age it was impressive. It would be interesting to see, as he grew older, if he'd be as powerful as Kord.

Emile brushed a stray tendril of blonde hair away from her face. She'd reminded him so much of Jaida when he'd first met her—still did, and the ache in his heart caused him to rub his chest. He hadn't saved his sister, and now, it seemed, he couldn't save Emile from having her magic taken.

He knelt and rested his hand on her shoulder. "I'm sorry this is happening."

"It's not your fault." She smiled at him. "It's better this way. Really."

"You're a brave kid."

"Can I still be part of the Paladin Guard? I'll fight as a Natural."

He swallowed and took hold of her hands. "Absolutely. We need more female fighters. You might even surpass your brother."

Emile's smile widened into a grin.

They observed the wyverns for a while longer, picking their favorites and talking about where they would go if they could fly anywhere. Their innocence was refreshing, and the tension in his shoulders lessened.

Embracing the Darkness

He'd grown to love these kids. Lander, too, even though he couldn't show it. Lander was already one of the best soldiers in his year, and Jasce didn't want a target on the kid's back for being the commander's favorite.

"Commander Farone, may I have a word?" Archduke Carnelian approached, frowning at Maleous and Emile.

Jasce nodded and then said to Emile, "I'll see you at the Sanctuary. You'll be fine." She wrapped her arms around him and then ran off with Maleous toward town.

He faced the archduke, who examined his wrist. "I can feel that, you know."

Jasce inwardly swore. He'd wondered if the Gemari could sense the crystal. He should've left the leather band in his room, but he recoiled at the idea of taking away the power that now coursed through his body. What the man would do with the information, Jasce wasn't sure.

Kill him.

Jasce stiffened and glanced over his shoulder. The area around the paddock was empty, and the handler had disappeared into the stable.

"Commander?" The archduke's brows furrowed, and the gem in his chest glowed.

Do it, now. No one will know.

Jasce flexed his hands.

A low growl brought his attention back to the wyverns. The large black one strolled toward them, its gold eyes focused on Jasce, and its lips curled into a snarl. The archduke's eyes crinkled around the edges as he rested a hand along the beast's snout. He made a few clicks with his tongue and the animal dipped its gigantic head and trudged to the other side of the paddock.

"You need to be careful, Commander. That isn't just a pretty bauble."

"I don't know what you're talking about."

Archduke Carnelian laced his fingers behind his back and ambled along the fence. Jasce followed, perplexed by the voice he'd heard and the lust for blood he hadn't felt in months.

"Gemaris have a relationship, so to speak, with magical crystals. We understand them better than you Spectrals." The man's eyes glazed as he stared at nothing. "There's always a balance with magic. And just like nature, if that harmony shifts, it will right itself. Sometimes aggressively."

"I can handle it," was all Jasce said.

The archduke raised a brow. "We'll see." He stroked his long beard as he peered over the outskirts of Orilyon. The sun drifted behind the clouds, creating a canvas of golds and pinks. There was a charge in the air and the smell of rain. "I've also seen the way Evelina watches you. She has ulterior motives."

Jasce scoffed. "Don't we all?"

"Yes, we do."

"Are you looking for the Heart?" He remembered what Queen Siryn said about not wanting the Gemaris to find it.

The archduke glanced at him out of the corner of his eye. "We've known about the Heart for eons and have been content to let its whereabouts remain hidden. But now, too many people are aware of it, and I fear it getting into the wrong hands. If someone obtains all four pieces, we wouldn't be able to stop them."

"Can the Stones be destroyed?"

"Possibly, but what effect would that have on our magic? The repercussions are unknown."

Jasce pondered that while two of the wyverns butted heads. They spread their wings and extended their claws as they battled for dominance.

"Anyway," the archduke continued, "I believe I've made my motives clear. A united Pandaren and Terrenus would be advantageous." His mustache quivered. "However, I do think you'd be a good choice for ruling in Queen Valeri's stead, despite your reputation." He smiled at him. "The Terrenians will support you, Commander, if that time comes."

"Why would you be on my side? I didn't think you approved of me or my methods."

"I may not, but I can tell you're a good man." He stole one last glance at the leather band and then walked toward the entrance to the wyvern paddock. "Don't go searching for the Empower Stone by yourself. If you don't believe me, ask your friend Amycus."

Embracing the Darkness

Jasce felt his jaw drop. It seemed Amycus knew more about the Heart than he was letting on. He'd be a fool not to gather as much information as possible before searching for the Stone. But how, without endangering those he loved?

He rubbed his neck. The Vastanes and the Terrenians supported his ruling Pandaren. He knew he couldn't trust Queen Siryn, and he wasn't too sure about the archduke. However, his Gemaris would make powerful allies.

He approached his horse and stroked Bruiser's mane. "You're still my favorite." The horse snorted and shook its head, its large brown eyes staring at the wyverns. He needed to get to the Sanctuary and try one last time to stop Maera from removing Emile's magic. He rode along the outskirts of the city toward the Bastion, and as he got closer, the peace he'd experienced with the rising sun dwindled. He frowned at a tremor in his hands. The sun, invincible in its quest to conquer the darkness, seemed to have been thwarted, and the hope he normally felt at a new day remained hidden in the shadows.

Chapter Twenty

The sound of equipment whirring had Jasce grinding his teeth. This was so wrong—why couldn't anyone see it? He paced the back of the room and tried to ignore the worried glances from Kenz. The chamomile and medicinal scent from the Sanctuary made his skin crawl. Tillie had her arm wrapped around Lander and whispered to him. He nodded as he tracked Jasce's movements.

Maera had been successful with her experiments faster than he thought possible and was smarter and more talented than Drexus ever was.

They'd been waiting for what seemed like years, and the helplessness he felt made him want to rip his hair out. He needed to do something, anything. And yet, there was nothing he could do besides charge into the room and vault Emile away. But to what end? Her magic was slowly killing her.

He understood the procedure was for Emile's benefit—she wouldn't survive the three types of magic flowing through her veins. But it still didn't sit well with him. He trusted Maera completely, but what if this operation fell into nefarious hands? Someone like Queen Siryn or Lord Haldron. Spectrals would be at a disadvantage, and if news of this got out and history repeated itself, Pandaren would be in another civil war before the end of the month.

At one point, Caston had come in to see how Emile was doing. The rest of Jasce's team had wanted to stay, but the room wasn't big enough. Caston said he'd provide updates and that they'd be waiting for them when the procedure was finished.

"You're going to wear a path through the floor," Kenz said, talking around a compact bevel trapped between her teeth. She'd brought a small scabbard with her and was carving detailed scrolls through the leather, alternating between the knife and bevel. It was a present for Emile after she woke from the procedure.

Jasce stopped pacing. "I can't believe we're doing this." Emile's petite body lay on the exam table while Maera and Kord worked, Maleous by his father's side. Amycus and Pilar assisted them, as well as a man Jasce didn't recognize. "It isn't right to take someone's magic."

Kenz removed the bevel from her mouth. "If Maera and Amycus could've found another way, they would've. Emile is safe, and that's all that matters."

"Is it, though?"

Lander's head shot up. "What's that supposed to mean?" He scowled at Jasce, which would be viewed as insubordination, but considering the circumstances, Jasce let it pass and continued his pacing.

Standing still wasn't an option. Jasce's hands trembled, and it felt like a million bugs were crawling across his skin. "What if the wrong people learn how to do this? Any Spectral could have their magic removed, lose their power against their will. There just has to be another way."

He thought about the power he'd used to save Emile and vault his team from the forest to the tavern. He'd tapped into a deeper level of magic, and now with the crystal warming his wrist, who knew what else he was capable of? And for someone to steal his magic? It was inexcusable.

Jasce rested his hands on his hips. Kord stood over Emile, his brow furrowed, as he continued to heal her while her magic was siphoned away. Rubbing his arms, he remembered the tubes that had stuck out of him while Drexus had done the same thing, and it made him cringe. He'd been powerless to stop it and had almost died. As if sensing his turmoil, Kord glanced over, his good eye piercing Jasce to the core.

Amycus said something to Maleous, who nodded and jogged out the back door.

"Something's wrong," Jasce said. He sat next to Kenz, afraid his legs would give out. She grabbed his hand and gave it a gentle squeeze. He stared at their entwined fingers, feeling powerless. Lander walked to the window and placed his hands on the glass. His shoulders bunched as he watched Maleous return with another physician. She pressed two fingers against Emile's neck and spoke to Amycus and Maera, who worked diligently, moving between Emile and the equipment and making adjustments. Jasce couldn't hear what they were saying, but they looked worried.

His heart pounded in his ears. "I can't just sit here while they slowly kill her." He pushed out of the chair and was about to enter the exam room when Tillie grabbed his arm.

"Jasce, wait. Look at Kord."

Kord's uninjured eye was closed, the other hidden under a patch. A muscle ticked in his jaw, but his face was calm. Maleous rested a hand on Emile's forehead as he added his healing magic to his father's. Maera said something and Kord nodded.

Amycus turned from the bed and found Jasce's stare. He gave a small smile as Maera escorted the two other physicians from the room.

Jasce closed his eyes. It was done. Emile's magic had been removed, and she'd survived the process. What the consequences were now, no one knew.

Kord wrapped an arm around Maleous and signaled that they could come in. Lander shot away from the window and ran through the door, practically barreling into Kord. Tillie and Kenz entered after him.

Kenz looked over her shoulder. "Coming?"

"In a minute," Jasce said, plopping down into the chair. He rested his elbows on his knees and stared at the marbled floor, attempting to swallow the fear that had gripped his mind and body. He locked his fingers together to stop them from shaking and inhaled a deep breath.

The memory of being strapped to Drexus's cold table occupied his thoughts—restraints compressing his muscles, tubes lodged in his skin. A groan slipped as it all came rushing back. The pain. The hopelessness.

I will never allow anyone to take our power again.

His head jerked up as he scanned the room.

Empty.

The others stood near Emile's bed. Tillie wiped a tear from her eye as she wrapped an arm around Maleous and Lander. Kenz hugged Kord while Maera and Pilar removed the tubes.

Jasce swallowed and glanced at the dark corners of the waiting room. He'd seen how the area around a shadow distorted when Commander Faez had Shade Walked during the collapse of the wall. The air was still.

Dread knotted in his gut.

Amycus approached him and sat in the chair Kenz had vacated. "She did well."

Jasce huffed. "You can't be on board with this."

The blacksmith leaned his head against the wall and stared at the ceiling. "If you asked me a month ago, I would've said no. But if it's the only way to truly help her . . ." He splayed out his palms and sighed.

Jasce rubbed his damp hands on his pants and thought about the voice he'd heard earlier.

Amycus lowered his eyes to the leather band on Jasce's wrist. "That's new." The blacksmith's knuckles whitened as he clenched his fist.

Frowning, Jasce stared from the band to Amycus, who seconds ago had seemed relaxed. He lowered his wrist to his side, out of view, and said, "Kenz made it for me."

Amycus licked his lips. "I . . ." He stood abruptly and headed for the door. "I have to check on something. Tell Maera I'll be back soon."

Jasce watched him hurry from the waiting room and weave through the beds in the Sanctuary, almost running into a Healer on his way out.

That's odd, Jasce thought.

Kenz peeked her head out the door. "She's waking up."

He nodded and looked over his shoulder again to peer into the shadows.

The voice he'd heard seemed hauntingly familiar.

∽

Embracing the Darkness

He stayed with Lander at Emile's side while his team came and went, but he couldn't make himself leave just yet. While Emile drifted in and out of sleep, he and Lander spoke of different training regimens. The kid was a natural leader and had some good ideas. Eventually, Lander mumbled about getting something to eat and left the Sanctuary.

Jasce watched him go, spotting the Vastane visitors who meandered through the Sanctuary with a Healer at their side. He slumped in his chair and sighed. Emile's face was calm, but her eyes darted back and forth behind her lids. He wondered what she dreamed about and hoped it was something peaceful. A stab of jealousy shot through him, unable to remember the last time he'd experienced a restful night's sleep.

"You're still here, I see," Maera said, approaching the other side of Emile's bed. Her blonde hair was knotted on top of her head, and her green tunic made her hazel eyes darken. "Don't you have a tournament to compete in?"

He rubbed the tightness from his neck. "I wanted to make sure she's okay."

"Your lack of faith in my abilities is annoying." He arched a brow and she chuckled. "I'm kidding, and I won't tell anyone what a softy you are."

He forced a smile and leaned forward. "I get she needed to have this done, but what are we doing? I mean, who's to determine who has their magic removed? Or prevent them from taking mine?" He feared this more than anything. He wouldn't be powerless, not when so much rested on his shoulders. His fingers brushed reassuringly against the leather band.

Maera pulled up a chair and focused on Emile. "I understand your concern. I've already talked with the queen about setting up protocols."

He stood, unable to sit any longer. "Yes, but Naturals might want to level the playing field. And what if the Vastanes get ahold of this? They're medically advanced enough to pull it off."

Maera bit her lip and focused on her intertwined fingers. "Jasce, they helped us perfect the procedure."

Ice formed in his veins, and he slowly turned. "What did you say?"

She stood and lifted her hands. "As you said, they're medically advanced. For Emile's safety, I couldn't refuse their help. Two of their medics oversaw the transfusion."

His stomach dropped.

Queen Siryn knew how to remove a Spectral's magic. She hadn't been in Pandaren long enough to have gained that knowledge from Maera. So how did she learn this, unless someone who was proficient in magic transferal taught her? There were only two people he was aware of, and Amycus would never work with the Vastanes. Which left Drexus. But he was dead.

"Are you all right?" Maera asked.

His fingers trembled, and his magic hummed. "I need to speak with the queen."

Worry filled her face as she padded to the other side of the bed and rested her hand on his arm. "She's already in the arena."

He took one last look at Emile, turned on his heel, and rushed out of the Sanctuary.

Rage threatened to overflow as the crystal warmed against his wrist. A breeze wafted through the corridor, making the torches flicker. The shifting light illuminated Drexus as he lumbered down the hallway with Jaida at his side. A sword protruded from his chest and when he smiled, blood stained his teeth.

Jasce tripped and almost fell as his former commander dropped to his knees.

"Where's your compassion?" Drexus asked, laughing as blood bubbled from his lips. Jaida's scream echoed through the caverns of his mind.

He blinked and the image disappeared. Resting his hands on his knees, he ordered himself to breathe and tried to still the tremors racking his body. A spider scurried along the ground, and cheers from the arena drowned out the ringing in his ears.

Find the Heart and no one will stop us.

He peered into the empty hallway and leaned against the wall, letting it anchor him to reality. Drexus was dead. His sister was safe, if he could trust Queen Siryn. He was exhausted. That's all it was.

A cackle drifted along the breeze.

"Shut up," Jasce growled, clenching his fists to stop the shaking.

Embracing the Darkness

"Commander Farone?"

He looked up. Lord Haldron scrutinized him with furrowed brows. Two of his guards flanked the noble, both staring at Jasce with wariness in their eyes.

What had they heard?

"Keeping tabs on me, Larkin?" Jasce asked, pushing off the wall.

The lord's eyes narrowed. "Not everything is about you, Commander. I'm on my way to the games."

He muzzled the anger burning inside him. Lord Haldron was someone who'd want a Spectral's magic removed. He forced away the thought of slicing his dagger across the man's throat and strode past him and his guards toward the arena. The last thing he should do was compete in a sword fight. He was having a hard enough time controlling his thoughts without a weapon in his hand.

A blade of lightning flashed through the sky, followed by a boom of thunder. Dark clouds, swollen with rain, blocked the sun. The heavens would unleash their fury and he'd be fighting in mud.

Perfect.

Chapter Twenty-One

Jasce entered through the arena's side entrance and scanned the seating area for the Pandaren queen. His gaze landed on Queen Siryn, who wore a crimson gown, her blonde hair cascading over her shoulders. She offered him a catlike grin, and he wondered when he'd become the mouse in this game of hers. His finger tapped the hilt of his dagger, and the desire to kill someone grew in intensity.

"Jasce, there you are. We've been looking—" Kenz stopped at his side and followed his gaze. Her lips drew into a flat line as she glanced between him and Queen Siryn.

"I was in the Sanctuary with Emile."

Kenz wrapped her arms around herself. She'd braided her hair and wore the chest piece Amycus had created for her. The hilt of her sword shimmered as it hung from one of her handmade scabbards. She narrowed her eyes. "What's going on?"

"Did you know the Vastanes helped remove Emile's magic?"

She dipped her chin. "Kord mentioned it."

Pain sliced through his palms as his nails dug into his flesh. "You both knew." It wasn't a question. It was another secret his future wife and his friend had kept from him.

"Please don't get mad. They had to do what was best for Emile."

He leaned forward and glared down at her. "Do not tell me how to react. This is twice now."

"Oh, that's rich. You haven't been the same since we returned with that Snatcher. Sneaking off in the middle of the night, staring at that Vastane hag."

He retreated a step, unable to remember ever being this angry at her. He didn't trust himself as the need to fight, to spill blood, coursed through him.

"Hey, you two. It's time—" Flynt jogged up and skidded to a stop. He stared between them. "Is everything okay?"

The muscle in Jasce's jaw throbbed as Flynt stood beside Kenz. "Not even close," Jasce said and stalked away, flexing his fingers, not realizing he'd wrapped them around the hilt of his dagger.

Jasce leaned against the wall as a Terrenian soldier sparred with the Balten consort. He'd known the Baltens were bred for war, but he had never seen them in hand-to-hand combat. Their sword fighting skills were renowned, and he almost felt bad for the Terrenian. Almost. The smug expression on the archduke's face melted into rage as Consort Lekov defeated his man. She was one of the most skilled fighters in the arena, next to Caston and himself.

Kenz had already competed, and he'd wanted to congratulate her on her victory over the Alturian commander but remained pressed against the wall. Two secrets she and Kord had kept from him, all because they feared how he would react. Did they still look at him as if he was the killer they'd first met in the dungeon? Did they not trust him?

He sighed. He felt her slipping away as the secrets and lies piled up between them. And now he was just as guilty, unable to tell Kenz about his sister. If Queen Siryn found out, he had no doubt she'd be true to her word and Kenz and his child would pay the price with their lives. He wouldn't allow that.

Which meant he couldn't tell her about Drexus's crystal or how he'd obtained it. That would lead to even more questions and accusations, and if anyone else knew he had it, they'd try to take it. That the archduke was aware of it, and hadn't yet told Queen Valeri, bothered him. What game was he playing?

Caston approached. His battle with Prince Jazari had been entertaining, and Caston had come away mostly unscathed. After a quick trip to the Healer's tent, the wound on his arm looked like a scratch. The prince's skill with the sword had been impressive, but he was no match for the ex-Hunter.

"I've watched Garan spar. He's strong, but not fast. You'll be fine," Caston said, leaning back and propping his foot against the wall.

"I'm not concerned." Jasce opened and closed his hands, willing away the tremors.

Caston glanced at him from the corner of his eyes. "Then what's bugging you?"

He ran his hand along the stubble over his jaw. "That anyone can remove magic, and my fiancée and best friend knew the Vastanes helped with the procedure." Scanning the other side of the arena, he found Kenz sitting next to Flynt and Delmira. He looked away when their eyes met. "How do they even know how to transfer magic?"

"I get that, but you need to clear your head." Caston pushed off the wall and blocked his view of the sparring rings. "We'll deal with this properly. Maera won't take advantage—you know that."

A loud voice broke through the cheers. "What's got the archduke so riled?" Jasce asked.

The Terrenian waved his hands and pointed toward the exit of the arena, his face getting redder by the minute.

Caston looked to where he was staring. "His top fighter didn't show, and he wants a rematch since Consort Lekov won."

Jasce frowned. This was the second event where a competitor hadn't shown up. "Did we ever find out what happened to the Balten soldier who was supposed to compete in the Gauntlet?"

Caston shook his head. "I haven't heard anything. Do you want me to look into it?"

"Yes. Quietly."

Caston nodded and handed him a collar. "Good luck."

The metal snapped shut and Jasce clenched his jaw, waiting for his power to disappear. A small pulse of magic fluttered inside him. He lifted his wrist. The sliver of the Empower Stone flickered as it fought the effects of the collar, and a smile tugged at his lips.

The crowd cheered when he entered the sparring ring. He inclined his head to Queen Valeri and the rest of the council members, holding Amycus's stare when the man's normally sparkling eyes filled with concern. Garan stood on the other side of the ring, twirling his sword. The Vastane soldier was similar in size to Kord, but unlike Kord, this man had the eyes of a killer. But so did Jasce.

Lord Haldron made an announcement that Jasce ignored as he cracked his neck, hearing a satisfying pop. He addressed his opponent. "Are you ready?"

Garan sneered. "Whenever you are, Commander."

The two warriors circled, analyzing each other. Jasce settled into his fighting stance and winked. Garan's jaw pulsed and his knuckles whitened as he squeezed the hilt of his sword.

The clash of steel echoed through the arena, and the crowd roared. Jasce dodged the bodyguard's attack and lunged. His feet were in constant motion, feinting and slicing under Garan's guard, as the clouds burst and large raindrops fell from the sky. He blinked away the water and tightened his grip on his sword.

Garan's attacks intensified, and Jasce grunted, barely blocking a strike behind his back. The oversized bodyguard was better than he'd thought.

A flash of red caught his eye. Queen Siryn laughed as she took a drink from her goblet, whispering something to one of her attendees.

Focus!

Jasce glanced at the judges. A hand wrapped around his arm and a searing pain cut through his distraction.

"You need to concentrate, Commander," Garan said, pulling Jasce close.

The need for more power mixed with suppressed rage crashed through Jasce as the crystal warmed his wrist and his magic hummed. Visions flashed through his mind. Lurching back, he wiped the rainwater from his face and shoved the images away. He grimaced at the laceration on his side. He'd chosen not to wear his armor, and his pride had cost him.

Embracing the Darkness

Garan twirled his sword. He smiled and glanced at his queen. "She is quite beautiful, isn't she? But aren't you engaged?"

Do not lose control.

"Shut up," Jasce growled. He wasn't sure if he was talking to his competitor or the mysterious voice.

Garan prowled on the edge of the ring while the crowd yelled, demanding more.

Jasce's body trembled with pent-up anger, and his fury made him careless as he swung his sword at Garan's head. The bodyguard laughed while easily dodging the strike.

Weeks of politics, lies, and secrets piled on top of his failure to find his sister, the threat of having his magic taken, the fear of being a father, and the traits he may pass down. It pressed in on him—a weight he wasn't sure he could bear.

Jasce lunged and slashed at Garan's chest.

Their blades crashed together. They stood nose to nose, only their swords separating them.

Raindrops clamored on steel, the thunderstorm muting the yells from the crowd.

Garan's scar twisted as his lips curled into a sneer. "Your sister's quite beautiful, too."

He's baiting you!

Jasce's temper exploded and all logical thought disappeared, along with years of training. He gave in to the fury. The sky split open, and with a rage-filled roar, he attacked.

Chapter Twenty-Two

The Back Alley Tavern, known for its reprehensible clientele, had a reputation for keeping locals and tourists away, which was fine with Jasce.

He sat on a rickety stool and tapped his finger on the sticky wood. Water dripped down his back from the rain and mud covered his boots. He looked awful, but he didn't care. He had wrapped a bandage around his waist, which was now soaked in blood, and his right eye was almost swollen shut. He mumbled a curse, unable to remember the last time someone had defeated him in a sparring competition. Queen Valeri had lost graciously, but she hadn't been pleased. He should've won that contest, no matter Garan's size or strength, but he broke his own rule and allowed his emotions to take over.

In the end, the Baltens scored the most points and were now in first place. Because of him, his team had lost the lead. The thought made him ill.

Replaying the sparring match in his mind, he tried to decipher when he'd lost the advantage. He remembered seeing Queen Siryn smiling and hearing a voice, then Garan grabbing his arm and a sudden pain in his side. A surge of emotions had ignited his restrained fury from discovering the Vastanes had assisted with Emile's procedure. He saw himself slashing through the Sanctuary, destroying everything and everyone. The vision shifted to him sitting on a throne and people bowing before him, his hand wrapped around the Empower Stone. He'd tried to ignore the images and focus on the fight, but the voice nagging him hadn't helped, even though it'd been completely accurate: Garan had baited him and Jasce had wriggled like a fish on a hook.

He knocked back the remaining whiskey and signaled the barkeep for another. He let out a shuddering breath and winced as his head pounded and his hands shook.

The barstool next to him creaked and Jasce sighed. "Can't a man be left alone?"

"Nope." Kord chuckled and reached out. "Besides, your wounds need tending."

He brushed off Kord's hand. His injuries could wait. Right now, he needed answers. "Why didn't you tell me about the Vastanes?"

"One, I had it under control. I'm in charge of the Sanctuary, remember?"

Jasce glared at Kord in the mirror. "And two?"

The Healer sighed. "You have so much going on. I wanted to spare you one more thing."

Jasce's knuckles whitened as he gripped the glass. "I'm not weak. You should've trusted me to handle it. You kept Kenz's pregnancy a secret, and now this. What am I supposed to think?"

"No one would ever accuse you of being weak. Stubborn and irrational, yes. But not weak." Kord rested his arms on the bar, grimacing at the stains. "With teaching the recruits, security for these tournaments, searching for your sister and the Snatchers, dealing with the council members and the other dignitaries, Kenz's pregnancy . . . it's a lot. Did you ever stop to consider that I was protecting you?"

"I don't need protecting," he said through clenched teeth.

Kord laughed. "Yes, brother, you do."

Jasce swiveled his head and regarded his friend. Kord had never called him brother before. He hadn't heard that word since before Drexus had taken him to the Watch Guard, when he'd had an ordinary life with a loving mother and sister.

"How'd you even find me?" he asked.

Embracing the Darkness

"Caston. He said you'd often come here when you were moody, back in the Hunter days. Now quit being a stubborn mule." Kord rested a hand against Jasce's side and immediately warmth flowed through his body, healing his wounds at a faster rate than normal. Kord shifted away and stared at him, his good eye doing that penetrating-into-his-soul thing that made Jasce squirm.

"Something's different," Kord said.

Jasce rubbed his thumb along the leather band. Queen Siryn said not to tell anyone about Jaida, but she never mentioned anything about Drexus's old ring. Jasce's eyes darted around the tavern. No one seemed to pay them any attention. He scanned the shadows but everything was still.

He lifted his wrist.

Kord's tankard was halfway to his mouth. "Kenz is doing well with her leather carving, but I've seen this before."

"Look closer. In fact"—Jasce unclasped the band—"hold it."

Kord narrowed his eyes but took it. His shoulders stiffened. "Whoa. What is this?"

Jasce eyed Kord carefully. "It's the crystal Prince Jazari was talking about."

"But how did you get it?"

"Someone gave it to me."

Kord arched a brow. "Who?"

Revealing Queen Siryn and Jaida would be too dangerous. "Someone. The who isn't important. I think it will lead us to the Empower Stone."

Kord slowly returned the leather band, unable to hide the shiver that coursed through him. "Who gave it to you?"

Jasce reattached the band and almost sighed as his power ignited. "I can't say. You'll just have to trust me."

Kord frowned. "Okay, but why? Why give it to you?"

Jasce shook his head. "Did you hear what I said? We might be able to find a section of the Heart. Imagine how many people you could heal."

Kord held up a finger. "Don't."

"Don't what?"

"Don't make this about anyone but you." Jasce bristled, but Kord continued, "You've always sought power, but you don't know what that crystal will do to you."

Jasce pointed to his wrist. "If I would've had this, you might still have your eye. Besides, all it's done is strengthen my magic." That wasn't totally true, but he could already see the concern on Kord's face. The trembling hands and constant ache behind his eyes seemed to be getting worse. But it wasn't anything he couldn't handle. He just needed to acclimate to the magic. He took another sip of whiskey and forced himself to relax.

"I don't like this." Kord scratched his jaw. "Have you told Kenz?"

"No. We seem to argue most of the time or miss each other completely."

"Well, I think you should tell her, and I want you to be honest with me if something happens with your magic." Jasce opened his mouth, but Kord interrupted him again. "I mean it. The second you feel, I don't know, *different*, you need to tell me."

"Fine," he said, raising his hands.

They were both quiet while they drank. Two Baltens entered the tavern, both nodding to Jasce and Kord. Seeing them made Jasce remember the sword fighting contest. He rested his elbow on the bar and rubbed his eyes.

"I still can't believe I lost."

Kord patted his back. "The experience is an essential part of the journey, not just winning and losing."

Jasce rolled his eyes. Kord and his sayings. Sometimes they baffled him and other times he wanted to simply smack the man.

"Speaking of losing," Kord said, facing him. "Not super happy about you promoting my sister to captain, especially in her condition."

"I share your worry, but she deserves it and is more than qualified."

"Yes, she is, but she's also a little impetuous, like someone else I know. Always needing to prove herself." Kord raked his fingers through his hair, making the ends stand up.

Jasce chuckled. "That she is. But holding Kenz back is like trying to keep the waves from crashing on the shore. I won't do that to her."

Kord grunted and signaled the bartender for another drink.

Jasce agreed with Kord, but he also knew he had run out of excuses

Embracing the Darkness

for not promoting Kenz. He just hoped that with the baby, she'd be more careful.

He counted the number of bottles in front of the gilded mirror behind the bar. Thinking about the tiresome meetings and other events occurring during the Gathering, he longed for the adrenaline rush he'd encountered when rescuing Emile and fighting the Snatchers. He had felt so alive. Something he hadn't experienced in a long time.

He had craved that rush as a Hunter—donning his mask and raiding villages. He gritted his teeth. That's not who he wanted to be anymore, but being the queen's lackey wasn't something he enjoyed, either. The image of Emile with tubes sticking out of her flashed in his mind. If the queen discovered he had Drexus's crystal, or if he found the Empower Stone, would she try to remove his magic? The thought had him squeezing his fists.

Jasce sighed, needing to focus his thoughts elsewhere. "Are you happy working in the Sanctuary, living in Orilyon instead of Carhurst?"

Kord wiped the ale from his lips. "I am. It was a bit of an adjustment, but I love the work I'm doing with the Healers and with medicine. I don't trust the Vastanes, but they do have valuable knowledge, and what we did to help Emile . . . I know you don't approve, but it was an important medical advancement. So, yes, I'm happy." He looked at Jasce. "Are you?"

"No, not really. I'm a warrior and not cut out for politics, and I really don't enjoy taking orders, especially from the queen." He stared at his hands and the slight tremor in his fingers. "All I wanted was a normal life with Kenz."

Jasce finished the contents in his glass, savoring the alcohol burning down his throat and warming his stomach. Thanks to Kord, his head and side no longer hurt, and he could see fully out of his blackened eye.

Kord swiveled on his stool. "Jasce, there isn't 'normal life.' Just life and what you make of it."

"And what am I supposed to make of it? I'm balancing on the edge of a blade. Every step I make toward a future with Kenz seems to be in the wrong direction. The idea of being a dad scares the hell out of me, and I'm constantly fighting my rage. It's always present. I wanted to slash my knife across Larkin's throat." He rubbed his temples. "I'm broken, Kord. A murderer, monster."

The Healer sighed. "Stop letting your past define you."

Jasce chewed on the side of his thumbnail. The line between his past and present blurred, obscuring his vision. The anger he'd worked so hard to defeat was becoming second nature again—the Angel of Death reborn from the ashes.

Jasce scrubbed his face. "I can't escape who I am, and I can't have a kid. What kind of father will I be? Kenz deserves better."

Kord took a long drink. The bartender lounged on the other end of the bar, cleaning glasses, while patrons played a quiet game of dice in the corner. "You know I'm protective of my sister, hence not happy about her promotion. However, if I thought you shouldn't be together, I would've mentioned it. You both complement each other beautifully." Jasce raised his brows, and Kord chuckled. "Not perfectly, but beautifully."

Jasce stared at the ink on his right arm. Besides the Watch Guard tattoo, which he'd had altered, the rest remained. Every kill, every job, was carved into his skin. A visual reminder of who he'd been, but also what he'd overcome, or at least, was trying to. He took another sip of his drink. His head swam from the alcohol, but his shoulders finally unhooked themselves from his ears.

"And you'll be a great father," Kord said. "I've learned that children need their dads to love their mother and protect the family. You're already doing both, Jasce. So give yourself a break."

Jasce processed his friend's words. Because of Kenz, he strived to be a man worthy of her love and respect. She was his lighthouse, but he was trapped in a storm and that light had dimmed.

He was still upset with her for keeping secrets. But what a hypocrite he was for keeping one from her.

It was time to tell her the truth, about the crystal, at least. He couldn't mention Jaida, not yet. But he could start here. He wouldn't lose the only good thing in his life.

He placed his empty glass on the bar. "Thanks, Kord."

Kord slid off the stool. "I'm always here for you. But next time you want to be alone, can you pick a cleaner tavern?" He grimaced at the filth on the floor and bar.

Jasce laughed. "I'll keep that in mind." His steps were lighter as he emerged from the tavern and headed for the Bastion in search of Kenz. He ignored the pounding against his protective shield blocking Spectral emotions. He wouldn't allow his past to have any leverage in his life. Not again.

Chapter Twenty-Three

Jasce pushed open the door to his suite and froze. Captain Reed sat with Kenz at the table, with the fire crackling behind them. He clenched his teeth and glared at Reed when they turned to face him.

Kenz crossed her arms and leaned back in her chair. "We've been waiting for you." She scanned his body, frowning as she noticed the blood on his tunic.

Jasce tore his gaze from the captain. Informing Kenz he'd been drinking probably wasn't the best response, even if he had been with her brother. "And why is that?" he asked.

He didn't know why it bothered him to have Reed in his rooms with his fiancée. He trusted the man with his life, but lately paranoia and suspicion clung to him like a noxious odor, and he found himself constantly looking over his shoulder.

Reed crossed an ankle over his knee and drummed his fingers on the table. "I needed to talk to you in private."

Jasce placed his swords near the door and sat across from the captain, whose eyes drifted to the dagger still on his thigh. "About what?"

"The Heart of Pandaren."

He raised his brows. Kenz set a cup of coffee in front of him, giving him a knowing look.

"Lord Rollant has contacts in Alturia and has known about the crystal for a while. We were searching for it the day the Watch Guard attacked Carhurst," the captain explained.

"So that's where you were." He had wondered about that for months. He'd almost died that day—would have if not for the woman sitting next to him. "Why are you looking for the Heart?"

Reed's gaze narrowed. "Because if a Spectral gets just one piece, they'd be unstoppable. Us non-magical folks wouldn't stand a chance."

Jasce held the captain's stare and rested his arms on the table. "Did you find anything?"

Reed shook his head. "But we have an idea of where two of the Stones might be."

Jasce paused as he raised the mug to his mouth, the contents rippling on the surface. The tremors in his hands had increased as the whiskey wore off. "Where?" His stomach tightened while he waited for Reed to answer.

The captain continued to strum his fingers on the table. The desire to crush the twiddling digits had Jasce fisting his hands to the point where his knuckles cracked.

"Does Queen Valeri know?" Kenz asked, her eyes darting between the two men.

"Lord Rollant's meeting with her now."

Jasce crossed his arms and went with a different tactic. "Why tell me?"

"Lord Rollant trusts you."

Jasce snorted.

"He does. He also thinks you may have seen a fragment of the Empower Stone."

He kept his face neutral and gave the man a taste of his own medicine. A log shifted in the fireplace. Kenz sipped his coffee while he waited out the captain.

Reed's lips curved into a smile. "I'm sure Prince Jazari told you the story of the missing sliver of one section of the Heart." Jasce nodded. "After Drexus's attack on Hillford, I explained to Lord Rollant the

Embracing the Darkness

power I'd seen, and we wondered if Drexus had it, maybe disguised as a ring or another piece of jewelry. But after you killed him, his body disappeared." The captain shrugged.

"Wait," Kenz said, turning toward Jasce. "You cut off his hand. Did you see a ring?"

He kept his arms under the table so Reed wouldn't notice the leather band around his wrist. "I was a little preoccupied." Technically, it wasn't a lie.

Reed narrowed his eyes. "Well, Lord Rollant has a theory that the crystal can locate the other pieces. We also suspect Drexus probably knew this. Since the Angel of Death was his closest confidant, we thought you might be privy to some information."

Jasce ignored the captain's remark. That's two people who'd said the crystal could find the pieces of the Heart. His magic pulsed inside him. The sliver had already increased the power rushing through his veins, and he still hadn't had the chance to really test it. But if he retrieved the Empower Stone? Who knew what he'd be able to do?

We'd be invincible.

Jasce's shoulders tensed. His eyes danced around the room, checking the shadows and dark corners.

Empty. Which he expected. Why he kept looking outside himself for the voice, he didn't know. The alternative wasn't something he wanted to consider.

Kenz followed his gaze and then stared at him, her eyes widening as if to ask if he was okay.

Reed unfolded himself from the chair. "If you think of anything, let me know. We need to locate the pieces of the Heart before they fall into the hands of someone like Drexus."

Jasce trudged to the door with the captain on his heels.

The man scanned his face. "You don't look so good."

His hand flexed on the doorjamb. "Yeah, I keep hearing that. Where do you think it is?" He inwardly rolled his eyes at his lack of discretion. He sounded desperate, and Reed knew it.

"There are rumors about the coast and the desert. If you know anything, I need you to tell me."

"I'll see what I can find out."

Reed nodded and walked down the hallway. Jasce closed the door and leaned against it. He ran his hands down his face as he processed everything Reed had told him.

"I'm sorry about the tournament," Kenz said, moving to the couch and tucking her legs beneath her.

"I can't remember the last time I lost."

"Nobody's perfect. You can't win them all."

"Yeah. Your brother said 'experience is an essential part of the journey, not just winning and losing.' Whatever that means."

He lumbered toward the fireplace and regarded the flames dancing along the wood. He hadn't become the most feared assassin in Pandaren by losing. Back when he was Azrael, defeat wasn't an option. He would never have allowed emotions to affect him the way they had today. The Angel of Death wasn't controlled by feelings.

Kenz fiddled with the hem of her shirt. "I'm sorry for what I said about you and Queen Siryn. I know nothing is happening between you two, but I see how she looks at you, and I don't like it."

"She's playing a game and trying to get underneath everyone's skin."

"Yeah, well, it's working."

He paced the room as rain splattered on the windows. Thunder made the glass shake. He stopped in front of the bookcase. "Where's that book you were reading? *The History of Pandaren?*"

Unfolding herself from the couch, she walked toward him and removed a leather book. "Why?"

He scanned the chapters as he settled on the sofa. "When I was young, my mother would tell Jaida and me stories to get our minds off my father's drunken tirades. One time she told us the story of the Heart of Pandaren. I remember thinking it was a stupid name." Kenz chuckled and sat next to him. Her leg pressed against his and he could feel her warmth through her leather pants. He finally found the page he was looking for—the royal family tree. "She said that a girl had accidentally dropped the Heart and a sliver of the crystal had broken off. She used it to become the queen—I think she was a Psyche. Anyway, the crystal was passed down through the royal family, just like Queen Valeri said."

Kenz traced her finger down the list of names. "King Valeri would've been the last one to have it."

Embracing the Darkness

"Right. Drexus must have taken the ring when he killed him, which is why the queen wanted proof of Drexus's death. She wanted that ring."

"So where is it now?"

He unhooked the leather band and held it in his palm. The voice growled its resistance, but he ignored it. "Here."

Kenz ran a finger over the crystal tucked between the leather straps. Her eyes widened and her bracelets ignited, the blue glow lighting up her face. "How long have you had that?" she whispered.

"About a week," he said, thumbing through the pages.

"I see. And why didn't you tell me?"

"Why didn't you tell me about the Vastanes helping remove magic?" He continued examining the pages for a clue to where the pieces of the Heart were hidden.

"Touché."

"The reason I didn't tell you is because a lot of people could get hurt if I did. Including you and our . . . our child." Even though he hadn't wrapped his brain around the idea of being a father, the need to protect the baby grew with every passing moment.

"Who else knows?"

"Kord and the archduke. I also think Amycus might know more than he's letting on." He snapped the book shut and tossed it onto the coffee table. Clenching his fists to stop the trembling, he leaned back and closed his eyes. The headache had returned with a vengeance as his frustration grew.

Kenz handed him the sliver, which he immediately strapped to his wrist. "How did you get it?" she asked.

He couldn't tell her about Queen Siryn, not yet. He needed more information and to verify that she really had Jaida and that she was safe. "I can't tell you." He opened his eyes but kept his gaze fixed on the ceiling. She slowly faced him and crossed her arms. "But I will. I need you to trust me," Jasce said.

They listened to the rain as it beat against the window. The couch shifted and she grabbed his hand, pulling him to his feet and leading him to the washroom.

"What are you doing?"

"Taking care of you. Now don't be stubborn." She nudged him onto a bench.

The corner of his lip lifted. "Stubborn, huh?" At least she hadn't called him a stubborn mule, like her brother.

She smiled and removed his shirt. His breath hitched as her fingertips brushed against his muscles. She retrieved a towel and filled a bowl with hot water, and the smell of jasmine drifted into the air to mix with her citrusy scent. He closed his eyes as she washed his face and neck and along his torso, ran her fingers through his hair, massaged his shoulders. The tension in his muscles slowly relaxed.

He rested his forehead against her stomach and wrapped his arms around her waist, thinking about the baby growing inside her. What if their child was like him, like his father? What if he failed at being a good dad? So many what-ifs and unknowns. So many people relying on him to do the right thing. He couldn't afford to make a mistake.

The image of Emile strapped to that table flashed behind his eyelids. "Promise me you won't let them take my magic," he whispered into her tunic.

Her fingers stilled. "Why would they? Jasce, you're one of the good guys."

He laughed, the sound bitter. "I'm not so sure anymore."

She lifted his chin. He could drown in the depth of those green eyes and die a lucky man. "We all have parts of our personality we don't like or are ashamed of, but you're not the man you used to be."

He wanted to believe her, was desperate to. He clung to her wrists. "Promise me."

Her brows furrowed. Lightly, she brushed his hair away from his face. He closed his eyes and leaned into the touch. "I promise." She knelt to remove his boots. "You've had a trying few weeks. You just need a break."

He opened his eyes and gazed at her. Her black hair hung loosely down her back, reminding him of the night sky. He tucked a piece behind her ear. "You're exquisite," he said, his voice hoarse.

Kenz pulled him to his feet, untying his pants. "So are you." She dipped the rag into the water and knelt to clean his legs. He shuddered

Embracing the Darkness

as she moved closer to his waist, unable to control how his body responded to her sensuous touch.

His pulse thudded, and his magic reached out to hers, wanting more. He held her hands and pulled her to her feet, halting her tortuous journey. "I need you."

She licked her lips. "I need you, too."

Trailing kisses down her throat, he removed her tunic and camisole. He admired her breasts and the slight lump on her stomach—his child. He swallowed and his eyes met hers.

She wrapped her arms around his neck and pressed her chest against his. He kissed her, softly at first, until the longing intensified. He was ravenous, starving—the need for her burned out of control. Picking her up, he carried her to their bed, removing her remaining clothing. His mouth never left hers as they became one.

His body trembled and something deep inside him writhed. The crystal on his wrist burned against his skin.

He groaned as they moved together. More, he thought. The urge to conquer and devour overwhelmed him, and all gentleness disappeared. All he wanted was more, *more*.

Kenz gripped his shoulders. "Jasce?"

He ignored her, taking instead, drowning in the feel of her, satisfying the desire, quenching the lust-filled rage. Harder. Faster.

An elbow connected with his jaw and indigo light blasted him into the wall.

He rushed forward like a crazed animal and crashed into her shield. He growled as her magic grated along every exposed nerve.

"What the hell is the matter with you?" she asked.

His chest tightened and black spots floated into his vision as her emotions pummeled him. Doubling over, he focused on his bare feet, anchoring himself to the wall to keep from falling. "Breathe, dammit."

In—air filled his lungs—out—and escaped between his clenched teeth. He peeked through a damp curtain of brown hair. Kenz perched on the edge of the bed with a blanket wrapped around her. Fear and anger radiated off her, slipping through the cracks of his protective barrier. As he rebuilt his wall, the pain in his head increased, and his hands shook while the crystal cooled against his skin

What was wrong with him? He'd never treated her like that before. Their love making had always been passionate and satisfying, but never volatile. And that's what he'd felt. Rage. He swallowed the bile rising in his throat.

Jasce collapsed into the nearest chair and rested his arms on his legs. His breath came out in labored gasps and echoed off the indigo light surrounding him. "I'm so sorry. I—"

He reached out to her but dropped his arm as she flinched and pulled the blanket tighter, woven armor protecting her from an enemy. He closed his eyes as a section of his heart cracked. "Please don't be afraid of me. Not again."

She lowered her shield. "Your eyes turned black," she whispered. "Like Emile's."

He retrieved his pants and slid them on, then paced in front of the bed, raking his fingers through his damp hair. His eyes changing wasn't a good sign and only meant one thing. He remembered Amycus's words the day he removed the magic-suppressing tattoo. *"I believe that if a Spectral were to receive another form of magic, they'd either go insane or die."*

He shook his head. He was fine and had been fine. It was the lighting that had made his eyes seem to darken. Nothing more. He pulled Kenz toward him and kissed her hair. "I'm okay, I promise."

She encircled him with her arms and nodded, but she remained silent.

The mounting stresses of the Gathering, the Snatchers, and his sister's whereabouts were piling on. And the lack of sleep. That's all it was. He was fine.

A laugh echoed inside his mind.

Liar.

Chapter Twenty-Four

Jasce received word from Queen Siryn the following morning. Almost a week had passed since they'd met, and his need to see Jaida grew every day. She was so close, somewhere in Orilyon, and it drove him mad not knowing where. She had consumed his thoughts like fire burning dried leaves to ash.

He breathed deeply and knocked on Queen Siryn's door. It parted, and Garan greeted him, dagger in hand.

"Your queen summoned me," he said, shoving past, stopping when the bodyguard gripped his shoulder. Jasce's magic spiked.

"Leave your weapons," Garan said as two other guards approached.

He glanced at the bodyguard and arched a brow. "I suggest taking your hand off me."

"Or what?"

He vaulted and within seconds, his dagger was resting across Garan's throat. "Or this."

The other guards rushed forward but Garan raised his hand. "Point made, Commander."

Jasce smirked, placed his swords and dagger on a table, and faced the living room. Garan cleared his throat and pointed to Jasce's boot. He pressed his lips into a thin line and removed the small blade.

"The other one, too." The corner of the guard's mouth rose into a half-smile, making his scar pucker.

Jasce handed him the other blade and opened his arms, twirling in a circle. "We good?"

Garan nodded and waved him through. The royal guest room was spacious and elegant, with tufted chairs surrounding a chaise lounge where the queen rested, dressed in a burgundy gown that hugged her curves.

"Enjoying the view, Commander Farone?" The queen's lips curved as she perused Jasce's body slowly. She signaled to a servant, who brought wine and glasses. "Sit and have a drink with me. You look like you need one."

He surveyed the grand room and marked the exits and any potential weapons.

"Sit, please. I promise I won't bite. Unless you want me to." She winked and took a sip of her wine.

Jasce lowered himself into a chair, his eyes never leaving hers. "I'm here to see my sister."

She laughed. "Well, you get right to it, don't you? There is something to be said for anticipation."

"I don't have time for games, Your Highness."

"Please, call me Evelina."

He glanced at the ceiling and took a deep breath. "Just tell me where she is."

"Now, why would I do that? This journey gives us the opportunity to learn more about each other, which would be beneficial to you."

"And why is that?"

She sipped her wine and licked her lips. "For many reasons, Commander, one being that you need me as your ally."

The queen sauntered to the window, revealing bare skin from the base of her long neck to the curve of her hips. "Just imagine what we could accomplish, you and I," she said, staring at the ocean as if she could see all the way to her island. "Uniting Pandaren and Vastane—even the Baltens would be fools to challenge us."

"Pandaren is powerful enough. Why would we need you?" he asked, rising to his feet, unable to sit still as his skin crawled.

Embracing the Darkness

Queen Siryn twirled around, a feral smile on her face. "Oh, Jasce. There's so much you don't know. Even your precious queen isn't aware of what the Vastanes can do." She crossed the room, resting her hand on his chest, and looked up at him under her lashes. "You could be such a powerful ruler, surely that appeals to you. Once you find the Empower Stone, you'll be unstoppable."

The power he had felt with only a sliver of the Stone had him wanting more. He couldn't deny it. And if he located a single piece of the Heart, he'd never be anyone's pawn again. The Vastane queen was right. No one could oppose him.

Her fingers stroked his chest and something oily lurched inside him. He remembered last night with Kenz and his rage-filled desires. By the hunger in her eyes, he'd bet Queen Siryn would savor the power and madness as he pinned her to the bed.

He stepped back and took in a tremulous breath. Pain throbbed in his head, and his chest cooled from where her hand had rested.

"Are you all right, Commander?" A light sparkled in her eyes as she watched him over the rim of her glass.

He cleared his throat. "All I want is my sister."

She tilted her head. "Are you sure about that?"

He held her gaze. "I'm engaged to Kenz."

A shadow flickered across the queen's face. "Funny. I was talking about the Empower Stone." She edged up on her toes and whispered in his ear. "You deserve so much more."

Jasce shivered as she teased his earlobe between her teeth.

Her meaning was clear. He could have a queen instead of Kenz. Be a king instead of commander. Sit on the throne with a piece of the Heart of Pandaren in his clutches.

Powerful.

Unstoppable.

Spectrals and Naturals bowing before him.

Queen Siryn stepped back, her eyes wide, and covered her mouth. "But what am I talking about? You're here for Jaida." She patted his arm and walked around him toward the door.

We deserve a queen.

He blinked.

Pull yourself together, he thought. He scrubbed his hands down his face and followed the queen. Garan waited with a collar. It wasn't silver like the ones at the Bastion, but a flat gray metal.

"So you don't get any ideas." Garan snapped the collar around Jasce's neck.

He cringed, expecting his magic to disappear, but as with last time, a kernel of power burned. The crystal pulsed, keeping his magic alive. Weakened, but alive.

With every bump of the carriage, the queen's body rubbed against his. The heat emanating from her had him gritting his teeth.

They had blindfolded him, which was ridiculous, as he knew the city by its smells and sounds. They passed the Meat Sector, then circled around the Steel District. The journey took longer than it should have with the twists and double-backing. He almost laughed at their ruse, but kept his mouth shut, allowing them to believe they were tricking him.

When the carriage finally ground to a halt, he had a good idea they were on the outskirts of Orilyon near the Textiles District. The hinges on a door squeaked and a musty smell laced with chemicals burned his nose.

"Mind your step," Queen Siryn said as Garan led him down a set of stairs.

At the base, the path sloped downward, and a ripple of heat wafted from a corridor. He stumbled and reached out his hand, trying to feel for the wall, but he brushed across empty air. Garan grabbed his arm. A groan reverberated through the hall.

"Who's down there?" he asked.

"The Spectral we caught with your sister," the queen said, her heels clicking as she passed him.

"Vale?"

Garan shoved him forward. "Let's go."

It took all of Jasce's self-control not to headbutt the bodyguard and break his arm. It wouldn't be a perfect execution with the blindfold, but it would be satisfying.

Embracing the Darkness

They finally came to a stop, and Garan removed the covering. Jasce blinked and peered into a cell, albeit a very comfortable one. A rug decorated the granite floor, the bed was draped with quilts, and a table and chair sat in the corner. If it weren't for the bars or lack of windows, the room would be cozy.

A young woman clothed in a simple blue dress sat at the table, the candlelight illuminating the collar on her neck. She twisted a long blonde curl around her finger as she read a book. "Garan, I've been waiting—" Her gray eyes narrowed when she looked up. "What is he doing here?"

"Jaida," Jasce whispered, gripping the bars. He cleared his throat and tried again. "Jaida, are you all right?" She looked uninjured. In fact, she seemed completely healthy—no marks on her, besides the collar.

His sister drummed her fingers on the table. She glanced at Garan and then fixed her gaze on the queen. "I'm fine."

"Of course she is. We wouldn't dream of hurting baby sister," Queen Siryn said, arranging her dress as she sat in a chair against the far wall.

"Why is she wearing a collar?" Jasce asked.

"Because I'm not a fool. Besides, baby sister needs to work on her control."

"Quit calling me that!" Jaida yelled at the same time Jasce growled, "Quit calling her that."

"It seems you two *are* related." She tapped her chin and examined Jaida. "You know, now that I look more closely, I can see the resemblance."

"You do love to hear yourself talk," Jaida said, the chair scraping as she stood.

"Careful." The queen's eyes sparked with anger as she pulled a metal device the size of a small dagger from the folds of her dress. Pleasure danced across her face when she pointed it at Jaida and pressed a black button.

Jaida cried out and dropped to her knees.

The bars jammed into Jasce's chest as he reached for her. He looked over his shoulder. "Stop! Evelina, please."

Jaida lowered her head, her palms flat on the rug, her back arching.

"Oh, I enjoy hearing my name on your lips. However, begging doesn't suit you." She lifted her thumb, and Jaida whimpered and sagged onto the floor.

"What have you done?" he asked, pivoting between his sister and the queen.

"We found one of those collars Drexus used, quite ingenious by the way, and made it better. Why just control the magic when you can control the person, too?" She looked at the device and then at him. "Just point and shoot." She aimed it at him, a smirk lining her face, but she didn't press the button. She stood, her gown swishing as she approached him. "That's why you need us. We always make things better." She trailed a red nail down his arm.

He turned from the queen and examined his sister. "Jai, are you okay?"

She lifted her head and wiped her mouth. A softness filled her eyes at the use of her nickname but quickly disappeared. Rising shakily to her feet, she sat in her chair. After brushing her hair over her shoulder, she finally looked at him. "Why do you care?"

"I've been looking everywhere for you—to fix this."

She laughed. "Fix this? Because of you, we are wanted criminals, and now we've been kept prisoner by this Vastane—"

"I wouldn't finish that sentence if I were you," the queen interrupted, her thumb resting on the button controlling the collar.

"We? Is Vale with you?" Jasce asked.

Jaida glanced at the queen and the device in her hand. A flicker of fear flashed through her eyes. "Yes, Vale is here. Somewhere."

"See, Commander, your sister is fine. I've completed my part of the bargain." Queen Siryn motioned to Garan and walked toward the stairs.

"What bargain?" Jaida asked, rising from her chair, her small hands fisted. She approached the bars, her eyes wide.

Jasce scanned her face, memorizing every detail. "I never got the chance to thank you for stopping him, for saving my life."

She swallowed. "Jasce, I . . ." She closed her eyes and took a deep breath, then whispered, "You can't trust her."

He loosened his hold on the bars, his hands stiff. The muscle in his

Embracing the Darkness

jaw ached as he stared at his sister, her gray eyes just like their mother's. "I'll be back. I swear."

∼

Wheels clattered along the cobblestones, matching the thoughts careening in Jasce's mind as they rode to the palace. His sister seemed fine, besides the collar around her neck and the fear that had flashed in her eyes. The queen was using Vale against Jaida. To what end, he didn't know. She still seemed angry with him, but he'd seen the concern when Queen Siryn had mentioned their bargain. Maybe one day, Jaida would forgive him for killing Drexus.

He leaned his head back, thankful for the blindfold so at least he could pretend he was alone. He had so many questions he wanted to ask his sister, especially about Drexus's ring. She'd taken it when they escaped the Bastion, so she must have realized its power. Did she know where the Empower Stone was? She couldn't—otherwise, Queen Siryn wouldn't need him.

Seeing Jaida in pain had almost broken him. But at least she was safe, relatively speaking, and now he had an idea of her location. And even though she wanted nothing to do with him, he'd get her out of that cell. Vale was another matter. The Earth Spectral could rot in there for all he cared.

The carriage jerked to a stop, and the metal gates of the palace courtyard squeaked open. The queen removed his blindfold, and he blinked against the brightness. Her face was so close, Jasce could see silver flecks in her eyes, feel her breath dance across his lips.

"You behaved yourself back there," she said. "But let me be clear: If you try to free Jaida, your precious fiancée will pay the price, as well as her brother and his entire family. Including those other two children."

Dread hollowed out his gut, and his anger spiked. He envisioned snapping her neck and then killing Garan. No one would know.

She trailed her hands over his shoulders, and he immediately grasped her wrists. "What do you think you're doing?"

"Just this." A snap and the collar fell onto the bench. "You really need to relax."

He closed his eyes and sighed as his magic rushed through him like a soothing balm. The queen's pulse thumped under his fingers, and the scent of her perfume clouded his mind. The image of killing her turned into visions of her moaning beneath him.

The queen raised a brow when he opened his eyes. "That's interesting."

"What?" he asked, his voice hoarse.

"I'm curious, Commander, have you enjoyed my gift?" Her breasts pressed against his chest. How did she get this close? Did he pull her toward him? He didn't remember his hands releasing her wrists and gripping her hips.

"Gift?" His thoughts were muddled, and desire made his mouth as dry as the desert. His body betrayed him, and they both knew it.

"The crystal." She leaned forward as if to kiss him and then whispered in his ear, "The power you must experience. I envy you."

Take her.

Jasce flinched.

"I can see the battle raging inside you. Wouldn't it be easier to give in?" Her breath caressed his face. "No one needs to know."

His resolve was slipping. His magic churned and chaos replaced the familiar hum. Wincing at the pain behind his eyes, he stared at his trembling hands. He needed to escape, flee from the temptation luring him like a moth to a flame.

Take her. Now! She wants you.

He bit back a groan. He could have her straddling him in seconds. The fight would be over, the release a relief.

"Stop!" He pushed her off him. Since he expected her to be angry at the rejection, confusion further addled his brain from the flash of victory that swept across her face.

"Your self-control is indeed impressive, Commander."

He released a shuddering breath, shoved open the carriage door, and indicated for the queen to get out. Garan stood nearby and helped her down. Jasce emerged and inhaled. The sweet smell of hay from the stable cleared his head from the queen's tempting scent.

She held his hand, rubbing her thumb along the leather band on his wrist. "Just remember your part of the deal. Bring me the Empower

Embracing the Darkness

Stone and your sister goes free." She glanced over his shoulder and smiled, then she sauntered toward the palace entrance.

He spun around and his stomach bottomed out. Kenz fisted her hands on her hips, her mouth open, hurt flashing across her face. Delmira stood next to her, biting her lip and looking away.

"Kenz, I—" he said, taking a step.

She raised her hand and an indigo shield rammed him against the carriage. She shoved past a guard and exited the courtyard.

He lowered his head. Queen Siryn knew exactly what she was doing. She had spun her web, and like a mindless bug, he'd wriggled right into the center of it.

Chapter Twenty-Five

Jasce searched for Kenz throughout the Bastion while trying to formulate an explanation for being with Queen Siryn. The queen wasn't bluffing—he'd seen the threat in her eyes, as well as a hunger that, for a moment, had matched his own.

His stomach clenched. Now that he was away from her, revulsion filled every part of him, whereas before, he'd been seconds from making the biggest mistake of his life. Surely his two magics weren't causing this reaction to the queen.

Jasce rubbed the back of his neck. He'd figure that out later. The need to fix things with Kenz quickened his steps. He had checked their rooms and the Sanctuary. Kord said he hadn't seen her and asked if everything was all right.

No, things were not all right.

He tried to imagine where he'd go if the situation was reversed. The tavern, which Kenz wouldn't do. She might visit Tillie. He'd check there after he went to the training yard.

He found her sparring with Flynt, who held his shoulder where a line of blood dripped down his arm. Kenz's face resembled the walls of the compound, impenetrable and unyielding. She lunged for Flynt, who barely raised his sword in time to block her attack.

The Fire Spectral caught his eye and shook his head. Jasce's lips curved. He appreciated the warning, but he'd sparred many times with Kenz, and she was usually angry. He wasn't worried.

"Flynt, go get that looked at," he said, retrieving a practice sword.

Kenz spun on her heel. Her eyes darted between Jasce and Flynt, widening at the blood on Flynt's arm.

"Flynt, I'm so sorry. Why didn't you say anything?" she asked, lowering her blade.

"It's okay, just a scratch." He nodded to Jasce and mumbled, "Good luck."

The courtyard was mostly empty, as it was time for the evening meal. Kenz's heavy breathing filled the silence while Flynt returned his blade to the weapons rack and headed for the Sanctuary.

Jasce twirled his sword and admired Kenz in her fighting leathers. Black curls clung to her damp neck and her cheeks bloomed with color. Her emotions were pulled taut like a bowstring, ready to release. Even her magic felt chaotic as it spun around him, taunting him.

"Can we talk?" Jasce asked.

Her eyes narrowed as she raised her sword, and the knuckles on her hand whitened. The teacher in him wanted to correct the tightness of her grip, but he thought better of it.

He stepped into his fighting stance. "Let's do this, then."

Her lips cut into a flat line. "Let's."

Swords clashed and steel rang through the courtyard. He allowed Kenz to unleash her anger and was pleased to see her skill continued to improve. He was reminded of the time in the desert after she and Kord had rescued him, when he'd commented on her being heavy-footed. That hadn't gone well.

"What are you smiling about?" Kenz asked, lunging and slicing her blade.

He easily dodged. "Just remembering when we first sparred. You're not favoring your right side anymore."

"So glad you approve." She slashed her sword again, which he parried.

"Are you ready to talk, or do you want to go another round?"

Kenz's chest heaved. "You're such an arrogant—"

Embracing the Darkness

"Yeah, I know." He spun out of the way, feeling the rush of air from her blade whip past his head. His patience faltered and a surge of anger pulsed through him. His arm trembled as he suppressed the magic that begged to be freed. This is why he only sparred with Caston, who had the speed, strength, and skill that matched his own. "We can do this all night, even though I do have other responsibilities."

"Is one of those responsibilities entertaining that Vastane hag?"

He squeezed the hilt of his sword. "No, I—"

"I've seen how she looks at you."

She lunged and he blocked.

"And how you look at her." She thrust her weapon at his chest, which he deflected. Tension coiled in his neck. With every attack, his anger grew.

"I'm not an idiot." She attempted a roundhouse kick.

The cord of restraint snapped. "Enough!" He ducked and spun on a knee, sweeping her legs out from under her. Her blade skittered across the dirt, and in seconds, he was on top of her, gripping her wrists above her head with one hand. The ground dug into his knees, and he could almost feel the Hunter's mask pressed against his face. He squeezed her wrists and savored the dominance.

Fear flashed in her eyes, and she gasped. The sound cleared his mind, and he immediately released her.

Horror twisted inside his chest as he stood.

She scurried to her feet and shoved him. "What's wrong with you?"

He regained his footing. "Nothing. I—"

"You tell me the truth right now. Or I'm gone, Jasce. I swear it."

He returned his sword to the weapons rack. A few soldiers practiced across the yard but kept to themselves. He could hear the seagulls squawking in the breeze and the rhythmic crash of the waves against the shore.

He turned and faced the woman he loved more than anything else. The woman who carried his child. What he was about to do could endanger them both. Would he be able to live with the consequences? But if he didn't tell her, he'd lose her for sure.

"She has Jaida," he whispered.

Kenz's eyes widened and her arms fell to the side. "What?"

"And if I tell anyone, she's threatened to kill everyone I love."

"But why?"

From the corner of his eye, he saw the air shimmer. He squinted into the shadows near the entrance to the yard and would have bet his two swords that a Shade Walker had been lurking nearby. Swearing, he grabbed Kenz around the waist and focused on his magic. Between heartbeats, they reappeared in their living room.

Kenz closed her eyes and breathed through her nose. "A little warning next time."

"Sorry. We had an uninvited visitor listening in." He poured himself a drink, offering one to Kenz who pointed to the bulge in her stomach. "Right." Swallowing the contents in a single gulp, he willed the tremors to stop. Not only were his fingers shaking, but his entire hand now quaked, making it difficult to pour the whiskey.

"Okay," Kenz said, sitting at the table. "Spill it."

Jasce smiled into his glass at her bluntness and a layer of weight peeled away from him. He was so lucky to have her. His nature of wanting to protect her warred with knowing she was as fierce as him. Thankfully, her soul wasn't tainted like his, and she didn't have a trail of corpses in her wake.

He sat and reached for her hand, then told her everything, from the meeting with Queen Siryn when she gave him the crystal to seeing Jaida for the first time in months. Kenz listened quietly, her eyes hardening when he mentioned the collar that had an electric shock to control Spectrals. For obvious reasons, he didn't tell her about the reaction he'd experienced in the carriage.

She ran her fingers over his wrist. "So, Jaida or Vale took the ring from Drexus, then got captured by the Vastanes. And now Queen Hag is essentially blackmailing you to retrieve the Empower Stone for her."

"That about sums it up."

"Why does she even want it? They don't have magic."

"She claims she doesn't want the Gemaris to get ahold of it. But I think it has to do with her lust for power. Trust me, I recognize it when I see it."

Kenz gave him a small smile. "Do you think it's safe for you to wear that?" She nodded her head toward the leather band.

Embracing the Darkness

He forced himself not to pull away. "I have a feeling I'm going to need all the magic I can get. I will do whatever it takes to protect my family." His voice sounded like a blade being sharpened on a whetstone.

She raised her brows, about to speak when he interrupted her.

"Is it so wrong that I want to protect the woman I love? The woman who's carrying my child?" He rubbed a thumb along her jaw. "Don't you understand? You are the light in my darkness. If I lose you, that monster lurking inside me will return, and I can't let that happen."

She kissed his palm. "Thank you for telling me. We'll figure this out. *Together*. Don't do anything stupid."

"When have I ever done anything stupid?"

She tilted her head. "Oh, I don't know. Maybe surrendering to Drexus to protect me and Kord. Sound familiar?"

He tapped his finger on his thigh. That had been a thought, to pretend to work with Queen Siryn and act like he was betraying Kenz, but she wouldn't buy it. And now that Kenz was informed, he didn't want to do this alone. He and Kenz were a team, partners, and they were stronger working together than ever being apart. "Okay, I won't do anything stupid unless we're being stupid together." He smiled and pulled her onto his lap. "I'm so in love with you, Kenz Haring."

She laughed and wrapped her arms around his neck. "Damn straight you are."

~

They had settled onto the couch, Jasce trailing kisses across Kenz's collarbone, when Caston barged into the room, followed by Maera and Prince Jazari.

Jasce jumped to his feet, his dagger already leveled at his Second's chest. "Ever heard of knocking? I almost impaled you with this."

Caston guffawed. "Your aim isn't that good."

Jasce arched a brow but didn't have the energy to argue or prove his Second wrong. He returned the knife to its sheath and strode to the table while Kenz rearranged her clothing, mumbling curses at Caston.

Maera mouthed *sorry* to Jasce and joined Kenz on the couch. He hadn't seen Maera since the procedure with Emile, and the Vastanes helping her remove magic still didn't sit well with him, especially when they had his sister and Vale. Who knew what they were doing to their magic?

He slid a look to Kenz, who gave him a shallow nod. They'd keep this quiet, for now.

The prince strolled around the room, stopping near the counter with Jasce's whiskey. "May I?"

Jasce nodded.

Caston plopped down at the table. "We have some information about the Snatchers and wanted you to know first."

"No offense to the prince, but why are you here?" Jasce asked, crossing his arms.

Caston scratched his jaw, an amused smile on his face.

"None taken," Prince Jazari said, and sat at the head of the table. "I received word from one of my messengers. It seems there was a similar creature, called a Lizak, that lived in the Charcose Islands."

"Where?" Jasce asked, unfamiliar with the name.

"You call them the Far Lands."

He glanced at Caston, who shrugged while Kenz and Maera joined them.

"Was? Does it not live there anymore?" Kenz asked.

"Supposedly, it's extinct. The last of its kind disappeared about fifteen years ago." The prince took a drink from his glass and sighed.

Jasce pinched the bridge of his nose. "And what does that have to do with the Snatchers?"

"It seems the Lizak has been modified," the prince explained.

"I'm sorry. What?" Jasce asked, dropping his hand to the table.

"The Snatcher Reed brought back had scars along its limbs. I almost missed them, they were so small, but they weren't random or defensive wounds. I really didn't think much about it," Maera said.

"It seems someone infused the Snatchers with the Brymagus plant." Caston stared at Jasce. "Like us with the Amplifier serum."

He felt his mouth drop open and quickly snapped it shut.

Kenz glanced at him and then at Maera. "Why would anyone do that?"

"What you should ask is how," the Alturian said, placing his empty

Embracing the Darkness

glass on the table. "The why is easy. Get rid of Spectrals and leave Pandaren at a considerable disadvantage."

Jasce stood and grabbed the decanter and some glasses. This wasn't what he needed. It was one thing to have some random creature hunting Spectrals, but another to learn someone had specifically created and unleashed these animals on purpose.

He took a long swallow of his drink. "Does the queen know?" he asked as the door opened.

"Does the queen know what?" Kord asked, followed by Amycus, dressed in his typical blacksmith clothing, minus the apron.

Kenz rolled her eyes. "Doesn't anyone know how to knock?"

Kord chuckled and rubbed the top of her head. She slapped his hand away. Amycus smiled at Jasce, but it didn't reach his eyes. His face was pale, and he looked like he'd lost even more weight.

Maera filled them in on her discovery with Prince Jazari adding the part about the possible origin of the Snatchers.

"And to answer your question," Caston said to Jasce. "Not yet." He slid a glance toward Maera, who gave him a small smile.

"We wanted your take on this," Maera said. "The queen's in the middle of negotiations."

Jasce motioned to the prince. "Negotiations you're currently missing?"

Prince Jazari waved him off. "She's meeting with the Baltens right now."

He tried to hide the tremor in his hand but caught both Kord and Amycus watching him. He finished the contents in his glass and poured another one, hoping the alcohol would help. "Who benefits the most with Spectrals out of the way?"

"Any kingdom with magic," Kenz said, wincing at Prince Jazari. "No offense."

He smiled, and his silver eyes shined. "Again, none taken."

Jasce observed the prince. There'd been no animosity between the Alturians and Pandaren. In fact, there'd been none with any of the kingdoms, besides the Vastanes, and that was over fourteen years ago. He wondered if it'd been the prince hiding in the shadows when he mentioned Queen Siryn having Jaida. If not, had he already been informed?

"I know what you're thinking, Commander," the prince said.

"I doubt it."

A loud thunk under the table caused Jasce to wince. Both Caston and Kord gave him a look. Amycus chuckled.

"I'll let you talk this through." Prince Jazari stood and paused in the entryway. "Commander, the Alturians are on your side. Remember that." The door shut behind him.

Amycus steepled his fingers under his chin and stared at the ceiling. "I don't think Nicolaus would have offered this information if he wasn't being honest."

"Unless he's trying to throw us off course," Caston said, spinning his dagger on the table.

Jasce focused on the blade's hypnotic rotation. If what the prince and Maera said were true, someone took the Lizak and transformed it into a Spectral-hunting monster.

More questions with no answers.

Caston's dagger continued to spin. Voices drifted into the back of Jasce's mind.

Kenz nudged him, and he looked up. All eyes were on him.

"What?"

"What do you want to do with this information?" Kord asked.

He took a deep breath, stood, and paced the length of the room. "Amycus, you have connections. See what you can find out about this Lizak from the Far Lands, or Charcose Islands, or whatever they're called. I'll inform the queen, privately. She needs to know and would have my head if I didn't tell her." He stopped pacing and stared at each person. "Keep this quiet and mind your surroundings. Right now, I don't trust any of the other kingdoms."

Chapter Twenty-Six

The Pit hummed with activity as everyone prepared for the third event: grappling. Four sparring rings, each with two judges, were set up in the middle of the arena with stations on the outside for Healers and other medical staff. The competition was simple: whoever tapped out first lost, and the winner would advance to the next level until only one remained. Someone started a pool for fans to place wagers on the competitors, four from each country. Jasce would fight along with Kord, Caston, and General Nadja. Kenz had insisted on competing, but thankfully her brother and Amycus had backed him in his decision to keep her from participating. With her being pregnant, there was no way he wanted her wrestling with anyone. She was irritated with him, but these days, who wasn't?

The judges asked each royal to pull two names to pair off the competitors. Jasce, still annoyed that he'd lost to Garan in the sword fight, would've liked another go at the bodyguard, but Kord drew him instead.

The judges gave each participant a collar. Jasce attached the cool metal around his neck and embers of his magic sparked. He smiled at the leather bracelet. He supposed he should remove it for the competition. A hand waved in front of his face.

Caston raised his brows. "Hello, you awake?"

Jasce hadn't slept well again, the nightmare intent on clawing its way to the forefront of his thoughts. He'd been bound to a wooden post with a collar around his neck while Snatchers attacked everyone he loved. A Hunter appeared out of nowhere, slashing his two swords through the beasts and eliminating them. Kenz, covered in blood, had rushed to him and wrapped her arms around him. The Angel of Death turned, lowered his mask, and smiled.

Jasce had woken with a yell stuck in his throat and his hand gripping his dagger. His entire body, drenched in sweat, trembled uncontrollably. Azrael had saved his family. Not him. He'd been powerless, useless.

Jasce shook his head, trying to clear the image from his mind. "Sorry. Did you say something?"

"I asked if you thought Kord will win?" Caston asked.

"He'll be fine."

Kord and Garan entered the ring. The Healer rotated his shoulders and cracked his neck.

Caston's eyes darted to the tent where Maera and her staff waited. She glanced over and gave a quick wave.

"What's going on between you two?" Jasce asked.

Caston jerked his head and a flush crept into his cheeks, something he'd never witnessed before with the ex-Hunter. "Nothing. Why would you ask?"

"You're a terrible liar."

His Second sighed. "You'd think as a former spy, I'd be better at it." He ran a hand through his hair. "She drives me crazy. I either want to shake her or kiss her."

Jasce laughed, remembering feeling the same way with Kenz. Still did. He directed his gaze at the Pandaren box and found her standing next to Queen Valeri, her bracelets glowing blue. "I totally get it. And would suggest kissing over shaking. Besides, Maera probably needs a good kiss."

Caston snorted. "Not sure I should take romantic advice from you."

Jasce slowly turned toward his Second, who raised a hand. "You two seem like you're at odds."

He crossed his arms as Captain Reed, who guarded Lord Rollant,

Embracing the Darkness

mumbled something to Kenz, and her smile lit up her face as she laughed. When was the last time he'd made her laugh?

"She's pregnant," Jasce said.

Caston's jaw dropped. "What? How?"

"I really hope I don't need to explain that to you."

Caston huffed and rolled his eyes. "That's not what I meant. How far along is she? Why didn't you tell me?"

"Not sure it's my secret to tell." He rubbed the back of his neck. "She's about four months. I found out when we hunted the Snatchers." The way he found out was a whole other issue.

"You don't seem thrilled."

He searched Caston's face. If anyone could understand, it would be an ex-Hunter. "My hands are drenched in blood. No matter all the good I've done, there's no escaping my past. I mean, what kind of father would I be? Who knows what traits I've passed on?" He glanced again at Kenz. "She deserves so much more than this."

General Nadja fought in the second ring with an Alturian. The crowd cheered as she spun and performed a perfect roundhouse kick. The Alturian's head jerked back and he fell to his knees. In seconds, Alyssa wrapped her long legs around his throat and twisted his arm behind his back. Kord still battled with Garan while a Balten and another Vastane guard grappled.

"Whenever my father drank, I became his personal punching bag," Caston finally said. "It was either me or my mother, and sometimes he got us both."

Jasce tore his eyes from Alyssa's victory and contemplated his Second. Caston never talked about his past. In fact, neither of them really discussed the time before they had become Hunters.

"Our choices define us, not our circumstances. I'll never be like my father. I'd never hit a child or the woman I love." He spied Maera walking to the far ring to check on a wrestler. "Anyway," Caston said, pushing off the wall as his name was called, "you and Kenz make a great team, and any kid of yours is lucky to have you both as their parents. You're a good man, Jasce. You just need to believe it." He patted him on the shoulder and strode toward the second ring.

Jasce thought about his father. He, too, had been a drunk, but he'd never hit his mother or his sister, even when he'd lost himself in a drunken rage. He'd done enough damage by betraying them to Drexus. Amycus had explained that Barnet had wanted to prevent Lisia from joining the resistance to fight against the Watch Guard. Had his father known, when he'd tried to stop Amycus from recruiting her, he'd sentenced Lisia to death and that his son and daughter would practically be raised by the very man who killed his wife? If only his father had known that everything Lisia did was to protect their Spectral children, maybe things would have turned out differently. Maybe they'd both be alive.

Jasce scanned the arena and found Amycus talking with Archduke Carnelian. He hadn't known the blacksmith long enough for him to be a father figure, but he could see him becoming one. He already considered him a mentor and friend.

He still needed to talk to him about the crystal, but strangely, the man had been difficult to get alone. As if sensing his gaze, Amycus's eyes met his then drifted to Jasce's arm. The archduke also stared at him and then resumed his conversation. Even from this distance, Jasce could see the agitation on his friend's face.

Thunder sounded in the distance, and a breeze brought in the cool, briny smell from the sea, threatening another rain-filled afternoon. More cheers rang out through the stadium as Kord finally bested Garan. Jasce automatically looked at Queen Siryn, who was focused on Amycus and the archduke and oblivious to what was happening in the arena. What were they discussing that had her so enthralled she had missed her best fighter compete?

Finally, his name was called. Pandaren soldiers saluted him as he marched to the first ring. He spotted Lander, Emile, and Maleous, who waved with enormous grins on their faces. He gave them a mock salute, causing them to laugh.

Emile seemed to be adjusting well to being a Natural. Maera had kept him up-to-date on her progress, and besides a few body aches and temporary amnesia when she first woke, she was a healthy kid ready to prove herself among the other recruits.

Jasce stepped into the ring and rolled his neck. Raaf, a Gemari,

Embracing the Darkness

based on the collar around his neck, nodded to him. They waited for the judges to ring the starting bell.

The two warriors circled, testing out each other's strengths and weaknesses. Raaf was strong but Jasce was fast. Fists flew and kicks hit with painful thuds. The Gemari maneuvered past Jasce's guard and landed a flying kick.

Jasce spit blood into the dirt and blinked away stars. He widened his stance, breathed deeply, and allowed fourteen years of training to take over.

Raaf attacked with a combination jab-cross. Jasce blocked it with his forearm, ducked, and seized the man's ankle, flipping him. Quickly, Jasce tackled him and put him in a chokehold. The man grunted, and a faint glow peeked out from beneath his shirt. Metal clinked, and excruciating pain burned through Jasce's side as Raaf punched him. Jasce's ribs cracked, forcing him to release the Gemari, who scurried across the ring and got to his feet. Metal hinges covering Raaf's knuckles disappeared and the light from his gem dimmed.

Jasce struggled to a knee, his breath labored, and glowered at the Gemari. The crystal on his wrist warmed, and he focused on his anger instead of the throbbing in his side. He couldn't afford another hit like that.

They stalked each other around the ring. Jasce switched tactics to lure the Gemari in close. Raaf charged, and Jasce side-stepped and shoved him to the ground. He winced as the slightest movement made his ribs burn.

Raaf growled and attacked again. Jasce wrapped his arms around the man's waist and threw him to the ground. Raaf's magic pulsed, and the Gemari landed another punch to Jasce's damaged ribs, causing him to yell.

A crack formed in the protective wall blocking Spectral emotions and an unquenchable rage boiled to the surface.

Kill him!

Jasce jolted and the Gemari used the distraction and twisted, forcing Jasce to his back. He delved into his magic and bucked his hips to get Raaf off him.

Focusing on the ground, he breathed through the pain. His magic surged, even with the collar, and the crystal grew hotter. Jasce looked up slowly and smiled. "I'm going to kill you."

Raaf shuffled away as he noticed the leather band with the crystal glowing inside.

Jasce tapped into his anger and speed, then attacked, landing kicks and punches and bringing the Gemari to his knees. He scissor-kicked his legs and in seconds had them wrapped around the man's neck.

"Nice try, using a fake collar," Jasce said, his voice sounding strange.

Raaf grunted, and Jasce squeezed until the man finally lay still.

"Commander!" a judge called out, ringing the bell. Other people yelled but he refused to release the Gemari.

Suddenly, Kord was in the ring, yanking him off Raaf, whose eyes were closed, his face blue. Another Healer, Pilar, rushed to the unconscious man, while Queen Valeri and Archduke Carnelian strode across the arena, followed by Kenz and the archduke's general, Tobias.

Jasce tried to pull free from Kord but stumbled, doubling over and gripping his side.

"Jasce, look at me," the Healer said, holding his shoulders.

He glared at Kord, whose eye widened. Removing Jasce's collar, Kord placed his hands on his neck and a familiar warmth ran through him. "Come on. Fight it."

The power subsided, and his hatred settled into a smoldering hostility. Kord's magic coursed through him, settling his mind, and healing his ribs. He shook his head and blinked. The crystal cooled against his skin.

Another judge marched into the ring, his face red, and pointed up at him. "You are disqualified!"

"What?" He stepped toward the man, who jumped back.

Kord grabbed his arm. "Jasce, don't." He nodded, staring over Jasce's shoulder.

He spun and swore under his breath. Queen Valeri stood on the outside of the ring, her hands fisted and jaw clenched.

Kenz's gaze shifted to the leather band on his wrist. The crack in his protective shield allowed her worry to wash over him. He ignored the growl from deep inside and quickly rebuilt the wall.

Embracing the Darkness

The archduke bent under the ropes and before Jasce could move, his enormous fist connected with his jaw.

"What's the matter with you? You almost killed my man!"

Pilar tended to Raaf, who lay prone on the ground. His face returned to its normal color, but there was slight bruising above the collar on his neck.

"They shouldn't be able to heal him. He's wearing a collar," Jasce said.

Archduke Carnelian narrowed his eyes. "Excuse me?"

The queen stepped closer. "Commander Farone, I want to see you in my quarters immediately."

"Wait," Kord said, releasing him. He knelt next to Raaf and removed the collar. "Your Majesty, this is a fake."

"What?" the archduke said, marching forward and taking it from Kord. His brows raised and then anger flashed through his brown eyes as he observed his soldier. "It seems my man cheated."

The queen gave Jasce a frosty look. "Even so, that's no excuse for Commander Farone's behavior."

Jasce fisted his hands to stop the tremors and also to regain control of his fury. The desire to lash out almost overcame him.

"You will report to my room when this is over," Queen Valeri said to him and returned to the viewing box. The archduke glared at Jasce and pointedly looked at the leather band on his wrist. He followed his soldier and Pilar to the Healer's tent. Fights broke out and cheers rang through the stands as Jasce and Kord left the ring.

Kord led Jasce to the other side of the arena, away from prying eyes and ears. He crossed his massive arms and waited.

"What?" Jasce growled.

"I don't think you should wear that crystal anymore."

"I lost my temper, that's all." Jasce put some distance between them.

"That's twice now, and both times you were wearing that. I think it's affecting your magic more than you want to admit."

"Why do you say that?"

"Because your eyes turned black."

Jasce glanced at the stands, his gaze flicking over the royal boxes. Archduke Carnelian hadn't returned to his place and Amycus was gone.

He found Kenz, who was watching them intently. She had said the other night his eyes had shifted. He thought about Emile, how her eyes had changed colors and the hallucinations she claimed to have seen, and he remembered the image of Drexus in the hallway. Maybe the crystal was making him crazy, making the chaos of his magic worse.

Just then, Kord's name was called for his second fight. "We'll continue this conversation later."

Jasce stared at the tumultuous sky and shook his head. Too much was resting on his shoulders. He couldn't afford to lose his mind.

We're stronger than that. Trust me.

The voice made him grind his teeth. It seemed, no matter what Caston said regarding his past, the monster he used to be still skulked in the shadows.

Chapter Twenty-Seven

Rain dripped down the back of Jasce's tunic as he observed a group of fifth-year recruits practicing. Throwing knives sung through the air, most completely missing the targets as the wet handles proved to be a challenge.

Three days had passed since the grappling trial, and the scathing lecture he received from the queen still grated on his nerves. He'd been disqualified from the final event, archery, and his presence was no longer required during the meetings. That part didn't bother him, especially when Caston swore and mumbled every time he had to go. What did bother him was Queen Valeri not trusting him to "act like a commander and not a brutish fool." It made him seethe.

Kord had suggested telling her it wasn't his fault, that his magic had reacted strangely. But that would mean revealing he had the sliver of the Empower Stone. He wouldn't divulge that secret—not when the queen could take the crystal and his newfound power, and possibly remove his magic in the process.

Besides, the side effects were manageable. He didn't approve of drinking on duty, but the alcohol soothed the ache in his head and settled his trembling hands. Unfortunately, the whiskey did little to curb his nightmares, which were intensifying in number and in clarity. Most were of him either sitting on a throne with the Heart of Pandaren or him donning the Hunter's mask and slaying anyone who opposed him.

An internal clock ticked. He was running out of time, especially with only days until the closing reception would bid farewell to the visiting kingdoms. He still hadn't been able to talk with Amycus. When he wasn't instructing the recruits, he was either researching every book about the history of Pandaren or vaulting to different areas along the coast, since the only information he had was that the Stone could be near the ocean.

In his last vault, he'd traveled as far as Havelock. When he returned to his rooms, he collapsed, and the throbbing in his head made him retch.

"That's it," Kenz had said, helping him to the couch. "You can't keep pushing yourself like this."

"I have to." He rested his arms on his thighs and breathed through the pain.

She rubbed his back. "I'm getting Kord."

"No. It'll level out. Just give me a minute." He could feel the worry flowing off her. The cracks that had formed in his protective wall were making it difficult to block Spectral emotions, especially Kenz's. He seemed unable to repair it, which provided access for the dark presence that whispered into the recesses of his mind. He finally admitted to himself that it was Azrael's voice goading him to use more magic, to push his limits, to kill. It made no sense, but it seemed the Angel of Death had returned and he was getting stronger.

Kenz had lifted his head and peered into his face. She swallowed, and fear replaced the worry. "I think you should take that off."

She reached for his arm, but he yanked it away. "No."

"Just for a few days. You need to give your magic a break." She bit her lip. "Please."

Fury had risen to the surface, but he forced it down. Maybe she was right. Removing it for a little while wouldn't alter his plans. He nodded and held out his arm. The Hunter inside him roared, but his animosity dwindled when she unclasped the band and put it on the nightstand.

A soldier yelling his name shook him out of his thoughts. Wiping the rain off his face, he glanced away from the recruits to where Lander

Embracing the Darkness

stood, waving him over and pointing toward the entrance to the Bastion.

"I'll be right back. Keep working," Jasce said over his shoulder as he strode across the courtyard.

Caston joined him and they both halted when they arrived at the entrance. A young man with sandy brown hair leaned against the wall, one hand resting on the bars blocking the entry. He slowly looked up, and Jasce couldn't believe his eyes. The man had grown gaunt, his arms covered in small wounds similar to what Jasce had when he'd been experimented on.

"Vale?" Jasce said.

The Earth Spectral reached for him and then collapsed.

Caston motioned for the guard to raise the gate. "Where did he come from?"

Jasce kept his face blank as he peered out into the city. He knew, but how did he escape? Or did he? This might be one of Queen Siryn's tricks.

Once the portcullis lifted, he pressed his fingers against Vale's throat. His pulse was slow and black lines resembling veins wriggled up the side of his neck.

"Let's get him to the Sanctuary," Jasce said, grabbing him under the arm and then addressing Lander. "Find Maera and Kord."

Lander saluted and took off toward the medical facility.

They had barely settled Vale on a bed in a private room when Kord and Maera ran over. Maera frowned at the marks covering his body.

"Look familiar?" Jasce asked, crossing his arms and staring at the man who had been with his sister these past months.

She trailed her finger along the wounds on Vale's arm. "Yes, but the markings are different. Same idea, though. Looks like someone's been playing with magic."

Amycus entered, talking with Maleous and another junior Healer. When he saw Vale, he ran over. His eyes widened as he stared at the marks on the Earth Spectral's skin.

"Where did you find him?" Amycus asked.

"He showed up outside the gates." Jasce watched as Kord placed his hand on Vale's forehead and closed his eyes. He yanked his hand away.

"What is it?" Caston asked.

"It feels like he has more than just his Earth magic. I'll need a Tracker to be sure. But there's something else, another power that's not Spectral."

Jasce stepped closer and stared at Vale as if trying to see underneath skin and bone. "What do you mean 'another power'?"

Kord's brow furrowed as he traced the black lines. Jasce resisted tapping his toe as his friend's mind worked.

"Like Balten magic, but also Gemari. I've healed both, and this feels similar," Kord finally said.

Jasce's head snapped up. "Caston, find Indago."

Caston nodded and left the Sanctuary.

Amycus crossed his arms. "What are you thinking?"

Jasce paced in front of the bed. "I'm not sure, but a competitor was missing at both the Gauntlet Run and the sword fighting event. First it was the Baltens, and then a Gemari didn't show up." He looked at Kord. "Remember? The archduke wanted a rematch."

Kord lifted Vale's arm, inspecting the scars, his mouth turning down at the corners. "You think they're related?"

Maera stopped examining the Spectral and looked up. "Are you saying someone transferred other forms of magic into him?"

"That's what it looks like," Jasce said. "We'll have more information when Indago gets here."

"But who has the knowledge?" Kord asked.

Jasce rubbed the scruff along his jaw. "I'll give you one guess. But the question is why?"

Kord dropped Vale's arm. "You think the Vastanes did this?"

He slowly turned. "Since they helped you remove Emile's magic, they obviously know more than they're telling us." But they had to get their information from someone. He glanced at Amycus, who frowned. Jasce shook his head. Drexus couldn't be alive. There was no way he'd survived the wound Jasce had given him.

"I wouldn't put it past Queen Siryn. She's always craved knowledge and pushed the limit on what's acceptable," Amycus said, his eyes shifting from Vale to Jasce.

Embracing the Darkness

Jasce didn't miss that the man's gaze drifted to his bare wrist. The muscle in Amycus's jaw ticked.

A junior Healer approached Maera. "Sorry to interrupt, but Pilar is late again. She was supposed to help with stocking the inventory."

Maera sighed and rested her hands on her hips. "That girl is going to drive me crazy." She looked at Kord.

"I've got this," he said.

"Have a team standing by in case we need to remove his magic. I don't like the look of those lines," Maera said, leaving the room.

Kord nodded and continued analyzing Vale.

"I'm going to help Caston find Indago," Amycus said, and he left the Sanctuary.

Jasce scanned the area as Maera followed the other Healer to the storage room. Most of the staff were busy with patients or organizing supplies.

"Are you doing okay?" Kord asked. His one green eye examined Jasce's body, stopping at the trembling flask.

He hadn't realized he'd taken it out of his pocket.

"I'm managing." Kord opened his mouth, but Jasce raised a hand. "Look, I've got this under control, and I have more pressing issues. I need to figure out where he came from," he said, nodding to Vale. "Jaida might be close. Plus, I need to locate Consort Lekov and the archduke to question them about their missing competitors. I don't have time to deal with whatever is going on with my magic."

"Not sure that's what I call managing," Kord said, pointing to the flask.

Jasce was about to argue when a groan sounded from the bed. Vale's eyes flickered open.

"Vale, can you hear me?" Kord asked, kneeling next to his face.

The kid blinked, and when his eyes found Jasce's, fear flashed through them.

Kord rested a hand on Vale's arm. "Vale, who did this to you?"

Again, Vale's eyes darted between Kord and Jasce.

"Give me a minute," Jasce said.

"I don't know if that's a good idea."

"I won't hurt him."

Kord sighed and stood. "I'll be waiting over there." He pointed to the end of the row and lumbered off, glancing over his shoulder.

Jasce sat and leaned forward. The kid's brown eyes came into focus. "I . . ." He licked his lips, and Jasce handed him a cup of water. Water dribbled down his chin as he drank, his eyes never leaving Jasce's. "I couldn't get her out."

"Jaida?"

Vale nodded. "The queen said they'd remove my magic if I came here, but I had to . . ." He winced in pain. "You're the only one who can save her."

"I will, but I need to find the Empower Stone. Do you know where it is?"

The Spectral's eyes drooped.

"Hey, stay with me, kid." Jasce shook his shoulder.

Vale gasped, and his eyes widened. "You can't give her the Stone."

"Why?" Jasce shook him again to keep him awake.

His brown eyes turned black, and the darkened veins swirled faster up his neck. He gripped Jasce's hand, his voice sounding strange. "You will not take my magic . . ." He moaned and his eyes shifted back. "It'll kill me." With a sigh, his head lolled to the side and his hand dropped to the bed.

Jasce swore and gave him another shake.

Kord jogged over and touched his forehead.

"Can you wake him up?" Jasce asked.

Kord shook his head. "No. For some reason, my magic isn't working. It's as if his body is fighting me. What did he say?"

Only Kenz knew the queen had Jaida, and for now he'd keep it that way. He wouldn't risk Kord and his family, too.

"Nothing. Just a bunch of incoherent sentences." Jasce stood and rested his hands on his hips. "I want a guard stationed at all times. No one talks to him but me."

Kord crossed his arms, but Jasce was already heading for the exit. He called over his shoulder as he left the Sanctuary, "Let me know when the Tracker gets here."

He needed to talk to Jaida and see if she was aware of Vale and the experiments. The question was how, without endangering everyone he cared about. He strode through the corridors to his room to retrieve the leather band. He'd need extra magic since he didn't know what or who he'd find.

"Jasce! Wait up."

He sighed and focused on the ceiling. This was a complication he didn't have time for. He scowled at the flickering torches. When had his fiancée become a complication?

"Hey," he said.

Kenz arched a brow. "Hey yourself." He forced a smile and continued down the hall with Kenz in step beside him. "Is it true? Vale?"

He glanced out of the corner of his eye. "News travels fast."

"Well, when you and Caston send a teenager to get help, people talk. Plus, everyone knows you were looking for Vale and Jaida. I just figured. . ." she paused, and he stopped walking.

"What?" he said, facing her.

She licked her lips. "I figured you're going to look for her, and I'm coming with you."

"Until Vale wakes up, we have nothing to go on."

This is what he'd been afraid of. How was he supposed to sneak into the warehouse with Kenz? If Queen Siryn caught them, she'd use Kenz against him or simply kill her, like she'd promised. He wouldn't allow that. But he had no clue how to keep her from going.

He was still pondering this when they arrived at their door. Wood fragments lay on the ground next to the broken lock.

Kenz spotted it and twisted her wrists, igniting her shield. Jasce's first instinct was to have her wait outside, but that would lead to an argument they didn't have time for.

He pulled his dagger free and slowly pushed open the door. He motioned to Kenz, and indigo light filled the entryway as they entered their room. After doing a quick sweep, he sheathed his knife. Empty.

"Whoever was here was obviously searching for something," Kenz said, standing near the armoire. "My throwing knives were in the drawer, not lying out in the open."

He stepped closer and picked up one of the blades he'd made for her in Carhurst.

"I wonder what they were looking for," she said, turning toward their bedroom.

Jasce swore and rushed into their bedroom, heading straight for the nightstand.

"What is it?" she asked.

"It's gone. The crystal." Fury pulsed through him as he returned to the living room.

Kenz rifled through the drawers and searched under the bed.

He scowled at the pile of ashes in the hearth. "I shouldn't have taken it off."

She stopped and faced him. "You couldn't have known this was going to happen."

He mumbled a curse. "It was safer with me than by the bloody bed." His tone was accusatory, but he didn't care. The countdown in his head was nearing zero. He needed to figure out what the Vastane queen was up to and make sure his sister was safe. If Queen Siryn had experimented on Vale, then she might have done the same to Jaida. The queen obviously wasn't aware of the side effects of having more than one type of magic. Or she didn't care.

Kenz searched through the bookcase. "Maybe you moved it?"

He sighed. "It's not here."

He plopped down in the chair and rested his arms on the table, unable to believe someone had broken in and stolen the crystal. It could've been the Alturians, but why break the lock, except to throw him off? The archduke was the most likely suspect.

He massaged the back of his neck. What if Kenz had been alone in here when the intruder had come? The slight swell in her stomach made the knot in his gut tighten. She was a capable warrior and able to protect herself. Logically, he knew this.

She sat next to him and held his hands. "We'll figure this out, okay? Together." She gave a quick squeeze.

He focused on their joined fingers. The familiar sensation of her magic didn't soothe him like it usually did.

"I need you to wait with Kord in the Sanctuary. Caston is bringing Indago to see what's going on with Vale." He studied the freckles across Kenz's nose. "Can you do that for me?"

Embracing the Darkness

"And what are you going to do?"

"Question the archduke and then find a way to talk to Jaida." He stood and retrieved his swords, strapping them on his back. He double-checked the knives in his boots and the dagger on his thigh.

Her brow wrinkled. "I don't think that's a good idea. The archduke already doesn't like you."

"Like I care."

She rose to her feet. "I'm going with you. You might need help, especially with Jaida."

"No."

She rested her fists on her hips and tilted her head. "No?"

"Don't you understand? If you're caught, Queen Siryn will kill you and our child." Kenz's hand drifted to her stomach. "You've got to trust me."

"I do trust you. I just don't want you doing this alone."

"I'm used to doing things alone." He saw the hurt in her eyes and sighed. Pulling her close, he kissed the top of her head. "I'll be extra careful."

"Don't do anything stupid."

He pulled away and traced his thumb along her jaw. "I won't." Turning, he marched toward the door. He would do whatever it took to protect Kenz, their unborn child, and his sister. And if that meant becoming the monster he loathed, so be it.

Chapter Twenty-Eight

He'd searched the Bastion, the palace, the wyvern paddock, and the arena for the archduke and the Balten general. Caston had intercepted him in his room, informing him that Queen Valeri had taken the royals to her beach home on a private island, with the Trackers, and wouldn't return until the following morning. Jasce had let out a string of curses and thrown a vase. He was succumbing to the anger that continued to build. He'd apologized to Kenz for losing his temper, and she'd been about to say something about his magic, but he'd stopped her. Not using magic wasn't an option.

The next morning, before the sun permeated the night, darkness surrounded Jasce as he vaulted through the streets of Orilyon. Without the crystal, he had to dig deep into his power to get across the city. Every time he stopped, the pain throbbed behind his eyes and his hands shook violently. Using magic and trying to keep Azrael at bay was causing the side effects to worsen.

He lay on the rooftop of a warehouse in the Textile District while his magic renewed itself and squinted through the waning night to the streets and alleys below. He'd waited until almost dawn before starting his search, figuring there would be fewer Vastane guards to contend with. He knew roughly where they were holding Jaida but wasn't sure of the exact building.

He bit back his frustration as he adjusted his position, the tile from the roof digging into his hip, and thought again about the disappointment on Kenz's face from his recent outburst.

The Angel of Death cannot have a conscience.

Jasce jerked and swiped his knife through the air. Blood pounded in his ears as he scanned the empty rooftop. Drexus had said those same words to him when he was Azrael. Then his commander had whipped him, landing him once again in the medical wing of the Bastion.

He inhaled a calming breath. "Keep it together," he mumbled.

A man strolled down the street, periodically looking over his shoulder. Jasce noticed the tip of a sword underneath a long overcoat. "A little overdressed, aren't we?"

Even though the sun hadn't crested the horizon, the humidity pressed down on Jasce like a wet blanket. The man glanced up and down the alley before entering a building with boarded-up windows.

Jasce scanned the area and vaulted across the street. Unsheathing his dagger, he cracked open the door. Two Vastane bodyguards sat at a table playing a dice game while the man who had just entered walked to the far side of the room and hung up his coat.

Jasce imagined the stairs Garan had led him down and envisioned Jaida's cell. He needed to appear somewhere in that area and hoped there wasn't a guard waiting for him.

With a deep breath, he focused once more on his magic and disappeared.

"What the—"

A soldier jumped and drew his sword. Jasce swore and used his speed to lunge for the man, grabbing his neck while he spun him around. The crack echoed through the corridor. A shooting pain jabbed through his skull and his hands shook as he dragged the body down the hall.

Jaida stood in the center of her cell with her hand covering her mouth. "What are you doing?" she whispered.

He listened for any noise from upstairs. "Look, I don't have a lot of time. Are you okay?"

Embracing the Darkness

She wrapped her arms around her waist. "Yes, I'm fine. But why are you here? If the queen finds you . . ."

"She won't. Is she experimenting on you?"

"What?" Jaida's brow furrowed. "No, she rarely comes down here. What's going on?"

He peered down the corridor. He had a choice to make—to either trust his sister or not. "Vale showed up outside the Bastion," he whispered.

She scampered forward and gripped the bars. "He what? How?"

"When was the last time you've seen or talked to him?"

"It's been a couple of weeks. Why?"

"He's been experimented on, Jai. I don't know for certain, but we think he has other types of magic in him, from possibly the Baltens and the Gemaris." A door creaked upstairs. "Listen, combining magic has side effects."

"Don't you have more than one type?"

He nodded. "I don't have time to explain, but it's not good."

Voices sounded from the top of the stairs, and he swore. He hated leaving her here and was tempted to vault her out. But if Queen Siryn found the empty cell, there were too many people she could kill to make him suffer.

Jaida reached through the bars and squeezed his arm. "She can't capture you. You're the key to everything. I'm just the bait. You need to leave me."

He wrapped his hand around hers. "I failed you before. I won't again."

She looked at their combined hands. "You didn't fail me."

The voices grew louder. He had to ask the one question he'd been dreading. "Is Drexus alive?" He monitored her face for any signs.

She glanced down the corridor. "You need to go. If they catch you—"

A guard's voice echoed off the dungeon's wall. "If we don't find that Spectral soon, the queen will have our heads."

"Poor Tellis," another guard said. "Garan almost killed him for not getting the collar on Vale in time. That Spectral just disappeared from the room."

Jaida's knuckles whitened as she gripped his hand.

Jasce leaned in. "I'll get you out of here once I find the Empower Stone."

She shook her head. "Don't go near that thing."

"Did Drexus know where it was?"

Jaida bit her lip. The torches flickered as shadows danced along the wall.

"Please, tell me," he whispered.

"Where did Drexus keep his biggest secret?" His sister retreated to the middle of her cell. "Now go."

He wanted to ask more, to press her on Drexus. Based on her reaction, he still wasn't sure if his former commander was alive or not. But the footsteps grew louder. He ran toward the dead soldier and, with a tug of magic, vanished as the two guards appeared.

With his draining magic, he couldn't vault far—just to the other side of the alley, where he dumped the body behind some crates. It wouldn't take long for the Vastane guards to find it. But by then, he'd be back at the Bastion.

Jasce rounded the corner and cold steel pressed against his neck. He gritted his teeth, scolding himself for letting his guard down.

"What have we here?" Garan asked. Jasce was about to vault when the bodyguard said, "She'll pay if you disappear. You're in enough trouble as it is."

Light crept across the alley, and the clatter of hooves sounded from a distant street as he ran through different scenarios. He had a pretty good idea of what Garan meant about Jaida paying if he vaulted. And if Jasce killed him, Queen Siryn would find out. He was out of options, except one.

Jasce turned and shoved the blade away. "I need to speak to your queen. I have some information and thought she might have come here first before returning to the palace."

Garan narrowed his eyes and was about to bring the sword back when Jasce reached out, grasped his wrist, and twisted until the bones cracked.

Garan grunted and tried to pull free. "How did you know where your sister was?"

Embracing the Darkness

"You actually think that jaunt through the city worked?" Jasce laughed and walked toward the end of the alley, away from the boxes and crates that hid the guard's body.

Garan grabbed him. "What are you up to?"

He scowled at the bodyguard's hand, fighting the urge to cut it off and shove it down the soldier's throat. "Whatever do you mean?"

Garan's scar puckered as he sneered. "You want to see the queen, then let's go see the queen."

Jasce waved him forward. "After you."

"Yeah, I don't think so."

Jasce rolled his eyes and walked next to Garan down the street. He needed to get away from the warehouse before the other guards discovered one of their own was missing.

He sighed. "This will take forever. Hold on."

Garan snapped his head around and gaped at him. He raised his hands, but Jasce caught his arm and concentrated on his magic. He vaulted through the city and finally appeared in the palace gardens.

He would've taken a sick pleasure in watching Garan stumble away and vomit if he hadn't felt like doing the same thing. It took all his self-discipline to stand up straight and manage the pain.

Garan wiped his mouth and took a deep breath. "You'll pay for that."

Jasce huffed and then tramped through the gardens, toward the side entrance of the palace. A nearby fountain gurgled and splashed onto the blue tiles surrounding it. Lush foliage lined the pathway and dew decorated the flowers like diamonds as the sun rose above the towering walls.

"Now, where's your queen?" He hid his shaking hands behind his back and continued to breathe through the pain in his head.

Why do you hesitate? Kill him.

Jasce stumbled as a surge of anger and magic pulsed through his veins.

Garan stopped walking, his brow furrowed.

A familiar laugh sounded behind him. He spun on his heel. The fountain splashed, and a breeze wafted through the rosebushes.

Your compassion makes us weak.

Jasce held his head and muttered, "Shut up."

"What's wrong with you?" Garan asked, surveying the empty garden.

"Nothing." Jasce licked his lips and continued walking down the path.

He'd used too much magic and was losing control. He sensed Azrael crawling out of the depths, his strength growing despite the fact that he no longer had the crystal. It seemed his protective barrier was damaged beyond repair.

The clock in his mind ticked faster.

Hold on, he told himself.

They slid up the back stairs, passing servants who were starting their morning shifts. Garan led the way down a corridor leading to the library.

The clatter of heels resonated off the walls as Queen Siryn came around the corner holding a book with her attendants trailing behind her. Her brows furrowed as she glanced between him and her guard.

"Your Majesty," Garan said, bowing.

Jasce crossed his arms. He wouldn't bow to her. Ever.

The queen arched a brow.

"I found him outside the warehouse. He claims he was looking for you," Garan said.

Jasce shoved past the bodyguard. "I can speak for myself."

The queen waved her attendants on. She focused on his eyes and gave him a coy smile. "It's fine, Garan. I'm sure my assassin won't try anything, not with his fiancée's life in the balance. Or his sister's."

He inwardly swore. She had him by the balls and they both knew it. Somehow, he had to convince her he was switching sides, that the power she offered was more alluring than what he had here.

"I was considering your offer," he said, stepping closer to the Vastane queen.

"Oh, really?" She glanced over his shoulder at Garan. "You may go."

"Your Majesty," Garan started.

"That will be all." Her voice left no room for argument. The corner of her lip quirked as she stared at Jasce. "Which offer?"

He waited until he could no longer hear Garan's boots clumping along the marble floor. "I can't work for Queen Valeri anymore. She doesn't appreciate what she has. But you would, wouldn't you?"

"I'm glad you came to your senses. But I'm sure your Shield isn't supportive of this plan." The sapphires in her crown gleamed as they caught the light from the torches.

"Things aren't working out there, either."

His magic pulsed as Queen Siryn trailed a finger across his chest and down his arm until her hand held his.

The Heart of Pandaren glowed as it sat on a pedestal near his throne. A gold crown rested on his brow. Spectrals and Naturals bowed before him, along with Queen Valeri and the entire council. Power like he'd never known coursed through him. And at his side, Queen Siryn wore a silver gown cut so low he could see her stomach. She smiled at him and squeezed his thigh.

Jasce blinked and stared at their joined fingers. A breeze made the torches flicker, and the cold stone dug into his back. When had she pressed him against the wall?

Get control of this, or I will.

He spun and switched their positions. Her grip on his hand tightened and her eyes sparkled. When she licked her lips, desire hit him so hard he almost groaned.

Take her.

The need to taste her, feel her against him, to remove the crown and run his fingers through her silky hair choked out any coherent reasoning. He tried to back away, but his body wouldn't obey.

"Stop fighting this," she said, looking into his eyes and running her hands up his arms. "What do you want?"

Azrael surged to the surface and forced Jasce into the background. "You," he whispered as he pressed his hips against her.

"I can tell." She stood on her toes and licked his neck from his collar to his ear.

"And a crown."

"You'll have it, Azrael." She lifted his shirt and trailed her fingers along his back.

He snarled and his mouth found hers, the kiss full of fury and the need for dominance. Images of taking her against the wall flooded his mind—lifting her skirts and feeling her heat surround him.

Silky fabric wove through his fingers as his knuckles grazed against her thigh.

Stop! Jasce pounded on the barrier that had previously kept the Hunter at bay. Azrael had taken over, and Jasce couldn't find the power to restrain him.

Quit being noble. No one will know.

"Jasce?"

A growl escaped his lips, and he lowered the queen's skirts. He turned his head, and even in the darkened corridor, he could see Kord's shaking fists.

The queen removed her hands from his back and stepped away, a catlike smile lining her face.

Jasce's will resurfaced, and he forced the Hunter back into the shadows. Pain erupted behind his eyes.

What was that? He hadn't had control over his thoughts or body. And now, when he looked at her, he was appalled at what had almost happened. It was like she had some sort of authority over his emotions or magic that manipulated his actions.

Magic?

He gaped at her and memories flashed through his mind.

He opened his mouth when Kord's hand gripped his shoulder and threw him against the wall. His back hit so hard he heard the stones crack.

"I'll leave you boys to it, then." Queen Siryn smiled and escaped down the hall.

"What the hell are you doing?" Kord yelled, his face looking savage with the eyepatch he wore.

Jasce swayed, and his chest tightened.

The Vastanes had magic.

Kord's fist came out of nowhere and connected with his jaw. Jasce's head smacked into the wall, and the pain brewing behind his eyes exploded. Blood pooled in his mouth.

Kord swung again, but Jasce quickly raised his arm to block the blow. "Kord, wait."

Embracing the Darkness

Kord growled and pounced on him, wrapping his arms around his waist and throwing him to the ground.

Jasce's breath whooshed out of his lungs. He dug into his speed and strength and managed to push Kord off. Standing, he grabbed Kord by the throat and lifted him. Kord's good eye widened as he gripped Jasce's wrist. The only sound was his toes scraping the ground.

"I need you to listen to me. Can you do that?" Jasce asked, fighting the Hunter's rage. Kord's brow furrowed, but he nodded, and Jasce released him.

Kord fell against the wall and rubbed his neck. "Talk fast."

Jasce pointed down the corridor in the direction the queen had gone. "She has Jaida."

Kord straightened and lowered his arms to his side. He glanced down the hall and then back at him. "What does that have to do with what I just saw?"

Jasce narrowed his eyes at the flickering torches. "I'm not sure, but I think the Vastanes have magic. I had no control when . . ."

"When what?"

"When she touched me." His pulse pounded in his neck as he recalled all the times he'd been with the queen. "That's it. She must have some sort of compulsion magic, like a Psyche's power. But she manipulates emotions or desires."

Kord crossed his arms and glared at him. Even with one eye, it was still threatening.

"Please, believe me. I'd never do that to Kenz or you."

Seconds ticked by. If his best friend didn't believe him, he wasn't sure what he'd do.

Then, slowly, Kord relaxed and let out a breath. "I believe you," he finally said. "But you're still an idiot."

Relief swamped him, and his shoulders sagged. "*I'm* an idiot?" Jasce spit blood onto the floor and winced. Kord's right hook really caused some damage.

Jasce caught a flicker out of the corner of his eye and withdrew his dagger. Kord jumped back as the Alturian prince emerged from the shadows.

"I tend to agree with the Healer."

Chapter Twenty-Nine

"Prince Jazari," Jasce said, his voice resembling a growl. "Sneaking around again?"

"Sneaking? That's a little unfair." The prince laid his hand on his heart. "Honestly, I was on my way to the library. Shade Walking is faster. Surely a Vaulter can understand that."

Jasce crossed his arms. "How much did you see?"

The prince winced. "All of it, I'm afraid."

He inwardly groaned and wiped the blood off his chin.

Kord shrugged and said, "He may be able to help."

The Shade Walker smiled, his teeth bright in the darkened corridor. "I can be very helpful, when the need arises."

"I'm sure those are your needs we're talking about." Jasce glanced down the hallway. How was he going to maneuver out of this? Now Kord and the prince knew Queen Siryn had Jaida, which meant her life and Kenz's teetered on the tip of a blade. One false move . . . but he couldn't think about that now.

"If I may," Prince Jazari said, wiping an invisible piece of lint from his shoulder. "You don't seem the type who craves power above all else."

Kord snorted, and Jasce threw him a look.

"I don't," Jasce said. But Azrael did—always had.

Jasce could feel time slipping as Azrael's influence grew. If he didn't locate the Empower Stone soon, he wouldn't be able to save his sister and might be too far gone to even care. And saving Jaida was only one of the many things he had yet to accomplish. It was essential that he find his leather band and whoever had stolen it. He also needed to talk to Indago regarding Vale's magic and Caston to see if he learned anything about the missing Balten and Gemari.

"Have any of your people disappeared?" Jasce asked.

The Shade Walker held his hands behind his back. "Why do you ask?"

"Call it a hunch."

Prince Jazari stopped walking, his eyes resembling steel. "Yes, a week ago, actually."

"Why didn't you report it?" Kord asked.

"At first, we didn't suspect anything, but when she failed to show up for guard duty, Commander Faez went searching. No one has seen Braya anywhere." The prince's silver eyes scanned Jasce's face. "If you have any information, you must tell me."

"A Balten and Gemari soldier were reported missing as well." Jasce rested his hands on his hips. "I have Caston looking into it, but I need your help with something else."

The prince arched a brow.

"I need you to talk to Queen Valeri."

"You're her commander. Why don't you talk to her?"

Jasce ran a hand through his hair. "I'm not on her good side right now."

"Ah. What would you like me to tell her?"

He zeroed in on the prince's face. "I think the Vastanes have magic."

Prince Jazari didn't seem all that surprised. "And what brought you to that conclusion?"

"Another hunch. I believe Queen Siryn can manipulate emotions or desires, but she has to be touching you."

The prince sniggered. "Are you certain you're not thinking below the waist?"

Jasce clenched his teeth. "Yes."

Embracing the Darkness

"Very well. I'll have my people look into it, and then I will speak with your queen."

Jasce scanned the prince for his missing crystal but couldn't feel it. That didn't mean the Alturians were innocent, but the prince didn't have it on him. "Thank you."

The man nodded and disappeared into the shadows.

"See how awkward that is—having people pop up out of nowhere?" Kord said.

"Yeah, yeah. I get it." Jasce walked along the corridor. "I'm sorry you had to witness that."

Kord rested a hand on his shoulder. "All is forgiven. I hope your jaw is okay."

"You really do hit hard, you know."

Kord's laugh drifted away. "Why didn't you mention the queen had your sister?" Hurt laced the deep baritone voice.

"Because she's threatened to kill everyone I love." Jasce pointed at Kord. "Including you and your family. So I thought it best to keep it to myself. Well, except for Kenz. She knows everything."

Kord nodded. "Makes sense."

"Glad you think so." He didn't hide the sarcasm in his voice.

"I take it Kenz doesn't know about Queen Siryn manipulating your emotions?"

Jasce shook his head. "I wasn't entirely aware until right now. I'm glad it was you in the hallway and not Kenz. She would've killed us both."

"Yeah, well, that's why I was looking for you. Kenz told me that the royals have moved the last competition to today. In less than an hour, actually."

Jasce stopped and turned toward his friend. "Why?" He didn't have the margin to deal with the archery tournament, and wasn't allowed to compete anyway, which was probably best. With his trembling hands, he'd be useless.

"Negotiations are finished, and with the rising tension, they thought it wise to wrap this party up."

"What a relief this nightmare is almost over."

"Umm," Kord said, wincing.

"What now?"

"Indago is waiting for you in the Sanctuary."

Jasce quickened his pace. "Why didn't you mention this earlier?"

"Seriously? When did I have the chance? In between punching you or dealing with the spying prince."

Jasce grunted as he strode down the corridor. He needed to talk to Indago and hoped Vale was awake. They made their way to the Bastion and arrived at the Sanctuary. Maera worked with another Healer in the back room while the Tracker towered over Vale with his eyes closed and forehead wrinkled.

"Indago," Jasce said, striding over to Vale's bed. The kid had a tube in his arm with some clear liquid flowing through it. He grimaced, blinking away the memory of the transfusions and Drexus whispering for him to hold on.

The Tracker lifted his head and focused his white eyes on Jasce. He raised his brows as he scanned his body. "Something's changed within you, Commander."

"Never mind me." He pointed at Vale. "What can you sense? Does he have the other kingdoms' magic in him?"

The muscle in the Tracker's jaw pulsed. "He has traces of the Balten strength and speed, along with Shade Walking and Gemari. How it was done, I do not know."

Jasce swore. Surely the Vastanes had to know combining this many types of magic would kill the Earth Spectral. Why do it, then?

"There's more," Indago said, lacing his fingers behind his back. "He seems to have a small trace of Healer magic, which is probably why he's still alive."

Dread coiled in his gut.

Maera approached with her brow furrowed as she read a patient's chart.

Jasce surveyed the Sanctuary. "Maera, did Pilar ever show up to work?"

She lifted her head and blinked. "What? Um, no, she didn't. Why?"

His spine stiffened. "Are you missing any other Healers?"

Kord's eye widened, understanding making his broad shoulders tighten. "Where's Mal?"

Embracing the Darkness

Maera bit her lip. "I haven't seen him. What's going on?"

Kord swore and ran from the Sanctuary.

Jasce called after him. "Check the bakery. I'll go to your house." He faced Maera. "Gather all your Healers and wait for me here."

He needed to get to Tillie as quickly as possible and would deal with the consequences later. Tapping into his magic, he felt the tug deep inside. He pictured Kord and Tillie's home and disappeared.

He arrived on the front step and an intense pain flashed behind his eyes. His hands trembled as he reached for the door. "Tillie! Mal!"

Tillie walked out of the kitchen, wiping her hands on a towel. She'd tied her hair in a knot, and a dusting of flour decorated her cheek. "Hi, Jasce." She stopped mid-stride and frowned when he almost collapsed in the doorway from the pain. She ran to him and held him by the elbow. "What's wrong?"

He swallowed the bile that burned his throat. "Have you seen Mal?"

"Not since this morning. I thought he was at the Sanctuary."

He raked his hands through his hair. Where else would the kid go?

Tillie grasped his hand. "You're scaring me. What's going on?"

She wouldn't believe a lie—she was too perceptive. "Someone is experimenting with magic again. We need to make sure all our Healers are safe."

The towel drifted to the floor, and he seized her arm as she tried to run past him. "Kord's on his way to the bakery. I need you to stay here in case Mal comes home. Where would he go?" She stared at the open door, her entire body trembling. Jasce gave her a gentle shake. "Tillie, think. Where else would he go?"

She jerked, as if remembering he was still there. "I . . ." She shook her head and tried again. "The wyverns. I heard him and Emile talking about them."

He squeezed her shoulder. "We'll find him."

She covered her mouth as tears trickled down her face. He closed his eyes and vaulted. Without the leather band, he had to stop once near the Garden District, making a young girl scream. He reappeared at the wyvern paddock and fell to his knees. His head felt like it would split in two. He slowly got to his feet, scanned the area, and released a huge breath.

Maleous and Emile leaned against the fence, and both jumped when he called out.

"Uncle Jasce, you scared the—what's wrong?" Maleous asked.

The kid grunted as Jasce pulled him into a tight hug. "I'll explain later. Emile, I need you to go to the bakery and find Kord. Tell him Mal is in the Sanctuary."

Emile looked at Maleous and then at Jasce. "Okay," she said and jogged down the street toward town.

He smiled at the boy. "Hold on."

Maleous's complaint disappeared into the void.

Kord finally made it to the compound, with Tillie and Kenz on his heels, and gathered his son in his arms. He buried his face into the kid's shoulder.

"Dad, I'm fine. Put me down."

Kord mumbled something and then released him. Tillie held him next and Maleous rolled his eyes.

"I'm so glad you found him." Kenz's smile dissolved as she approached Jasce. "How much magic did you use?"

"I did what I had to." Jasce avoided her stare and watched Tillie fuss over Maleous.

Maera rushed into the Sanctuary, her chest heaving. "Pilar is missing. No one can find her, and she didn't report in last night."

Jasce swore.

Kenz reached for his arm. "What's going on?"

Warning bells tolled as screams sounded from the arena.

"Now what?" Kord asked.

Flynt ran in as soldiers sprinted by, strapping quivers of arrows to their backs. "Snatchers, heading for the arena."

"The tournament," Jasce said. Fear ignited inside him as he watched Kenz tighten the straps on her chest piece. "Kenz."

"Don't even ask," she said as she strode past him.

He grabbed her arm. "Please be careful," he said, glancing at her stomach.

Embracing the Darkness

She rested her hand on his cheek. "I will, I promise."

Jasce tried to extinguish the fear as he watched her exit the Sanctuary. He pulled a soldier aside. "Watch him," he ordered, pointing to Vale's room. "No one goes in, and no one goes out. Understood?" The soldier saluted and jogged into the private room. He then addressed Kord. "Get Tillie and Mal out of here." The muscle in Kord's jaw ticked, but he nodded and led his wife and son out the back entrance. He longed for the sliver of the Empower Stone as more screams sounded from outside. As he strode out the door, he said, "Maera, get ready. You're going to have a lot of visitors."

Chapter Thirty

Swearing, Jasce sprinted up the arena stairs, taking them two at a time while barking orders to his soldiers. At the top of the wall, Caston stood with a squadron of archers, the metal arrowheads shimmering in the sun. Screams echoed from the town below as dark shadows skirted through the side streets. With the tournament, the Spectral members of the Guard had congregated in the Pit—a magical beacon leading the Snatchers to their next meal.

Jasce yelled at the competitors below. "Protect the royals!"

Caston adjusted his armor and glanced at the town as General Nadja skidded to a stop beside them. "What about the rest of the people in the arena?"

"Get as many out the side entrance and move everyone else to the higher levels."

She saluted and ordered a group of soldiers to follow her.

Black shadows took shape, and Jasce quickly counted fifty as they rushed the Pit, some trying to climb the walls while the others attacked the gates.

Caston grabbed a crossbow and peered over the wall. "Surely they can't get through. They're not that strong, are they?"

"I hope not," Jasce said, searching for Kenz. She and Flynt were leading people through the back entrance with Aura and Breena, a Water Spectral, providing cover. He vaulted to the other side to make sure the way was clear right as a Snatcher dashed around the corner, heading for Kenz and Flynt. "Shield!"

She raised her hands and formed a barrier just as the creature rammed into it, causing the light to flicker. It lurched to its feet and stalked toward her.

Jasce found a crossbow and released the arrow. With his trembling hands, it only pierced the beast in the leg. More Snatchers appeared. He clenched his teeth, willing the tremors to subside. He couldn't afford to miss again.

I can help.

He weakened the barrier blocking Azrael and allowed the Hunter's power to work alongside his. As Jasce focused on his magic, the pain in his head lessened and his hands stilled. He let out a slow breath and concentrated on the Snatcher's white eyes. The arrow hit true. Dust settled around the twitching body as Kenz sliced her sword through its neck.

Flynt launched fireballs while Aura, her hair fluttering in the wind, sucked the air out of any creature that got too close. Breena shot streams of water and knocked them off their path, which allowed the people time to escape. The creatures didn't seem interested in the fleeing villagers, their attention focused on the Spectrals.

Prince Jazari appeared out of the shadows with a bow and a quiver of arrows slung over his shoulder. "What can I do?"

Jasce eyed him. "Stop as many as you can to allow the people to get to safety."

The prince ordered his guards to shoot the creatures scurrying around the side of the arena.

"Aim for the eyes," Jasce said, and the prince nodded, relaying the information to his soldiers.

A scream had him turning as Snatchers barreled into the arena.

"I've got this, Commander. Go," Prince Jazari said. Jasce looked down at Kenz and the prince gripped his shoulder. "I'll protect her with my life."

Jasce nodded and faced the arena.

Embracing the Darkness

A Fire and a Water battled two Snatchers, halting their progress while an Earth pelted rocks at three others. An Air raised his hands to suffocate one Snatcher, but it didn't stop. Before Jasce vaulted, the creature landed on the Spectral, silencing his screams.

Jasce reappeared and drew his swords. His magic pulsed. The creature reared up, its mouth open, teeth stained with blood. He pivoted, and with a graceful arc of his blades slashed through the Snatcher. Its head skittered along the cobblestones. A roar sounded from the remaining Snatchers as more bounded through the gates. Another Fire Spectral fell, her flames bouncing off the creature uselessly as it sliced her throat.

General Nadja and the Paladin Guard formed a wall of steel and shields while the Amps used their swords, strength, and speed to fend off the creatures slinking along the inside of the Pit. Jasce ordered the Earths to continue launching rocks and dirt cyclones to slow their pursuit.

On the balustrade, Caston and the other troops shot arrows at the Snatchers that crested the top, having used their lethal claws to scale up the rock face. Maera and her Healers dragged the injured from the fray.

The Balten guards fought alongside Consort Lekov. Their speed and strength made them invaluable as more Snatchers entered the Pit. King Morzov and his two Khioshkas, Arseni and Dasha, defended the other side of the arena. Indigo light and green fire surrounded the king as his beasts ripped the creatures apart.

Consort Lekov tipped her head back and yelled. Her body shook as what looked like an apparition emerged, twice her size, wielding a dual-bladed ax. The Defender flanked the consort and, working side by side, they slashed down every Snatcher that approached.

Garan and three of his men ushered Queen Siryn from the arena while light shot out of the Gemaris' chests. Glowing swords, axes, and maces appeared from their magical crystals as they charged the Snatchers. Over the city, wyverns dove from the sky, picking off the beasts one by one.

Delmira joined Jasce and cast her yellow light around the injured Spectrals. "Whatever you're going to do, do it fast." She gritted her teeth as a creature attacked her shield.

"Who's protecting the queen?" He pivoted and slashed at a Snatcher, who skittered back, piercing him with sightless white eyes.

"Amycus," Delmira said. "Do you want me here or with the queen?"

"Here."

Jasce reappeared in the Pandaren box as Amycus hurled his red fireballs. He slowed down a few of the Snatchers, but they still advanced, cutting off the exit. There was no way for the royal guards to get Queen Valeri to safety, and Jasce's magic was draining fast. If he was going to vault her out, he'd have to do it now and leave Amycus by himself.

Four Snatchers converged onto the box and one leaped, its claws aimed for Amycus, who raised his hands. The Snatcher crashed into a wall of air. Jasce spun with his sword and cleanly removed its head.

Queen Valeri's guard yelled as a Snatcher attacked. He clutched his chest and fell to his knees. Two other guards protected the queen as she drew her dagger, her jaw set and brown eyes hard. Jasce planted himself in front of her and engaged one of the larger Snatchers. It lunged forward and knocked him into the wall. A snap had him yelling, and his arm bent at an unnatural angle. His sword fell and clattered to the ground. The creature pinned him, snapping its jaws inches from his throat.

Using his Amplifier magic, he shoved it off with his good arm. He gritted his teeth, clutched his dagger, and jammed it into the creature's eye. With a yelp, the creature fell, taking Jasce over the railing.

More Snatchers surrounded the box, intent on Amycus and the queen.

Another guard yelled as she tried to fight a creature that snuck past Amycus. It swiped its massive claws across her throat, and her blood splashed onto Queen Valeri's dress.

Jasce slid out from underneath the dead Snatcher and struggled to his feet.

Amycus used the four elements—fire, earth, water, and air—and launched everything he had in a display of power Jasce had never seen before. The creature dodged and swiped its claw at Amycus's throat as he created a wall of air. The Snatcher hit it and ricocheted off. Queen Valeri raised her blade, but its momentum knocked her to the ground

Embracing the Darkness

with a sickening crack. Jasce hoisted himself over the railing and used his uninjured arm to stab through the creature's chest.

The queen lay crumpled on her side as blood pooled around her head. He pressed his fingers to her neck and breathed a sigh of relief. Her pulse was weak, but at least she was alive.

Wyvern shadows blocked the sun, and their roars sent the Snatchers fleeing from the arena. Amycus stared out the gate, his brow furrowed. He turned and his eyes widened at the growing puddle of blood.

"Get Kord, have him meet me in the Sanctuary," Jasce said as he wrapped his unbroken arm around Queen Valeri. He delved into the place where he imagined his magic lived while allowing Azrael more access to his mind and body. He focused on the beds and equipment.

A Healer named Brighid yelped when Jasce and the queen appeared out of thin air. He grunted when they landed, and the queen's body slid from his grasp. A sharp pain radiated from his shoulder down his arm.

"Help me," Jasce said, getting his feet under him and gently lifting the queen. Brighid helped carry her to the nearest bed and immediately rested her hands on the queen's head to stop the bleeding.

Where the hell was Kord?

As if Jasce's thoughts summoned him, the Healer ran through the doors of the Sanctuary, followed by Amycus and Caston.

"I can't get it to stop." Brighid's bloody hands shook as she looked at Kord.

"It's okay, I've got this," Kord said, taking over, his eye closed and brow furrowed.

She stepped back, knocking into Jasce, who swore. She studied his face and then his arm. "Your arm's broken."

"I'm aware."

The girl shook her head and touched him, leaving bloody handprints on his sleeve. Warmth radiated and he stifled a curse while the bones slowly mended together. He was used to Kord's healing, which worked quicker and with little pain.

She removed her hands, and he rotated his shoulder. "Thank you."

"You're welcome." She bit her lip and regarded Kord. "Why isn't she healing?"

Time ticked by and nothing happened. Jasce scanned the queen's body and noticed blood on her lower leg. "Dammit," he said, ripping away the fabric. A deep scratch cut through her shin.

Kord looked to where Jasce indicated, his mouth going into a flat line. "This complicates things."

Amycus rifled through the jars on a shelf and returned with rags to clean the wound.

Maera ran in, followed by Captain Reed. Her green tunic was splattered with blood. She pressed her fingers to the queen's neck. "She's losing too much blood." Maera scanned the room, but all the Healers were helping the wounded.

Reed approached Jasce. "What's going on?"

Jasce explained what happened while Amycus knelt next to Queen Valeri. "Lorella, stay with me now."

Kord opened his eye. "My magic can't get through the venom."

Pain lined Amycus's face as he looked at Jasce. "I'm sorry."

Jasce's brow furrowed. "This wasn't your fault."

Amycus pressed his lips together and lifted his sleeve. Jasce's leather band containing the sliver of the Empower Stone lay on the blacksmith's wrist. The crystal's glow faded as its magic waned.

"You?" Jasce whispered. Anger exploded to the surface as he lunged for Amycus.

Caston grabbed him and pulled him back.

Shame lined Amycus's face as he handed the leather band to Kord. "Try this."

Kord's large hand dwarfed the band and his shoulders stiffened. "Will the crystal's power counteract the venom?"

Amycus focused on the queen. "There's only one way to find out."

Jasce vibrated with suppressed fury while Caston kept an arm across his chest.

"Is that the crystal I specifically asked you about?" Reed asked, his face reddening.

Jasce looked out of the corner of his eye and said through gritted teeth, "Not now, Reed."

Kord quickly wrapped the band around his wrist and placed one hand on Queen Valeri's head and the other on her leg. The crystal glowed.

Embracing the Darkness

Seconds ticked by. Everyone watched the queen and Kord.

The blood loss slowed, and her leg partially knit together.

Maera looked warily at Kord's wrist and then at Amycus. "She's stabilizing, but we need to flush the venom from her system."

Jasce struggled against Caston's hold. He wanted to wrap his hands around the old man's throat and squeeze until the light faded from his eyes. How dare he steal from him.

"Jasce, calm down," Caston said.

He looked over his shoulder into Caston's narrowed eyes. Caston tilted his head toward Jasce's hand, clutched around his dagger.

Amycus sagged in the chair, and when he lifted his head, sorrow swam in his eyes. "I'm sorry," he said again.

"Sorry?" Jasce growled.

Maera stepped between them. "What's going on?"

Kord peered at the leather band, the crystal completely dark. The queen was still unconscious, but some of her color had returned.

Reed crossed his arms and paced back and forth, glaring at Jasce.

Jasce winced from the pain behind his eyes as he quickly rebuilt the wall forbidding Azrael access to his mind and magic. His body shook, and bile surged up his throat. Breathing deeply through his nose, he settled his thoughts and emotions. Rage simmered, but it no longer threatened to explode.

He glanced over his shoulder at Caston. "I'm fine. Let go."

Caston released him. Taking another calming breath, he led his Second by the arm away from the wide-eyed stares of Kord, Maera, and Brighid. "I want to know how those things got in."

"I already checked. The doors held."

Jasce went completely still. "What do you mean?"

"Someone let them in."

He looked over his shoulder at the wounded. Moans and the smell of blood wafted through the air. "Who would do that?"

Caston followed his gaze, stopping at the queen. "Do you think it was an assassination attempt?"

"Maybe. But how could you guarantee what the Snatchers would do? I wonder if they're attracted to the crystal." He pointed toward Kord's wrist.

Caston crossed his arms. "Yeah, that's something you forgot to mention. How long have you had it and when, exactly, did Amycus take it?"

He glared at the blacksmith, who held the queen's hand, his head bowed. "Why he took it is the question. Anyway, that's not important right now." Caston raised his brows and opened his mouth to argue when Jasce cut him off. "I need to talk to Vale. He is the key to all of this. I know it." He took a step and stumbled into the wall.

Caston gripped his arm. "Hey, are you okay?"

He closed his eyes, inhaled a calming breath, and nodded.

"No, you're not."

"I used a lot of magic, that's all." Using the Vaulter and Amplifier magic while attempting to inhibit Azrael had drained him. He couldn't deny tapping into Azrael's strength had given him an edge, but at what cost?

Unwanted emotions bombarded him. Fear, anguish, pain—they all crashed against his deteriorated wall. Azrael pushed against the barrier, trying to break free. Jasce tipped his head back and focused on the ceiling tiles. He counted his heartbeats, willing them to slow.

Kenz rushed in and scanned the room. Worry and anger made him groan as he bent over and rested his hands on his knees. Her magic contended with his, making his entire body tremble.

"What's wrong?" she asked, approaching him.

"His magic is drained," Caston explained.

"Jasce?"

He held out his hand. "Just give me a minute." He felt exhausted and completely exposed. Taking deep breaths, he slowly rebuilt his defense, brick by brick, silencing the emotions overwhelming him and suppressing Azrael. Jasce straightened, blocked the pain, and opened his eyes, hoping they weren't black.

He finally focused on Kenz, seeing the blood splatter on her face. His stomach dropped as he scanned her body for wounds. "Are you hurt?"

"No. One of them got through my shield, but it missed. I cut its ugly head off."

Amycus stood and approached him. Kenz frowned as Caston immediately grabbed Jasce's arm, pressing him against the wall. Kord got to his feet and wiped the blood from his hands.

"What's going on?" Kenz noticed the band on her brother's wrist. "Where did you get that?" She glanced from Kord to Jasce.

Jasce pushed against Caston, whose grip was like iron. "Amycus was the one who stole it." Bridled fury vibrated through his body.

Her eyes widened. "Amycus, why?"

Amycus opened his mouth and then snapped it shut.

Caston moved between the two men. "This is not the time or place." He indicated all the Healers and patients.

Jasce held Amycus's stare and then addressed Maera. "I want the queen put in a private room, guards stationed at all times."

Maera and some other Healers wheeled Queen Valeri into a room in the back. Jasce left Kenz and Amycus and stalked to the other side of the Sanctuary toward Vale's room. The Spectral needed to start talking, and now. He shoved open the door and stopped so suddenly Caston and Kord almost ran into him. Caston swore at Vale's empty bed. The soldier who'd stood guard lay crumpled on the floor, his neck twisted at an abnormal angle, with broken cuffs beside him.

Jasce bit back a curse. "This day just keeps getting better and better." He stormed from the Sanctuary. "Find him!"

Chapter Thirty-One

Jasce's boots thumped as he stormed through the corridor toward the command room. After a thorough search of the compound and surrounding area, there was no trace of Vale—he had completely disappeared during the chaos of the Snatcher's attack. Jasce wanted to rage at the failure. Vale was the key to finding the Empower Stone, and now he was gone.

The Sanctuary overflowed with the injured, the queen was still unconscious, and everyone looked to him for answers. Answers he didn't have. He wondered for the tenth time if the attack was a well-timed distraction for Vale to escape. Did that mean Queen Siryn was behind it? Did she have something to do with the Snatchers? More unanswered questions had him grinding his teeth.

He pushed open the doors and found his team waiting. Aura and Flynt stood next to the fire, talking with Delmira. Caston and Alyssa were examining the map of Pandaren, both with frowns on their faces, while Kord, Kenz, and Amycus sat at the table.

Upon seeing Amycus, Jasce clenched his fists.

As if sensing the fury radiating off him, Amycus looked up and half-stood. "Jasce, I—"

"I'll deal with you later." His hands trembled and pain throbbed behind his eyes. As everyone took their seats, he trudged to a counter in the corner and poured himself a drink, keeping his back to the room, which had gone silent. He swallowed the contents in one gulp and refilled his glass. The warmth spread through him and soothed his nerves. Turning, he walked to the table and sat.

"How many Spectrals did we lose?" Flynt asked. Amber eyes that usually glowed were like dull embers. The battle had drained everyone's magic. Everyone except Kord. Jasce could feel the effect of the crystal clenched in the Healer's large hand. The urge to take it had him leaning forward.

"Twelve," Caston said, rubbing his temples.

Flynt swore and rose from the table to pour his own drink. Kenz leaned into Kord as if needing his strength.

"We were fortunate for the wyverns, otherwise that battle might have had different results," Aura said.

Jasce peered into the amber liquid. "Did our lookouts get an idea of which direction the Snatchers went?" Even though they had stopped them, it had not been a victory, and he was done being on the defensive. It was time to launch an attack on these creatures, and with the visiting kingdoms, they could combine their strengths and destroy the Snatchers for good.

Caston scratched at his goatee. "One group headed toward the desert, but another broke off, going north up the coast."

Jasce's eyes flicked toward his Second. North, up the coast? Dread landed in the bottom of his stomach like a steel ball and the internal clock ticked faster and faster. He didn't have time for more meetings, but he needed a plan. He'd never admit it out loud, but he also needed a team for what he wanted to do. It would be foolish to tackle this on his own.

You doubt our strength?

His hand shook as he brought the glass to his lips. It was getting more difficult to block Azrael's voice.

"The coast?" Delmira asked. "Why would they go there?"

Caston leaned forward. "Let's start with what we know. Someone let those things in."

Embracing the Darkness

Alyssa drummed her fingers on the table. "Who has the most to gain by disrupting the tournament?"

"Do we even know if it was about the tournament? Seems overkill," Delmira said.

Kenz lifted her head. "Maybe it was about the Spectrals."

While everyone discussed theories, Jasce glared at Amycus. The blacksmith held his stare.

Jasce tore his gaze from the man and interrupted the conversation. "The Snatchers were a distraction, allowing Vale to escape. That's the only explanation that makes sense. The timing is too perfect."

Kord and Kenz stared at him as if telling him it was time to spill the truth. Jasce sighed. So much for keeping Jaida and the crystal a secret. Now more lives would be at stake.

Kenz reached across the table and squeezed his hand. "It's okay."

"What's okay?" Flynt asked, his eyes darting between Kenz and Jasce.

Getting to his feet, Jasce paced the length of the room. "What I'm about to tell you stays here. Otherwise, people will die. Is that clear?"

Everyone nodded, confusion lining their faces.

"A few weeks ago, after we returned with the Snatcher, Queen Siryn informed me she had Jaida and Vale," Jasce said.

The table erupted into exclamations. Jasce waited until they settled down to continue. "At that time, she gave me Drexus's ring. In it is a sliver of the Empower Stone, which enhances magic and can also lead to the pieces of the Heart. The only way to free my sister is to find the Stone and give it to Queen Siryn."

"And you didn't tell us because . . . ?" Caston asked. His jaw pulsed, and fury filled his eyes.

"Because she threatened to kill me and my child," Kenz said, resting her arms on the table.

"Child?" Delmira and Aura said together. Smiles grew on their faces.

Kenz nodded. "We wanted to wait to tell everyone once things settled down."

Caston leaned back and crossed his arms. "You still should've told me about the queen holding your sister prisoner."

Jasce rested his hands on his hips. "You're right. But can you try to understand that she threatened the people I love? I thought I was doing the smart thing. Until, of course, my lovely fiancée called me out."

Kord nudged his sister and smiled. "If it's any consolation, Caston, I just found out about Jaida a little while ago."

Caston's eyes narrowed as he regarded Jasce. Finally, the man nodded.

"I agree with Caston," Alyssa said. "As your generals, you should've kept us informed." She raised her hand as Jasce opened his mouth. "However, I'm also aware you're used to working alone, and that habit can be hard to break. Just don't let it happen again."

Jasce raised his brows. Caston snorted while others muffled their laughs.

"Duly noted," Jasce said.

Jasce turned as the door to the command room burst open. Reed stormed in, followed by Maera, who'd changed out of her bloody clothes.

"You better have a good reason for lying to me," Reed said, standing toe to toe with Jasce.

"Be careful," Jasce said through gritted teeth.

"Or what?"

Caston pushed up from his chair, and Kenz's bracelets glowed.

Reed glanced around the room. "You saw what that crystal did with Drexus's magic. And now all of you are comfortable with an ex-Hunter with two types of magic having a piece of the Empower Stone? Are you crazy?"

Jasce's lips curved into a smile.

Caston swore and rushed between them, placing a hand on Reed's chest. "I'd step away, Captain."

Kord stood. "He doesn't have it, Reed. I do."

"And before that, Amycus had it," Jasce said. It was taking all his willpower not to run the captain through with his sword. How dare he question him in front of his team. Small fingers interlaced with his, and he looked down into green eyes.

"Fight it, babe," Kenz whispered, squeezing his hand.

Jasce grew weary of the battle within himself, but as he felt the heat

Embracing the Darkness

from Kenz's hand, he willed himself to find the strength to keep fighting Azrael and complete the mission.

He turned away from Reed and stared at Amycus. "Why did you steal it?"

Amycus sagged in his chair. "I didn't want history to repeat itself."

"What are you talking about?" Kord glanced around the room. "And will you all sit down? You're giving me a headache."

Jasce kept his gaze on the blacksmith as he sat. Reed pulled up a chair on the other side of the table while Maera sat next to Amycus. Caston mumbled under his breath, grabbed a drink, then joined them.

"Talk, old man," Jasce said, leaning back and crossing his arms.

Amycus straightened. His scarred hands rested on the table as he looked at everyone. "When Drexus started his reign, something had to be done to stop him. He was too powerful, and Spectrals didn't know how to fight. I broke into the palace one night and stole his ring. That's when I visited Terrenus. If anyone had knowledge about the Heart of Pandaren, it would be the Gemaris. The archduke told me the crystal would lead me to the Empower Stone, but there would be consequences."

"What consequences?" Aura asked. The group raptly paid attention to every word the blacksmith spoke.

He licked his lips. "I tracked down the Stone using the crystal, and it triggered the other three elemental powers inside me, which is why I'm now able to use all four types equally. But I wasn't experienced in them and I..."

Maera placed a glass of water in front of Amycus. He took a sip and continued. "I wasn't familiar with the magic or the amount of power the Stone unleashed." He swallowed and closed his eyes. "I killed someone. A good friend."

Kenz covered her mouth. Kord pulled her close, sadness making the skin around his eye tighten.

Amycus's breath shuddered. "Drexus eventually found me, but not until after I threw the Stone into the sea."

"Where?" Jasce asked.

Everyone turned to him. Reed cursed under his breath.

Tears lined Amycus's eyes. "With two different types of magic, I have no idea what it will do to you."

Jasce leaned forward. "I'm willing to take that risk to free my sister. Now tell me where you last saw it."

"Don't you get it?" Maera said, her face turning red. "He's trying to protect you!"

"Protect me?" Jasce laughed, the sound harsh in the silent room. "Do explain how stealing that crystal is protecting me."

"He's dying."

A collective gasp traversed around the table. Kenz shook her head, and tears streamed down her face. Kord rubbed her back, his eye darting between his sister and Jasce.

"I analyzed his blood," Maera continued, grabbing the blacksmith's hand, "and all four elements have merged, causing an imbalance. His magic is slowly killing him."

"Amycus," Kenz said, trying to hold back a sob.

Jasce stared at his fiancée, and then his eyes met Kord's. He hadn't known the blacksmith long. The grief squeezing his heart couldn't compare to what Kenz and Kord must have felt.

Flynt held his head while Aura stared blankly at the table.

"Isn't there something you can do?" Delmira whispered. Flynt looked up, unable to hide his sorrow, and wrapped his arm around her.

Maera shook her head. "We've tried everything. The Empower Stone did something with the four elements. Every time we try to remove his magic, it's almost killed him."

"You haven't tried with me present," Kord said. Anger had replaced the sadness.

"I didn't want you involved. I was trying to keep you as far from this as possible," Amycus said.

"How can you say that? Not involved?" Kenz swiped at the escaping tears. "You're part of our family!"

The tears Amycus had tried to repress flowed freely. He got out of his chair and walked around the table. Kord and Kenz immediately jumped to their feet and embraced the blacksmith. Jasce stood, unsure of what to do. The woman he loved and his best friend were hurting. The man he admired, his mentor, was dying.

Embracing the Darkness

Compassion makes you weak.

He closed his eyes and blocked Azrael's poisonous words. He grimaced at the pain in his head. Azrael's power grew with each passing moment.

"Jasce."

Jasce's eyes flew open. Amycus reached for him and Jasce gripped his hand. His calluses matched Jasce's—warrior, blacksmith, friend.

The next thing he knew, Amycus was pulling him into the hug. The sensation comforted and scared him at the same time. He wanted to retreat, yet he also longed to burrow in and never leave.

Amycus grabbed Jasce by the back of the neck. Dark circles lined his eyes, more gray than blue. "I'm so sorry I took the crystal."

"I understand why you did." Jasce squeezed his shoulder.

Amycus swallowed and wiped the wetness from his face. Hearts heavy, they all returned to their seats.

Focus on the mission, Jasce thought as he cleared his throat. "The Vastanes are behind all of this, but the only proof I have escaped during the attack. The Snatchers need to be destroyed and the Empower Stone found before anyone else gets it."

Caston leaned back in his chair. "But why does Queen Siryn want it?"

"The Vastanes have magic. They can control your emotions or compel you. I'm not entirely sure. It's almost like a Psyche." Jasce spun his glass while he gauged everyone's reactions.

Most were stunned speechless.

Maera fisted her hands on the table. "But why help us with Emile? Why offer their medics to assist?"

Kord crossed his arms. "Maybe to see how much we knew. Get a layout of our system."

"Or get access to your Healers. Queen Siryn must have kidnapped Pilar to help keep Vale alive for the experiments." Jasce finished his whiskey. He glanced at the bottle in the corner and wanted another, but he needed to be sober for whatever was coming their way.

"So this is what we know for certain." Kenz ticked each finger. "The Vastanes are able to transfer magic and remove it; they possess magic and want the Empower Stone; and they have Jaida and, most likely, Vale locked away. Am I missing anything?"

"They've developed collars that suppress magic but also send some electric shock to immobilize the wearer," Jasce said.

Flynt swore. "Why aren't we killing them all, now?"

Jasce glared at the Fire Spectral. "Because my sister's life is at stake."

"Can't you just vault in there and get her?" Alyssa asked.

"They've moved her. I checked after the failed attempt to locate Vale. I did find, however, the bodies of our missing competitors."

Maera straightened in her chair. "What about Pilar?"

He shook his head. "No sign of her. I don't know if she's alive or not."

Kord cursed under his breath and glanced at Maera, who covered her mouth as tears filled her eyes.

"But how do the Vastanes know how to transfer magic?" Aura asked, her voice piercing the silence.

Jasce glanced at Amycus, whose lips were pressed into a flat line. He figured they were both thinking the same thing.

Amycus sighed and shook his head. "It's the only way."

Rage boiled inside Jasce because the old man was right. There was no other explanation for the Vastanes to have the knowledge they had. Failure crashed against his resolve, and a part of him wanted to release Azrael. But he wasn't sure if he'd be strong enough to control the Hunter once he was free.

"What's the only way?" Reed asked. The captain had remained quiet since he'd barged in, and Jasce almost forgot he was there.

Jasce fisted his hands and said through clenched teeth, "Drexus is alive."

Chapter Thirty-Two

After everyone had settled down over the news of Drexus, they devised a plan. Two teams would be sent out: Alyssa would lead a group to the desert, and Jasce would lead one to the coast. After everything was decided, Jasce, Kord, Amycus, and Maera returned to the Sanctuary to check on Queen Valeri. Thankfully, flushing her system had worked, and Kord was able to heal her.

Kord had taken the crystal and worked on Amycus, too. The blacksmith's color returned and the shadows under his eyes disappeared. Maybe, with enough time, Kord could heal him completely while using the sliver of the Empower Stone. Or if they retrieved the entire piece, who knew what Kord could do? There was still a chance for Amycus. Kord might even be able to get his sight back.

There was no sign of Pilar. Queen Siryn and her people had left the palace, and no one knew where they were. Jasce sent a squadron of guards to lock down their ship in the harbor, which was strangely vacant as well. After being updated, Queen Valeri agreed with their plan to hunt down the Snatchers while secretly searching for the Empower Stone. The tricky part was that Jasce and his team would have some additional guests on their journey.

Reed wasn't letting Jasce and the crystal out of his sight and had informed Lord Rollant of everything. Having Reed along didn't bother Jasce. The soldier was an accomplished fighter and knew what the Snatchers were capable of. The lack of trust, however, grated on his nerves.

Archduke Carnelian had insisted on going, and based on the look he received, Jasce wasn't fooling the Gemari with this quest. The Balten consort and one of her soldiers, Michail, were also joining them, along with the Alturian commander.

With the magical strength of his team, Jasce was confident of his chances of destroying the Snatchers once and for all. Finding the Empower Stone was a whole other challenge.

Jasce's mind replayed all of this while he rubbed his hand down the ebony flank of his horse. Bruiser snorted and his muscles quivered under the touch. He smiled, holding a sugar cube for the horse to nuzzle.

"Sorry, you can't go this time," he said, reaching for another cube. The sunrise created a soothing glow in the stables that didn't match the storm running through his veins. They were leaving later than he'd wanted, and that incessant countdown in his head continued to tick.

Not knowing where Jaida was or if she was safe was tearing him in two. Whether or not Drexus was truly alive also had him seething.

And a battle raged inside him. Azrael's strength was growing, even without the crystal, which Kord still possessed after healing the queen and Amycus. It seemed whatever crack had opened in Jasce's wall, the Hunter had gotten through and intended to stay.

The notion made no sense to him. He wished Emile was around to ask if she experienced the same thing when her magic was making her crazy. But Tillie had taken Maleous and Emile out of the city. Lander, who was at the age to decide whether to go or stay, had stayed with the Guard. Jasce saw a lot of himself in the kid and didn't know whether or not that was a good thing.

Movement out of the corner of his eye had him turning as Kenz, Kord, and Amycus entered the stable. Jasce frowned. He usually sensed Kenz's magic, but he hadn't this time.

"We've already discussed this, and you're not going," Jasce said to Amycus. Amycus's brows raised. He'd wanted to come with them, but Jasce had said no, and the queen had actually agreed with him.

Embracing the Darkness

Kenz ran her hand down Bruiser's neck. "That's not why we're here."

Jasce licked his lips. "Then what? I couldn't talk you two out of going, which I just don't understand, as I am your commanding officer."

Kord leaned against the wall with his arms crossed. "We wanted to ask you to listen to us and try not to get angry."

Jasce tilted his head, then glanced at Kenz, who reached for his hand. He motioned for them to continue.

"We don't want you wearing the crystal during this mission," Amycus said.

Jasce opened his mouth to argue, but Kord interrupted. "Hear us out. Your two magics are affecting you, and *this* makes it worse." Kord pulled the leather band out of his pocket, and Jasce found himself drifting closer. Kenz squeezed his hand. He stared at their joined fingers, and pain throbbed behind his eyes as Azrael scratched against the diminishing protective barrier.

Amycus stepped forward. "It also might be wise for you to wear a collar until this is all over."

"You want to suppress my power?" Anger swirled in his gut. "If you think I'm going to wear one of those while Kenz and my child are at risk, then you've truly lost your mind."

Amycus opened his hands. "I don't know how that Stone will affect you. Look what it did to me. Magic has to have balance, Jasce, and I feel yours is at its tipping point."

Jasce swallowed the rage and reminded himself they were looking out for his best interests. But he needed his magic now more than ever, and he'd do anything to protect Kenz and the baby she carried, even sell his soul, if there were any willing buyers. He'd find a way to get his leather band back and deal with the effects of the Stone. He was powerful enough to handle it.

He finally nodded. "Tell the others to gear up. We leave in ten minutes."

Kord and Amycus shared a look and then exited the stable, but Kenz stayed behind, helping him move Bruiser to his stall. With a final scratch on his velvety nose and one more sugar cube, they walked into the morning light.

She touched his arm. "You gave in too easily. What's going through that thick skull?"

Jasce forced a smile and tucked a stray hair behind her ear. "Promise me you'll stay out of the fray." She had agreed to be their sharpshooter, which was the only reason he and Kord hadn't locked her up in the dungeon.

She adjusted her bow along her back. "I will, but answer my question."

"If everything goes as planned, you'll have nothing to worry about." He hugged her and breathed in the citrus scent he loved so much. He reached for her magic, but it did nothing to comfort him this time, and the darkness inside him squirmed.

Hold on a little longer, he thought as they made their way to the wyvern paddock. He ignored the wary glances Kenz gave him and shoved the guilt away at the lie he'd just told the woman he loved.

The wyvern's powerful wings cut through the air like a blade through smoke, and Jasce couldn't stop from grinning. As a kid, he'd heard tales of the Terrenian wyverns and had dreamed of flying ever since. The rocky coast passed underneath them as they glided north, and the wind caressed his face, driving all thoughts of Amycus's warning out of his mind. He temporarily forgot the pain in his head and the tremors in his hands. Kenz's arms wrapped tightly around his waist, and every now and then she'd laugh, a sound that lifted his spirits even more.

Based on the direction the Snatchers had gone, the information Amycus had provided to where he'd thrown the Stone into the sea, and Jaida's last words—*go to the place where Drexus kept his greatest secret*—they flew north toward the Arcane Garrison. That was where Drexus had revealed that Jaida was not only alive but also a powerful Psyche. A great secret, indeed.

Villagers from Dunstead scattered as the group soared over the coast, the wyverns' shadows dancing over the tin rooftops. The sea grew brighter, resembling a field of diamonds as they neared the garrison.

After the destruction of Drexus's medical facility and with Queen Valeri resuming control, Jasce had turned the compound into a haven for Spectral children who'd lost parents during Drexus's reign. He visited when he could, trying not to look into the eyes of the older kids who recognized him as one of the reasons they were without family. As a Hunter and the Angel of Death, he'd killed or captured many Spectrals, and the guilt he felt made his stomach twist into knots. It had been his idea to turn the garrison into an orphanage, but the gesture wouldn't wash the blood from his hands.

Sentiment. Compassion.
You are weak.

Jasce forced Azrael's voice to the recesses of his mind. Helping those children didn't make him weak. He knew that.

Commander Faez, who'd ridden with Kord, hopped off the wyvern, her short hair standing in all directions and cheeks red from the wind. "That was absolutely magnificent! Nicolaus would've loved that." She shivered and her magic pulsed, making her almost disappear among the shadows cast by the wyvern.

The archduke and Tobias helped everyone secure their animals as a group of children rushed to the gates to get a better look at their visitors. A short, plump woman pushed through the kids, a smile on her face. "Commander Farone, what a surprise."

"Ms. Drehden," he said, giving a quick nod, aware that all eyes were on him. He had to lean down as she pulled him into a hug. He had never told Kenz or Kord that he funded the orphanage or visited as often as he could. Why he'd kept this secret to himself, he didn't know. He figured it was his penance to those whose lives he'd altered.

"Thank you for your recent gift, even though I'm not sure I totally approve." Ms. Drehden released him and looked over his shoulder at the other visitors, a crease forming between her wrinkled eyes.

"Well, at least they were wooden swords. Next will be bows and arrows," he said, giving the woman a wink. He then made introductions.

Kenz approached him after shaking hands with the caretaker. He kept his gaze on the kids as they edged nearer to the wyverns, their eyes wide and mouths open. "Why wouldn't you tell me about this?" She waved her arm at the former garrison.

A small garden nestled against the compound with flowers lining the walkway. It looked so inviting, unlike when he'd knelt on the ground, blood dripping from his face as Bronn had used his body as a punching dummy. Too many horrible memories had filled this place. All the experiments, Nigel dying in his arms, seeing his sister for the first time in years after thinking she was dead, being held prisoner in the dungeon alongside Kenz, Kord, and Emile. Too much blood and pain. It had taken months for him to move past it, and turning the garrison into an orphanage had brought him a semblance of peace.

"It was my burden to bear," was all Jasce said.

She sighed and grabbed his face. "When will you learn your burdens are now mine?" She kissed him hard and then smacked his cheek gently. "This is remarkable. I'm very proud of you."

He swallowed the knot in his throat as Kord walked by and patted him on the shoulder.

"Commander," the archduke said as he approached. "Let's not play games. We all know you're searching for the Empower Stone. You obviously didn't listen to Amycus."

Jasce crossed his arms. There was no sense denying it as Consort Lekov and Commander Faez stared at him with knowing looks. "Fine. We are hunting the Snatchers, but first we need to find the Heart, per Queen Valeri's orders."

The archduke snorted. "How obedient of you."

Jasce ignored his response. They didn't have time for the cat-and-mouse game they were playing. He held out his hand as he spoke to Kord, "The crystal should lead us to it."

Reed approached, shaking his head. "No. You cannot give it to him. The council agrees—"

Jasce widened his stance. "Do you actually think I care what the council thinks?"

"Give it to me. I can control it," Archduke Carnelian said, holding open his hand. The gem on his chest pulsed as Kord unwrapped the leather band and gave it to him. Tobias's gem also glowed while he kept

Embracing the Darkness

a wary eye on Jasce. Just like with Kenz's bracelets, the Gemari was readying his magic.

Jasce sensed the magic as it flowed around him, like a sensual embrace that promised more. Azrael seemed to stretch his arms as his power spiked. He winced from the pain in his head and knew everyone could see his hands and arms shaking.

Kord touched his forehead and warmth rushed through him, easing the pain to a dull ache and stilling the tremors. "Keep fighting it. I'm here."

Reed's jaw muscle ticked as he watched Jasce level out. Kenz steered him away to join Consort Lekov and Michail. Commander Faez eyed the crystal and took a tentative step back.

Jasce led his team through the entrance of the garrison and down the hallway to the forge. "I remember stairs leading to a tunnel, which I thought odd at the time. There were bars blocking it, but that shouldn't be a problem."

As he stepped into the abandoned workshop, memories flooded his mind with a vengeance. He'd worked on recreating Flynt's bombs to kill Drexus. Unfortunately, all his plans had crumbled when Kord and Kenz had tried to rescue him. He trailed his finger through the dust lining the table. The day they had drained his magic, almost killing him, still haunted his nightmares. Unable to move, powerless to stop Drexus. Incapable of helping Kenz as Bronn tortured her. The memory of being completely defenseless made his breath hitch.

Focus on the mission. Soon, we'll be invincible.

Longing cut through his resolve. He was running out of time.

The crystal glowed, and the archduke grunted as they moved toward the stairs. "This seems to be the way."

Jasce used his strength and ripped the bars out of the wall, then lit the torches that led them to the tunnels below the compound. As they progressed through the corridor, the air became wetter, and the smell of the ocean tickled his nose. The crystal glowed brighter—a beacon of light in the oppressive dark of the tunnel.

Jasce stopped listening to the archduke telling Kord about Gemari magic and thought about the four sections of the Heart. It seemed Drexus had found the Empower Stone, but why he hadn't used it, he didn't know. His thoughts drifted to when he'd first seen Jaida use her magic. He'd often wondered about his sister's power. Did Drexus use the crystal on her? Queen Siryn was correct when she said Jaida seemed unhinged, but was that a result of the piece of the Heart affecting her?

After more twists and turns, the sound of dripping water echoing off the cave walls stopped, and the tunnel lightened. He blinked against the light and reached for his dagger as they emerged.

The orphanage stood in the distance, and the sea crashed against the rocks and cliffs. The beach tapered off, away from the garrison. Clouds billowed on the horizon, and the smell of the ocean mixed with the threat of rain.

The archduke held out the crystal and closed his eyes, pivoting until he found the direction he wanted. As they traipsed across a rocky section of beach toward the cliff face, the gem glowed brighter. He knelt near a wall of hard-packed sand and ran his fingers along an almost invisible edge. He motioned to Tobias, who used his dagger to deepen the groove.

"It's in here," Archduke Carnelian said as he stood and handed the leather band to Reed, who slid it into his inside pocket. "I'm sure you can feel it." He looked pointedly at Jasce.

Jasce stayed still, even though he wanted to move closer. He sensed the others watching him warily as the hum of power embraced him.

Tobias and Michail removed a boulder blocking the entrance, and a whoosh of air billowed out of the hole. A wave of magical power washed over them. Jasce bit back a groan and focused on the clouds while Kord moved closer to him. Kenz's fingers entwined with his.

An object the size of a small melon, wrapped in cloth, lay in the center. The crystal's magic pulsed, and Commander Faez's body flickered as the shadows enveloped her. Tobias grabbed her and pulled her from the opening. Consort Lekov arched her back and Michail stumbled. Both of their eyes glowed. Reed dragged them away.

The archduke looked from the crystal to Jasce, and his eyes widened.

Jasce felt himself moving forward, a laugh erupting from somewhere inside him as he reached for the crystal.

"Jasce, stop," Kenz said, igniting her shield to block him from going any farther.

Embracing the Darkness

Azrael, the Angel of Death, peeked out from the depths, craving blood. His lips curved into a smile. "Lower it." His voice sounded different, harsher.

Kord swore and stood between him and Kenz.

Silver flashed, and someone forced him to the ground. He yelled as Tobias and Reed held him down while Kord latched a collar around his neck.

"I'm sorry," Kord whispered.

He thrashed on the ground, grabbing hold of Tobias's wrist and snapping it. The soldier cried out and fell off him. Jasce jerked back his elbow and connected with Reed's face. With a shove, he got to his feet.

"How dare you!" He sensed Azrael trying to break free from the collar's suppression, wanting to cling to the power emanating from the crystal.

Kord slowly stood, wincing. "It's for your own good."

Jasce wiped his mouth, his magic silenced. He felt helpless and out of control at the same time.

"This is necessary," the archduke said to Jasce. "Because of your two magics, the Heart affects you the most. It's for your safety and ours." He removed the Stone from its hiding place and blew off a layer of dust covering the tan fabric.

Jasce kept his face blank as a small tendril of his magic stirred. Usually, with the collar on, he felt nothing. But with the Empower Stone so close, the device couldn't completely block its power. Deep inside, Azrael smiled.

Tobias kept his sword trained on him, grimacing from the pain of his broken wrist. Kord, with his eyes on Jasce, moved to Tobias's side and healed him. Sadness and fear warred on Kenz's face. She had allowed them to suppress his power.

He turned his back on them.

We don't need them, Azrael said.

And he agreed.

Chapter Thirty-Three

Screams sounded from the orphanage. Jasce shielded his eyes from the sun emerging through the clouds, barely able to discern Ms. Drehden's head of gray hair as she peeked over the wall and pointed to the south. He sprinted up the hill, followed by Reed and Kenz.

A dust cloud billowed on the horizon as the Snatchers ran along the beach, their massive claws kicking up sand.

"How did they know?" Reed asked.

"Must be the Stone," Kenz said.

Jasce swore and pivoted, judging the distance between the approaching creatures and the Arcane. "And the kids. We need to keep the Snatchers away from the garrison," he said, sliding down the hill, scattering rocks as he returned to the waiting group. This is what he'd feared when he heard the creatures were heading north. Not only was the Empower Stone a magnet of magic, so were the Spectral children behind those walls.

"What's your plan?" Kenz asked, running beside him.

A knot twisted in Jasce's gut and fear replaced his anger. How could he protect her and the child she carried along with all the Spectrals at the orphanage? If the attack at the Bastion proved anything, those creatures could climb the Arcane walls with little effort.

Jasce skidded to a stop in front of the rest of the group and addressed the archduke. "We need your wyverns to slow the Snatchers down. Give me the Empower Stone and I'll lead them away."

"No," the archduke said. "I will not relinquish the Stone into your hands. You can't handle the magic, nor do I trust you with that kind of power."

"We don't have time to discuss this. Those kids' lives are at stake!" Jasce yelled, pointing to the Spectrals looking over the wall.

Archduke Carnelian glanced over his shoulder, his jaw muscle twitching, and then addressed his soldier. "Tobias, take the Stone to Orilyon."

Consort Lekov drew her sword. "We will hold them off." She faced Michail. "Do whatever needs to be done to protect the orphanage." Michail saluted and sprinted toward the tunnel, followed by Tobias with the Stone. The archduke jogged after them to get the wyverns into the air.

Jasce spun toward Reed. "Remove the collar."

"Are you nuts?"

"I can't protect anyone without my magic. Take it off now, or I'll make you." He seized his tunic and pulled him close. "Do you understand?"

Reed pushed him off and looked at Kord, who dipped his chin. Shaking his head, he handed Jasce the key. He unlocked his collar, palming the leather band he'd taken from inside Reed's jacket, and suppressed a shiver as his magic surged.

The pain that exploded behind Jasce's eyes almost dropped him to his knees as he fought to control Azrael.

Hold on, he told himself.

"Kenz, you and Reed stay here. Don't use your shield unless absolutely necessary. Remember, aim for the eyes." He drew his swords from the scabbards on his back and glanced at Kord.

He crossed his arms over his massive chest. "I'll watch over her."

Kenz rolled her eyes at her brother and then approached Jasce. "Don't lose yourself. Please."

He nodded, and with one last look at the woman he loved, he

sprinted up the hill toward the sound of crashing waves and pounding claws.

"I'm coming with you," Consort Lekov said, running beside him as Commander Faez followed, flitting between the shadows. Having a Balten warrior and a Shade Walker at his side provided some amount of comfort.

Jasce counted twenty Snatchers as they emerged through the dust. The leader slowed to a stop and raked its lethal claws through the sand. Its white eyes peered past him to the walls of the Arcane and snarled.

"We need to hold them off until the wyverns arrive." He figured fifteen minutes, maybe ten if the archduke sprinted through the caverns. The crystal pulsed in Jasce's pocket, and Azrael answered with a seductive caress. He hadn't liked leaving Kenz and Kord on the hill, and fear had him glancing over his shoulder.

He shook away the images of lethal claws attacking Kenz's shield and cutting through Kord's face like paper. Those beasts would not get past him, and if he had to become a monster to defeat the ones approaching, then so be it. Attaching the band around his wrist, he lessened the barrier holding Azrael and welcomed the extra power.

He faced the consort and commander. "Not one of them gets by."

The Shade Walker disappeared into the shadows of the boulders and shrubbery.

Consort Lekov drew her sword. "If I need to release my Defender, I will. Be ready." Her eyes glowed as her magic pulsed and swirled around him.

Jasce embraced his power, felt the tug, and vaulted. His swords came down with lethal quickness, removing the lead creature's head. Roars echoed through his ears.

One down.

He disappeared again, using his power to lure the creatures away from the Arcane. The surf flowed over his boots, and the cold water immediately soaked his feet. He hoped the soft sand and waves would slow them down.

Arrows flew from the shadows and the hill. Snatchers crumbled, the shafts vibrating from their eyes. Kenz's and the Alturian's aim were perfect.

Half of the creatures followed Jasce, his magic and the crystal a beacon drawing them in. He concentrated on the bunching muscles and outstretched claws as he timed his attacks. Flipping in the air, he landed behind a Snatcher. It dodged, but not fast enough. A wicked slash cut through its side, and it cried out as it limped through the surf, turning the white foam red.

Two more attacked. He vaulted while spinning and lunging and slashed both swords. Another head bobbed in the waves. Water splashed as the second Snatcher charged. It stopped just out of Jasce's range and snarled. He wiped the salt water from his eyes and circled the beast.

An arrow whizzed past his head, and a roar sounded behind him. Water sprayed into his face as a creature with the shaft lodged in its eye sank below the waves. He used the distraction and his speed to dispatch the one that had been circling him.

Jasce saluted Commander Faez and vaulted again, reappearing next to a Snatcher the consort was battling. Slicing his two blades, he cut through the creature's neck. He dodged as blood spurted onto his armor. The consort shoved him out of the way and stabbed one in the chest. He and the Balten warrior stood back-to-back, working in tandem, and killed the remaining Snatchers.

Blood soaked into the wet sand and a longing he hadn't experienced since he'd donned the Hunter's mask seized him. As the Angel of Death, every kill had strengthened him, and the lust for blood filled him with purpose.

"You fight very well," Consort Lekov said with an appreciative smile.

He returned his swords to their scabbards and surveyed the carnage. "You too."

Commander Faez joined them, slinging her bow onto her back and brushing the hair off her face.

"Commander Farone, look at me," the consort said, concern lining her face.

He slowly turned his head and the Balten consort gasped, taking a step back. Commander Faez swore and grabbed his shoulder. "Your eyes," the Shade Walker whispered.

Embracing the Darkness

He figured he looked like a monster, with his eyes turning black and blood covering him.

Relish your power. Unleash your magic.

"You're not supposed to have that." The Shade Walker stepped closer and held out her hand. "Give it to me."

"I don't think so," he said, his voice gravelly like the sand they stood on.

A vibration through the beach had him looking across the horizon. Dust swirled beyond a dune, and a string of Balten curses flew out of Consort Lekov's mouth as a second hoard of creatures crested the hill. "We can't hold off that many."

"No, we can't," Jasce said, examining the skies. Where were the wyverns? Surely the archduke had made it back to the main gate of the Arcane.

Steps pounded behind him, and he wheeled around. Running toward them were Reed and Kenz, her crossbow loaded.

Panic rushed through him. "What the hell are you doing? I told you to stay on the hill."

"Someone needs to protect you, too." She stopped short when she saw him up close and fear flickered across her face. "Fight it," she whispered.

"I will do what I need to do. Now go back."

"No."

"We don't have time to argue." Reed pointed to the creatures barreling toward them.

"Dammit, Kenz," Jasce said. He had half a mind to vault her away from the battle. But then he'd leave the others alone, and they wouldn't survive.

"Look!" Commander Faez said, a relieved smile tugging the corners of her mouth.

Jasce let out a breath as enormous shadows flew overhead. The archduke and six wyverns banked around the dune and dove for the creatures. The wyverns roared with their talons outstretched, greedy for prey.

Jasce and his team sprinted toward the front where the wyverns attacked the Snatchers. Kenz and Commander Faez loaded their crossbows and arrows whooshed past him. Consort Lekov yelled, and her Defender emerged with its dual-bladed ax to fight alongside her.

Jasce traveled through space, slashing his swords with each vault, moving like shadow and smoke, never in one place for more than a breath before disappearing again. He lost himself to the magic, allowing it to take control with each swipe of his blade, and the wall holding Azrael crumbled with each slice, with each kill. The crystal made his power thrum with limitless energy. He couldn't remember ever feeling this powerful.

A scream had Jasce pausing. Commander Faez fell as three creatures jumped onto her. Kenz ran toward her, igniting her shield to ram through the beasts and push them off the fallen commander.

The Snatchers got their legs under them and raised their heads, blood dripping from their teeth and claws.

Ice flowed through Jasce's veins.

Kenz stood in front of the commander, who lay facedown, her body torn and broken.

"Kenz, no," he whispered as the Snatchers surrounded her.

Another cry had him turning. Consort Lekov knelt. Her Defender had disappeared with the draining of her magic. A few Snatchers seemed to sense her weakness and circled her.

Reed yelled and slashed his way through to the consort. Wyverns streaked overhead, and Snatchers roared.

Kenz's magical barrier flickered as the three Snatchers took turns testing her shield's strength. She pivoted and stabbed one, immediately raising her shield again.

A creature attacked Jasce from behind, knocking him to the ground and sending his swords flying. He maneuvered onto his side and lifted his leg while keeping the snapping jaws away from his neck. He grabbed his throwing knife and with a shout, pushed the Snatcher off and stabbed it in the eye.

He looked at Kenz and swore as two more Snatchers had joined the group. Blood dripped down her nose, and she winced with each strike. He'd never be able to take on five by himself.

I can save her.

The Snatchers ferociously swiped their claws against Kenz's shield.

Embracing the Darkness

Jasce fumbled through the sand, searching for his swords. His heart pounded in his ears.

Release me.

She dropped her sword and held both hands up. Her arms trembled as she backed into the boulder. Jasce heaved a sigh when his fingers wrapped around the hilt of his blade.

With a collective roar, the creatures collided with Kenz's shield.

"Kenz!"

The light sputtered and then disappeared.

Let me free!

The restraint he'd held in place for the past months disintegrated.

He vaulted mid-sprint, and in the space between nothingness and death, Azrael was unleashed. The Angel of Death broke free from his bonds and attacked with a vengeance Jasce had never felt before.

"Kenz, please. Wake up." Jasce held her as blood coated his face and hands. He'd slayed the remaining creatures and vaulted to the Arcane, calling out for Kord. The fear and worry flowing off his friend made him recoil.

He kept envisioning the Snatchers breaking through her shield with their claws outstretched and maws opened. Jasce—or was he Azrael?—had slashed through them with unrestrained violence, but one creature had rammed Kenz, smacking her into a boulder and tearing a chunk of flesh from her side. He had almost retched seeing the blood pour from her.

Kord placed his hands on Kenz's body. A muscle pulsed in his jaw. "I need you to put pressure on the wound."

Blood oozed through Jasce's fingers as he pressed his ear to her chest and listened.

"Kord," Jasce said as dread knotted his gut.

"I know," Kord said. "The venom is blocking my magic."

Jasce glanced at the crystal on his wrist covered in dirt and blood. There was still a spark of magic glowing inside. He removed it. "Use this."

Cassie Sanchez

Grabbing it, Kord closed his eyes and placed his hands on Kenz's chest. Jasce rested two fingers against her neck.

Reed and Consort Lekov limped onto the rooftop, both freezing when they saw Kenz lying in a puddle of blood.

Jasce brushed the hair away from her face. "Come on, honey. Don't you quit on me."

His heartbeat pounded in his ears as he waited.

Her color slowly returned, and her breathing evened out. Relief washed over him as he felt a faint pulse. The blood seeping from her wound slowed.

He was about to breathe a sigh of relief when Kord's breath hitched.

"Oh no," Kord whispered.

"What? What's wrong?" Jasce asked, his eyes scanning Kenz.

"The baby," Kord said, looking up, tears in his eye. He dropped the leather band. The crystal, a black void, clinked onto the roof.

Jasce's shoulders sagged, and his hands fell to his lap. Helplessness clamped around his chest as he tried to breathe.

Reed approached, raking his hand through his hair. Ms. Drehden ran through the back entrance, followed by the orphanage doctor, who pushed past Jasce and rested his fingers on her neck.

"Take her inside," the doctor said.

Kord held Kenz and got shakily to his feet. His shoulders hunched as if the weight of the world pressed down on him.

Jasce picked up the crystal and held it out. "Kord, can't you . . . ?" He couldn't finish the sentence. If there was any hope, Kord would still be trying to save the baby.

A tear slid down Kord's cheek. "I'm sorry," he whispered.

Jasce stumbled back as they took Kenz inside.

The sound of the crashing surf eclipsed the slamming of the door. Black spots crept into the corner of his eyes. He couldn't breathe as the rage he'd tried to contain exploded. Tipping his head back, he roared and then fell to his knees. He squeezed the band, his knuckles turning white. "You said you would save her."

And I did.

"The baby. You weren't fast enough."

Embracing the Darkness

You shouldn't have hesitated. Besides, what would that child have become with you as the father?

Jasce rocked back and forth. "Shut up. Shut up. *Shut up.*"

A hand rested on his shoulder. "Jasce?"

Bile surged up his throat and he retched.

Reed gripped him by the elbow and lifted him to his feet. "Look at me, Commander." Reed gave him a shake. "Look at me!"

Jasce raised his head, not seeing anything but Kenz's blood soaking into the sand. He hadn't been fast enough. He hadn't protected her or his child. And deep down, Azrael was right. His feelings toward being a father had terrified him. Had he hesitated? Was it his fault the baby hadn't made it?

He pushed away from Reed and lumbered to the wall, staring along the horizon where the sparkling water of the Merrigan Sea mocked him.

He glanced at the commander emblem on his chest. With a violent rip, he tore the patch and threw it on the ground.

"I'm done," Jasce said, and he vaulted away from the pain and failure.

Chapter Thirty-Four

He didn't go far as the sun began its descent, the shadows growing longer and the night air cooling. The wind ruffled his hair, and the peaceful lapping of the waves caressing the shore, along with the soothing cry of gulls, counteracted the tempest raging inside him.

A vice tightened around his heart, and for the first time since he was a child, fear sank its claws into him. It had been too easy to give in and allow Azrael control. He'd lost himself to the monster within, and for what? He hadn't protected Kenz or the baby, and he'd lost his child before he'd even had a chance to truly wrap his mind around being a father. And Kenz—why did she have to be so brave, so stubborn? His plans crumbled apart like sifting sand, and his failure to protect those he loved wrapped its spindly fingers around his throat and squeezed.

He bent over and moaned, gripping his chest. Physical pain he could deal with. But this? The loss and grief sliced like a dagger through his heart. Maybe Drexus was right. Compassion made you weak, and so did love.

The Angel of Death didn't suffer these emotions, and what he needed now more than anything was to have a heart of stone. He didn't want to think about what Kenz might feel when she awoke or about the loss of their baby.

He wrapped the leather band around his wrist. He still had a mission to complete.

Opening his mind once again to Azrael, he buried the heartache, along with the part of his humanity he had recently embraced and surrendered completely to the Hunter.

Blackness crept into his vision, and he fell to his knees. He yelled as the sliver of the Empower Stone finally set Azrael free.

The Angel of Death stood. "At last," he said, his words drifting across the sand. He pushed Jasce's presence behind the protective wall he'd spent weeks trying to break through. The pain in his head and the trembling of his hands ceased. Azrael had finally won the battle for dominance.

He glanced at the orphanage. He wanted to get back to Orilyon and the Empower Stone. But he had something he needed to do first.

Commander Faez lay facedown in the sand, the surf brushing up against her as the tide came in. Even Azrael wouldn't leave her to be eaten by the vultures that would soon feast on the flesh of the Snatchers. No warrior deserved that.

He picked up her broken body. If it weren't for the gashes across her neck and through her stomach, she looked asleep. Peaceful. The part of him that Jasce still occupied envied the serenity she now had. With a growl, Azrael strengthened the wall and blocked the sentiment.

He vaulted toward the Arcane where the archduke and the wyverns waited, along with Consort Lekov and Michail. The consort removed her mantle and, without words, they both wrapped the commander's body.

"I'll take her with me, but we need to return to Orilyon," the archduke said.

Azrael looked over his shoulder at the orphanage, the sun casting it into shadows. "Give me five minutes."

Archduke Carnelian shook his head as he stared into Azrael's eyes. "I warned you—about magic and balance. You're flirting with disaster."

Azrael leaned forward. "I'm stronger than I've ever been, and I will stop anyone who gets in my way."

The archduke's face reddened, but Azrael ignored him. Memories of

Embracing the Darkness

being held prisoner and having his magic drained flooded through his mind while he walked toward the medical facility.

Drexus had destroyed much of the compound, but one room had been restored. Thankfully, the exam tables and transfusion equipment were gone, as well as the chains that had confined Kenz to the wall.

He hesitated in the doorway. Kenz slept on a cot while Kord sat, staring at the floor, his damaged eye uncovered. Reed talked quietly with the doctor and Ms. Drehden in the corner. The caretaker turned and her eyes widened as she covered her mouth. He looked down at the blood and sand, and who knew what else, covering him.

Reed approached with his hands raised as if Azrael were a trapped animal ready to pounce. "Kenz is fine. The doctor gave her a sleeping drought so she can rest." He peered over Azrael's shoulder at Kord, whose arms rested on his knees, his head bowed in defeat.

"We need to get back," Azrael said.

"Did you hear what I said? Kenz is still healing. We can't have her flying on a wyvern right now."

He gritted his teeth. "Yes, I heard you. But I have a mission to finish."

Reed crossed his arms. "So, this is the Hunter I've heard so much about. Azrael, the Angel of Death, returns. Is that why your eyes are black?"

Azrael's hand moved to his dagger as he stepped forward. Reed swallowed, but he held his ground.

"Jasce," Kord said.

He gave one final glare to Reed and strode to the other side of Kenz's bed. "Can I vault with her?"

Kord looked up, sadness lining his face. He wiped away a tear and reattached the patch that covered his damaged eye. "Can you vault that far?"

"I can with the crystal."

"Do you think that's a good idea?"

"She'll heal faster at the Sanctuary."

Kord raked his fingers through his hair. "I meant for you."

Azrael crossed his arms and stared at the Healer. He probably should leave Kenz at the orphanage, but Jasce had permanently altered something in both of them by loving her. It was an emotion Azrael simply couldn't block out.

Kord slumped in his chair. "Don't do this."

"Don't do what?" he asked, trying to keep the bite from his words. He didn't have time for this conversation. The Stone was probably at the palace by now.

"Don't go back to who you were. You're worthy of love and—"

Azrael raised his hand. "Stop." Taking a deep breath, he continued, "Can she vault or not?"

Kord's mouth drew into a flat line and he nodded.

"The archduke is waiting for you and Reed." Azrael reached for Kenz and paused. Her magic, though weakened, recoiled from him.

Kord stood and opened his palms. "Don't let him win."

"I've already won." Azrael held on to Kenz and focused on the power flowing through every muscle, every heartbeat.

Brighid yipped, almost dropping a tray of food, as he and Kenz materialized out of thin air. He placed her on a nearby bed, and without looking up, spoke to the Healer. "Get Maera. Now."

Footsteps sounded as Maera jogged over. "I'm here. What happen—" She covered her mouth as she focused on Azrael's eyes. He knew they were as black as onyx.

"The Snatchers attacked. Kord did what he could." He looked away from Kenz and concentrated on the machines along the back wall. "The baby didn't make it."

"Oh, Jasce," Maera said, reaching for him.

He shrank from her touch. "Kord will be here soon." He took a few steps toward the door. "Anything happens to her, and you'll be the one who pays," he said, then he left the Sanctuary, not caring about the shock and fear that had flickered across her face.

He strode to the barracks to wash off the blood and gore and dressed in a black tunic with leather pants. Strapping on his armored chest piece, he returned his swords to his back and his dagger to his leg. He instinctively reached for a skull mask before remembering that he'd destroyed them all when first arriving at the Bastion as the new commander.

"Sentiment," he mumbled as he strode toward the palace. He

Embracing the Darkness

needed to tell Prince Jazari about Commander Faez, find the Empower Stone, and free his sister. Once Jaida was safe, he'd take the Stone for himself. The crystal's power had revived his magic, and he'd never felt stronger. He couldn't imagine the power he'd have once he acquired a single piece of the Heart.

Dusk had settled and the night sky glittered with the emerging stars. He entered the palace and grabbed his dagger when a red flame flickered to life.

Amycus leaned against a pillar. "What happened?"

Azrael sheathed his blade and crossed his arms. "We were attacked. Commander Faez is dead. Kenz was injured and lost her baby."

Amycus's shoulders slumped, and he reached out. "I'm so sorry."

He huffed and stepped back. "Why does everyone keep saying that? It's probably better this way."

Amycus's mouth dropped open. He snapped it shut and peered at him. Sadness washed over his face. "I see." He gazed over the empty courtyard. "Where's the crystal?"

"Tobias flew it back."

"Not that one."

Azrael clenched his jaw and tapped his finger on the hilt of his dagger.

"Give it to me. Please," Amycus said, holding out his hand.

"No."

Amycus took a step forward. "Can't you see what it's doing to you?"

He pulled his blade free, and his knuckles whitened on the hilt as he stepped closer. "This is my true self. The sooner you and everyone else accept it, the better."

Fear flickered across Amycus's face, replaced just as quickly with anger. A shield of air formed between them.

Azrael's lungs tightened. "I wouldn't do that if I were you."

"Or what, you'll kill me?"

He vaulted behind the Air Spectral and placed his dagger against his throat. Taking a full breath, he said, "I need that Stone to free Jaida. Now, where is it?"

"I don't know."

"Do not lie to me."

Footsteps echoed on the steps behind him. "Drop the dagger."

Azrael looked over his shoulder. Caston and the two guards flanking him had drawn their swords as they walked down the stairs from the queen's living quarters.

He lowered his blade but didn't return it to its scabbard, something Caston noticed. Caston whispered to his guards, who glanced nervously at Azrael and returned the way they had come. Azrael followed them with his eyes and the corner of his lip turned up.

"As your Second in Command, why am I not the first to know you've arrived?" Caston asked as he approached. He scanned Azrael's face and his eyes narrowed.

"You're no longer my Second."

"What?" Caston asked, his voice like steel.

"I've relinquished my command. I'm sure Queen Valeri will approve." He was done working for her anyway, for he wasn't someone's lackey or pawn. He was the Angel of Death and the most powerful Spectral in Pandaren.

Azrael sidestepped Amycus to continue down the corridor, but Caston took hold of his arm. "What are you talking about?"

"What part didn't you understand?"

"Jasce, why?" Amycus asked.

"Do not use that name, and the 'why' doesn't matter. Now, if you'll excuse me, I need to talk to the prince."

"He's in the War Room. The royals and nobles are discussing sending out another squadron of soldiers to search for the Vastanes," Caston said.

Azrael rubbed a hand down his face. The last thing he needed was another meeting.

Caston crossed his arms and glared at him. "So the Angel of Death has returned. I didn't realize Jasce was so weak."

Azrael stepped closer and held the man's stare. "Be careful."

"Or what? I remember how you were. I wasn't afraid of you then and I'm not now. Take your arrogant swagger somewhere else."

Azrael smirked but shoved the anger away. He respected the man for standing up to him and didn't have the time or desire for a fight.

Embracing the Darkness

"Where's the Stone?" he asked as he marched down the hall toward the War Room.

"Safe," said Caston, sneaking a glance at Amycus.

He hadn't figured they'd tell him where it was, but he'd find it. And he had a good idea of where it might be.

Guards lined the corridor and saluted as Azrael strode past. He pushed open the doors into a room of chaos. Council members argued with the other dignitaries while Queen Valeri sat in her chair, her jaw set. She still looked pale, and shadows darkened the skin under her eyes. A Healer remained next to her, resting his hand on the queen's arm. Tobias leaned against the wall with his arms crossed, and the gem in his chest glowed like a full moon in a cloudless night.

The room fell silent as Azrael, Amycus, and Caston entered.

Azrael singled out Prince Jazari and pulled him aside. "Your Highness, Commander Faez died valiantly protecting the Spectral children from the Snatchers."

The prince kept his face blank, but Azrael saw the shadow of grief flicker through his silver eyes. "Her body?" His voice was hoarse, barely a whisper.

"The archduke is bringing her back, along with the others. They should arrive soon."

The prince swallowed. "Thank you for taking care of her."

"Commander Farone, report," the queen said, her tone making him clench his fists.

Azrael explained what happened at the Arcane, and when he finished, he stepped forward. "Queen Valeri, I resign as commander to the Paladin Guard." He bent down and whispered. "I no longer work for you."

Her shoulders tensed, and he smiled as she reached for the dagger hidden in her bodice. Caston moved closer, his hand resting on the hilt of his sword.

Azrael was about to leave when a commotion outside the room made him stop. Reed and the archduke argued as they marched down the hall with Consort Lekov and Michail in their wake. The wyverns had made good time.

The soldiers standing guard shut the door behind them.

Archduke Carnelian strode toward the table. "I insist you hand over the Empower Stone to the Terrenians."

The consort walked to King Morzov's side and whispered in his ear. The king glanced at Azrael and nodded, unhooking the strap over the hilt of his blade. Azrael arched a brow. No one in this room was a match for him, not with the crystal warming his wrist.

"And why should you have the Stone, Kraig?" King Morzov shoved his chair back and towered over the Gemari.

Prince Jazari jumped in between the archduke and the Balten king, resting his hands on their chests. "Until we study it further, no one kingdom should take it."

The archduke scowled. "Oh, and I assume the Alturians—"

"Enough!" Queen Valeri slammed her palms on the table, causing the council members to flinch. "We have other pressing matters, like the location of the other team and the whereabouts of Queen Siryn."

The doors opened again. Paladin guards lay crumpled on the ground.

"Look no further." The Vastane queen entered, her arms outstretched, followed by her bodyguards. Lady Wuhl screamed as a Snatcher crawled in, chained to Garan, who rested his hand on its leathery skin. The council members scrambled away from the table.

Azrael pushed off the wall and drew his dagger while Caston shoved Queen Valeri into her chair and stood in front of her, his sword drawn. Amycus raised his hands, and the air shimmered around the queen. Sweat beaded on his forehead.

The Snatcher swiveled its head toward Azrael and growled.

Queen Siryn sat at the other end of the table, straightening her skirts. Her silver crown sparkled, and a smile danced on her lips. "Commander Farone. Were you able to attain it?"

"He's no longer commander, and I will remind you that you are in my palace, under my authority," Queen Valeri said.

"That's unfortunate, for you at least." Queen Siryn scanned Azrael from head to toe, victory making her eyes sparkle. "It's a shame you never appreciated the most powerful Spectral in Pandaren. Maybe a change of scenery would appeal to the Angel of Death?"

Azrael gripped his dagger and approached the Vastane queen. Her

Embracing the Darkness

guards withdrew their weapons and Garan loosened the Snatcher's chain.

As he neared, she stared into his eyes and then held up her hand, halting her men.

"About time," she said. Triumph flashed across her face. "Now, where is the Stone?"

Archduke Carnelian approached Queen Siryn, giving Azrael a wary glance. "Why do you even want it? You don't have magic."

Azrael's eyes shot to Prince Jazari, who winced when their gazes met. Of course the prince hadn't had a chance to inform Queen Valeri about the Vastane's magic, and even if he had, would the queen have believed the prince if she knew the information had originally come from him?

Warning bells sounded from the harbor. Caston peered out the window and swore. Another set of bells rang from an outpost on the edge of the city.

"What's going on?" Queen Valeri asked.

Queen Siryn strummed her red fingernails on the polished table. "Yes, well, you're being invaded. By sea and by land. Right now, my Daeloks—that's their true name—are in the city and will destroy everything unless I get the Stone."

Prince Jazari stepped forward. "Are you saying those creatures belong to you?"

"Yes. Thanks to some interesting experimentation using Drexus's methods, we were able to transform the Daeloks into lethal magic hunters." She glanced at Azrael. "You, of all people, should've recognized the tactic."

Azrael vaulted through space and appeared next to the Vastane queen with his dagger pressed against her throat. "How dare you attack the Bastion."

She slowly lifted her chin, exposing more of her neck as if taunting him. "You're stronger than I thought, but I knew eventually you'd surrender. You just needed an extra push."

His shoulders tightened. "What are you talking about?"

He'd been so focused on wanting to slit her throat, he hadn't noticed when the leather band unhooked from his wrist. She held it and smiled cruelly at him. His arm shook and he watched in horror as he slid his dagger into its sheath.

His mind and body were no longer under his control.

"You're now mine," the queen whispered. She squeezed the leather band and then gazed at all the royals. "You asked, Kraig, why I wanted this piece of the Heart. How about a small demonstration—just so you know I'm serious."

The archduke's mouth dropped. King Morzov removed his sword from its scabbard, his eyes not on Queen Siryn but on Azrael.

His body moved on its own, despite every nerve and muscle spent fighting it. The room erupted into chaos as Azrael drew his sword, the lust for blood and power overcoming him as he advanced toward the archduke, who raised his hands, stumbling back in shock.

Azrael's weapon came down and crashed into a glowing ax in Tobias's hands. Azrael grimaced, but his body pivoted and spun, dragging his blade across Tobias's stomach even as he tried to halt the sword's momentum. The soldier looked at the gaping wound and his eyes widened, his weapon disappearing as his knees collapsed into a growing puddle of blood.

Azrael bit back a curse. He'd liked Tobias, respected him, and hadn't wanted to hurt him. A Healer ran to the wounded soldier as Azrael glared at Queen Siryn. "Stop this," he managed through gritted teeth.

The Vastane queen narrowed her gaze and sweat glistened on her forehead as she pointed at him.

Lord Haldron released Lady Darbry and stuck out his chest. "You're in league with her, aren't you?"

Azrael peered over his shoulder, his hand involuntarily tightening on the hilt of his sword.

"Haldron, shut up," Caston warned, keeping himself between Azrael and Queen Valeri.

The noble's face reddened. "I knew we couldn't trust you. Making you commander was the biggest mistake this council ever made!"

Fury blasted through Azrael at the brazenness of this inconsequential man. In less than a heartbeat, he traveled through the void and reappeared in front of Lord Haldron. Lady Darbry screamed and backed into the wall as he thrust his sword into the noble's chest.

Embracing the Darkness

"Do you know how long I've wanted to do that?" With a sickening squelch, Azrael slid his weapon free, and the nobleman crumpled.

Caston swore, lunged forward, and stepped into his fighting stance. Reed jumped in front of the remaining nobles while Amycus reinforced his air shield to protect the queen.

Prince Jazari appeared out of the shadows with his sword raised. "Commander, fight it."

Caston's eyes darted from the prince to Azrael. Azrael's shoulder twitched.

Queen Valeri stood. "That's treason!"

He glanced between Caston and the queen. "Do you actually think you can stop me? Any of you?" He caught Amycus's stare. The old man's arms shook as he held his shield. Sadness washed over his face.

Queen Siryn raised her hand, and Azrael's body stiffened. His feet moved across the room, past the growling Snatcher. He stopped next to the Vastane queen. "Do you understand now, Lorella?" she asked. "I command the Angel of Death. It looks like you're under my authority."

Lady Darbry sobbing into Lord Rollant's shoulder was the only sound in the room.

Queen Siryn tilted her head as she addressed Queen Valeri. "You have until dawn to consider. The Empower Stone for the lives of your people. Seems an easy trade." She pushed back from the table and signaled her guards. "Come, Azrael. We've made our point."

Azrael sheathed his sword and followed the Vastane queen.

"You can't trust her, Jasce," Amycus said, finally lowering his hands.

He looked over his shoulder. "That's no longer my name."

Chapter Thirty-Five

The door to the War Room snapped shut, silencing the cries and yells of the nobles and dignitaries. Azrael tried to fight against the control the queen had over his mind and body and didn't notice Garan stalking up behind him until a collar clicked shut around his neck. He spun but was too late to stop a guard from shackling his wrists, while another removed his swords and dagger.

Azrael growled at the queen. "We had a deal."

The queen simply smiled and led her soldiers and the Snatcher out of the palace and toward the boardwalk where the waves caressed the docks. Warning bells continued to ring as four Vastane warships bobbed in the harbor.

Azrael was still seething as they walked up the stairs to one of the boat-building facilities. He scowled at the soldier who fondled his blades as they entered a room. He needed to get those back, along with the leather band she had taken. And the only way to do that was to convince her he was on her side.

Queen Siryn reclined on a red satin fainting couch and ran her hand down her shimmering gown. "I think that went well, don't you?"

"Up until you put these on." Azrael raised his wrists. "I accepted your offer, remember?"

The queen tapped her lip as she regarded him. "We'll see." Keeping her eyes fixed on Azrael, she said, "Garan, darling, you may remove the cuffs."

"I don't think that's a good idea," the bodyguard said.

"I don't pay you to think." Her blue eyes flashed as she glared at her guard.

Garan mumbled something incomprehensible and inserted a key into the cuffs.

"Thanks, Garan darling." Azrael winked as the restraints clambered onto the floor. Garan's face reddened and his fists clenched. "I need to talk to the queen privately. Do you mind?"

He opened his mouth, but Queen Siryn interrupted. "Wait outside." The guard glowered and then stomped toward the door.

She licked her lips and patted the cushion next to her. Azrael sat and surveyed the room. "It's quite an accomplishment keeping your power hidden," he said, "especially from my Trackers."

She removed the pendant with the ruby from a silk pouch. "This blocks your Trackers from sensing our magic."

He eyed the pendant. "Does every Vastane have this ability, whatever it is?"

"How did you figure it out?"

"I'm not just a pretty face." Azrael assumed the leather band with the crystal was somewhere in the folds of her dress. "But you know your magic won't work while I'm wearing this collar, right?"

She trailed a finger down her neck into her bodice and pulled out the crystal. If he could somehow trick her into giving it to him then, with time, he'd have the strength to break the collar off and he'd—

Desire replaced that thought as he stared at the low dip in the front of her dress, revealing ample cleavage.

"You want me," she said. He hadn't realized she held his hand.

"Yes." His voice was strangled as he tried to pull away, but his body had a mind of its own as he slid next to her.

She trailed her tongue on his lower lip as her other hand ran up his thigh. His body betrayed him, and his lust, whether it was for power or for her, dominated his resolve. With her touching him, he couldn't resist.

Embracing the Darkness

Fight it!

Azrael lurched back and out of her grasp.

Don't let her control you.

Rising from the couch, he walked toward the bar, where he poured himself a drink and collected his thoughts. With the leather band, her compulsion worked despite him wearing the collar. If she was that powerful with just the sliver of the Empower Stone, he didn't want to imagine what she could do with the whole thing. He'd been under Drexus's thumb and then Queen Valeri's. He would not allow the Vastane queen to have power over him. At least he and Jasce—the sentimental fool he was—agreed on that. He couldn't deny it had been Jasce's voice telling him to stop.

A swish of fabric had Azrael turning.

"You are very impressive. Most men can't resist once I have control of their minds."

The alcohol burned his throat as he drained the contents of his glass. "Wouldn't you rather have me of my own free will?"

She took the glass from him and refilled it. "I don't trust you yet. I'm sure you understand. Plus, I wanted to see what I could do with you wearing that collar." Turning, she wandered to the window and stared out over the harbor. "Granted, you are much more compliant when you aren't wearing it. That's something I need to fix." She whispered the last sentence as if talking to herself.

Azrael grabbed another glass and filled it.

"Where's the Stone?" she asked, returning to the couch.

"Where's my sister?"

"Even as the Angel of Death, you still care for her." She tilted her head and smiled. "She's safe. Once I have the Stone, I will release her, as promised."

"I think I know where it is, but I'll need the crystal." Azrael stared at her over the rim of his glass.

"I'm not sure that's a good idea, my fierce assassin."

He stalked over to her and pulled her from the couch. "Do not toy with me."

He inwardly swore when his hands touched her arms and another wave of desire coursed through him. This time, he lounged on a throne with her at his side, and all the dignitaries bowed before him. The Heart of Pandaren, whole and glimmering with power, sat next to him.

The door burst open, and Queen Siryn cursed when the connection between them broke. Azrael let out a shuddering breath that caught in his throat as Amycus was shoved to the ground.

"Look who I found snooping around," Garan said, gripping Amycus by the hair.

The blacksmith winced in pain. Bruises already covered his face.

Queen Siryn huffed. "Mr. Reins. This is a pleasant surprise, even if the timing was poor."

Azrael stepped away from her. His muddled brain was making it difficult to align his thoughts.

"Jasce, you can't join her. Please . . ." Amycus grunted as Garan punched him in the stomach.

"Don't touch him," Azrael growled and lunged for the bodyguard.

His entire body spasmed as electricity coursed through him. He reached for the collar around his neck, but the shock wave zapped through him until his knees hit the floor with a crack. He gritted his teeth as he glared at her.

"You will remember your place." She lifted her thumb, and the pain stopped. "Looks like Jasce still has some sway on you. But not for long."

Azrael slowly rose to his feet. He could kill her with his bare hands, and even though Garan would run him through, it would be so satisfying to watch the light leave her eyes. But he needed to free Jaida. And he had to find out once and for all if Drexus was alive.

He stared at Amycus, surprised by his initial reaction when the old man had come into the room. Queen Siryn was right about one thing: Jasce still had a presence within him and, once again, his compassion had led him into trouble.

"Now, get me the Stone," the queen said. "Garan, go with him, and meet me and Mr. Reins at the warehouse." She handed the device and the sliver of crystal to her bodyguard, then ran her hand up Azrael's chest and pressed her lips against his, running her tongue along the seam. He winced when she bit his lower lip, drawing blood. "No hard feelings."

Embracing the Darkness

He wiped his mouth as she sauntered into a private room, shutting the door behind her while guards yanked Amycus to his feet.

Azrael tried to dodge the fist, but it came too fast and connected with his jaw. Garan kicked him in the stomach. Grunting, he fell to one knee and struggled to take a breath.

"That should also keep you in your place," Garan said.

Azrael rose to his feet and glared at the man. "I'll kill you for that."

The bodyguard sneered and shoved him toward the door. "Let's go."

Infiltrating the palace wouldn't be a problem. Azrael knew all the servants' entrances, and at this time of night, they'd be empty, especially with the queen's guards occupied with the Snatchers and trying to get the citizens to safety. They ran through deserted hallways and up four flights of stairs. He smirked as Garan bent over, his chest heaving.

"Where are we?" the bodyguard asked in between breaths.

"Quiet. Queen Valeri's study is down that hallway. I have a hunch the Stone is in there." It was the most logical place to start. Caston and the other guards had come from this direction when he first arrived at the palace. He remembered the crooked painting of the bowl of fruit—the one that hadn't matched the others. He'd thought it was out of place and now wondered if it hid a secret compartment. It'd be the perfect spot to hide something valuable.

He peeked around the corner. Two guards stood watch in front of the door leading to the study. Azrael backed against the wall. "There's two of them," he whispered. "We need to dispatch of them, quietly."

Garan nodded.

Azrael sprinted around the corner and then slid on his knees, avoiding the first soldier. He jumped to his feet and blocked a punch from the other guard before wrapping his arm around his neck. The guard tried to claw at Azrael's face but soon lost consciousness and slid to the floor.

Garan wiped off his bloody dagger and replaced it in his boot. The first soldier slumped down the wall, leaving a bloody smear.

Azrael pushed open the door, wincing at the squeak of hinges. They both glanced over their shoulders and listened for the sounds of footsteps.

"You stand guard while I go in," Azrael said.

Garan crossed his arms. "Do you think I'm stupid?"

"Yes, but what does that have to do with anything?" He bit back a curse as Garan rammed him into the door. Azrael grabbed the lapels of Garan's jacket and shoved him away. "We don't want anyone sneaking up on us. Besides, where do you expect me to go?" He pointed to the collar around his neck.

Garan scowled and then released him. "Hurry."

Azrael waited for the door to shut and his eyes to adjust to the darkened room.

"Idiot," he whispered, smiling as he hid the stolen leather band in his pocket. An ember of his magic sparked to life thanks to the crystal. It wasn't enough yet to vault or remove the collar, but soon.

He skirted around the gurgling fountain and removed the painting. A wooden box, banded in iron strips, lay in a hole in the wall. He let out a relieved sigh as he felt magic emanating from the safe. He withdrew it from its hiding place and turned it, trying to find a way to pry it open. If only he had a dagger or his magic.

A flutter of movement caught his eye. He pretended to return the painting, then lurched to the side and jabbed his fist into the shadows.

With a yank, he pulled the Alturian prince from the darkness. Prince Jazari raised his palms.

Azrael released him. "What are you doing? Garan's right outside."

"I followed you from the War Room to the docks and then here."

"Impressive," Azrael reluctantly admitted.

"Indeed." The prince straightened his jacket and stared at the box in Azrael's hand. "Now, what's your plan?"

Azrael lifted a brow, surprised the prince assumed he was unwilling to join Queen Siryn. A sense of relief had him lowering his shoulders. The control the queen had over him when she had the crystal had made him rethink his tactics. He'd be a fool to tackle her army and her lethal pets on his own.

He glanced over his shoulder at the closed door. "Listen fast.

Embracing the Darkness

They're taking me and the Stone to a secret location where they're hiding my sister. Follow us and then get Queen Valeri and the Paladin Guard. If she uses that Stone—"

The door creaked open, and Garan entered. "What's taking so long?"

Azrael glanced to where the prince had been but all that remained were shadows. He hoped the Shade Walker would come through. As he walked around the fountain, Garan raised his sword. Azrael rolled his eyes and batted it away.

The guard snarled. "Give it to me."

Azrael couldn't kill him because he still didn't know where Jaida was. Swearing, he handed over the box. Garan put it on the floor and used his dagger to break the hinges. Inside lay the cloth-covered Stone.

Garan licked his lips and stood. "I could make you do anything I want."

Azrael pointed to the collar. "Not with this on."

The man scowled and then slipped the Stone into a satchel draped over his shoulder. Azrael breathed a sigh of relief when the guard didn't notice the leather band missing from his pocket.

Soon, he thought. Once his sister was free, Queen Siryn would regret the monster she had awakened. They all would.

Chapter Thirty-Six

They had moved Jaida to a new building on the east side of the Textiles District. The stench of dye from a nearby processing center made Azrael's nose burn.

The guards shoved him inside the cavernous room and slammed the door behind them. Azrael memorized each of their faces and made a silent promise to kill them all once his magic was free.

A sly grin spread across Queen Siryn's face as she leaned against a dusty table. She had changed from the silk gown into brown pants and matching tunic, the same as her guards.

Amycus stood on the other side of the table, his eyes hard and jaw set. He too wore an electric collar, the metal dull and gray. His hands were bound behind his back, his cheeks were sunken, and the lines around his mouth deeper. "You won't get away with this," he said to the Vastane queen.

"Do shut up." She motioned to Garan, who pointed the device at the blacksmith and pushed the button. Amycus cried out and dropped to his knees, his head thrown back, causing the veins in his neck to bulge.

Before Azrael's mind caught up with his body, he stepped in front of the old man and grimaced as electricity flowed through him instead. Amycus slumped and his breath rattled in his chest.

The queen raised her hand and the current stopped. "That was foolish, Commander."

Azrael inhaled. "I need you to quit showing off and release my sister."

The queen's eyes narrowed to slits. "It seems I'm going to have to teach you some manners once we return to Vastane. Now, where's my Stone?"

Garan took it from his satchel and placed it on a table. Everyone retreated when he removed the covering, but Queen Siryn's eyes sparkled as pale blue light shone from beneath a layer of dust, and a ripple of magic pulsed through the air.

Amycus rose to his feet and whispered, "Why did you do that?"

"To test a theory," was all Azrael said. He had wondered how the device knew which collar to affect. It seemed one had to be in its line of sight, which he expected. He hadn't, however, liked how his body had instinctively reacted to protect the blacksmith. The Angel of Death wasn't a hero.

Queen Siryn frowned at the section of the Heart that resembled a small block of ice. "Doesn't look like much." She traced her fingernail along two different clefts where parts of the crystal were missing. Azrael frowned and glanced at Amycus. According to the story, only one sliver had broken off.

Amycus peered at it, the skin tightening around his eyes. "Be careful. You have no idea what it will do to you."

She glared over her shoulder. "Thank you for your concern, Mr. Reins." She focused back on the Stone and her lips parted. "Commander, can you feel it?"

Yes, he thought. "Not with this collar on. Want to remove it?"

Amycus shot him a look, his brow furrowed, and then quickly returned to staring at the Stone.

"I think not. You're much too powerful."

"We had a deal. You release Jaida and I come with you. Remember, side by side, ruling all of Pandaren?"

Turning, she looked him up and down. "Yes, and I will keep my end

Embracing the Darkness

of the bargain. However, I never said *how* you'd rule by my side." She walked around the table and stared at the Stone.

He clenched his fists. Amycus opened his mouth but snapped it shut as Azrael pointed at him. "Don't say it."

Amycus shrugged and whispered. "I'm assuming you have a plan."

"I always have a plan." The leather band in his pocket grew warmer the closer he stood to the Stone. The suppressed embers burned to life, and his magic stirred. Soon, he'd have the power necessary to get them out of this mess.

Queen Siryn placed her hand on the crystal and gasped. Closing her eyes, she inhaled a shuddering breath. When she opened them, their color had shifted to a royal blue. "Let's try this again."

She focused on Azrael. Suddenly, his fingers wrapped around Amycus's throat. Amycus grabbed his wrist, his eyes wide.

He yanked the blacksmith closer.

"Kill him," Queen Siryn said.

He clenched his teeth and tried to break the connection between him and the queen, but all he wanted to do was kill the old man, to crush his windpipe. To end his life.

"Fight it," Amycus wheezed. "You're stronger than her." His face reddened and his eyes rolled back.

Stop! A voice from deep inside yelled. He released Amycus, who stumbled and gasped for air.

Azrael inwardly swore. With the Stone, the queen's power was so strong the collar was almost ineffective. If it hadn't been for Jasce's lingering presence, Azrael would've killed the blacksmith.

Victory danced in her eyes as she released the Stone and addressed Garan. "It works. Lorella will kneel at my feet and gladly surrender Pandaren, and the remaining kingdoms will follow suit. No one will stop me." She peered out over the warehouse, as if imagining herself already on a throne.

Impatience coursed through Azrael, but he kept his feet stationary. "Your Majesty," he choked out, "my sister."

The queen stepped away from the table and rolled her eyes. "Yes, fine. A bargain is a bargain, after all." She sauntered toward the door leading to the prison cells below.

Garan signaled to the guards. "Watch him," he said, pointing to Amycus, then pushed Azrael toward the stairs. As they descended, the air grew cooler and mustier. He passed a dark corridor and remembered the other warehouse and the hallway that had pulsated with heat. *The Spectral we caught with your sister* had been the queen's words. He had thought she'd meant Vale, but what if it had been Drexus?

"It must have been annoying to have Vale escape. Didn't quite plan for that, did you?" Azrael asked.

Queen Siryn's back stiffened, and she slowly turned. "Not everything goes as planned, as you know."

"He won't survive with that many types of magic in him."

She snorted. "Like you care."

"I don't. But Jaida will."

She narrowed her eyes and then continued walking along the corridor, finally stopping outside his sister's cell. "Hello, puppet. Look who I brought."

Jaida's head whipped around. She glanced between the queen and him, then settled on Azrael. "What are you doing here?"

"It's quite delicious," the queen said, threading her hand through Azrael's arm. "He's trading himself for you. You're very fortunate to have someone care for you that much."

Jaida stood and approached the bars. "What does she . . . ?" She settled on his eyes and covered her mouth. "What's happened to you?" she whispered.

He stepped away from the queen. "I'm fine," he said to his sister and then addressed Queen Siryn. "Now, let her go."

She brought out the device that controlled the collars. "Brother and baby sister better behave or . . ." She mimicked pushing the button. Garan unlocked the cell door.

Jaida tensed as Azrael drew her into a hug. Neither one had touched the other for thirteen years, and the contact was foreign to both of them. He whispered in her ear. "Use the crystal to remove your collar." He pulled back and ran his hands down her arms, interlocking his fingers with hers. Her brows furrowed. When he released her, her hand clutched the leather band and her eyes widened.

Embracing the Darkness

"That's so endearing, but we're running short on time. Let's go," the queen said, waving to the stairs.

Azrael widened his stance. "Am I not staying here?"

The queen's laugh echoed off the walls. "Of course not. I wouldn't leave my best weapon locked in some dungeon."

The muscle in his jaw pulsed. Jaida's breath came out in quick gasps due to the crystals power, and he hoped she could hold on a little longer. Eventually, Garan would realize the crystal was missing and they'd search him first, but they wouldn't think to suspect Jaida.

The four of them walked up to the main floor and found Amycus kneeling with guards surrounding him, each holding a sword.

Amycus lifted his head when Jaida emerged through the doorway. "Jaida."

Azrael figured his sister must have been around six when she'd last seen Amycus, before Drexus had changed both of their lives.

Jaida's steps faltered as she gazed upon the blacksmith. "Hello, Amycus."

"What a happy reunion. Might as well add one more piece to the puzzle." The queen looked knowingly at Azrael. "Even though his methods were crude, he really is brilliant. Too bad he won't be much use to anyone anymore."

Azrael approached Queen Siryn. "Where is he?"

The smirk melted off the queen's face. She flicked her wrist, and a guard opened a side door. Two soldiers emerged, pulling along a tall man with short black hair. Azrael would recognize him anywhere, even if his body had wasted away to half its size.

Amycus swore. He and Azrael had both suspected he was alive, but to see him in the flesh and mostly whole still shocked them.

Drexus's dark eyes scanned the room. They first landed on Jaida, but the relief in them dissolved as he focused on Azrael. His jaw clenched. Where his right hand used to be was a metal claw.

"Are you okay?" Jaida struggled against the guard holding her.

Azrael snarled and then turned to the queen. "How is he still alive?"

"Well, it took a lot of Healers, poor souls." She shrugged. "Death really does taint everything you touch."

Azrael stared at his former commander. All this time, the man had been alive, if barely, and had told the Vastanes how to transfer magic. He closed in on the Fire Spectral, his teeth bared. A shot of electricity had Azrael's body going rigid, and it took everything he had not to fall to his knees. Not in front of Drexus.

"Easy, Azrael. I can't have you killing him, yet." The queen smiled at both men. The current stopped, and he let out a breath.

Drexus inclined his head. "Azrael? What *has* happened to you?" His voice sounded like he'd swallowed knives.

He bared his teeth at Drexus. "How could you help them?"

The queen ran her fingers through Drexus's short hair. He snarled and pulled away from her. "He really didn't have a choice. Not when I had his precious Right Hand," the queen said, then she added, "Figuratively and literally." She laughed at her own joke and flicked her fingernail against his metal claw.

"Have you seen what they did to Vale? They could've done the same to Jaida!" Azrael reached for Drexus, but Garan's sword pressed against his chest and electricity shot through him. He couldn't stop his legs from buckling.

The queen tsked at him. "You really are stubborn."

Blood pooled in his mouth, and his tongue throbbed. He glowered at the queen, who finally lifted her thumb.

Drexus's face revealed nothing as he gazed at him. He glanced at Jaida and then toward the table where the Empower Stone lay unprotected. A shadow flickered across his face.

"You need to stop doing that," Azrael said through clenched teeth, getting to his feet, and spitting a glob of blood onto Garan's boots.

Queen Siryn paced around them like a lioness stalking her prey. "Give us a little credit. Our medical knowledge is more advanced than yours. But poor Drexus is no longer a Fire Spectral. He now knows what it feels like to be a Natural, to be what he despised." The queen waved her hand. "Anyway, Jaida was never in danger. So you see, I've kept my side of the bargain. Now it's your turn."

Magic or no magic, Azrael was going to kill his former commander. The desire for revenge that had driven him for so many years burned like a torch in the night. Drexus needed to die. Azrael forced his gaze from

Embracing the Darkness

Drexus and stared at the queen. "I'm here, aren't I? What more do you want?"

She lifted her brow. "Lots more, but we don't have time for that."

Two Vastane guards rushed in and bowed. "They know, Your Majesty."

"Didn't take them as long as I thought," she said. "No matter. Garan, prepare the troops. Chain up Drexus and Mr. Reins—they may be useful."

Azrael faced the queen. "My sister."

Jaida wrapped her arms around herself, worry swimming in her eyes as she glanced between Drexus and her brother.

"Once we are free from this dreadful place, I'll release her. Once I know where your true loyalties lie, which shall be tested soon enough." She patted his cheek. "Your Paladin Guard is on its way."

Chapter Thirty-Seven

Azrael followed Queen Siryn out of the warehouse onto the cobblestone street. Lamps burned low, the sun peeking over the horizon and illuminating the Vastane soldiers. Howls followed by screams echoed through the alleyways as the Daeloks drew near. Jaida stood next to him and took hold of his hand. He stared at their joined fingers, remembering how he'd held her hand when they were children. How she had looked up to him, trusted him. This is what he'd wanted since he first discovered she was alive, but a hollowness now carved through him.

Azrael regarded the burst of color slicing through the clouds; pink, orange, and purple set the sky on fire. "The light chasing away the darkness," he whispered. A breeze brushed across his face, and a scent he knew all too well washed over him.

The sound of boots and shields rumbled through the dawn. There she was, as the Paladin Guard emerged. She'd braided her midnight hair and wore her chest piece over a beige tunic and forest-green leather pants. Her face was pale, but her jaw set as resolve filled her eyes. Kord had obviously done his work to heal his sister, at least physically.

What had Kenz thought when she'd woken and he wasn't there? Guilt threatened to swamp him. She deserved so much better.

Azrael shook his head. He couldn't allow those emotions to take root, not when there was so much at stake, so he once again forced Jasce to the background, behind the protective barrier.

Kenz's eyes found his and then narrowed when Amycus was led out of the warehouse, followed by Drexus. Gripping her sword, she stepped forward, but Caston called the troops to a halt.

Jaida squeezed his hand. "Isn't that the woman you love?"

He gave a slight nod.

"Then what are you doing here?"

He tore his gaze from Kenz and looked down at his sister. "I had to rescue you. There was no other way."

She gripped his shoulders. "I can take care of myself. You got me out, now go to her."

Azrael's smile didn't reach his eyes. "You're not out of this yet." But by the time the sun crested the top of the buildings, she would be. He swore it. "I need you to break these collars. Just a slight crack so no one notices. Can you do that?"

She bit her lip and looked at her hand, knuckles white as she gripped the leather band.

"Jasce!" Kord's yell broke through the din from the marching soldiers. He held his sword at his side and sorrow distorted his face. His eye flicked to the collar around his neck. The rest of his team stood by him: Flynt, Aura, Delmira, and Reed.

Caston was on one side of the queen, while General Nadja was on the other. Queen Valeri sat astride her horse and glared accusingly at Azrael as two Vastane guards wheeled out the Empower Stone. The penalty for treason and the murder of a noble was death. If he made it out of this alive, what method of execution would she choose?

"This is a blatant act of war, Evelina. Theft, kidnapping, betrayal. Is this truly what you want?" Queen Valeri asked.

"This is what I've always wanted, ever since you killed my father." Queen Siryn smiled, but hatred stormed in her eyes. "When this is over, you'll be kneeling. All of you will."

She motioned to her guards, who drew their weapons. Archers appeared on the top of the warehouse while the Daeloks slithered into the light and surrounded the Paladin Guard. She removed the covering

Embracing the Darkness

from the Stone and Azrael stepped closer, bringing Jaida with him. Power rippled through the air.

"Look around you, Lorella," Queen Siryn said with her arms spread. "The Daeloks will rip your Spectrals to shreds, my army will destroy your Paladin Guard, and I have the Angel of Death at my disposal." Murmurs rattled through the Pandaren soldiers. Lander pushed through the line, his eyes wide. Many of the soldiers Azrael had spent the last few months instructing wore looks of shock and betrayal. Their reaction caused a stirring inside him, feelings he didn't understand. He shook his head. To finish the mission, he couldn't afford these emotions breaking free.

"Evelina, don't do this," Amycus said from behind him. A fist struck flesh and his body hit the ground. Kenz stepped forward, but Kord held her back. Azrael slowly looked over his shoulder and memorized the face of the Vastane guard who stood over Amycus.

"Surrender. Unless you want your streets bathed in blood," Queen Siryn said. "You are outmatched."

"Now," Azrael whispered to Jaida. "Break the collar."

She licked her lips and then glanced at Drexus, whose mouth twisted into a smile.

Azrael's collar vibrated. Garan walked toward them, his eyes narrowed as he gripped his sword.

"Hurry," Azrael whispered.

"I'm trying," Jaida said, her eyes closed. The metal groaned and two cracks sounded.

His magic slowly awakened, and Jaida gasped as the suppression stopped. She turned her head and focused on Amycus. His shoulders stiffened, and he glanced around until his gaze met hers.

"When I say run, you run," Azrael said out of the corner of his mouth. "She can't use her compulsion on you. Understand?"

"What about you?"

"Don't worry about me."

Jaida rolled her eyes. "That's stupid."

A sharp jab caught Azrael in the ribs. He grunted and was about to retaliate when Garan grabbed his sister.

The scar puckered menacingly as Garan smiled. "What are you two whispering—"

A whoosh of wings swept overhead as the wyverns landed on the rooftops across from the warehouse. Vastane guards yelled and backed away from the beasts and roars resounded from the Daeloks.

The archduke touched down in the middle of the road, and his wyvern reared back on its hind legs. "You cannot have the Stone."

King Morzov, Consort Lekov, and the Balten soldiers emerged from the other end of the street while Prince Jazari and his Shade Walkers appeared out of the shadows.

Queen Valeri leaned forward in her saddle and smiled. "It seems we aren't outmatched after all."

Queen Siryn's nostrils flared as her gazed drifted over the wyverns and the other kingdoms. She rested her hand on the Stone and her magic pulsed.

Jaida groaned and held her head.

Azrael scanned his sister. "Jaida, back away," he said, but Garan blocked her path. She banged into his chest and whimpered. The power was too much for her.

"Garan, move. The Stone—" Azrael tried to retrieve the leather band, but the bodyguard backhanded him and then wrapped his arm around Jaida's waist.

Queen Siryn focused on the wyvern. It bucked and knocked the archduke to the ground. Roaring, it charged the front line of Pandaren soldiers. Screams rang out as its massive jaws snapped and claws ripped through the guards like paper.

Archduke Carnelian yelled, and the gem in his chest ignited. A crossbow emerged and in seconds, a bolt sliced through the air. Azrael's hair fluttered as the arrow streaked by. With another wave of Queen Siryn's arm, one of her guards blocked the arrow with his body.

The wyvern shook its head and flew to the top of the building. The archduke shouted a command to his soldiers, and gems blazed as weapons burst forth.

The Balten warriors marched forward, their eyes glowing as they engaged the Daeloks. Wyverns took to the skies. Caston raised his sword and gave the order to charge.

Embracing the Darkness

Human yells mixed with the roars of the creatures.

The Paladin Guard hurtled toward the Vastane soldiers while the Alturians flitted in and out of shadows, advancing from behind and shooting their crossbows with lethal accuracy. Azrael scanned the ground for a weapon to free his sister from Garan.

A tremble coursed through the streets. Pebbles vibrated, and plumes of dust drifted through the morning light as a fissure snaked along the cobblestones. The ground shook, and soldiers stumbled. Queen Siryn released the Stone and braced both hands on the cart. Azrael drifted closer just as the windows in the warehouse shattered.

A man emerged from the shadows.

"Vale," Jaida whispered, and tried to pull free of Garan.

Vale's eyes, the color of onyx, focused on Jaida and then surveyed the crowd. Drexus stepped forward, but a guard yanked him back. Black veins lined Vale's skin, and Azrael could practically see the magic shimmering around him.

"Release Jaida and Drexus," Vale said, his voice sounding as if more than one person was speaking.

Queen Siryn's lips flattened. "I'd wondered where you'd gone off to."

The ground continued to shake, and the black lines on Vale's skin swirled. A glowing dagger flew from his hand and spun through the air. One of Queen Siryn's guards pushed her out of the way. The blade sank into his chest.

The Vastane queen's face twisted in rage as she scrambled for the Stone and pointed at Vale, who halted mid-stride, struggling against invisible restraints. A squadron of Vastane soldiers advanced on him with their weapons drawn.

"No!" Jaida yelled, finally pulling away from Garan, who raised his sword. Azrael ran for the guard and tackled him.

"Jasce!" Amycus pointed as Jaida ran toward the queen.

Azrael spun. Magic from the Stone shimmered over Jaida, and her entire body stiffened. She clenched her teeth and her collar clattered to the ground.

All sound stopped as if sucked into a void. Jaida threw her head back and raised her arms. With a scream, the world shattered, and magic like Azrael had never felt before erupted from his sister.

"Kenz, shield!" Azrael yelled before the shock wave hit.

Creatures and soldiers alike flew backward, crumpling, their limbs twisted in unnatural directions. Queen Siryn screamed and hid behind her guards, whose bodies went rigid, their eyes bulging from their skulls. Vale disappeared into the shadows while Drexus maneuvered out of the soldier's grasp and dove for cover.

Kenz and Delmira threw up their hands, and indigo and yellow light erupted, creating a massive shield around Queen Valeri and the Paladin Guard to block the destructive waves of Jaida's magic. The wyverns beat their enormous wings and took to the skies as buildings crumbled. Men and beasts were thrown backward like rag dolls.

Amycus staggered to his feet, ripped away his broken collar, and raised trembling arms. Debris bounced off a wall of air.

Vastane soldiers, with weapons drawn, shoved past Azrael toward Jaida. Her hair whipped around her face, and her magic thundered. She focused on the advancing soldiers and sent another shock wave.

Wooden beams and shards of glass from the building behind them soared toward Azrael and the guards. He'd never get out of the way in time.

He glanced over his shoulder for one last look at Kenz and grunted as he was shoved to the ground. A wall of air and fire exploded in front of him.

Amycus hunched with his hands raised as the shock wave battered his body, his magic focused on protecting Azrael from the blast. With a final yell, Amycus was launched across the street.

Debris skittered along the road as the air settled. Jaida's eyes rolled to the back of her head, and she collapsed. Azrael sprinted toward her, gathering her in his arms, while the leather band he'd given her clinked onto the cobblestones.

He grabbed his collar and yanked it off. Holding her, he stared at the carnage, blinking as he tried to take it all in. Daeloks and soldiers from both sides lay unmoving, their bodies broken. The building behind him was leveled, leaving a cavern where it had stood. Heavy beams were strewn across the street like matchsticks.

Embracing the Darkness

A labored wheeze made him turn. Amycus lay on the ground with a wooden beam trapped on top of him. His chest rose slowly, and blood stained his lips. Azrael gently laid his sister down and ran to the blacksmith, pushing the board off him with a groan and feeling for his pulse. He scanned the area for Kord. Indigo and yellow light sparkled through the dust and fire. Blood dripped from Kenz's nose as she held her shield in place, protecting those from the blast. Her eyes found his and then dropped to Amycus's broken body.

"No!" she screamed.

"Jasce," Amycus whispered, squeezing his hand. "Don't give in."

"Shhh. Kord's on his way," Azrael said.

Amycus grimaced as his body tensed. "Don't embrace the darkness. Promise me."

The hand in his loosened its grip and fell to the street. Amycus's head dipped to the side and blue eyes that normally sparkled dulled, staring blankly at the lightening sky. The remaining nighttime stars faded into the sunrise.

Chapter Thirty-Eight

A cry exploded through the settling dust and boots pounded on the ground as all hell erupted. Swords crashed against shields. Terrenian soldiers yelled, and their wyverns roared. The sound of their enormous wings vibrating the glass of surrounding buildings was thunderous as they descended upon the remaining Daeloks.

Caston led the charge and the Spectrals attacked. Cyclones of fire and dirt eliminated the Vastane archers on the roofs while Amps battled alongside General Nadja and the Naturals on the ground. Delmira shielded Kord and his Healers along with Queen Valeri and the other council members.

Indigo light glowed as Kenz pushed past a squadron of soldiers to get to Amycus. Her sword cut through anyone who stood in her way while Flynt covered her with fireballs that blasted against the Vastane shields.

Queen Siryn backed away from the fray as her guards fell at her feet. Vale had disappeared into the shadows and Drexus lay unconscious by an overturned wagon.

Azrael closed Amycus's eyes. "Rest easy now, my friend," he whispered. He swallowed the grief, blocking Jasce's presence and not allowing the emotions to take over. He wasn't done yet.

He approached his sister. "Can you get up?"

She held her head. "Did I kill him?"

"Can you get up?" he asked again, not wanting her to think about what she did, needing her clear of the battle raging around them. He was about to lift her to her feet when a hand grabbed his arm and yanked him back.

Caston stood over him with a sword pointed at his chest. Azrael glanced at his sister and shook his head, warning her off as she stood.

Azrael inched closer to a fallen soldier and his abandoned weapon.

"I'm ordered to arrest you for treason. Will you surrender?" A look of pleading flashed across Caston's face.

"What do you think?"

Caston heaved in a breath. "So be it."

Azrael kicked up the sword just as Caston brought his down. Sparks flew, and the clash of steel vibrated through his arms. Caston lunged, aiming for Azrael's stomach. He parried and spun. The two former assassins moved in a lethal dance, their blades blurring through the morning light.

Kenz's cry had him turning, and his heart twisted seeing her kneeling over Amycus. Kord knelt next to her, holding his bleeding arm while Flynt and Aura kept the Snatchers and other soldiers away.

A burning heat sliced through Azrael's chest, and he stumbled, wincing as blood stained his tunic. Caston spun, bringing his foot around and connecting with his jaw.

Blood spurted from his mouth.

Azrael's head jerked back as Caston's fist crashed into his face. The cobblestones dug into his knee. Stars floated in his vision, and blood dripped down his nose and chin.

Caston grabbed a collar from his pocket and reached for Azrael. He halted mid-stride. His eyes widened and his shoulders stiffened. Crying out, a bone cracked and the collar he held fell to the ground.

"Get away from my brother." Jaida's hair fluttered, and her eyes pierced through the dust and smoke.

Caston's jaw pulsed as his feet lifted off the ground. Azrael remembered all too well the pain of having your body stretched, powerless to get free.

Embracing the Darkness

"Let him go," Azrael said, getting to his feet.

Jaida tore her gaze from Caston.

Azrael wiped the blood from his face. "Let him go."

Caston's toes touched the ground and then he bent over, resting his hands on his knees. He looked up. "I have to bring you in. I'm under orders."

Azrael tapped his boot with his sword. "You'll have to kill me. I will not be her prisoner." He gripped the hilt and focused on the magic pulsing through his muscles.

"Please." Caston grimaced.

Azrael stared at the carnage and chaos surrounding them. "Get my sister out—" His shoulders tensed. The need to protect his sister was replaced by a sudden desire to kill the man in front of him. He lurched forward.

Caston swore and raised his weapon.

Rage surged through Azrael, drowning Jasce's compassion that had snuck through. From the corner of his eye, Queen Siryn knelt by the Stone, her hateful gaze on him.

With a roar, the Angel of Death attacked.

Caston blocked and stumbled, trying to regain his balance. Azrael vaulted and Caston barely lifted his blade in time to block the strike before he disappeared. Materializing at Caston's side, he elbowed him in the face, and blood spurted from his nose. Azrael flipped over him, spun, and slashed through his leg. The soldier cried out and fell to one knee.

Don't do this!

Azrael's arms shook, and his knuckles whitened. Another surge of magic flowed over him, and he moved with unfettered speed. The killing blow careened toward Caston's neck.

Resignation flashed in Caston's eyes as he attempted to block the strike.

Azrael gritted his teeth as his blade sunk into an indigo shield, centimeters from slicing flesh.

Kenz had her hands raised, eyes shining like emeralds.

Jaida rose to her feet and waved her arm. The Empower Stone flew away from the queen and landed next to a wagon covered in flames. Queen Siryn's face twisted in fury.

Free from the queen's compulsion, Azrael lowered his sword. Shame washed over him—a feeling the Hunter wasn't accustomed to, a feeling that wouldn't go away.

He jerked as Jasce's presence reached from the depths and pounded on the wall. Memories flashed through his mind: when he first saw Kenz, enamored by her beauty; her fingers scraping over his wet skin as she helped him remove his armor. He shuddered, thinking of her gentleness as she stitched up his back and saved his life. The first time they made love, the feel of her body against his. When he asked her to marry him.

Azrael grabbed his head. "Stop!" He didn't know if he was talking to Jasce or himself. Where was the line separating the two? All he knew as he gazed at the woman he had loved was that he wasn't worthy of her affection. He'd made too many mistakes, and she deserved better.

Kenz's arm shook as she held her shield in place. "Jasce, come back to me. Please."

Caston struggled to his feet, anger and pain warring in his eyes.

The sounds of battle surrounded them. Morning mist clung to the street as the sun peeked over the horizon. Flynt, Aura, and Kord fought off a Snatcher and a Vastane soldier. Grief and sorrow lined their faces.

Azrael stumbled. The fight with Caston had weakened his magic and emotions flowed around him: despair, fear, anger, betrayal.

He groaned and rested his hands on his knees. A squadron of Vastane soldiers separated him from Jaida and were quickly advancing on Kenz and Caston.

Kenz lowered her hand, and her shield disappeared. "Let us help you."

He breathed deeply as sweat trickled down his back and remembered how Amycus had taught him to block Spectral emotions. He closed his eyes and rebuilt the barrier, brick by brick. He couldn't afford to feel the vulnerability, not when he still had a job to do. Not when lives depended on him being ruthless.

Kenz's shoulders hunched, and Caston swore as Azrael stood to his

Embracing the Darkness

full height. From the corner of his eye, he saw Garan stalking toward Jaida.

He wiped the blood from his face. "My fight isn't with either of you." He vaulted as Jaida screamed.

She covered her mouth and looked away as a sword tip erupted through Garan's chest. Azrael gripped his shoulder, withdrawing his blade with a sickening sound, and spun him around. Blood gurgled from the bodyguard's lips.

"I told you I'd kill you," Azrael said, watching the light leave Garan's eyes. He cleaned his sword on the dead man's tunic and surveyed the battle, then scanned the area for the Empower Stone and found it lying right where Jaida had sent it.

"Jaida, stay here," he said, and he removed a satchel from a fallen soldier. Vaulting to the Stone, he forced himself to place it inside the bag, hoping the fabric would subdue some of its power.

"Give it to me."

He whirled. Queen Siryn's hand fisted around the leather band that Jaida had dropped. Her normally perfect hair was knotted and dirty, and a gash lined the side of her face.

"No." He squeezed the hilt of his sword.

Anger marred her beautiful face. "So much for trusting you."

"You should've known the monster you unleashed would never bow to you."

"We'll see." Her brow furrowed as she raised her hand. Azrael tried to vault, but dread crashed over him. His body was frozen except for his hand releasing the strap holding the satchel.

The queen's lips curved as she walked over and picked up the Stone. "If you won't bow, then I'll kill everyone you care for. You will be my slave and live out your miserable life knowing you failed."

She held the Stone and then shot her hand forward. Azrael's body went rigid. "Don't you see? I can control every part of you. Break you from the inside out."

Azrael cried out as the bone in his arm cracked. His sword clattered to the ground.

He needed to vault before the pain became too much. He concentrated on the magic of the Empower Stone and his hate, but the queen's power held him in place. A loud pop sounded, and he yelled as his shoulder dislocated.

Kenz shouted as she and Caston battled a squadron of soldiers while trying to get to him.

Azrael focused on her beautiful face and the love they had shared. He remembered laughing with Kord and Caston, and the pride he'd felt training the recruits, the approval in Amycus's eyes. Grief and love battled through him, the vulnerability and compassion so much more powerful than his most violent rage.

Azrael roared and disappeared. He resurfaced next to the queen and in one fluid motion he spun, kicked the Stone out of her grasp, and grabbed the sword with his left hand. She raised her palms and tried to retreat. He swung the blade and fulfilled his promise. Her scream was silenced forever as he removed her head from her body.

He stood over the former Vastane queen, not sure how he'd found strength in the emotions he'd once considered weak.

The Paladin Guard cheered as the Vastane soldiers fled down the streets. The Baltens and Alturians joined the Guard as they pursued on horseback, not allowing any to escape while the wyverns continued picking off the Snatchers.

As Azrael scanned the clearing for Kenz, a shimmer in the shadows near Queen Siryn's body caught his eye. Swearing, he searched the ground for his leather band, but it had disappeared.

"Drexus, no!" Jaida screamed.

Pain coursed through Azrael as his back arched. He stared in shock at the tip of a bloody sword protruding through his armor. The blade slid free. He gripped his chest and fell to his knees. Blood dripped from his hands as Drexus stalked around him.

"I believe this makes us even," Drexus said. He picked up the Stone and placed it in the satchel, then anchored it over his shoulder.

Jaida sobbed and crawled to where Azrael knelt. She covered his hand with hers and stared at Drexus. "Why?"

He glowered at her. "Choose, my dear. Me or him?"

Azrael coughed, and blood bubbled from his lips. "Go. Queen Valeri will take your magic if you stay." He swayed, and she wrapped her arm around him. "There's nothing for you here." He sat on his heels as crimson stained his tunic. He blinked, trying to stay upright and conscious.

"You're here," she whispered.

"Is this your choice, then?" Drexus asked, anger filling his dark eyes.

A tear slid down Jaida's cheek.

"Drexus Zoldac, you are under arrest!" Queen Valeri shouted as her guards ran toward them.

Drexus glanced at the soldiers and then at Jaida. His expression hardened as he turned and sprinted through the smoke.

Tears streamed down Jaida's face. She gasped as Vale emerged from the shadows across the street. His black eyes cleared for a second, the warm brown full of sadness.

She choked back a sob. "Vale."

Vale's gaze flickered to Azrael. With a nod, he grabbed Drexus as the soldiers drew their swords and crossbows. Arrows bounced harmlessly off the wall as they disappeared into the darkness with the Empower Stone.

The world tilted, and Azrael fell, his head bouncing on the ground. He blinked and tried to lift his arm when soldiers yanked Jaida to her feet and attached a collar around her neck.

He heard his name yelled from a distance.

A delicate hand pressed against the hole in his chest. "Stay with me."

He gazed into the most hypnotic green he'd ever seen. Hair resembling the beauty of the night sky framed a face with freckles dusted across her cheeks.

"I'm so sorry." His heart slowed as his life bled out of him. A roar from deep inside clawed out of the depths, holding on, clinging to the slowing rhythm.

Feet shuffled, and someone gently nudged Kenz out of the way.

"Don't you die on me, you stubborn mule," Kord said, his voice muffled.

This time, it wouldn't be enough. Death had smiled at Azrael for the last time.

Chapter Thirty-Nine

Azrael woke to the sound of whirring equipment and hushed voices. He blinked against the brightness and winced from the pain shooting through his chest and back.

"Wiggle your toes."

A tall man stood at the end of his bed with his arms crossed. Black wind-blown hair accompanied one bright green eye, the other covered with a patch. He was huge, yet he had a kind face.

Tearing his eyes from the stranger, he looked at his toes and moved them.

The man let out a breath and uncrossed his massive arms. "Good. I wasn't sure if you'd been paralyzed. Drexus caused some serious damage and one of those Snatchers got me, so I couldn't heal you right away. We had to—"

"Who are you?" Azrael licked his dry lips. His voice sounded like he'd swallowed the entire Desert of Souls. "Where's the physician?"

The man's brow furrowed. "What?"

Azrael tried to sit up, but the cuff around his wrist clanked against the bars on his bed. He yanked once and then swore. "What's going on? Where's Commander Zoldac?"

Concern flashed through the man's eyes. He raised his hands and slowly walked to the side of the bed. "Easy, Jasce. You've been out for almost three days. You need time to heal."

"What did you call me?"

The man sat across from him and rubbed his jaw. "I called you Jasce."

"How do you know my name?" His arm shot out and he grabbed the man by the tunic. "I'll ask again, who are you?"

The man's lips drew into a straight line. "My name is Kord Haring. I'm a Healer. I'm also your best friend."

"I've never seen you before in my life."

"What's the last thing you remember?"

Azrael eased back onto the pillows and surveyed the medical facility. It seemed different from the last time he was here, when he'd sparred with Bronn, who got a lucky shot and sliced his arm. He'd been waiting to undergo the procedure to give him magic and wondered if Drexus had perfected it yet.

He answered the imposing man, wondering what a Spectral was doing in the medical wing.

"That's the last thing you remember? What about being rescued from the dungeon, or Carhurst, or the Battle of the Bastion?"

Azrael's brows lifted. "There was a battle and I missed it? When did that happen?"

Kord shook his head. "What about Kenz?"

"Who's Kenz?" The blood rushed in his ears. Something was terribly wrong, or someone was pulling a sick prank. "Go get the physician in charge. Now."

"That would be me." Kord leaned back in his chair.

A commotion over the Healer's shoulder had Azrael raising to his elbow. He quickly bowed his head. "Your Majesty."

Queen Valeri arched a brow. "Proper manners won't get you out of this mess, Mr. Farone."

Kord stood and raised a finger. "Your Highness, we have a problem."

Azrael sat up straighter in bed. "Mr. Farone? I'm Second in Command of the Watch Guard."

Embracing the Darkness

The queen glared at him. "You have been stripped of all authority and are no longer commander of anything, nor a member of the Paladin Guard."

Azrael's heart thundered in his aching chest. He was losing patience. Someone had better start answering his questions soon. "What the hell is going on? Where's Drexus? And why am I chained to this bloody bed?"

The queen rested her hands on her hips. "You're chained to that bed because you're guilty of treason and the murder of Lord Haldron. Thankfully, Tobias survived. However, Drexus has escaped again—with the Empower Stone, I might add. If your magic hadn't made you lose your mind, you'd be hanging from the gallows right now. But thanks to Mr. Haring and a few other council members, you're still breathing."

"Treason? With all due respect, Your Majesty, I was following orders of Steward Brenet and Commander Zoldac."

The queen crossed her arms and frowned at Kord. "Mr. Haring, what's going on?"

The Healer sighed and raked his fingers through his already messy hair. "It seems Jasce has forgotten everything after he received the Amplifier serum."

"How is that possible?"

"My guess is that because his inherent magic is Vaulter, which is a mental magic . . . when we removed it along with the Amplifier, it affected his memory." Kord chewed the inside of his cheek as he observed him. "Emile experienced a very minor case, but nothing like this."

"Mr. Farone has no memory of the last year?" the queen asked.

"I'm sitting right here. And my name is Azrael." He fisted his hand, his neck aching as he glanced between the two.

Kord rubbed his forehead. "It seems so."

The queen tapped her lip while Azrael tried to keep the scowl off his face. He didn't answer to her, hadn't since Drexus had taken over. But it seemed she was in power now.

"I want guards on him at all times, and when you've cleared him, he's to be escorted out of my Sanctuary."

Kord interrupted. "But Your Majesty, this wasn't his fault. Queen Siryn made him kill Lord Haldron."

"We've been over this, Kord. I'm sorry." The queen's gown fluttered in her wake as she exited the room.

Azrael felt his mouth hanging open and snapped it shut.

Kord plopped into the chair and rested his arms on his knees. "What a mess," he mumbled.

Azrael scooted to a sitting position, the metal cuff on his wrist clanking in the silence. Punished for crimes he didn't commit? Or at least, didn't remember committing. He had so many questions bouncing around his head, he didn't even know where to start. But one thing kept coming back to him. "Did you say I had magic? Vaulter?"

The Healer looked up. "Yes, you had Amplifier, thanks to Drexus's experiments. But we also discovered you had latent Vaulter magic." He pointed to Azrael's arm.

The place that used to have the tattoo his mother had given him was now a scar. A knot formed in his stomach.

"That tattoo had Brymagus plant in the ink and blocked your inherent magic. The two types eventually caused you to go crazy," Kord explained.

"Crazy?"

Kord scratched the stubble along his broad jaw. "Crazy."

"And you somehow removed both types?"

"Yeah. Maera and me." Azrael was about to ask who Maera was, but Kord continued, "She is our top physician and had perfected Drexus's procedures."

Azrael gritted his teeth. "And you didn't think to ask me before taking my magic?" Even though he couldn't remember having magic, who were they to remove it?

"I had to. I'm sorry. The two magics would have eventually killed you, and I couldn't let that happen."

Azrael swallowed the anger. Then he noticed the tattoos on his other arm, specifically the one on his right hand—the space reserved for the Fire Spectral who had killed his mother and sister.

"I found him? How can I not remember this?" Azrael looked from the tattoo to the Healer. His purpose since becoming a Hunter was to

Embracing the Darkness

find and kill the Spectral with black fire. Based on the mark on his hand, he'd done it. He'd completed his mission. But who had it been? He was about to ask when blonde hair caught his attention. His blood turned to ice as his mother appeared in the doorway.

"Please, just let me see him," the woman said. Her voice sounded different. A man behind her with copper-colored hair spoke to the soldier at the door. With a nod, the two entered, and the woman jogged toward him.

He swallowed as his chest tightened. Not his mother—his sister. It wasn't possible. She was dead. She'd been dragged behind a burning cottage, her screams silenced. The man with black fire had killed her, along with his mother.

Kord stood and raised both hands. "Hold on."

The other man walked over. "It's fine, Kord. Her memories have partially returned. Let her see him."

"Jaida?" Azrael whispered. He scooted back as she came to the side of the bed and threw her arms around him.

"I've been trying to visit you since they brought you in."

He gripped her shoulder and pushed her away. "How are you here? Alive?" He tried to breathe but couldn't seem to remember how. Black spots floated in his vision.

Jaida's forehead creased as she stared at Kord. "How much has he lost?"

Azrael tried to focus on the pain his nails left in his palm. Panic, like he hadn't felt in years, rushed through him. "I can't breathe," he wheezed.

"Everyone back up," Kord said. Azrael thrashed under Kord's touch as he yelled to a nearby staff member. A warming sensation flowed through him, but he struggled to pull free as a needle punctured his skin.

"Hang on, buddy. We'll get this sorted out," Kord said.

A fuzziness washed over him, and his heartbeat slowed. He fell back onto the pillow and tried to force his eyes open. Gentle fingers caressed the hair from his face, and gray eyes full of worry stared down at him before he drifted off into a drug-induced haze.

Cassie Sanchez

∽

Azrael opened his eyes and focused on the ceiling. Based on the chamomile and harsh antiseptic smell, he was still in the medical facility. Metal clanked as he moved his arm, and a soft snore came from his side.

A woman hunched in a chair. Her cream tunic was wrinkled, and a sword leaned against the table. Her boots laced up to her knees and dark green pants clung to muscular legs. A warrior, even with the fancy bracelets on her wrists.

For a guard, she wasn't doing a very good job, Azrael thought, watching her sleep.

She jerked and blinked. "You're awake."

"As are you."

The corner of her lip quirked. "Do you remember me?" Hope shone in brilliant green eyes, similar to the massive Healer. Freckles decorated the bridge of her nose, and her midnight hair lay in a braid down her back.

He slowly shook his head. "Sorry."

She gave a sad smile. "I'm Kenz."

He swallowed. He couldn't remember seeing a more beautiful woman. "Yeah, that big guy mentioned your name. I'm supposed to know you?"

She bit her lip and looked away. He had this unnatural desire to pull her to him and take away the pain that he had obviously caused. She wiped a tear from her eye and huffed out a laugh. "That big guy is my brother, and I'm your fiancée." She looked down at her folded fingers. "Or was."

Fiancée? He was engaged? What the hell happened in the last year? His sister was alive, Drexus was who-knew-where, and he'd proposed to this woman?

He rubbed a hand down his face. "I'm sorry."

"I'm glad you're okay. You had us worried."

He glanced around the facility. "I'm still unsure of what happened. All I know is I had magic, and now I don't, and everyone keeps calling me Jasce. Supposedly, I'm a traitor." The thought left a bitter taste in his mouth. He wasn't a traitor. A killer, yes, but not a traitor.

Embracing the Darkness

"We'll work on the queen, but there's so much to tell you." She stared at him as if trying to figure out what to say. She swallowed, and resignation filled her eyes. "I'm not sure I'm the person to do it."

"Is Jaida really alive, or did I imagine that?"

She took his hand and squeezed. "She is. Drexus kept her hidden."

His chest tightened and he willed himself to breathe through the rising anger and the sting of betrayal. "Why would he do that?"

She bit her lip again and looked toward the door. Even through his confusion and the drugs they'd given him, desire flared as he examined her mouth.

Get a grip, he thought.

A soldier marched in and nodded to the guard standing nearby. "You're relieved," he said as he strode past. The guard saluted and exited the room.

"Caston." Finally, someone Azrael recognized as a fellow Hunter. He noticed the symbol on his tunic. "They made you commander?"

Caston smiled. "Don't look so surprised."

"You might as well be king. I'd be less shocked with all I'm learning right now."

Kenz stood. "I'll let you two catch up."

He caught her hand before she could leave. The contact was comforting in a way he couldn't explain. "Wait. Will I see you again?" He had no idea why he asked that, but somewhere deep inside him, he knew he didn't want her to go.

She squeezed his hand. "Yes."

He watched her weave through the empty cots and then peeked around Caston to keep her in view until she disappeared through the doorway.

Caston chuckled. "Well, at least some things don't change." He sat in the vacant chair. "How are you feeling?"

He arched a brow. "How do you think?"

Caston crossed his ankle over his knee and stared at him for a long time. "I need you to remember your training."

"My training?"

"As a Hunter."

"I haven't forgotten that."

Cassie Sanchez

Caston nodded. "Good, because you're going to need it after I get done telling you everything."

Chapter Forty

The following days were a blur between consciousness and whatever drugs they'd given him to make him sleep. Discovering Drexus had been the one who betrayed him and killed his mother had made him throw up the lunch he'd forced down. He'd experienced every emotion from rage to disbelief to grief. He was physically and emotionally exhausted, especially after hearing the recounting of the most recent events. Who would've thought having magic would've changed his life so drastically?

During the darkness of night, when he was alone in the Sanctuary, he'd decided to go back to his given name. After all, it was Drexus who'd changed it to Azrael. Hatred simmered inside him for his former commander, for the lies and betrayal. If he ever saw the man again, Jasce would end him once and for all, even if he lost his own life in the process.

Kord had visited, along with a few other Spectrals he didn't recognize. Jasce's stomach tightened into knots whenever Kenz came to the Sanctuary. Stories were told, many with him in it, that he couldn't remember, but he found himself laughing along with his friends. He'd never experienced friendship as a soldier or Hunter. Bronn had been the closest thing, and he'd betrayed him.

Cassie Sanchez

Jaida came by twice a day, always with that Fire Spectral in tow, and every day more of her memories returned. Why his hadn't, no one knew. Some suspected it had to do with his two types of magic and the time spent with the Empower Stone. He and his sister recounted their adventures in the forest when they were kids, and she cried when she told him about the events at the Bastion months ago, and about losing control of her magic and killing a man named Amycus. He didn't remember any of it, but he felt her pain and remorse—something he wasn't accustomed to feeling.

The day of Amycus's funeral finally arrived. It was all that was talked about between the Healers and other medical staff.

Shackles rattled as a soldier led Jasce out of the Sanctuary and across the courtyard. He shied away from the sunlight, still warm even as it started its descent. The monsoon season had passed, and the summer breeze from the ocean blew strands of hair off his face. He passed a group of recruits who looked at him with wide eyes. A few started to salute, out of habit, and then lowered their hands. Jasce kept his eyes forward.

He thought about how Kenz, Kord, and Caston had all argued against having him chained. He'd watched in admiration as the three had stood up to the queen.

"Your Majesty," Kord had said. "He can't be held responsible for this. He's not a criminal."

"I understand your concern. But he's proven he'll do anything to rescue his sister or have power. He should've told you about the effects the magic was having on him," Queen Valeri replied.

Kenz crossed her arms, and anger flashed in her eyes. "He did. We knew everything."

Damn, she was fierce, he thought, his stomach tightening.

"Yes, and as captain, you should've mentioned that. Both you and Caston are lucky I don't strip away your ranks."

Jasce leaned forward, the metal cuff clanking. "Your Highness, please. I'll wear the shackles. Don't take your anger out on them. They were just following orders. My orders." He was guessing at that, but he'd do whatever he could to keep the fallout from landing on Caston or Kenz.

Embracing the Darkness

Kord had rested his hands on his hips and smiled at him. Jasce frowned, not understanding what that look was for.

The queen arched her brow and then left the Sanctuary.

Caston shook his head. "She doesn't realize you could get out of those cuffs in seconds."

Jasce snorted. "True."

Kord and Kenz had laughed in agreement, but how they knew he was capable of picking locks and getting out of restraints, he had no idea.

Footsteps sounded behind him, bringing him back to the present, and the guard holding Jasce tightened his grip. He fought the urge to twist away and elbow the man in the face. He'd already been warned. The queen was giving him some leeway to attend the funeral from afar. It was a show of mercy he wouldn't take advantage of.

"Wait!" A teenage boy, dressed in uniform with water droplets dripping from his hair, ran toward them.

Jasce shifted awkwardly as the chains connecting his feet scraped along the ground. He hissed out a breath at the sharp pain that ran through his back and leg. The Healers had done all they could. Kord had said he couldn't heal him right away due to some creature called a Snatcher and when the soldiers had transported him to the Sanctuary, more damage was caused. The weakness and lingering pain were most likely permanent, even though there was some hope he'd fully recover. Even still, Jasce was done being poked and prodded, and the queen's patience had met its limit.

The boy skidded to a stop and saluted. "Commander, are you all right?" His eyes scanned Jasce's body. Obviously, the Guard knew about the sword that had pierced through his chest.

"No need to salute. I'm not your commander."

"You'll always be my commander, sir." The boy rubbed his forearms. "Is it true you don't remember anything?"

Jasce swallowed, giving a quick nod. "It's true."

The boy stared at his feet and then looked up, jutting out his jaw. "The name's Lander." He held out his hand.

Jasce's chains rattled as he shook the boy's hand. "It's nice to meet you, Lander. I'm Azrael—or Jasce." He sighed and massaged the back of his neck, his cuffs scraping his skin.

The guard holding him cleared his throat. "I'm sorry, sir, but it's time."

He glanced over his shoulder and nodded, then focused on the boy. "Keep training hard."

Lander saluted again. Tears filled his eyes, and his body jerked forward. Jasce stiffened as the teenager wrapped his arms around him.

Lander gave one last squeeze and ran off in the direction he'd come.

"He's right, you know."

Jasce looked at the guard. He thought he recognized him from his time as a Hunter. "About what?"

"Many still consider you their commander and would follow you into any battle."

He lifted his brows. "Many, huh?"

The soldier laughed. "Not all, but yeah. Many. Including me."

"You fought under Drexus?"

"I did. The name's Darin."

"Darin," Jasce repeated and shuffled toward the gates leading out of the Bastion.

"You were an amazing commander. Better than Drexus any day."

"Thank you." At least he'd done one thing right, he thought. The last year had been a tumultuous list of events. Kord had filled in a lot of missing information from Caston, and Jasce could understand how they'd quickly become friends. Kord's lighthearted manner and easy-going smile was refreshing. Kord had even brought his family in to see if they'd jar his memory.

He was tired of seeing the disappointment on everyone's faces and would be glad when this day was over.

The Fire Spectral—Flynt, if Jasce remembered correctly—led Jaida across the courtyard to join him for the funeral. He'd learned that she was under house arrest, too, and her magic had also been removed. Even worse, because of her association with Drexus, she'd been banished from Pandaren. He'd tried to convince the queen to change her mind, but she would not yield.

Shock filled Jasce every time he saw his sister. It would take some

Embracing the Darkness

time before the reality of the situation settled in his mind and heart. Protecting Jaida gave him a purpose and having his revenge on Drexus kept him focused but waking up and learning that his life had completely changed, left him hollow inside.

They made their way past the arena to an open field surrounded by the Guard. A vacant pyre lay in the middle, a stark reminder of life's ending place. Wood, fire, ash.

Queen Valeri sat on a small throne surrounded by nobles Jasce wasn't familiar with, plus the other kingdoms that had attended the Gathering. Two large white cats lay next to a redheaded man with a gold circlet on his forehead. A fierce-looking woman sat next to him dressed in full armor. Those must be the Baltens, he thought.

Darin pointed out the other dignitaries, mentioning the Alturians decided to leave early to return their commander's body to their island. Before they left, though, the prince had argued for leniency toward Jasce to the queen. It was strange to feel indebted to a man he neither knew nor remembered.

Jasce recognized the blonde woman, Maera, from the Sanctuary, the one responsible for taking his and his sister's magic. He wasn't too sure how he felt about her, even though she'd been kind and was trying to find a way to get his memory back.

Murmurs rippled through the crowd as Darin led Jasce and Jaida up a small hill, away from the spectators. He noticed General Nadja, who saluted as he walked by. He'd always admired her discipline and strength and wasn't surprised she'd advanced in the ranks.

The Balten king whispered something to Queen Valeri, who lifted her head and stared at Jasce. She nodded and resumed talking with the Archduke of Terrenus while the king made his way across the field with his cats walking by his side.

His eyes drifted over Jaida and then focused on Jasce. "Commander," the king said, his voice a deep baritone.

Jasce inwardly cringed at the use of his old title. "Your Majesty."

The king absently stroked the cat's ears. "Lorella's told me your sister is to be banished, and you're going with her."

"Yes. Until I figure out . . ." He looked over the field, his eyes resting on the pyre. "There's a lot I need to sort out," was all he said.

"Both Consort Lekov and I agree you are welcome in Balten."

He looked at Jaida, who shrugged, and then said, "That's very generous of you."

The king chuckled. "I'm not that altruistic, my boy. You're an excellent warrior, and we could use a man like you. Plus, I think we could learn from each other."

"Learn what?"

"Come to Balten and find out." With a wink and click of his tongue, he strode across the field. One of the enormous cats looked over its shoulder, her red eyes probing. She wrinkled her nose and then loped after her master.

A horn blew, and the flaps of a tent opened. His former team came out carrying a pallet with Amycus's body wrapped in white fabric. The swish of clothing whispered around the clearing as everyone rose to their feet. Based on what many had said, Amycus had stood up to tyranny, trained Spectrals to fight for their freedom, and been an inspiration.

Kord and Kenz led the procession with Flynt, Aura, Delmira, and Caston. Jaida grabbed Jasce's hand and held on tightly. A breeze blew in the salty air from the ocean while the sun warmed his skin.

"It's my fault he's dead," she whispered, tears trickling down her face.

"It sounded like it was an accident. No one holds you responsible."

"I'm not so sure about that."

He wished he could comfort his sister, but he didn't know how. He barely knew her and had been trained to block out useless emotions, as Drexus had called them. All he felt was emptiness.

Amycus's body was handed to the soldiers, who reverently placed him on top of the pyre. Kord, Kenz, Delmira, and Aura found their seats. Kord slid an arm around his wife and pulled her close. Caston sat next to Maera and whispered something to her. She dabbed her eyes and rested her head on his shoulder.

Queen Valeri stepped forward and lifted her chin. "Today, we honor an amazing man. Amycus Reins was a dear friend to my late husband and a loyal soldier to the end. He was a brilliant blacksmith who always had a twinkle in his eye. Not only did he fight for Spectrals, but for all of Pandaren. His wisdom and strength will be sorely missed." She cleared

Embracing the Darkness

her throat and took a wavering breath. "May you find peace, my old friend, as you are welcomed home."

She motioned to Flynt, who signaled to the other Fire Spectrals. Clicking his wrists together, he ignited a green spark and created a sphere of fire. He floated a fireball to the Spectral next to him, who caught it. Green fire morphed into blue. Soon, flames of every color surrounded Amycus. With another blast of the horn, the Spectrals launched their fire.

The crackling of wood filled the silence as the blaze snaked its way up the pyre, consuming everything it touched. Jasce clenched his teeth. Images of black fire destroying his cottage and circling his dead mother invaded his mind. And now he knew who that fire belonged to.

His heart thumped wildly in his chest, unable to believe Drexus had been the one. His mentor and commander had lied to his face for thirteen years and used him as a pawn to do his killing.

"Are you okay?" Jaida asked, scanning his face.

He pressed his lips together and nodded.

Queen Valeri approached the burning pyre and bowed her head. Kneeling, she placed something on the ground. She straightened her gown, and with one last glance at her friend, she left the field. Many of the Guard and all the Spectrals followed suit, placing a variety of metal objects near the flames in remembrance of the blacksmith. The royals and the remaining spectators filed out, accompanied by the cry of seagulls and the crash of waves. The field was silent as smoke billowed into the sky, and what remained of the blacksmith everyone revered disappeared in the breeze.

Before leaving, Kenz leaned into Kord, and they both turned in Jasce's direction. His heartbeat quickened as she trudged up the hill toward him. Her hair resembled an onyx waterfall flowing down her back, and she'd replaced her pants and tunic with a purple dress. She looked pale, and the longing to remove her sorrow overcame him.

He retreated a step.

Kenz shot a look at Jaida and anger filled her eyes. Jaida swallowed and squeezed his hand. "I'll be waiting over there." She walked away with her head lowered.

"Darin, could I have a minute?" Kenz asked.

Darin looked warily from Kenz to Jasce and then followed Jaida, giving them space.

She stood next to him with her fingers interlocked behind her back. The smoke drifted into the darkening sky, and the sun kissed the horizon, turning the sea into molten glass.

"I'm sorry for your loss." He grimaced and cleared his throat. The platitude sounded hollow and offered no comfort.

She wrapped her arms around herself. "I'm leaving. I just wanted you to know."

"Why?"

"Why am I leaving or why am I letting you know?"

Jasce's lips curled into a smile. "Both, I suppose."

"The queen is sending a team to hunt Drexus. I volunteered, along with Aura, Caston, and a few others."

A part of him longed to go with them, the familiar desire for vengeance making his heart pound. It didn't matter that he had no recollection of the events of this past year. Drexus had ruined so many lives, and the man would pay for his crimes, but he'd meant what he said to the Balten king. He needed to figure things out, plus there was Jaida to consider.

"And why are you letting me know?" Jasce asked.

She lowered her arms. "Because I love you."

"I—"

She placed her fingers on his lips, and the desire to kiss her almost brought him to his knees. "You need time to heal—physically, emotionally, deep in here." She rested her hand on his heart. His lips were cold from the absence of her touch. "And so do I. It's too much for you to bear right now, but one day, you and I will talk. Maybe then, we can try again."

He tried to swallow, but his throat had swollen shut. What else could be said that was too much for him to handle? What was she protecting him from?

A lightning bug blinked past them, and Kenz watched it flitter into the distance. She gave a half-smile. "Those are my favorite." With one last look at him, she turned. "Goodbye, Jasce."

He was speechless as she disappeared around the corner of the

Embracing the Darkness

Bastion. Another lightning bug glowed in the twilight. "Goodbye, Kenz," he finally managed as he faced the sea. The sun made its final appearance and dipped below the waves, ending another day.

Footsteps scraped along the dirt, and Darin cleared his throat. Jasce glanced once more at the smoldering wood on the abandoned field. It felt as if a part of his soul had died, carried away among the smoke and ash, forever lost to the night.

Chapter Forty-One

Caston released him the next morning, escorting him to the washroom and giving him a change of clothes. Neither spoke as Jasce strapped on new armor. He ran his fingers along the metal and leather straps. Supposedly, he and Amycus had perfected the design, and the entire Paladin Guard now wore replicas.

Caston handed him his two swords and dagger. "Found them at the docks. Thought you'd want them, as you have an unhealthy relationship with your accessories."

A chuckle escaped Jasce's lips. At a loss for words, he slid the weapons into their scabbards, exited the Bastion, and made his way to the stables. Jaida was waiting, brushing one of the guard's mares. His old horse, Bruiser, shook his mane and stomped his hoof. Jasce raised his brows.

"I talked the queen into at least giving you your horse," Caston said, rubbing his neck.

"How'd you manage that?"

"I told her it would take you a lot longer to leave by foot."

Jasce snorted and then stared at the Bastion. He had spent much of his life behind those walls, and he'd most likely never see them again. He wasn't sure if he was relieved or not.

He'd accepted King Morzov's offer to travel with them to Balten. At least he wouldn't know anyone there, besides Jaida, of course. He was tired of seeing the looks of pity or disappointment on the people who visited him.

Jasce had trained as a warrior for so many years, he wasn't sure what he was going to do next. Heal, like Kenz had said, and figure out who he was now that he was no longer the Angel of Death, nor was he a soldier in the Guard. Based on the armor he wore, he knew he had some talent as a blacksmith and supposed he could do that. He had enjoyed working with Nigel, after all.

It all seemed so foreign, though. Even his given name.

He peered out the gate toward the city. "What am I going to do?"

"You're going to keep moving forward."

Jasce hadn't realized he'd spoken out loud. "I'm adrift at sea with no bearing in sight."

"I remember something you said to me months ago. You said, 'Your mistake is thinking without magic, I'm defeated.'" Caston crossed his arms. "You've always been confident, to a fault at times, but Jasce, you aren't defeated. You're a warrior and a survivor. Maybe you are broken right now, but you'll find your way. You always do."

Jasce examined the ex-Hunter. "Caston, I'm . . ." He choked on the words, his emotion tightening like a fist around his throat.

The soldier grabbed Jasce's forearm. "Get your head on straight, because I suspect we're going to need you in the months ahead."

Jasce focused on their joined arms. He didn't see how he could help them if he was leaving Pandaren.

Caston released him. "This isn't goodbye, and Jasce . . ." Jasce lifted his head. "I'll keep an eye on Kenz, protect her with my life." Caston gave him one last smile and disappeared inside the Bastion.

Jasce swallowed the lump in his throat. The vow Caston made gave him a comfort he didn't quite understand. He simply nodded and walked toward his horse. For the first time in his life, he didn't have a plan. There was no mission or job. He was truly adrift, but at least he wasn't alone.

He approached Jaida. She had a lightness to her, an inner peace that he hadn't attained. She'd only suffered from a brief episode of amnesia

Embracing the Darkness

but had since regained most of her memory and didn't seem upset about surrendering her magic.

"For the first time in years, I don't feel like I'm losing my mind," she had said one day when he'd asked her about it. Jasce envied her. His mind was a jumbled mess. Vengeance for what Drexus had done battled with the feeling that he was damaged, inside and out.

"You good?" he asked, running his hand down Bruiser's mane.

She lifted her face to the morning sky. The sun shone through her golden hair, making it glow. "Yes. You?"

He almost answered with the same lie he'd responded to everyone with these last few days, but he shook his head instead. "Not really." He hopped onto his horse, grimacing as he swung his injured leg over the saddle.

The hairs on his neck rose and he turned. Kord walked across the courtyard with a leather book clutched in his hand.

"I found this in Amycus's rooms and thought it might be helpful," Kord said, handing the book to Jasce, who frowned. The journal was worn and the leather soft. It was very old. "I took out a few pages for Kenz and myself, but the rest is yours."

Jasce cleared his throat. "Thank you." That seemed to be the right thing to say. A part of him didn't want to explore the blacksmith's mind and past, but that was the cowardly part. Maybe this journal could help unlock his memories, or at least give him direction.

Kord gave him a sad smile. "This isn't goodbye," he said as he turned away.

Jasce watched the Healer return to the entrance of the Bastion. Flynt, Aura, and Delmira stood next to him. Aura blew him a kiss, and the breeze whispered across his cheek. Delmira waved, and Flynt inclined his head. Jasce didn't miss the Fire Spectral's eyes darting to his sister. Jaida smiled, and a blush crept into her cheeks.

Jasce scowled at her. They might not know each other very well but he understood that look, and his brotherly instincts kicked in. "That's a big no."

"What? Why?"

"I don't think I like that Fire Spectral."

She giggled and clicked her tongue. "You don't even remember him."

He shook his head and looked at the man who had called him a friend and memorized his features, from the black, wind-blown hair to the kind smile. He nodded to Kord, who nodded back. Jasce sensed his gaze long after he and Jaida left the Bastion.

What did the future hold for an ex-Hunter? He would make a life with his sister at his side, maybe find a forge in Balten. She would be safe, and he had to admit he was curious about what the king had meant about learning from each other. One thing he knew for sure was that he wanted to face Drexus again. For thirteen years, revenge had fueled him, and the loss of his magic or his memories would not eradicate the desire to see his former commander again. And kill him.

He and Jaida were silent as they rode through the streets of Orilyon and out through the southern gates. The sun warmed his face, and the smell of the ocean tickled his nose. He'd miss that smell and the heat. But a change of scenery would do him good, and hopefully he would heal, not just physically, but emotionally and mentally.

As Jasce and Jaida rode past the outlying farms, she shifted in her saddle and raised her brows. "So, which way?"

"South to Balten."

"It's cold there."

"I'll get you a fur-lined cloak."

"Too bad we don't have a Fire Spectral to keep us warm." Her eyes sparkled as she grinned.

He jerked his head to the side. "Seriously?"

She kicked her horse and laughed as the wind blew through her golden hair. Jasce glanced over his shoulder toward Orilyon. His eyes drifted over the palace and stopped on the Bastion. Silver flags waved in the breeze in honor of Amycus. Somewhere deep inside of him, the need to make the blacksmith proud fluttered to the surface and filled his heart.

"I'll do my best, old man," Jasce said. And with the start of a smile, he faced forward, leaving his past and, hopefully the darkness, behind.

Where To Now?

Thank you so much for reading *Embracing the Darkness*. I hope you're enjoying the world of Pandaren and Jasce's story. If so, please consider leaving an honest review with your preferred retailers, on Amazon and/or Goodreads. As an indie author, I rely on my amazing readers to help spread the word about my books. Your support means so much - thank you!

To stay in the loop with The Darkness Trilogy, please stop on by my website and sign up for my newsletter at www.CassieSanchez.com

Acknowledgments

Can you believe it? Two books written with a third on the way. Who would've thought? I want to first and foremost thank God, who's given me a purpose and creativity to write fantasy.

Here's to my fabulous Beta readers. I can't tell you how much your encouragement, ideas, and mostly, your time with reading and providing feedback meant to me. Thank you, Alyssa Ford, Darin Rasberry, Elaine DeLand, Jared Kenwood, Karla DeGroft, Janine Goff, Linda Jeffreys, Linda Pino, Tracey McClain, and Mom.

To my editor, Rachel Oestreich. Who knows where this story would've gone without you? Thank you for keeping me on track and focused, and for fixing my lousy grammar. A big thanks to Laurisa Brandt and Anna Frantz for doing a final proofread and being another set of eyes on this project.

I also want to thank my Instagram Street Team – you know who you are. Your promotion, support, reviews, and encouragement have kept me moving forward. Thank you for spreading the word about the Darkness books.

I couldn't do any of this without the support of my family and friends; for being in my corner and for your excitement over my writing. Tyler and Chase, you are my gurus for all that's magical and sometimes geeky. And to my awesome husband, Louie, who's made this all possible. You're my biggest fan and the best shoulder to lean (or cry) on. I wouldn't be on this journey and publishing my second book if it wasn't for you.

Lastly, to my fans (which sounds so awesome to say), thank you for believing in my world, my characters, and this story. If it wasn't for you, these books wouldn't have seen the light of day.

Keep the magic alive.

About the Author

ABOUT THE AUTHOR

Growing up, Cassie Sanchez always wanted superpowers and to be a warrior princess fighting alongside unlikely heroes. Suffice it to say, she lost herself in books, from fantasy to sci-fi to a suspenseful romance. Currently, Cassie lives in the southwest with her husband, Louie, while pestering her two adult men-children. She can usually be found drinking too much coffee while working in her office with her dogs, Gunner and Bullet, warming her feet. When she isn't writing about magic and sword fights, she enjoys golf, spending time with friends, or partaking in a satisfying nap. You can visit her online at Cassie Sanchez.com.

facebook.com/cassiesanchezauthor
twitter.com/CSanchez_Author
instagram.com/CassieSanchezAuthor

Made in the USA
Middletown, DE
02 March 2024